The
Deadfall

LILLY BLACK

BOOK I of
LILLY BLACK'S GODS OF EARTH SERIES

© 2018 by Lilly Black

Cover Design by Lilly Black

Photo by Irina Alexandrovna

www.lillyblackauthor.com

2018 First Print Edition

Learn more about Lilly Black and her other works at:

www.lillyblackauthor.com

Acknowledgements:

For my husband.
When you read it, you aren't going to like Olivia's storyline at all,
but surely you know by now that all heroes, no matter their
name or backstory, are only ever you.

Special Thanks:

to Author Amy Leigh Napier, who always finds all the
mistakes I miss because she's awesome,

to Margie for encouraging me and
Keira for ignoring her and slacking off with me,

to Nilisha for helping me understand
more about where Ravi comes from,

to all the wonderful ladies who helped me with the ARC,

to George R., may he rest in peace,
for setting me on a collision course with this book long ago,

and

to all of the horrible people who drove me to destroy the world.

LILLY BLACK'S
GODS OF EARTH SERIES

Book I: The Deadfall

Book II: Coming Soon

Since I am going out of town today for a long weekend with my oldest and dearest girlfriends, last night Reid was determined to do what he always does when we're going to be apart. He has just the slightest streak of insecurity when it comes to me, and it shows itself at times like these. No way was he going to send me out into the world to get drunk with the girls for three days without twenty orgasms to remind me that no other man could ever please me like he does.

It wasn't necessary. I already know how good I have it. But I'm not one to turn down twenty orgasms either.

If you've read this series of journals from the beginning, you already know that's just a typical Tuesday in my sex life, but if you just flipped straight to the last entry, you're probably going to call bullshit, Dani. Fifteen years ago, before I met Reid, I know I would've been right there with you. It's not bullshit, though. I am, without a doubt, the luckiest woman alive and not just because he's such a generous and magnificent lover. He's a wonderful husband. I've never understood how people always say that marriage is hard work. Marriage isn't hard work at all, and maybe all those people who say it is just aren't doing it right. My marriage is everything I could ever possibly want, and I don't think there's any way I could be happier. But you didn't ask me to journal my undying love, did you, Dani? You just want the juicy parts, so here you go.

Bon Appétit!

Last night after my shower, I came out of my bathroom into our bedroom wrapped in a towel, planning to put on one of several new lingerie acquisitions that arrived in yesterday's mail, but Reid was waiting for me right outside the door. I gasped, startled when I saw him out of the corner of my eye, and it made him smile as he came at me, deliciously naked and unashamed, his well-toned body almost as hard as his perfect cock. It had been a while since he had his hair trimmed, and growing just below his ears now, I could still see the blonde strands from working outside all summer mixed in with his messy, light brown locks. Every part of Reid is beautiful to me. I love the sharp angles of his face, the sun-kissed color of his skin, how smooth his chin feels right after he shaves.

As I ran my fingers along his jaw line, he leaned forward, trapping me against the wall with one hand as he loomed over me at six feet to my petite 5'3". Then he grabbed the corner of my towel where I had it tucked in above my breasts and yanked it away with a grin. I stood naked before him as he looked me over head to toe with predatory green eyes, and every sign of arousal in my body came on like he flipped a switch. My nipples tightened into pink dots, my clit was hard and aching, and I could feel myself growing wet inside as I anticipated what he would do next. The thing is, I never know what he's going to do next because even after fifteen years together, Reid and I have never fallen into a rut. We've never even gotten past the honeymoon phase, and even when he does things he's done a thousand times, there's always some new, little trick to it to keep me surprised.

Tonight, he started by kneeling down before me and lifting my foot, kissing it softly at first then sucking my toes into his mouth. It's never been an erogenous zone for me, but knowing how much he gets off on it is what turns me on. And he does get off on it. I could feel his cock twitching against my other ankle as he worshipped my foot, running his tongue up the side and around the heel, nibbling at the back of my ankle. When he moved on to my leg, he placed my foot on his shoulder, and as his tongue made its way to the spot where I really wanted it, he pushed into me until my leg was bent over at the knee, dangling down his back, his gorgeous face looking up at me from between my thighs.

Without breaking eye contact, he slowly extended his tongue toward my clit, and my legs began lightly trembling as I begged for more inside my head. He moved in closer. I could feel his breath, humid against my most sensitive flesh, but just before he would have reached the target, he turned his head to the right and bit me on the thigh, sending shockwaves of pain and pleasure through me.

He hummed in approval as he heard my breath catch, and though I whined in disappointment, it was just a part of the game.

"Patience, my love," he teased, punishing me by going even slower as he worked his way down my other leg, and he knew it was torture because I was so ready, I could feel it on my inner thighs, and finally, half way to my knee, he stopped teasing, suddenly spreading me open with his thumbs and brushing his tongue gently over my clit.

I shuddered, my fingers winding their way into his hair as he began to make soft swirls with the smooth underside, slowly coaxing the pleasure out of me, and when he had taken me as far as the position would allow without the ability to spread my legs, he placed one hand against my belly and pushed me into the wall to keep me balanced as he raised my other leg onto his shoulder.

Then he began to stand, lifting me up until I was more than five feet off the ground, but I wasn't concerned about my precarious position. Reid's strong. He makes me feel like I'm as light as a feather as he effortlessly moves me around to suit his desires, and all the while, his tongue never stopped, pressed right against my clit as he slid his hands behind me to carry me to the bed.

Then he dropped me, letting me fall on my back on the mattress, and as I watched the black, corseted babydoll nightie I had laid out to wear slide off the edge on his side, he went to his knees at the foot, pulling me to the very

2

end, straight into his face, his hands on my inner thighs, pushing them wide apart. He moved fast, flickering over me as my fists grasped the sheet in balls, the orgasm coming for me so quickly, nothing could've stopped it.

"Oh, Fuck!" I moaned, and bearing into me, he gave me the last, little jolt I needed, his grip on my thighs intense as I screamed his name and pushed myself forward into his face. He pushed back, guiding me beyond the first orgasm to a second and a third, each more intense than the last. My body seized as I praised him in deep groans and inarticulate cries, my mind ravaged by impossible pleasures that only Reid could ever give me. And his lust for making me come was inexhaustible, not stopping until I pulled away, giggling euphorically.

"Was that alright?" he asked with a smirk on his face, and it only made me laugh harder until he abruptly flipped me over, driving his cock into me from behind and chasing the laughter right out of my mouth. He didn't tease, immediately fucking me hard and fast, gripping my shoulders, forcing my back into a sharp arch, and as his body crashed into mine, it took him seconds to bring me to orgasm again, my entire being exploding against him just as he breathed the command in my ear: "Come for me, baby."

"Oh, my God," I cried, shuddering as I flooded his cock with hot, wet validation of his absolute power over me. He gave me a moment to savor it before he started again, repeating the process with slight changes each time - grabbing my hips, pulling my hair, running his fingernails down my spine as he made me come over and over, and when I thought he was finished with me, he got down off the bed, dragged me to the end, and flipped me over so suddenly I felt my long, wet, blond hair strike him like a whip. Unfazed, he pulled my ass off the edge and put my legs on his shoulders, then as he slid his cock inside me again, he sucked my toes into his mouth. As I felt him grow harder, I knew I could end him so quickly, but I didn't want it to be over yet. We were going to be away from each other for three nights - an eternity by our standards - and I needed to send Reid off feeling as supremely sated as I felt.

As he began fucking me, I gave him a few more seconds with my foot before pulling it away and wrapping my legs around him, caging his arms at his side. He held onto my thighs, and I let his glorious cock take possession of my will once more, my mind lost in the sensation of soft skin stretched over steel gliding rapidly against the enkindled flesh inside me, each stroke a step closer to heaven. I felt it approaching, and knowing how close Reid was, I held my tongue, trying to be as quiet as possible so I could get that cock in my mouth before he reached his end, but my body betrayed me, quaking, practically vibrating as he drove me to madness. And he didn't stop. He just kept fucking me relentlessly, another orgasm building upon the last as I felt Reid's cock reach that critical mass.

"Oh, God, yes!" I screamed, and together we erupted, the ecstasy shooting into my veins like a narcotic as he filled me with his undying lust.

"Oh, fuck, Liv," he groaned, thrusting gently now, wresting the last of the bliss our bodies had to give until he finally leaned forward and collapsed over me.

"God, I love you," he breathed, his voice barely audible, his lips softly brushing the side of my face as he nuzzled into me, and I echoed him in my own whisper, so high I could only think of two things.

I love him more than the limited words of my native tongue could ever express.

And,

God! Three days is going to be an eternity!

T Minus 3 Days and Counting
9:00 AM Friday Morning

Olivia finished writing the most recent chapter and slipped her sex journal into her suitcase along with the other two volumes from the last three months. It seemed like a silly exercise in the beginning when Dani asked that she, Liana, and June start writing in them, but as she began to chronicle every experience she had with her husband, she realized that maybe she had found just the thing they had been looking for. She and Reid had always said they were so good at sex they should get paid for it, yet neither of them really wanted to go into porn or prostitution. Writing erotica was something she'd never considered, but now she realized it might be her best bet for turning their extraordinary sex life into cash flow. She had been very thorough in her writing ever since, and now that she was going off for a weekend with the girls, it had been important to Reid to give her a lot to write about last night.

Olivia gathered her luggage, and began dragging it down the hall from her bedroom toward the lodge. She and Reid had a private home that was attached to their rustic, seven-room hotel, which made the lodge look bigger and more impressive, and though they had a private entrance, they seldom used it. Her friends would be meeting her in front of the lodge anyway, and when she dragged her suitcases into the hallway outside their bedroom, Reid was there waiting to carry them to the lobby. She watched him with a lusty stare as he effortlessly lifted them both, his muscles flexing beneath his shirt.

"How many weeks did you pack for?" he teased, and she giggled.

"You know I always over-pack," she said as she followed him down the hall. He set down her bags by the front door of the lodge and turned to face her, putting his arms around her and looking down into her eyes.

"I'm going to miss you," he whispered.

"*I'm* going to miss *you*," she echoed, then she leaned in close, her lips by his ear, "but when I get home on Monday..."

"When you get home on Monday, you're going to be exhausted and hung over," he corrected her. "So, I'll make you dinner, and pencil you in for a proper fucking on Tuesday."

"You're so romantic," she said with a roll of her eyes.

"You wouldn't have it any other way, my love," he said, kissing her on the forehead. He was right, of course. In the romance department, Olivia was extremely low maintenance, but if she hadn't been, then Reid would have learned to be more romantic. He had loved her from the first moment he saw her, and every day together thereafter only reinforced their belief that they were made for one another. They had met in college when they were in their early twenties, and even after fifteen years together, their sex life was as exciting as it was when they were first discovering each other.

"Ink," she called out to him as she walked back down the hall for something she forgot. "Not pencil."

Reid smiled. Knowing her libido, it was probably safe to ink Monday in as well.

Liana & June

"What the fuck is that thing?" Liana demanded, her amber eyes flashing in fear as she stood behind the driver's side door of her ten-year-old SUV, refusing to leave the safety of the car. She glared up at the second story, front deck of the log-cabin lodge at Olivia and Reid's compound, and staring back at her were the menacing, green eyes of Evil, the full grown, melanistic jaguar, who sat regally surveying her pride lands from the banister. Evil came to them as a cub seized in a drug raid by cops in Reid's hometown of Charleston, WV, and she had been raised as part of the family alongside their only child, Savannah. Evil was as gentle as a kitten as long as no one threatened Savannah, but all Liana ever knew about that species of great cat were the old wives tales spun by her Argentinean grandmother who grew up in fear of them coming out of the Amazon in the night to eat babies.

5

"You're perfectly safe," Reid promised as he approached the car to carry her bags inside, and her teenage son, Rey started to open his door.

"Don't you dare!" she shouted at him, then she turned to Reid. "Could you maybe put it in a cage first?"

He laughed and called out to Olivia on the walkie-talkies they used to keep in contact while working around the compound. She was already heading upstairs onto the deck before he even spoke, and when she reached the banister, she smiled down at Liana as Evil began to rub her head against Olivia's. Reid gave her a look, gritting his teeth, and she knew exactly what to do.

"Come on, Evie," she said. "Let's go to your room." The cat jumped down off the railing, her tail swishing as she followed Olivia inside, down the stairs, and to her "room", which was connected to the master suite. She had her own indoor area with a bed, central heating and air, and a cat door to a large outside enclosure. It's where she lived when there were guests on the property, whether they were staying in the lodge suites or one of the cabins. Reid and Olivia had closed the business for this long weekend, but since Olivia's friends were leaving their children with Savannah and Reid, they knew Evil wouldn't be able to roam the grounds.

"Evie is safely locked away," Olivia announced as she came back into the lodge to find Liana already inside, standing by the door, her hands on her curvaceous hips. With bronze skin, and long, wavy brown hair, Liana was beautiful now that she wasn't terrified of Olivia's youngest, and furriest, child. "I can't believe you didn't even want to pet her."

"Seriously, Oblivia?" she demanded with a roll of her eyes, then she laughed and hugged her old friend.

"I've missed you," she said, laughing with her. No one had called her Oblivia in years, but apparently it still applied because she couldn't imagine how anyone could look at Evil and not immediately want to cuddle with her.

"I've missed you, too," Liana said, and they sat down to catch up while they waited for June to arrive since Reid had taken Rey to the stables where Savannah was feeding the horses. Back in Columbus, GA, Liana and Rey lived on an army base, so he was very excited about spending a weekend horseback riding, fishing, and hanging out with Reid and Olivia's beautiful, blonde daughter even though his mother had already warned her seventeen-year-old son that Savannah was too young for him "no matter how old she looks in her Instagram pictures."

Savannah had heard a similar warning from her mother because Rey Navarro was known for being a bit of a player, and there was no question what fourteen-year-old Savannah thought of the muscled, Latin boy with the dark eyes and messy hair. Good thing Reid was staying there to kick his ass if he crossed the line. Plus they were going to have four younger boys to look after once June arrived with her brood.

About ten minutes later, just as Olivia was about to give Liana a quick tour of the lodge, the buzzer rang on her walkie letting her know someone was at the outer gate. Assuming it was June, she went ahead and set all three to open in sequence, and she and Liana waited on the porch until June's shiny blue minivan pulled up beside Liana's car.

"What is this place? Fort Knox?" June complained as she stepped out of her vehicle with four boys, ages six to twelve, falling into a line behind her. The three older boys had their father's brown hair and blue eyes, but the youngest had green eyes and red hair like their mother. June's friends were all jealous of her full mane of gorgeous strawberry-blonde hair, and her freckled skin was milky pale and absolutely flawless. She had a willowy figure and a strange beauty about her even though she rarely wore makeup. It was something she could never see for herself. All she ever saw was orange hair and freckles, both of which made her feel like the ugly duckling of the group, but today, it was the furthest thing from her mind as Liana came rushing toward her.

"Junie-bug!" she cried, throwing her arms around her old friend.

"Oh, my goodness, LiLo! It's so good to see you!" June cooed back.

Liana's maiden name was Lopez, and since she had silly nicknames for everyone, they started calling her LiLo back in middle school. Nicknames were her thing, along with being the group peacemaker, and any time June and Olivia were in the same room, they were going to need a peacemaker. Olivia had very little patience for June's judgmental attitude, and June had something to say about everything Olivia did.

"June," Olivia said coldly.

"Olivia," she replied as Liana helped carry in her bags. Once they were all inside, while the adults talked, the boys stood by quietly holding their suitcases, so quietly it creeped Olivia out, but she didn't let it show. It was too early to start an argument, and she wanted the boys to be able to enjoy their weekend here with Reid and Savannah. She understood that it was wrong to second guess how anyone else parented their children, but she was sure these kids were far too sheltered since their mother considered *everything* a sin.

"Would you boys like something to drink or a snack?" she asked them.

"They're fine. They had a snack in the car," June snapped. "Seriously, though. What is this place? Why all the security? Are you guys running a cult or something?"

"I think they're doomsday preppers," Liana said with a wink.

"You're both wrong. Well, sort of," Olivia said, then she went on to explain. She and Reid had always wanted to have a place in the mountains where they could farm and have lots of animals, and when Reid's grandmother passed away and left them an inheritance, they built their dream compound - five hundred acres with a natural spring on a mountaintop in West Virginia, including green cabins operating on renewable energy, stockpiles of food, water, and weapons, greenhouses, livestock, and a tall fence around the main complex. They weren't doomsday preppers, but they did believe that once the polar icecaps melted, sending millions of Americans inland, they needed to be on high *and secure* ground.

"40% of the world's population lives within sixty miles of the ocean. We could end up with a huge number of refugees, depending upon how quickly the melting accelerates," Olivia said.

"That's not going to happen. God is never going to destroy the world by water again. It's in the Bible," June said dismissively.

"Well, we have a bunker under the lodge if he destroys it by fire," Olivia said with a crinkle of her nose just as she heard a buzz on her walkie. She looked down and smiled, entering the code to open the gates, then she turned to Liana. "Ready to hit the road?"

"Which one of us is driving?" Liana asked.

"None of us," Olivia said cryptically, and when she led them out front, a deep red Hummer limousine was coming up the drive.

"Day-um!" Liana exclaimed, but all June had for Olivia was a disapproving glare. Though it wasn't clear exactly what she didn't approve of, she was sure spending the extra cash on this limo for the sake of their newly-divorced friend, Dani, who was meeting them in Pittsburgh, was somehow sinful.

That was the purpose of this adventure.   Dani, the fourth bestie in their group since Kindergarten, finally had the paperwork that made her divorce from her alcoholic, waste-of-flesh husband final, so they were all getting together for the first time in ten years to celebrate. And Liana was ready to get started. As Reid and Rey helped the chauffeur load their luggage into the back of the limo, she checked the mini bar to make sure they had some good vodka and Olivia's favorite dark rum.

When they were ready to leave, Liana threw her arms around Rey. Olivia hugged Reid and Savannah tightly, and June went down the line of her boys oldest to youngest to remind them of the rules before leading a quick prayer for their safety and kissing each of them atop the head. They would be breaking the first of many rules before the Hummer made it off the Anders property as Savannah and Rey led them straight to the game room and introduced them to the Xbox.

It took over four hours to get from Olivia's compound in the mountains near Pipestem, West Virginia to the airport in Pittsburgh to meet Dani after her flight from Indianapolis, and though June and Liana had already been stuck in their cars driving from North Carolina and Georgia, they were all reenergized when they saw Dani coming out of the terminal looking like a million dollars. She always did. Since they were teenagers, Danielle Templeton had learned to do flawless makeup and never looked back. With caramel skin, long, straight, jet black hair, and a thin, perfect figure, Dani came off like a model or a New York socialite...until she opened her mouth to speak and her façade was betrayed by her upbringing in West Virginia.

"Now, that's what I'm talking 'bout!" she shouted as she scoped out the long, red limo while her best friends in the world hung out the window, beckoning her to them. She got in, Liana mixed her a Jack and coke, and the party got started as the chauffeur drove them to downtown Pittsburgh where Olivia had booked the biggest suite on the highest floor of the tallest hotel. She wanted nothing but the best for Dani.

They were going to be there for three nights, living like queens with in-room massages, spa appointments, and shopping during the day, and partying at night, including front row tickets to the band that had been Dani's favorite for twenty years - ParraJax. Dani knew about the concert, but she had no idea she was going to be seated in the sweat zone. That was a fun and expensive surprise they'd all pooled their money on, though June contributed very little since she had to hide what they were really doing from her husband. She was going to feel guilty about it the whole time, but Liana had always been good at talking her into things. Olivia was traditionally the leader of the group, but she just had no patience for June. June had even called her up once during the planning phase insisting that if they were going to engage in drinking and other debauchery, they should schedule a church visit on Sunday morning for balance.

"This trip is not about you," Olivia had told her. "It's about Dani."

Then as the limo passed the convention center in downtown Pittsburgh en route to the hotel, June got her chance to throw those words back in Olivia's face. On the roster outside, it said, "Comic Con featuring Aleksander Hellström."

"Is that why you picked Pittsburgh?" Liana teased her.

"I had no idea. I swear," Olivia said as she stared out the window at the sign. She wasn't the type to lust after famous people, but there had been a few men who had caught her eye over the years. Aleksander Hellström was one of them. The 36-year-old actor, who played a demon on the television adaptation of some comic book Olivia had never heard of before the show, was well over six feet tall, blonde, blue-eyed, Swedish, and absolutely beautiful...just like she liked them, and though no one would ever know she was starstruck, she was blushing on the inside at the idea of being in the same room with him. But it was just a fleeting fantasy. There was nothing Aleksander Hellström could offer her that would ever lure her away from Reid. Olivia was the only one in their quartet who was truly in love with the man she married. Their relationship was so good, it was almost annoying.

"We should see if we can get tickets," Liana suggested in response to the wistful look on Olivia's face, and that's when June jumped in.

"Uh, I don't think so," she said glaring at Olivia. "This weekend isn't about you. It's all about Dani, remember?"

"Psh! I get to go to a Jax Bonham show! I don't care if we spend the rest of our time digging ditches," Dani said. She was starstruck and didn't care who knew it. "If you want to go see him, Liv, I'm down with it."

"Nah. It's okay," Olivia said. "I'll just pretend it's him when we get those in-room massages this afternoon."

Him and Reid, she thought to herself. That was a fantasy she'd had for a long time, but it's something she could never admit to anyone because it made her feel like a slut. As open-minded as she was, she just couldn't get past it. It didn't matter anyway. It was the one thing Reid couldn't handle. Even though he knew no one else had ever been able to make Olivia's body do the things he could, the thought of seeing another man touch her tweaked his insecurity in wildly irrational ways.

T Minus 2 Days
Saturday

Last night, the women had planned to take it easy, ordering a room service dinner and catching up with each other, but after a few drinks, Dani talked them into going downstairs to the hotel bar, which eventually led them to other bars where they partied until three out of four of them had pretty much guaranteed themselves hangovers in the morning.

It was almost noon on Saturday before they finally rolled out of bed, and teetotaler June had already been up for hours. She had ordered everyone a room service breakfast around eleven before they switched to the lunch menu, reheating everything in the microwave for them, and as they ate, they slowly began to feel human again. Afterward, June wheeled the breakfast cart into the hallway, and Dani decided to use the downtime to bring up the reason she had asked them to start journaling their sex lives.

"Did you all remember to bring your diaries?" she asked

"Yes, for what it's worth," Liana grumbled, and the others nodded.

"Can I have them?"

"Before I hand over a book about my private love life, I'd like to know what you plan to do with it," June said.

"I'm glad you asked because it's more than just what I told you on the phone. I'm actually doing a study and writing a book about how beliefs affect the sex lives of women in and outside of marriage," she explained.

"What beliefs specifically?" June asked, suspicious that she might be the main case study.

"Religious beliefs, slut shaming, all sorts of things really. It's not aimed at any particular thing. I have fifty women in my study, including you guys."

"Well," Liana said as she pretended to put her hand inside her pocket and offer Dani absolutely nothing. "Here's mine."

"You haven't had sex once in the past three months?" Olivia asked, feeling sorry for her.

"She's not married," June said. "I think it's commendable."

"And I think you're a tight ass," Olivia said. "In fact, I'll bet you five hundred dollars right now that I could flip to any page in your diary, and it will be straight up missionary sex, five minutes max, lights out."

"You don't know anything about my private life!"

"A thousand dollars," Olivia said.

"My husband and I have a healthy, fantastic romantic life, and I have four children to prove it!"

"Five thousand dollars."

"Shut up, Olivia! I'm not a tramp. Whatever!" June cried, and when Olivia took in a breath to speak, Liana jumped between them, ever the diplomat.

"Hey, at least you guys are getting it," she said. "Dani could have asked us to start keeping track five years ago, and mine would still be empty."

"I told you in the beginning. Bob counts!" Dani teased.

"Who's Bob?" June asked.

"Her battery-operated boyfriend," Dani said with a wink.

"Fine! I'll get the damn book," Liana relented, and despite the tension between Olivia and June, they all laughed. Then when Olivia retrieved hers from her room, three completely filled volumes, they laughed harder, even June.

"I may have been a little more detailed than you needed me to be," Olivia admitted, but she explained that she hadn't done it to brag. She intended to convert that diary into an erotic novel once Dani was finished with it.

"It's going to take me a damn month to read all this, but I'll be sure to return them. Anyone else want them back?"

"As long as my name's not on it anywhere, you can keep mine," June said.

"You can burn mine," Liana insisted.

"Fuck that!" Olivia said. "We're going out tonight after the concert, and we're going to get both you and Dani laid."

"Are you willing to bet five thousand dollars on that one?" Liana asked, and Olivia threw a sofa cushion at her as she rolled her eyes. No way was she taking that bet. Liana was ridiculously picky when it came to men, or at least that's what she would have her friends believe.

Saturday Night

Jax Bonham. Dani had been in love with the lead singer of ParraJax since she and her friends were teenagers. They were in their mid-thirties now, but unlike the other acts from their youth who were just reliving their glory days in bars and at music festivals, ParraJax had continued to put out good music and remained just as popular as they were when their first album went platinum. And Jax Bonham had held up really well too.

On the stage right in front of them, he looked like a god - tall and lean with a muscular core and chest that everyone in the audience got to savor once it became too hot for his shirt. His upper arms were covered in tattoos as blue-black as his shoulder-length hair, which was wet with sweat from the hot lights above. His eyes were a brilliant shade of blue and his features well defined, and even at nearly forty-years-old, he was as beautiful as he had been in his twenties. And to Dani, he was perfect.

Mesmerized, she watched him as everyone else in the world began to disappear until there was only Jax and his music, performing just for her, and on the last song, when they played the power balled, *In My Arms*, and he reached out to touch hands with the fans on the front row, he paused and locked fingers with her. Time froze as Dani felt herself drowning in a deep well of blue eyes that stared back, mirroring her own dreamy adulation, the words of the song coming out of his mouth by muscle memory alone, but as the woman beside her started grabbing at his hand for her turn, he had to let go. He gave her a smile and moved on, not even looking at the woman whose hand he now held as his eyes lingered on Dani, and from that moment, she was walking on air.

When the limo picked them up after the show, she begged the others to have drinks in the bar at the Kemp Hotel where the band was staying, and though hanging out in another stuffy hotel bar on the off chance that Jax Bonham might stop by seemed like a long, boring exercise in futility, the others agreed to go for their friend's sake. Fortunately, when they arrived, they found that the Kemp's bar wasn't stuffy or boring. It was like a night club, and it was packed.

With an obscene tip, Olivia managed to get them a table, and they were quickly ordering rounds of shots and hitting the dance floor. June, of course, refused to drink anything, but at least she was willing to go out and dance with them in a group until men started showing up and whisking her friends away from her. She acted disgusted by it, especially with Olivia because she was married, but in truth she was jealous. Men never asked her to dance. She thought it was because she was the plain one. In the company of Liana's hourglass figure, Dani's head-to-toe model-like perfection, and Olivia's gorgeous girl-next-door appeal, she still felt like a flat-chested teenager, but that wasn't the case at all. Even though she didn't wear much makeup or dress as sexy as the other women, June wasn't homely. It was the vibe she put off that kept men from approaching her. Her stance and expression said "move along, nothing to see here."

When the others finally returned to their bored friend at the table, before she had a chance to intimate that they were acting like sluts and Olivia had the chance to tell her where she could shove her prudery, the waitress showed up with an unsolicited round of drinks.

"Did you order these?" Liana asked June, earning herself an incredulous stare.

"They're from the gentleman in the corner," the waitress explained, pointing to a well-dressed man who sat surrounded by people in the large, elevated corner booth across the room. When Olivia made eye contact with him, he raised his glass to her and gave her what she interpreted as an arrogant smirk. She smiled and nodded to thank him then proceeded to ignore him.

"What an ass," she said.

"A man buys you a round of really overpriced drinks, and he's an...a-s-s," June said, dropping her voice as she spelled the last word as if she was afraid of some sort of cosmic punishment for cursing.

"He's sitting over there like he's holding court, and I'll bet he thinks this round of drinks is going to make our panties drop, so yeah, he's an ass."

"You did promise to get us both laid," Liana said.

"What?" Olivia asked. "Do you think he's pretty?"

"I think I've had too much to drink," she said with a giggle, and they quickly got lost in conversation and forgot all about the arrogant man in the corner booth until Olivia got up to go to the ladies' room and ran into him en route.

"I didn't introduce myself earlier," he said, extending his hand. "I'm Jonathan Kemp, Jr."

"Nice to meet you, Mr. Kemp. Olivia Anders," she said, shaking his hand loosely, hoping he'd get the idea that she could not be less interested.

"You and your friends should join us. I own this hotel," he said awkwardly, his polished appearance dissolved by his need to advertise.

"I thought you said you were Jonathan Kemp, Jr. Doesn't that mean your father is the Kemp in Kemp Hotels?" she asked. She normally wouldn't be so confrontational, but she was getting lit and he was getting on her nerves.

"I'm his only heir. What's his is essentially mine."

"Well good for you," she said. "If you'll excuse me." She hurried down the hallway toward the restroom, leaving him stunned in her wake, and once inside, she wasted as much time as she possibly could, wanting to make certain he'd be gone when she came out.

After that, it seemed Mr. Kemp Jr. had, thankfully, lost interest in her. Dani had also lost interest in hoping for Jax Bonham to show up, specifically because she saw a picture of him on social media signing autographs in another Pittsburgh bar. So they called their limo driver, took their last sips, and got up to leave, but in the narrow hallway that led to the lobby, someone was waiting for Olivia.

"Oh, Miss Anders..." Kemp sang her name like a school yard chant as he approached her, singling her out and blocking her way with his arm against the wall in front of her. Her friends were several paces ahead before they realized what was going on and stopped in their tracks, shocked at his audacity.

"Olivia!" Dani called back as Kemp stood, obstructing their view.

"I was hoping we'd have a chance to get to know each other before you left," he said. "I'd love to give you a tour of the hotel."

"I appreciate the offer, but beyond the bar and the lobby, which I've already seen, there really isn't much left, is there?" she asked with a spiteful glare.

"There's my suite. I think you'd really enjoy..." he paused and leaned in objectionably close "...the view."

"No, thank you," she said, then she attempted to push past his arm, which he held firmly in place. Angry, Olivia cleared her throat, and said, "Excuse me." It should have been obvious that she had no interest in what he was offering, but he didn't seem to understand. Instead of letting her pass, he put his other hand on her hip and moved into her personal space.

Olivia was a strong woman, but this was not a familiar situation. No man had ever had the nerve to just come up and touch her without permission before, and though she was on the verge of losing control on him, the shock of the situation made everything seem to move in slow motion. Dani and Liana, however, had decided they were going to kick his ass, and they could have too. They had taken self defense courses together in high school, and during military training, Liana had kicked lots of men's asses. But before they took their first steps, someone else entered the hallway.

Aleksander Hellström.

Standing a head taller than Kemp, Aleksander immediately moved himself beside Olivia, looking down on her aggressor with fierce blue eyes and a confidence that told Kemp his only option was to yield.

"Get your hand off her, put your arm down, and walk away," Aleksander said.

"Who are you? Her husband?" Kemp demanded, releasing his hold on Olivia's hip but continuing to block her path with his arm.

"I'm just a guy offering to educate you since you seem to be confused about the meaning of the word no, but if you turn out to be a slow learner, I'm going to be the guy who teaches it to you the hard way."

Kemp held firm for a second as he studied Aleksander's face, but realizing he was outmatched, he raised his arm. Olivia immediately hurried past him to join her friends.

"It doesn't matter," Kemp said. "I have a hundred little sluts just like her lined up to get in my bed."

He looked over his shoulder to give Olivia a smirk, but when he turned back, he nearly crashed into Aleksander, who was now blocking his path like he had blocked Olivia's.

"Why'd you have to go and do that?" he asked. "I was going to let you walk away, but the first thing you do is call her a slut because she didn't want to sleep with you? You need to apologize."

"I don't apologize," Kemp said with a cocky tone, and furious, Alek grabbed him by the neck and slammed him against the wall.

"Did I do something to give you the impression that it was optional?" he demanded, glaring into Kemp's eyes as he held him there, the tips of his shoes barely touching the ground, and now that Aleksander could see that he was genuinely scared, he leaned in close and spoke softly. "Don't embarrass yourself anymore than you already have. Tell the lady you're sorry, and you can go back in there and keep right on ruling your sad, little kingdom without anyone knowing you nearly pissed yourself out here. Okay?"

Kemp looked around to see if there were any employees who might help him but found no one in sight.

"Fine. I'm sorry," he said grudgingly, and Alek realized it was probably the best he was going to get out of him unless he wanted to put his fist down his throat, which he decided to forego for Olivia's sake. It was obvious to anyone that she just wanted to get as far away from Kemp as possible, but she couldn't leave while Aleksander still stood there defending her. He let Kemp slide back to his feet, and the second he released his grip, the smaller man hurried off down the hallway.

"Are you okay?" Aleksander asked as he caught up with Olivia and her friends. They all walked out into the street.

"Yeah, I'm fine, thank you," she said, maintaining a calm façade even though she was screaming inside. The creepy encounter with Kemp had been completely overshadowed by the fact that Aleksander Hellström had come to her defense, and now here he stood before her in all of his tall, gorgeous, blonde glory concerned for her well being. The only thing wrong with Olivia at the moment was that she was utterly enamored against her will and better judgment.

"I apologize for intruding," he said. "I'm sure you're perfectly capable of taking care of yourself. I just couldn't stand by and watch him treat you like that just because his daddy owns a hotel or two."

"And I don't know how to thank you. I was so taken aback, I honestly didn't know what to do."

"No thanks are necessary."

"Still, there must be something..."

"You don't owe me anything," he insisted, though inside his head, he was begging for her to push the issue. He wanted her to do something - anything - so he didn't have to walk away from her because the timing made it impossible for him. No matter how bad he wanted to, he couldn't come onto her right after Kemp's creepy behavior, and Olivia didn't want him to slip through her grasp so easily either.

"I can't just let your noble deed go unrewarded," she said, the words pouring out of her mouth without a thought of what they might imply.

"What did you have in mind?" he asked, but when her entire body squealed in excitement at the thought of him saying those words to her, she realized she had to get away from him. She and Reid had a solid marriage and a sex life that couldn't be outdone by the best one night stand, and because of that, no other man had ever even given her a passing thought of what might lie beneath the zipper of his jeans. But this was Aleksander Hellström. He was no man. He was a god!

"If nothing else, I would, at least, like to buy you a drink to show you my appreciation, but the thing is, tonight we're celebrating my friend Dani's divorce. Our plans could really be hindered by having a man so..." *[mouth-wateringly fuckable!]* "... handsome with us if you get what I mean," she said, trying to part ways while her subconscious mind insisted that she leave the door open, and she felt like an ass for what she just said. "God, I'm sorry. I must sound like a total jerk saying that after what you did for me."

"Shhhh...I understand," he assured her. "At least let me see you safely to your next destination, and if we see each other again, you can buy me that drink."

"Okay," Olivia said, biting her lip as she motioned for him to follow. They headed down the street toward where the limo was waiting for them, and the other women were snickering and whispering to each other as Olivia and Aleksander talked.

"My name's Alek, by the way," he said, extending his hand to shake hers.

"Olivia," she said. "And this is Dani, Liana, and June."

"Ladies," Alek said, dipping his head and smiling, and when he made eye contact with June, she blushed, her eyes chased away. She didn't watch his show or have any idea who he was, but even she couldn't deny that he was drop dead delicious.

"Well, this is us," Olivia said when they came to the limo.

"Then I'll leave you to it. Have a lovely evening, ladies," Alek said, his eyes lingering just a little longer on Olivia than perhaps they should have.

"We're in town a couple more days. Maybe we'll see you around," she said, and as she heard it come out of her mouth in a shamelessly flirtatious tone, she felt a deep pang of guilt.

"I'm here until Monday," he said, "and I'd really like that." Then he flashed his smile and walked away, leaving Olivia thoroughly disgusted with herself as she swooned in his wake.

"Oh, my freaking God!" Liana growled, fanning herself with her hand as they sat in the back of the limo while the driver pulled away from the curb.

"You know, you did promise to get LiLo and me laid," Dani teased Olivia.

"If I can't fuck Alek Hellström, none of you bitches can," she said, trying to pretend she was unaffected by June's self-righteous glare and her own moral compass. But she was affected. Whether she gave a shit or not about what June thought, she still felt horrible. Maybe it was natural for other people to be tempted but not for her. Her marriage was as idyllic as marriage could get.

So why was it that she couldn't even trust herself to have a drink with Aleksander Hellström?

"Would you stop?" Dani whispered in her ear with an exasperated sigh.

"What are you talking about?"

"You got all hot and bothered, and now you're feeling guilty," she said, and Olivia snarled at her. Dani had always been good at knowing what was going on inside Olivia's head, and now that she was an experienced psychologist, there was no hiding anything from her. "It's perfectly natural, and it doesn't make you a bad wife. I mean, did you see those muscles? Damn, girl! You'd be blind not to want that."

"I didn't," June sniped.

"You wouldn't know what to do with it anyway," Dani said dismissively.

"Well, I would, and since Olivia screwed me out of that opportunity, the next round's on her," Liana said, trying to defuse the situation before June could respond.

"Let's start with a toast from the mini bar," Dani said, opening it up and grabbing the bottle of Goldschläger. She also pulled out four shot glasses.

"You won't be needing that fourth glass," June informed her.

"Please, Junie-bug," Liana begged. "Just one shot to celebrate Dani's divorce?"

"You know I can't," she protested.

"I'm not asking you to get hammered. It's just one, little drink," Liana pressured her.

"But..."

"Oh, for fuck's sake," Olivia said impatiently. "When you go to confession, you can tell the preacher I made you do it."

"We don't really go to confession," June explained, but when Olivia looked at her with a scowl, her eyes rolling back in her head, she relented. "Fine. But just half a glass."

"You got it," Dani said with a sly grin as she reached into the bar and pulled out a beer stein, and even June burst into laughter.

T Minus 15 Hours
Sunday

June woke up with her first hangover since she was in high school. After her joke, Dani had poured her half a shot glass as requested, but once she did that, the others pressured her to do more. She

18

stubbornly resisted, forcing them to pretend to twist her arm, absolving her of the responsibility for the sin of it.

In total, she only had about six shots all night long, but since she had barely drunk more than a few glasses of wine in over fifteen years, it didn't take much. She loosened up and for a few, brief hours became the Junie-bug they all remembered and loved. This morning, however, she was back to her new self, claiming her nausea and headache were the wages of sin.

"What you need is a little hair of the dog," Dani suggested as they rode in the limo toward the cafe where they planned to have brunch before shopping.

"I'm never drinking again," June said.

"Pounding Goldschläger probably wasn't the best course of action when you never drink, but I know what will make you feel better," Olivia said, and as soon as they were seated in the restaurant, she ordered four mimosas, banking on June not knowing they had champagne in them. She didn't know, and though she thought they tasted funny, her lack of experience with alcohol allowed her to keep up as Olivia ordered four more rounds, leaving her feeling much, much better than she had earlier.

After brunch, they walked down the street toward the first of several boutiques they had found online, excitedly talking about their plans for later tonight when a sudden, heavy wind started to blow. Dani fought to keep her perfect hair from becoming a tangled mess, but it got so strong, they all had to duck into a doorway to wait it out as leaves and debris began to swirl over the sidewalk in front of them. Though they could see people walking on the other side of the street as if nothing was out of the ordinary, the wind on their side trapped them there, and when Dani turned around to fix her hair in the reflection of the shop window where they'd taken shelter, she noticed the signage and drew her friends' attention to it.

Madam Levinia's Parlor - Futures Foretold - Spells Cast - Wishes Granted

"Oooh," Olivia said sarcastically, rolling her eyes as Dani hummed the Twilight Zone theme song, but Liana was a little more superstitious than her friends. And of course June was fairly certain it was the work of Satan.

"We're going in," Dani said.

"I don't think we should," Liana protested.

"I know we shouldn't! It's witchcraft!" June exclaimed.

"And now it's *definitely* happening," Olivia said. She was going to vote against it since she didn't like the idea of paying charlatans to fill her head with bullshit, but June had to go and say something asinine. And she wasn't finished.

"I'll wait out here for you. I can't go in there," she insisted.

"What do you think is going to happen, June? Is a portal to hell going to open up and swallow us all?" Olivia demanded impatiently. "Nothing is going to happen. She's going to tell us what she thinks we want to hear, and we're going to leave poorer yet no more enlightened than when we entered."

"She's probably right," Liana said with an uneasy giggle.

"Bitches," Dani said, putting her foot down. "Jax Bonham is still in town, you promised to get me laid, and this lady casts spells. Get...the fuck...inside." She held the door open, and the others walked past - Olivia laughing, Liana massaging the cross on her necklace between her thumb and forefinger, and June silently praying for forgiveness for things she hadn't even done yet.

When the door closed behind them, it took a minute for their eyes to adjust. It was so dark, all the decor in shades of deep, rich jewel tones and black. The furniture was antique with gilded, intricately carved arms and legs, and a thick, velvet curtain hung across the back, creating a narrow, cozy waiting area. As they looked around the room at the curiosities displayed on the walls and shelves, it only reinforced the opinions each had going in, and though not all of them were nervous about being there, they all nearly jumped out of their skin when they heard a voice.

"Can I help you, ladies?" Madam Levinia asked, suddenly appearing through the break in the curtain. Dani took a deep breath and gathered herself, holding out her hand as she approached the old woman whose face was covered in deep trenches of wrinkles extending into thin lips that no longer lent themselves to adequate application of the dark, red lipstick she wore. Her eyes were a milky, dull blue with a cataract in the left one that made the pupil an even lighter color than the iris.

"I hope we're not intruding. My friends and I just sort of stumbled in here by accident," Dani began.

"There are no accidents, child," Levinia said. "I've been expecting you."

Olivia was so annoyed by how typical this all seemed, it was killing her to keep her mouth shut, but for her friend's sake, she bit her tongue and pressed on when Levinia invited them to follow her behind the curtain. Olivia had to prod June who was frozen in her tracks, but Liana's fascination seemed to have overridden her superstition as she walked trancelike behind a very exited Dani.

Madam Levinia sat down at a round table with five chairs. In the center was the obligatory crystal ball, and in front of the old woman was a deck of tarot cards with a black pentacle on the back. Olivia enjoyed the look on June's face when she noticed them because she knew June had no idea what distinguished one five point star in a circle from the next. June automatically assumed it meant Satanism, and she grew ever more anxious as her eyes adjusted to the even dimmer room and she realized the motif was repeated throughout, including a faint representation on the table top with the points between the chairs.

"You want a love spell," Levinia said to Dani with an enduring certainty that left her nodding in astonishment, but Olivia was unconvinced. Dani was a woman in her thirties, no wedding ring on her finger, hanging out with the girls on Sunday afternoon...it seemed like a logical guess.

"And what about your friends?" the old woman asked. "I don't think you're the only one who could use a love spell."

"I'm married," June snapped as if she was offended.

"Same here," Olivia added. "The last thing I need is a love spell."

"You, sweet red-haired girl, are not as happy as you deserve to be, and you, golden haired lady, you deny yourself something you deeply desire."

"Oh! Do me next!" Liana clucked excitedly after hearing the old woman pretty much nail her friends.

"Your strength and independence have left you lonely, but Madam Levinia can help you all." She rose from the table, picking up the tarot cards and taking them to a nearby bookshelf that housed hundreds of other decks, some in their original boxes, some tied together with rubber bands, some wrapped in silk handkerchiefs, all shoved in haphazardly, and without even searching, she pulled one out, sending a swirl of dust particles into the already stale air. In the corner, she lit candles and incense, then she wound up an old victrola that started playing a soft, scratchy recording from the 1940's that seemed somehow both juxtaposed with the scene and perfectly congruent.

When she sat back down and unwrapped the tarot deck from the silk, on the back of the cards were four silhouetted figures on horseback. Without looking at them, Levinia pulled one card from the deck and laid it face down in front of each of the women.

"Yours is the King of Staves," she said to Liana before even turning it over to reveal that it was, indeed, the King of Staves. "Positive masculine energy."

"You, however, need the King of Cups. Freedom of desire," she said as she gazed eerily at June, the light blush on her cheeks betraying Madam Levinia's accuracy as she turned over the card.

"Hmmm...that's strange," Levinia said when she saw that it was actually the Queen of Cups.

"Somethin' you're not telling us, Junie-bug?" Dani asked with a wink, making her friends giggle, but June scowled as Madam Levinia reached into the deck and pulled out another card. It was the King. Without a word, she moved on to Olivia.

"You seek the King of Pentacles," she said. "Ultimate fulfillment."

"Oooh..." Dani said, teasing her friend until she looked up to find that Madam Levinia's eyes were now fixed on her.

"And you, my dear," she said, turning her card face up, "you deserve the honesty and transparency of the King of Swords. You've suffered long enough."

As the heady scent of incense wafted through the air, even the skeptical Olivia was silenced by Levinia's words and insights, though somewhere in the back of her mind she was certain there was a trick to it. June and Liana looked nervous, but Dani was still excited as the old woman pulled a sealed bottle and what looked like four thimbles down from the book shelf. The bottle was glass with red jewels inlaid in the aged and fading gold paint on the outside, and the thimbles were tiny cups in different colors. She poured a drop from the bottle into each cup, doled them out to the women, and bade them drink.

Olivia's cup was white, Dani's red, June's black, and Liana's a pale grey. As the women looked at each other, uncertain about drinking some odd, clear liquid that a strange gypsy crone had placed before them, she laughed and turned the bottle up, waterfalling its contents into her mouth to show them there was nothing to fear.

"Well...bottoms up," Dani said first, holding her thimble aloft before drinking it. It tasted like water, and when she didn't even make a face, the others followed.

"Good. Good," Levinia said as she collected the cups and set them aside, then she instructed them to hold hands. "Now you must speak the name of the man you desire so the spell may be cast upon him." She looked first at Liana.

"Aiden LaCroix!" she said enthusiastically. He was her favorite Greyhawks hockey player. He was a puck bunny's dream - 6 feet tall, chocolate brown hair, dark brown eyes that almost looked black, and he'd never lost a tooth or a chance to score on the ice. He'd been her ideal since the first moment she saw him at a game in New York on vacation, and what made him even more enticing was the fact that he was well-known for avoiding the hockey groupies. He was so gorgeous, he could have been walking around with a supermodel on his arm, but he didn't seem like that kind of guy. Liana liked that. She also liked a challenge, and when Levinia's eyes started to move on to June, she drew them back with an important condition.

"I don't want a love spell, though," she said. "Just bring us together somehow so he'll have to get to know me. I'll do the rest."

"Yeah! Same for all of us!" Dani blurted out, and Levinia smiled, her teeth crooked and yellow as she nodded to accept their stipulation.

"And what about you?" she asked June. "What man would you like to fall into your lap?"

"Uhhh...I don't know..." she hesitated, but Liana smacked her leg and gave her an impatient look. "Okay. Jobe Stricklan."

"The TV preacher?" Dani demanded, and Olivia rolled her eyes because of course, she picked Jobe Stricklan! Her batshit crazy husband probably didn't let her watch much else, and if you had to fuck a televangelist, it may as well be the only one out there who was semi-attractive and less than a hundred-years-old.

But damn, he was skeevy!

"There's one more thing," June added, "we're both married, so however this works, it can't be cheating. I would never commit adultery." Levinia gave her an irritated look then moved on to Olivia.

"And what about you?" she asked.

"Ummm..." Olivia began, biting her lip and looking down at her hands. "Maybe Kai Rivers...or...."

"Or what? Hers is Aleksander Hellström," Dani barked. "Next!"

"Wait!" Olivia called out because she wasn't finished. Even though she didn't believe in magic, she felt guilty for even playing along at this point, and she had to do something to assuage that guilt so when she told Reid the story - because they told each other everything - she wouldn't have to see that faint, insecure look in his eyes that still reared its head even after fifteen years of proving that she wasn't really out of his league. "I'm okay with Alek Hellström, but it has to be a situation where it won't negatively affect my marriage."

"Tall order," Levinia said with a cackle.

"Oh! Amina Vašilić!" Olivia shouted out as it dawned on her how to make this whole thing okay with Reid. Amina Vašilić was a Bosnian-born actress whom Reid considered the most beautiful woman on the planet (next to his wife of course), so as long as Reid got her in exchange, Olivia was free to indulge in this silly fantasy. "It has to be a situation where Reid also gets to be with Amina Vašilić."

"Are you finished?" Levinia asked impatiently.

"Yes, ma'am," she said, giggling as June looked at her with wide-eyed surprise, and the gypsy turned her attention to Dani.

"Jax Bonham," she said resolutely. "And no monkey paw bullshit! I don't want to fall in love with him then I die of cancer or he gets hit by a train on our wedding day." Then she paused. She wasn't finished, but she needed to choose her next words carefully because she wanted to cover Olivia's husband without covering her own ex or June's husband, whom she doubted June truly loved anyway. "None of us dies, and the men we love can't die either, you feel me?"

"And our children," Olivia added. "None of our children can die."

"Enough!" Levinia snapped, holding her hands up in the air before calmly and softly adding, "You must leave room for the magic to work its will."

Satisfied with their caveats, the women fell silent, and Levinia reached for Liana's hand with her left and Dani's with her right. Dani took Olivia's,

Olivia took June's, and June completed the chain. Then the old gypsy began chanting in an unfamiliar tongue, her eyes closed tight, her body swaying, and as she grew louder, the music seemed to fade until they could barely hear it at all. The reek of the incense filled their nostrils, its thick, grey smoke creeping over the table top like morning mist in a valley, enveloping and drawing their attention to the crystal ball in the center. Olivia's eyes were caught by images of fire and blood and death, but when she squinted to focus on the ethereal wisps, they became nothing but reflections of candles and smoke.

Liana watched the old woman herself, and though she continued to sway, her eyes closed toward the ceiling, she looked back at Liana at the same time, eyes open, her cataract replaced by a tiny, black pupil, her face young and beautiful, her hair no longer the silver wires of the crone but full and black as coal, cascading over her shoulders. She winked at Liana, then the image was gone.

Each of the women saw something she could not explain. To Dani, Levinia seemed to soften like a kind grandmother while June saw a vision of a Christlike figure that she took as a warning, but as their brains tried to process the last illusion, the next was already begging their attention, leaving them all utterly disoriented when the same violent wind that drove them into the shop in the first place began to kick up. The candles blew out, leaving only threads of sunlight from the storefront illuminating the small room through cracks in the billowing velvet curtains, and the old woman's hair flew in long, grey strands, striking their flesh like the tendrils of a whip as the currents grew stronger and stronger until its sound was all they could hear above Levinia's incantation. The needle of the victrola was forced across the record, the tarot cards blew off the stack one by one, and lastly the Kings flew off the table and vanished from sight before the wind abruptly died. The curtains fell into their static position, blocking out the light, and in the dark room, they could hear the sound of cards and other small items hitting the floor.

"The words are spoke. The magic set free. The spell is cast. So mote it be!" Madam Levinia cried, her words devolving into cackling laughter, and then there was only darkness.

When Olivia woke up, it was already dusk. Disoriented, she looked around the hotel room, and the red, glowing numbers on the digital clock caught her eye. It was 7:45 PM. She didn't even remember lying down for a nap. In fact, she didn't remember anything after Madam Levinia's spell - not paying the old woman, not leaving her shop, not riding back to the hotel. She stood up and realized that she was still dressed in the clothes she had worn to brunch, and she walked out into the living room of the suite to find June and Liana already there, looking just as confused as she was. Then Dani appeared in the doorway to her room rubbing her temples.

"What the hell happened?" Dani asked, thinking she was the only one with a large chunk of her afternoon missing. She wasn't. None of them remembered a single thing from the same point in time.

"I think that old bat dosed us," Liana said.

"That's not possible," Olivia protested.

"Please," Dani scoffed. "You mean to tell me you didn't feel like you were trippin' balls in that place?"

"No, I did, but it's only been about five hours. We'd still be tripping."

"Maybe it was the mimosas," June offered. "There was alcohol in those, wasn't there?"

"A tiny bit of champagne. There's no way mimosas could've caused this," Olivia argued as her phone pinged. She grabbed it from the table. It was a text from Reid.

Did you lose your sat phone? he asked, and while the other women continued to ponder the loss of the past five hours, Olivia called her husband.

"It's somewhere in my luggage," she said of the satellite phone after greeting him. The whole family had sat phones because cell coverage wasn't always a given on their mountaintop. "Why?"

"I've been trying to call you for the past five hours, and when I couldn't reach you on either phone, I looked them up to see where you were."

"And?"

"And the cell phone was traveling while the sat phone stayed in one place, then when I checked again, it was the opposite. It kind of freaked me out." It was freaking Olivia out too as she looked through her missed calls to see that he had tried her ten times. She hadn't heard it ring once, but she didn't want to worry him.

"That's weird. I must have turned my ringer off on the cell. I'll check the limo for the sat. Why were you trying to get a hold of me? Is everything okay?"

"I had to come to Charleston this afternoon. Liza lost Mom again."

"Oh, babe, I'm sorry," she said. Reid's mother had Alzheimer's and had been living with his sister for about two years, and six months ago, she had begun sneaking out and wandering around town.

"It's okay. We found her, but I'm going to go ahead and spend the night down here so Liza can have a break. Are your friends okay with me leaving Rey and Savannah in charge of the kids?" he asked, and Olivia walked into the other room.

"Probably not, but what June doesn't know won't hurt her," she said with a laugh. "Did you make sure Savannah knew Sally and Bella are still banned?" Sally and Bella were Savannah's best friends and worst enemies, and Olivia was sick of the drama, sentencing Savannah to a weekend without them so she didn't have to deal with the phone calls while she was away. Of course, Savannah was convinced that meant Sally and Bella would spend their weekend talking shit about her, which her mother informed her was all the more reason to find new, more loyal friends.

"I made her promise," Reid said. "Besides, I don't necessarily consider this a good thing as a father, but she seems very content to hang out with Rey."

"Are you sure it was a good idea leaving them alone? He seemed like a player."

"Nah, he's a good kid. Plus I told him you'd feed him to Evil if he touched our daughter."

Olivia laughed. "Then take your time, and give your mom a hug for me, okay? We probably won't be back home until tomorrow afternoon."

"I'll make sure I'm back before you. I love you, baby."

"I love you, too," she said.

As soon as they hung up, Olivia called the chauffeur to see if her satellite phone was in the car, hoping he would know more about what happened after they left Madam Levinia's, and *did he ever!* Olivia had brought him the phone when they got back to the hotel and asked him to keep it handy, telling him she was going to need it later, and before that, they had shopped for more than two hours, filling up the trunk of the limo with bags they said they'd sort out later.

"Did you notice anything off about us?" she asked, and he hesitated for a second before speaking.

"You all seemed pretty drunk, ma'am," he admitted bashfully.

"Really? We were only drinking mimosas at lunch."

"Well, I don't know how many you had, but they put some kind of liquor in them at the Cafe Concourse. My mother got smashed there on just three at my sister's bridal shower," he explained with a laugh.

"Oh," Olivia said, relieved.

"Will you be needing the car again this evening?"

"We'll be leaving for dinner in about an hour, I guess, but I don't know where we're going to go after nine on a Sunday night," she said, thinking out loud.

"This is my hometown. When you're ready, just let me know what sounds good, and I'll find it for you."

"That would be fantastic. Thank you!"

She hung up and explained to her friends that they'd all been drinking hard liquor at lunch, and though Olivia couldn't figure out how she didn't taste it in the mimosas, it still seemed like the best explanation, especially considering the fact that they finished their afternoon shopping as planned. And, of course, whether it accounted for everyone's complete lack of memory or not, it was much easier to digest than the wild ideas that had been going through all of their minds since they woke.

Sunday evening was their last night together in Pittsburgh, so the quartet left for dinner dressed to kill. Dani, who had to be at the airport at 9:00 am, brought her suitcases with her so she wouldn't have to bother with a bellman when she rolled out of bed in the morning, and with little room in the trunk due to their shopping spree, the driver put her luggage in the front seat, promising to shuffle the items in the trunk to make it fit while they were at dinner.

"I just hope he doesn't get bored and read my sex diary while he's waiting for us," June said after he dropped them off at a pub that was still serving food.

"I just hope June's sex diary doesn't bore him so much that he reads mine," Olivia sniped, winking at June as if she was kidding.

"Well, since we're all about to meet the men of our dreams according to one magical gypsy, I have to insist that you all continue journaling your sexploits for me," Dani said.

"Shit, girl! If that spell works, I'll video it for you," Liana said enthusiastically while June gave their information to the hostess.

"Don't hold your breath on mine," Olivia said. "Alek Hellström may be in Pittsburgh, but I doubt Amina Vašilić is within a thousand miles of West Virginia."

"That reminds me," Dani said, grabbing her arm as the hostess motioned for them to follow her to a booth near the bar. "What was that Kai Rivers shit?"

"Kai Rivers is still hot," Olivia argued.

"Yeah, but you haven't mentioned him since we were nineteen, and the other day, I stood right on the streets of Pittsburgh and watched Alek Hellström melt your damn panties."

"Maybe I just want it all," Olivia quipped, kissing the air in Dani's direction as they sat down - Olivia and Dani on one side, Liana and June on the other, facing the entrance.

"Madam Levinia did offer her ultimate fulfillment," Liana said with a sly grin.

"Psh!" Dani balked. "I'd bet anything that - even if Reid was standing right there telling her to fuck Alek Hellström *or* Kai Rivers - Olivia wouldn't have the balls to go through with it."

"Lucky for me, I don't have to worry about that bet because there's no such thing as magic."

"Don't be so sure," June said, her eyes suddenly large as she stared back toward the door. The others followed her gaze to see Aleksander Hellström walking in.

"Well, well, well," Dani said, grinning ear to ear.

"Coincidence," Olivia insisted, but half an hour later it was harder to argue when Alek, who had been surrounded by swooning fans, noticed Olivia sitting at the table not far from his barstool. He got up immediately and walked toward her.

"Olivia," he said with an enthusiastic smile.

"Alek," she replied, swallowing her own excitement as she looked up at him - so tall and fair like a golden god.

"I believe you owe me a drink," he said as a crowd of women watched his every move.

"It seems I have an opportunity to repay my debt and return the favor since it looks like you're the one who needs rescuing this time," she said, indicating the lovesick fans with a quick nod as she inched subtly closer to Dani on the booth bench, hoping he would take a hint and sit.

"May I?" he asked, and she cleared more room, forcing Dani against the wall.

When Alek sat down close to her, Olivia watched the faces of his fans fall, and though she couldn't see Dani's face, she could feel her smirk as the sensation of Alek's bare arm against hers sent electricity coursing through her, settling between her thighs.

The waitress cleared the dishes, they ordered drinks and made small talk, and Olivia wrestled with her conscience, thinking about Reid with his poor, disoriented mother while she sat in a bar with a man who effortlessly conjured erotic visions inside her head. That's why she had almost picked Kai Rivers. Kai was still hot, but he did not do this to her. He was just a fantasy from her teenage years, and Reid would understand that when he heard the story of Madam Levinia's. Reid wasn't going to understand this. While most men would laugh it off if their wife had a crush on a famous actor, most men assumed their wives would never have a chance. Not Reid. He knew what Olivia was capable of, and her confidence was something she couldn't hide. Men were drawn to it, even men like Alek, and because of that, she was glad at least June stayed as a witness to prove that nothing inappropriate happened since Dani and Liana were now too busy mingling and dancing, determined to end their friender-bender with a literal bang.

Then Liana came back to the booth alone and slumped down into her seat beside June.

"What's the matter?" Olivia asked.

"I lost my wingman," she grumbled as she pointed with her eyes at Dani who was sitting at the bar with Jax Bonham! He was wearing an untucked silk shirt with the top three buttons undone, his jet black hair a wild mess that hung to his shoulders, his eyes a piercing blue that stood out from all the way across the bar, and he had his arm around Dani as he fed her the cherry from the top of her drink.

"When did this happen?" Olivia asked.

"I watched him come in about an hour ago," June said.

"Yet you didn't think that was worth mentioning to your best friend who's been crazy about him since the seventh grade?" Olivia demanded.

"It worked itself out," she said with a snide crinkle of her nose, bored, annoyed, and wanting to just go back to the hotel and watch TV.

"It sure did," Liana said. "I just wish I didn't have to wait so long for my spell..."

Olivia shot her a very clear *shut the fuck up* look, not wanting to have to explain to Alek that there was a possibility that he was there because of some voodoo rather than a genuine attraction to her. She didn't believe in it, but she wasn't sure about his beliefs. Though he had a perfect American accent, he was Swedish, and she really knew very little about Swedes beyond a few words she had learned in high school to hit on a hot, blonde exchange student.

"I just meant I'm bored is all," Liana said, trying to cover up her faux pas.

"Well, Canada is a long way away," Olivia whispered with a wink. "But you know what you should do? You should get our chauffeur to join us. His name's Mitch. He's a nice guy, and he's been sitting in that car waiting for us while we have a good time all weekend."

"I think that's a great idea," Liana said. The same thought had crossed her mind. Not only was he a really nice guy, he was polite, respectful, *and safe*. She didn't feel like he would put the moves on her, and despite that she agreed that the goal of the weekend was to get laid, the truth was she didn't want to get laid. Well, she did. She wanted to be kissed and licked and fucked like the world was ending, but there was a reason she had spent the last five years of her life committed to Bob. It was why she feared that even if the gypsy brought Aiden LaCroix into her life and he fell madly in love with her, she'd still be stuck with Bob in the end.

But there was no reason the sexy chauffeur couldn't act as Bob's fluffer for the night.

Mitch was a good looking guy - tall, light brown hair with a well-groomed beard, a little older than Liana but not too old to get her attention, and he was happy to spend his evening *with* her rather than in the car waiting *for* her. For hours, they sat at the bar keeping each other well entertained, but as she threw back drink after drink, he only nursed a single beer himself. Right beside them, Dani kept Jax Bonham's attention solely on her, despite that they had to pause their conversation every three minutes so he could sign an autograph or pose for a picture. Alek had to endure similar interruptions, though with much less frequency as he angled himself inward, keeping his back to the crowd while he and Olivia got to know each other. They learned that they had a lot in common, and though he seemed to have little in common with June, he chivalrously included her in the conversation as she sat there feeling like a third wheel. Then just as he and Olivia had gotten into the deep, philosophical subject of the imaginary world of the demon character he played on television, his cell phone alarm went off.

"Fuck," he groaned. "I have to get to the convention center."

"At one in the morning?" Olivia asked, suspicious that it might be a ruse to rescue himself from her.

"We're doing a promo in full makeup at 5:00 AM, and you wouldn't believe how long it takes to get my horns on," he said apologetically, then he looked up at her, suddenly excited. "You could come with me."

"I would love to, but I can't. We're leaving in the morning," she said with a pout.

"Then I guess this is goodbye," he said as he stood, and when he reached for the hand closest to him, her left, he held it as if he couldn't decide whether to shake or kiss it. "I've really enjoyed your company tonight, Olivia. I'm sorry it had to end so early."

"Me too," she said, and just as he was about to ask for her phone number, he noticed a set of rings he hadn't before. His eyes lingered on them for a moment, then he forced a smile.

"Have a safe trip home," he said.

"Have fun getting...your horns on," she said, barely resisting the urge to tell him to have fun getting horny, but as she sat there looking up at him, he realized what she almost said as if he could read her mind. A grin spread across his face.

"It's no fun at all when I'm alone," he said, then he crinkled his nose before heading toward the door, and she was glad he didn't look back to see the blush on her cheeks as she watched his perfect ass walk out of her life, leaving her guilt-ridden and wishing Reid was waiting for her back at the hotel.

On the other side of the bar, Dani was about to experience the same disappointment. Gino, the ParraJax crew member most hated by any fan who had ever partied with the band, had come to wrangle Jax. The bus was leaving for Cleveland in half an hour.

Jax grabbed a pen from the bartender and wrote his private cell phone number on Dani's palm, then he put his hands on her shoulders, bracing her as he pulled her in for a kiss. Slowly their faces moved toward each other, their eyes closed, Dani began to tremble, and Jax Bonham slipped his smooth, wet tongue between her lips. Her hands went to his head, twisting her fingers in his long hair as they attacked each other forcefully, ravenously. He grabbed her leg, hoisting it up over his hip, and with her dress riding up to expose the crotch of her panties, she could feel his cock, hard and yearning for her just as her suddenly throbbing clit yearned for him. At this point, she would not have had the power to stop him if he had tried to fuck her right there in the middle of the crowd, and Jax felt just as weak.

This man who couldn't leave the safety of his hotel or limousine without droves of women begging to fulfill his every possible fetish or fantasy found himself in unfamiliar territory, wanting Dani so desperately, he could have fallen to his knees and begged for her, but even more delicious was the idea of dreaming about her for the next two weeks as he waited for the tour to take him to Indianapolis where they'd planned to meet. Summoning what little willpower he had, he pulled his lips from hers, tracing them along her face toward her ear, and with his cock still rubbing against her, he whispered.

"Don't wear anything special when we meet in Indianapolis because when I get my hands on you, I'm going to rip your clothes to shreds and use them to tie you to my bed, then I'm going to make you come until you beg me to stop because making you come is all I'll be able to think about for the next two weeks."

He thrust his cock against her as he bit down on her ear lobe, and when he started to softly grind into her, he heard only the slightest moan escape her lips as an orgasm seized upon her right there in the bar in front of everyone. Her breath grew heavy, her body quaked, and a very satisfied smile spread across the face of Jax Bonham as he slowly teased her through the aftershocks.

"Call me," he breathed, pressing himself against her once more before he allowed Gino to finally pull him away, leaving her flushed and exposed but too high to feel embarrassed until she realized how many people were looking at her. Suddenly shy, she covered her mouth with her hand and scurried away from the bar to the booth where June and Olivia giggled at her, having watched the entire scene.

Once Jax was gone, Dani asked if they could call it a night. June had been ready to leave since dinner was over, and Olivia had been bored since Alek left. After drinking all night, she thought she would be nicely hammered rather than racked by guilt, but she hadn't even managed to catch a buzz. In fact, the only one of them who seemed tipsy at all was Liana. She had sucked down a lot of shooters, hoping she could talk herself into inviting Mitch up to their room, but even if she had gotten herself obliterated enough to make such a bold move, it would not have worked. Mitch was a nice guy. He would have refused to take advantage of her in that state.

With Liana draped over him as he walked her out of the bar, he helped her into the back of the limo and asked the others if they would like him to stop to get her coffee on the way back to the hotel. While they debated it with their stubborn, drunk friend, Olivia noticed something strange going on down the street. There appeared to be some sort of brawl on the sidewalk involving about ten people, and each time someone new came out of the club nearby, they were drawn into it.

"Olivia!" Dani shouted. "Get your ass in the car! Let's go!"

"What's the hurry?" she asked as she closed the door behind her, bummed that their vacation was essentially over.

"You need to help me decide if I should text Jax or not," Dani said, then as Mitch pulled onto the road, she excitedly told her friends everything about her time with the lead singer of ParraJax, omitting the fact that he made her come in the middle of a crowded bar. "And now I want to call him so bad...just to make sure it's real. But I don't want to look desperate. I don't know what to do."

"Well, you could tell him I spilled a drink and smudged the ink, so you wanted to make sure you had the number right," Liana suggested as she reached to open the limo's bar.

"You're cut off," Olivia said, smacking her hand.

"I'm going to do it," Dani said, and she tapped out a text.

This is Dani...just making sure I got your number right.

With a deep breath, she hit send, but Jax didn't text back. He called.

"Hello?" Dani said, suddenly grinning as she bit her lip and twisted her hair in free hand. Giggling, the others tuned her out, talking among themselves as Jax told Dani he regretted not getting her number the minute he got on the bus because he would have called her already. He also regretted not sneaking away with her and letting the bus wait for him. He was, after all, the star, and that star was as taken with Dani as she was with him.

Olivia thought it was cute, but it made June anxious. She wasn't even comfortable with what they did at Madam Levinia's when it was all just a joke, but now that it seemed like the spell was coming to fruition, she didn't like the implications for her immortal soul.

"We shouldn't have done that," she said.

"Done what?" Olivia asked as she stared out the window at another street fight, this one involving fewer people, but two of them had a third down on the ground, really attacking him.

"Messed with witchcraft," June said.

"Shut the fuck up, June," Olivia groaned with an impatient eye roll as she leaned forward so Mitch could hear her better. "Is it common around here to see this many people fighting in the streets?"

"Not unless there's a WVU-Pitt game going on," he said with a laugh. "That's the fourth fight I've noticed since we left the bar. Maybe it's because of the comic convention...young people not used to drinking..."

"Maybe," Olivia said as she sat back in her seat. They had decided not to stop for coffee, so a couple of minutes later, they were in front of their hotel, but Mitch couldn't pull the car under the awning because it was too congested. That was weird too. It was a busy hotel, but there was no reason there would be so many cars clogging the way after 1:00 am on a Monday morning even with the comic convention in town. The really weird thing was, there seemed to be some sort of altercation happening here as well.

"Stay put, ladies," Mitch said. "I'm going to see what's going on before I let you out of the car."

Liana was almost passed out, and as Dani argued with June about the spell she allegedly cast on Jax, Olivia's focus was locked on the activity under the hotel awning. She noticed that all of the cars appeared to be left running with their doors open, and as Mitch approached the valet stand, she saw several people rush him, knocking him to the ground. They seemed wild, mindless, and terrifying, and that *something is amiss in the universe* feeling suddenly flooded her system with adrenaline.

We have to get the fuck out of here! her every instinct told her, and without even thinking, she crawled through the window separating the cab from the back and slid into the driver's seat, throwing the car in reverse and backing up just enough to be able to move it out of the circular drive.

"What are you doing?" June demanded.

"Making sure we don't get blocked in," she answered as she drove into the fire zone in front of the hotel to get as close to Mitch as possible, then she cracked the passenger side window. "Mitch! Come on! Hurry!"

He looked up, and as he shoved a man off of himself and tried to make a run for it, he realized someone else had a hold of him. It was a woman lying on the ground with her arms wrapped around his ankle. He struggled to pull away, but instead of letting go, she clutched him tighter. He could feel her fingernails digging into his flesh just above his sock, and as he bent over to free himself, she bit him, taking a hunk out of his calf. He screamed in agony, but he couldn't let his wound slow him down because more were coming. With his other foot, he kicked the woman in the head until he could pull free from her, and even though he shouldn't have been able to put weight on the leg that had been bitten, he couldn't even feel the pain as he raced to the car with others running after him.

"Go! Go! Go!" he shouted as he rolled into the backseat, pulling the door closed behind him. Olivia hit the gas and tore off onto the street where she could now see people wrestling and chasing each other everywhere.

"What's the quickest route to the hospital?" she asked Mitch as June and Dani tried to clean his wound using vodka from the mini bar.

"Doesn't matter," he said.

"Of course it matters!" Liana cried. She had abruptly sobered up and began taking care of him. "We're taking you to a hospital!"

"Look at what's going on around you, ladies. What do you think the hospitals will be like?"

"What *is* going on around us?" June asked as they all turned their attention to the world outside where things were growing increasingly chaotic. People were running in the streets - way more people than should have been awake after 1:00 AM on a Monday morning - and now emergency vehicles were lining the sides of the roads. Flashing lights. Sirens. Gun shots.

"No!" Dani cried as she watched a man tackle a woman and take a bite out of her face, the shreds of muscle stretching like cheese on a freshly baked pizza as he pulled away. She covered her mouth as her chest began to heave.

"Pull over!" Liana shouted. "I think Dani's going to throw up!"

"I can't," Olivia insisted as she stared ahead, her eyes glazed because running down the walk in front of the convention center was Alek Hellström. She knew it was him by the shape of the horns on his head, his face covered with the prosthetics from his demon makeup, and he was wearing a white t-shirt that was spattered in blood.

Speechless, everyone in the car watched him being chased across the lawn, and despite all of the potential threats between them, Olivia had tunnel vision as she sped forward on an intercept course, terrified that she might see him go down right before her eyes when someone caught up to him from behind. Alek turned, swinging at the man with a prop from the show - a large bow with a pentagram in the center, and as the man went down, June spoke, her voice carrying a weight beyond its power in the eerie silence of the limousine.

"Behold," she whispered. "A white horse, and he who sat upon it had a bow and a crown, and he went out to conquer."

For a second, everything seemed frozen, her words hanging in the air like the narration of a bad dream until Olivia was abruptly awakened by the anger they provoked.

"Shut the fuck up!" she snapped at June as she slammed on the brakes and cut the wheel, slinging the car toward Alek and the two crazed people who tailed him, their eyes glassy, their teeth gnashing violently. Olivia rolled down the passenger side window and called his name.

"Hurry!" she cried desperately, and when he dove into front seat, his face in her lap, she hit the gas, rushing away before his pursuers could grab his legs.

"Thank God you were here," Alek breathed as he righted himself on the seat and began peeling the horns, mask, and cowl from his head and face.

"God?" June butted in. "I don't think *God* is the reason we were in the exact right place at the right time, huh, Olivia?"

"Stop it, June!" Dani demanded.

"Why? Afraid to admit it? We did this! It's what happens when you summon demons!"

"There's no such thing as demons!" Olivia hissed.

"Then what would you call it when people start eating each other in the streets?"

"I don't know, but if you don't give it rest, I'll throw you out the fucking window and you can see for yourself!" Olivia snapped at her, and June scowled as she slumped back in her seat.

"Maybe it's some kind of virus like mad cow disease," Liana suggested, trying to keep the peace. "Or bath salts. Remember that video of the man in Florida who was on bath salts and bit someone's face off?"

"It's not bath salts," Alek said as he pulled the bald cap off his head, releasing his gorgeous blonde hair. His demon costume was pretty bad-assed, but his human character was what Olivia liked best about the show.

"How do you know it isn't bath salts?" she asked him.

"I watched someone get bit and become one of them," he said. "It may be a virus, but if it is, it acts fast." He had been in the makeup chair when a man came running into the backstage area and attacked a member of the FX crew. The security guard had to shoot him to stop him, but before he died, he managed to bite the makeup artist on the neck. She fell in the scuffle and bled out, then a few minutes later, she got back up, infected. It was a chain reaction from there, and Alek had run with two crew members, both of whom were attacked and bitten along the way. He didn't want to abandon them, but having seen firsthand that one bite was all it took, he knew they were beyond his help.

"If that's the case, why haven't I contracted it yet?" Mitch asked.

"I don't know," Alek said.

"Maybe it depends on where you were bitten or how much you weigh?" Liana offered. "It doesn't matter. We're taking you to the hospital."

"I need directions," Olivia said, catching Mitch's eyes in the rearview.

"We could try Ruby Memorial in Morgantown. Do you know how to get there?"

"I can get us there once we're in West Virginia, but I'm not that familiar with the area in between," she said, and Mitch sat up and looked out the front window at the traffic. Now that more people were aware of what was going on, there were more cars on the road.

"Take the next left," he said. "The main roads out of here are going to be a clusterfuck. We can go through Uniontown. Alek, would you reach into glove box and hand me my gun."

"What do you need a gun for?" Liana asked as Alek pulled it out and gave it to him. When the glove box was open, Olivia saw her satellite phone in there as well.

"I don't need the gun," Mitch said to Liana. "I want you to have it. If I get sick and attack you, I want you to shoot me."

"I can't shoot you!" she protested.

"I'll hold the gun," Dani said, but she didn't really plan to use it either. Surely if it was a virus, it could be cured. Death was permanent. If he started showing signs of it, she could use the gun to force him to get out of the car. Then they could just put him in the trunk for the rest of the trip to the hospital. For no more than she understood about the situation, it seemed like a sound plan. Then her phone rang.

"Jax!" she said excitedly when she answered.

"Dani? Oh, thank God!" he said. "You have to send us help."

As Mitch directed Olivia through the backstreets toward the road that would lead them to Uniontown, PA, Jax spoke to Dani from the lavatory of his tour bus. He was calling her because his screen was busted, and though he had been blindly trying to call 911, he finally hit the right sequence to redial the last call.

They had been travelling on route 51 toward interstate 70 when the bus driver had spotted a car coming straight at them from the opposite direction. It had been weaving all over the road, and to avoid a head on collision, he had swerved onto the shoulder and lost control, crashing the bus into a large tree.

"We were all shaken up, but everyone seemed okay except the driver. He was slumped over the wheel. Our manager went to check on him, and he just freaked out and attacked him. He bit him - tore his fucking throat out, Dani. It was the most terrifying thing I've ever seen. We rushed him and held him down, but it was like he was on PCP or something. Even when we beat the shit out of him, he just kept fighting. Then our manager got up and was acting the same way. Jacky got bit. Richie got bit, fucking everybody...Jesus! It's just me and a couple of girls now. We're locked in the bathroom, and they're all out there trying to tear down the door. I don't know how long we can hold out. Can you send the police?"

"I don't think the police are an option. You don't know what it's like out here," Dani said. "Where are you?"

"Somewhere on the side of Highway 51. My phone is smashed. I can't get our exact location."

"Hold on," she said, then she turned to Mitch. "Where's Highway 51?"

"We're heading there right now. It's the road we're taking to Uniontown."

"We're on our way, Jax," Dani said. "Just hold tight. We'll figure something out."

Without even asking for anyone else' opinion, Dani told Olivia and Alek to keep their eyes open for the bus as she stayed on the phone with Jax. She could hear the girls crying as their tormenters banged against the door, trying to get to them, and she heard Jax soothe them, promising them that their savior was on her way. She didn't know how she was going to do it because, by her count, there were at least six infected men standing between her and that small tour bus bathroom, but Jax was getting out of this alive. The gypsy promised. No man they loved would die, and she was sure she was falling in love with him already.

Once they got south of Pittsburgh, Highway 51 was deserted. Whatever was going on in Steel Town didn't seem to be overflowing into the surrounding areas, so their best guess was that Jax's bus driver must have contracted the sickness somehow before the band left town.

June and Liana had tried to look up similar events on their phones, but neither could get a strong enough signal to use the internet. Liana called her son, Rey to check on the kids, and while all of June's boys were already asleep, Rey and Savannah were still up watching a movie. Otherwise everything seemed perfectly fine on their mountaintop, so Liana didn't mention what was happening in Pittsburgh because she didn't want to worry the children, but when she hung up, it occurred to her that they didn't mention Reid.

"Is Reid home?" she asked Olivia.

"He should be," she said, then she reached for her satellite phone in the glove box. There were several missed calls from him, and the ringer was silenced. She turned it on.

"Did you turn off the ringer?" she asked Mitch as she dialed Reid's sat phone.

"I put it in there exactly as you gave it to me," he said. She didn't remember turning it off, but then again, she didn't remember giving it to Mitch either. She looked down at the phone sadly as the call ended with no answer. Then it rang.

"Hello?"

"I can't talk right now. It isn't safe," Reid whispered. "I'm trying to get back home, but there's been some sort of outbreak here. I'll call you when I can. I love you."

"I love you," Olivia said, but Reid hung up so quickly, she wasn't sure if he even heard her.

"What's wrong?" Liana asked.

"Reid had to go to Charleston to check on his mother. He said there was some sort of outbreak there too, so whatever this is, it isn't restricted to Pittsburgh."

"Oh, God! The children!" Liana cried.

"I'm on it," Olivia said, and she dialed Savannah's number.

"Hi, Mom," her precious, fourteen-year-old sang as she picked up.

"Savannah, I need you to listen to me very carefully," Olivia began, and though she projected a strong façade, inside she was falling apart. "Something bad is happening out here. We're heading back from Pittsburgh right now, but I don't know how long it will take us to get there, so I need you to wake up the boys and take everyone into the panic room in my bedroom. Keep your gun on you, and give one to Rey if he's comfortable with it."

"Mom, what's happening? You're scaring me," Savannah said.

"There's nothing to be afraid of. If you do everything I say, you'll be fine..."

There was a panel in the panic room that controlled everything on the property. Olivia instructed her daughter to kill all of the lights, lock everything down, and not to open the gate for anyone but her or Reid. "If someone comes and you feel like you have to use the gate defense, do not hesitate. Your safety is the most important thing on this planet. Do you understand me?"

"Yes," she said meekly.

"I mean that. I want you to watch the surveillance monitors and call me immediately if you see anyone pop up on any of those screens, and if someone comes to the gate, I don't care who it is, if they do not have a child in that house, they are your enemy," Olivia said. "Take some snacks, blankets, and pillows into the room, and don't let the boys get scared. Be strong and try to make it fun for them, and before you know it, we'll be there with you, okay?"

"Okay."

"I love you, baby. You can do this."

"I love you, too, Mom," Savannah said, then she thought of something, something that would make her feel safer than the panic room and the guns. "Can I bring Evil into the room with us?"

"No. I'm sorry. It just isn't safe."

"But, mom..."

"I get it, Savvy. She's my baby too, but there are other children there, and we have to respect their parents' wishes."

"I understand," Savannah said, but she really didn't. Evil had been her little sister for so long, she didn't remember a time without her, and she trusted that cat more than most humans. Still, she would do as her mother said.

Savannah immediately told Rey the plan, but unwilling to just shut everything down and hide in a panic room without explanation, he first turned the channel on the television to a news network. He was immediately sorry. They had been expecting to see that there was some sort of civil unrest that was causing Olivia to overreact, but instead what they saw were the serious journalists their parents watched every day reporting on an unidentified outbreak that was making people behave erratically, attacking, biting, and in some "as yet unconfirmed" cases, cannibalizing others. They were uncertain if it was caused by a virus or a drug at this point, but whatever it was, there were stories coming in from various major cities along the eastern seaboard.

"Okay. There's something going around. Big deal," Rey said, ever cynical.

"A virus or drug that's making people act like rabid animals."

"So? We're in the middle of fucking nowhere. Why do we have to hide in a panic room?"

"Because my mom said to, and if my mom said to, there's a good reason for it."

"Can't we just watch for their car and go in there when they get here? They'll never know," he said, annoyed by what he saw as a silly waste of his time, particularly when he had hoped the movie they were watching would end in a kiss with Savannah. She thought he was cute too, but right now, she had a responsibility.

"I don't care what you think, okay? I'm in charge here, and we're going to take the kids into the panic room and wait for our parents to come home. Do you know how to use a handgun?" she asked.

"I guess, but..."

"But nothing. We'll do what we have to do to keep us all safe until my mom or dad gets here and takes over. Got it?"

"Yes, ma'am," he said, impressed with how an otherwise laid back fourteen-year-old girl had suddenly taken charge so forcefully. She led him to the gun safe, handed him a .357, and gave him a box of bullets along with a quick tutorial. Next she went to the kitchen for snacks, then she woke up the boys. Once they were all inside the panic room, she opened the control panel, shut off all of the interior lights, and armed the security at the upper gate. As the boys sat on the floor on their blankets watching the pictures on multiple monitors behind Savannah, she explained that since her dad couldn't make it back, sleeping in there was something she wanted to do just to be on the safe side, and they seemed to buy it until the oldest of June's sons, Noah, noticed something moving on one of the screens.

"Is that your dad?" he asked, and Savannah turned to see a man creeping across the lawn near the front of the lodge. Fear flooded her system. Whether this was a regular person or one of the violent maniacs they saw on television earlier, he was a stranger on the property, and she knew they couldn't just hunker down in the panic room and let him do whatever he came to do. Even if they were safe inside, when their parents returned, he could hurt them...or worse.

She whispered her concerns to Rey, and together they decided that he had to be dealt with. They took Noah out into the master bedroom where they told him their plan, warning him to keep the doors locked and watch the monitors while they were gone.

"Don't scare the little ones, but this could be serious," she said. "If we don't come back, use the satellite phone mounted on the wall in there to call my mom. She's speed dial one. If we do come back, and we're not *ourselves*, don't let us in."

"How will I know?" he asked, and she paused, unsure of what to say.

"You'll know," Rey said, thinking about the footage he saw on the news. "*You'll know.*"

"If you're unsure, make us answer questions to get in, and no matter what, do not open that door for anyone but us or one of our parents, okay?" Savannah told Noah exactly what her mother had told her.

"Yes, ma'am," he said respectfully.

"One more thing," she added. "Do you know how to shoot a gun?"

"Yes. My dad taught me."

"Here," she said, pulling a small handgun from the back waistband of her jeans. Earlier, Rey had seen her strap one in a shoulder harness, but he didn't even notice her stashing the extra. "Take this. The safety is on. Do not even point it unless you absolutely have to."

"Yes, ma'am," he said, and Savannah and Rey left the boys in the panic room so they could go confront some strange man on the property. Rey tried to act brave, but in truth they were both terrified as they walked through the Anders residence and into the lodge.

"Do we need night vision goggles or something?" he asked as they approached the front door.

"Nah, the moon's almost full," she said. "You ready for this?"

"Bring it on," he said, and she opened the door. They stepped out onto the porch holding their guns in front of them, and they saw the intruder's face peeking around a bush on one side.

"Come out or I'll shoot," Savannah shouted, her voice strong and authoritative even as she had to struggle to keep her knees from knocking together.

"Yes, my lady," the intruder said with flourish, taunting her as he came into full view. He was a skinny man with dirty hair and scabs on his face, and when he spoke, he jerked, making Savannah think he might be a meth addict. It was a growing problem in the area due to poverty and unemployment, and her parents had educated her on the warning signs after a string of robberies in a nearby town.

"What are you doing here?" she demanded, straightening her posture to try to intimidate him.

"I'm a friend of your daddy's. He asked me to come by."

"Shall I wake him for you?" she asked with a skeptical glare.

"We both know he's not in there, little girl," the man said with a creepy laugh.

"I'm holding a gun, and you're unarmed. I don't think it matters where my father is."

"Oh, but it does," he said as he inched forward, and though she tensed, she never took her gun off him, keeping it aimed at his chest because the head was too easy to miss.

"I don't want to shoot you," she said.

"Then don't. I'm just a guy looking for a place to hide until morning so I don't get infected, then I'll be on my way."

"I don't *want* to shoot you," she repeated, "but I will if you don't get off my property right now."

"Come on, kid. I just need a safe place for the night. I'll sleep in the barn," he said as he moved ever closer, his attitude disturbingly cavalier for someone with two guns trained on him.

"And if I believed you, I might let you, but I don't," she said.

"So what do you think I came here for, hmmm?" he asked as he took another step, narrowing the gap between them to just a few yards.

"Do you think I'm here to rob you?"

He took another.

"Kill you?"

And another.

"*Rape* you!?" he roared, suddenly rushing toward the kids. Rey pulled the trigger only to find that he forgot to take the safety off as Savannah froze in terror, but just before he could get his hands on them, Evil lunged out of the shadows and took him down, landing on his chest at the bottom of the stairs and tearing out his throat with her teeth. Blood gushed upward like a fountain as he gurgled then quickly died.

Savannah burst into tears, and Rey put his arms around her from behind while she watched the cat dismount her kill. She walked a few steps toward the porch, then she scratched at the ground, slinging grass on the body behind her. She didn't want to eat the man. She was protecting her sister. She always would, and when she was finished posturing, she hurried up to Savannah, rubbing her head against her leg, seeking praise for her accomplishment.

"Good job, Evie," Savannah said, scratching her behind the ear. "Let's get you cleaned up."

Though her mother had told her not to, once Savannah cleaned the blood off the great cat, she took her into the panic room.

"Does anyone know how Evil got loose?" Savannah asked, looking at June's boys, and Jeremiah, the eight-year-old gave her a sheepish glance.

"I peeked in her door earlier tonight. I just wanted to see her, but I promise I shut it back all the way," he admitted.

"You have to lock the door. She knows how to work the knob," Savannah said.

"I really am sorry," Jeremiah said.

"Well, you shouldn't have gone in there, but this time, it was a good mistake. She saved our lives." Savannah petted Evil atop the head and when the boys joined in, the jaguar rolled over on the floor like a giant house cat. Savannah just knew they were safe with Evil in there. She'd tell her mother later. Sometimes it was easier to ask for forgiveness than permission, which is what she had told the boys when she introduced them to video games the day their mother left for Pittsburgh. They loved video games, especially the violent ones, and now that the world was getting more violent than ever, Savannah thought maybe she and Rey had done the right thing.

"I see the bus," Alek said as the limo sped down Highway 51.

"Where?" Olivia asked, slowing down.

"Up ahead on the right." He pointed, and her eyes followed until she could see the very top of it off the side of the road where it had run down a hill into a thicket of trees. She pulled off onto the gravel shoulder, and in the backseat, she could hear Dani trying to call Jax to let him know they had arrived. She had planned to keep him on the line until they got there, but the call dropped, and now the lines had become so busy, there was no reestablishing the connection.

Leaving Liana in the back with Mitch, everyone else got out to discuss how to get Jax and the two girls off the bus without disturbing the infected. Before closing the door, Dani handed Mitch's gun to Liana.

"No, you take it," Liana said. "You might need it."

"You might need it too," Mitch insisted, then he turned to Dani. "Why don't you use the rifles in the trunk?"

"There are rifles in the trunk?"

"The ones you bought today. Remember?"

No. She didn't remember. Dani popped the trunk and looked inside to find that the shopping they did this afternoon was the quickest way to get on a government watch list. They had gone exclusively to gun shops and Army-Navy surplus stores. There were multiple rifles, thousands of rounds of ammunition, bows and arrows, knives, swords, and Kevlar vests.

"What the actual fuck?" Dani wondered aloud, and though Olivia was just as confused by it, when she saw the cache, she smiled from ear to ear.

"Lock and load, motherfuckers," she said as she went to work filling the magazines. Before Olivia passed out the rifles, Dani opened her suitcase and handed her friends clothes and shoes. Hers was the only luggage they had, but since they were wearing fuck-me pumps and mini dresses, she figured it wouldn't really matter if her jeans were a little loose on Olivia's narrow hips and a little tight on Liana's curves. At least they all had the same size shoes. June, who's idea of dressing sexy already meant jeans, didn't need anything beyond the rifle Olivia gave her, but Dani tossed her shirt away.

"What are we going to do?" June asked. "We can't just go on that bus and start shooting people."

"We'll shoot them in the leg if we have to," Olivia said.

"Why don't they just crawl out the bathroom window?" June suggested.

"They already tried, but Jax said the window is too small," Dani said.

"Does anyone know if there's a bedroom at the back of the bus?" Alek asked.

"Let's shoot out the window and see," Olivia said.

"You could hit someone!" Dani protested.

"I'll aim high," she promised, then she shot at the window, pointing the barrel upward so the bullet exited through the roof. It left behind a small hole surrounded by spider-webbed glass, but it was large enough for Alek to look through. When he peeked inside, he found that there was indeed a bedroom, and it was vacant with the door closed. He had Olivia fire two more shots to make a triangle, then they were able to push on the glass, causing it to shatter into the bedroom.

"I need something thick to cover the bottom edge before we can climb in," Alek said, and Dani grabbed a Kevlar vest out of the trunk. With the butt of a rifle, he removed as much of the remaining glass as possible, then put the vest in place. "Who's going in?"

"I am," Dani said.

"I will," Olivia offered, but Alek shook his head.

"I get the feeling you're the best shot. I need you out here in case the noise draws any infected from the outside," he said, but they were in the middle of nowhere. It felt more like he was saying he wanted to keep her safe. That wasn't necessary, but she was flattered as she helped him hoist Dani into the bus. Then Alek gave Olivia a smile and climbed in.

Once inside, they looked for something to use as a battering ram to push the door open and force the infected down the hallway so they could release Jax and the girls from the bathroom and retreat through the bedroom window, but as the sound drew the infected to the door, Alek realized there was a problem with their plan. On the other side, they knew there were at least six men, and the door was hinged to swing inward. If they were to open it, the infected could easily force their way in before any battering ram could push them back. Already outnumbered, they really needed physics on their side.

"Okay, what if we do this," Dani said. "You climb back out, sneak around to the front of the bus, and then I'll open the door and lure them all in here. I'll jump out the window, and then you should be able to just slip down the hall and lock them in the bedroom."

"I think it sounds like a great plan except for one thing," Alek said. "There's no way in hell I'm going to let you stay in here by yourself. You climb out, and I'll lure them in. Then you can be the one to rescue Jax Bonham."

"Are you sure?" she asked.

"I'm sure. It'll be safer for me to jump out the window. I'm taller. I don't have as far to fall," he said with a wink, and Dani smiled. This guy was famous, wealthy, and sexy as hell, but he was also a genuinely good person.

She couldn't believe the risks he was willing to take to rescue others from standing up for Olivia back at the Kemp Hotel to everything he was doing for Jax.

He helped her back out the window, and waited for the signal. When Dani was at the front entrance to the bus, she motioned for Olivia to let Alek know, and he took a deep breath and unlocked the door, slowly turning the knob and releasing it. Then he jumped back, letting the infected who had been pressing against it fall onto the bedroom floor. He climbed up on the bed and stood in the middle taunting them as they clambered to their feet, and he was surprised by how they ran into the bed then stood around it grasping at him as if they couldn't figure out how to climb onto it. There were seven of them, including Gino, and as they gnashed their teeth and moaned, it was terrifying to know that if just one of them fell onto the bed, they might all realize they could crawl toward their intended victim.

Keeping his distance, Alek looked down the hallway and saw Dani creeping along with her back against the wall. She made it almost all the way to the door when her hair got caught on a dimmer switch, startling her. She let out a yelp, barely even audible, but *they* heard it. Two of the infected at the foot of the bed turned and began walking back toward her.

Alek knew he had to do something. He held out his hand to tell Dani to freeze, then he knelt down on the bed and started yelling, calling the infected back to him, reaching out and waving in their faces, giving them hope that they could catch him, and once they all were focused on him again, Dani grabbed the knob and pulled the bedroom door closed, slamming it loudly, hoping to lure at least some of them away from Alek. It caught the attention of one, who quickly lost his balance and fell onto the bed.

Growling and groaning with his head right by Alek's thigh, he tried to sink his teeth through the thick denim of his jeans, and Alek abruptly propelled himself backward, landing on his ass against the back wall on the pile of broken glass. As he scrambled to his feet, the others discovered that they could crawl onto the bed, and suddenly they were all encroaching upon him. Panicked, he turned away and tried to dive headfirst out the window when he realized one of them had a hold of his shirt and would not let go.

"Alek!" Olivia screamed, terrified. "Get out of there!"

She reached for his arms, but he was being pulled back. He fought hard, kicking them in their faces as they bit at him, yet they were undeterred, one even taking a chunk out of the rubber sole of his combat boot. They seemed to have no pain receptors, and as they tried to grab his legs, he twisted and squirmed until he finally managed to slip his arms through the holes in the t-shirt and let them yank it off him. Once it was gone, he jumped out the window and straight into Olivia's arms. She was so relieved, she nearly burst into tears.

"Are you okay? Did you get bit?" she asked as she hugged him tightly before she realized what she was doing and let go with an embarrassed laugh.

"I'm fine," he assured her, looking down into her eyes and smiling, pleased by her reaction. Then Dani came around the side of the bus with Jax and two girls who looked like they couldn't be a day over eighteen. Jax had one arm around Dani, and in his other hand, he was carrying a katana. His manager had bought it at the comic convention the day before as a gift for his son. It was a real steel replica from some anime series he was crazy about, and Jax had used it to protect himself and the girls as they fought their way toward the bathroom earlier. Wearing a deep red, silk shirt with black pants, he made Dani think of a sexy pirate on the cover of a romance novel, but he gave a much different impression to June, who went instantly from muttering a prayer under her breath to quoting scripture.

"Behold," she said when she saw him. "A red horse, and he who sat upon it carried a great sword to take peace from the Earth."

"Shut the fuck up, June," Olivia hissed under her breath as she led the way back to the car.

Olivia pulled the limo onto Highway 51, following the course that Mitch had given her to get him to the hospital, and while they talked in the back seat about what had happened leading up to Jax being locked in the bathroom, Olivia struggled to watch the road as the glow of the dashboard illuminated the muscles of Alek's core. For a fleeting moment, she forgot about everything - the crazed cannibals, the distance between her and her child, her marriage - but all of it quickly came crashing back down on her, racking her with guilt and anxiety. She didn't even know if Reid was safe, and she was sitting next to the only other man on Earth who could tempt her. It was certainly uncanny that she ended up right beside him in this situation, but she wasn't willing to admit that she and her friends had caused this. It was coincidence.

"Here," June said, luring Olivia out of her thoughts as she passed Alek a t-shirt. "The less skin you have exposed, the safer you'll be."

"Thanks," he said as he wondered where it came from, then when he slipped it over his head, he realized it belonged to one of the women because it was extremely tight. Dani had pulled it out for June in case she wanted to change out of the frilly blouse she wore clubbing, but she wasn't willing to do it with the men in the car, even if they promised to look the other way.

"So where are we going?" Jax asked, catching Olivia's eyes in the rearview mirror.

"To a hospital in Morgantown to get Mitch's leg looked at," she answered.

"Not anymore," Liana said, her voice haunted.

"What do you mean?" Olivia asked as all the eyes in the backseat turned to Mitch.

"He's dead," she whispered. "I was just talking to him. I looked away for a second, and...he's gone." She started crying, and Dani put her arm around her as June moved to sit beside Mitch and check his pulse. She couldn't find anything.

"What should we do?" Olivia wondered aloud as she pulled to the side of the road.

"Are you sure he's dead?" Alek asked, and June nodded. She was a nurse, sort of. She didn't have a nursing degree, but she had worked in a doctor's office since she left college as the receptionist and was eventually moved into a role where she took vitals and performed other nursing duties. She was definitely the closest thing they had. Dani had a doctorate, but her medical training was restricted to fixing what went on inside the brain. Liana had planned to go into medicine when she joined the army to pay for college, then she ended up making a career out of the military. She was tough as nails and had seen actual combat, but she had never lost the part of her personality that desired peace above everything and considered all life precious. Mitch dying in her arms was more than she could bear.

As she mourned him, June went into action, asking Alek and Jax to move him to the ground outside the limo so she could perform CPR. Olivia was impressed as she watched her fight to revive the man, taking charge of the situation in a way the usually meek woman never did, and though it seemed like it was no use, just as June was about to call it, Mitch's eyes flew open. They were glassy, and he seemed disoriented, like he couldn't focus at first.

Then he grabbed her by the shoulders and started to sit up, his mouth open, his teeth bared as they lunged for her face. Alek quickly pulled her off of him, and before Mitch could get to his feet, they all hurried into the car. He staggered after them, banging on the window, clawing at it as if he didn't understand that he couldn't tear through glass.

"Oh, God!" Liana cried to see him like that. He was so different, so inhuman, that it seemed death would have been a preferable alternative, but even though she was the best shot despite Alek's assumption about Olivia, she couldn't bring herself to do it because she was still thinking like Jax. He held out hope for his band mates, believing that our society was too powerful and advanced to be taken down so easily, and certain that there would be a cure for the sickness, neither of them thought any of the infected should be killed if it could be avoided.

"Drive," she begged Olivia, and Olivia looked at Alek for guidance, feeling terrible about the idea of taking off in Mitch's car and leaving him to whatever fate befell the infected. Alek nodded. He didn't know if it was the right choice, but it was the only choice. Olivia pulled back onto the road.

"So where are we going now?" Jax asked.

"Home," Olivia said. "We're going to my compound in Summers County, West Virginia. There's plenty of food, solar power, clean water, and a fence. We'll be safe there until the government gets a handle on this."

Neither Alek nor Jax argued. It was more about wanting to spend the time with Olivia and Dani than believing it was necessary to hole up in a solar-powered compound, but neither of them saw the harm in it...unless, it suddenly occurred to Alek, the man who wore the match to that ring he had seen on Olivia's finger would be there.

"Are there infected there?" he pried. "Have you spoken with your family?"

"My daughter's on our mountaintop near Pipestem, so they haven't seen anyone infected yet, but it's definitely in Charleston already."

"It's everywhere," June said, holding up her phone. She had been trying to call her husband since the beginning, but he wasn't answering. He had finally responded by text, saying that there were hundreds of incidents reported in Asheville and Charlotte, the cities nearest to the little town where they lived. She replied that she was going to stay at Olivia's with the children until they knew what was going on, but the outgoing message was still spinning its wheels.

"Has anyone else heard anything?" Olivia asked.

"Our phones were left on the bus," one of the girls who came with Jax said. Her name was Penny, and she was a petit redhead who looked like June might have when she was younger if she had worked out and wore sexier clothes. Of course, at the moment, Penny just looked like a scared, little girl who had been playing in mommy's closet.

"Do you have someone you need to call?" Olivia asked, offering the use of the satellite phone, and though it made the rounds to almost everyone in the car, since they were trying to contact landlines and cell phones, very few actual connections were made. The girls, Penny and Brittani, texted their parents to say that they were safe since they had been on the bus travelling with the band through several cities, and as Olivia navigated the backroads toward her old college town, one response came through confirming that Syracuse, New York was not immune to the outbreak.

Once they made it to the outskirts of Morgantown, Olivia knew her way around and was able to get to Interstate 79 South fairly quickly. With

Morgantown being home to a famous party school, she had expected to find more traffic because of students staying up and going to the bars, but while they saw several wrecks, emergency vehicles, and infected running around, their route seemed fairly clear. They experienced the same luck as they drove south on 79, heading toward route 19 to Beckley that would take them to Interstate 77 and ultimately to Summers County. Though they could have taken 19 directly to Pipestem, the road first went through Beckley, and remembering the streets of Pittsburgh, she thought the Interstate would be safer. At least in the middle of the night before the whole country had woken up and realized what was going on, they were likely to encounter fewer people, and thus fewer of the infected, while driving ninety miles an hour with no stop lights. If the 79 was any indicator, they stood a reasonable chance of having large stretches of interstate to themselves.

About twenty minutes outside of Morgantown, Olivia noticed that the limo was low on gas. She wasn't looking forward to having to stop to pump it. As they passed through Fairmont, the gas stations that could be seen from interstate had been overrun, but she remembered a station off an exit coming soon where there wasn't anything else but a two lane country road for miles in both directions. As she approached the exit, she told everyone what they needed to do, and once they were at the station, they all got out with their rifles. Liana and Alek stood guard by the limo while one of the girls pumped gas, and the rest went inside with specific lists, including buying all the gas cans they could fit in the limo so they wouldn't have to stop again. The car held a lot of people, but it was a gas hog.

Inside, there was a young Indian man running the register. He was handsome and managed a smile, but it was clear that something was bothering him beyond the fact that in a hostile political climate his store had just been descended upon by an armed group. Dani assumed it had to do with the outbreak, but when she pressed him, it turned out he knew nothing about it at all. He was distressed because his father was in the back complaining of chest pains and the ambulance he called over an hour ago had not come.

"My friend's a nurse," Dani said. "She could take a look at him."

"Would you, please? It would be very much appreciated," he said, and though it was obvious that June didn't want to do this, when Dani narrowed her eyes in an unspoken threat, she reluctantly agreed. Part of June's problem was that she didn't know the difference between Hindu and Muslim, nor did she know the difference between Muslim and terrorist. On a normal day, Olivia and Dani would have realized what was going on and forced her to learn it, but today, they were preoccupied. Olivia was collecting all of the most valuable items the convenience store had to offer like bandages and medication while Dani was determined to help the attendant's father.

"I'm Ravi, by the way," he said as he led her and June to the backroom and opened the door. "This is my mother. She doesn't speak any Engli..." he trailed off when he saw his mother weeping over his father, who had apparently passed away.

"How long?" Dani asked the elderly Indian woman, and Ravi translated. When she said it had been only a few minutes, Dani turned to June. "Can you try CPR?"

"I don't know if I should," she said, and though Dani gave her an angry look, assuming it had to do with some closed-minded belief, this time it was different. "I gave mouth to mouth to Mitch, and he was infected. What if I'm infected? If I revive him, I could pass the virus to him, and..."

"What virus?" Ravi asked.

"There's been some kind of outbreak, and if it's a virus, she's right. She could be infected," Dani explained quickly then turned back to June. "Tell me how to do it. You do the chest compressions, and I'll give him mouth-to-mouth."

As June began to explain the process, Ravi's mother's face suddenly lit up with joy and she gasped, drawing the attention to her husband, who had begun to blink.

"He's alive!" she cried in Hindi, and as Ravi translated, Dani noticed the glassiness of his eyes.

"He's infected," she whispered, and then just as Mitch had done before, the old man grabbed his wife, gnashing his teeth. Dani pulled at the woman, but she didn't understand. She resisted, leaning in toward her husband whose mouth closed around her nose, biting it off, and Ravi cried out.

"Help me!" Dani demanded of the young man who had frozen in shock, and robotically, he obeyed. He helped her try to pull his mother to safety, but even as blood poured from the hole in her face, she fought them, choosing instead to give in to her fate, lying down beside the monster that was once her beloved husband as he chewed and swallowed her flesh. For a second, time seemed to stand still as Dani watched the scene, realizing something about the infected that she hadn't before. They weren't attacking people because they were out of their minds with violent rage. They were hungry, and they saw people as their food source.

June grabbed Dani by the back of her shirt, jolting her from her daze as she pushed everyone out of the backroom and slammed the door.

"But my mother," Ravi said weakly because even as the words came out of his mouth, he knew there was no saving her. He just didn't know what would happen next, that his mother would be infected and come for him if he opened that door. They explained what they had seen in Pittsburgh and what had happened to Mitch, then using the latest evidence they had gathered from the death of Ravi's father, they extrapolated that these blank-eyed cannibals were not actually infected at all. They were dead. Mitch had no pulse before he woke up and tried to take a bite out of June, and while they didn't have definitive proof that Ravi's father had been dead, his resurrection seemed identical to the last one they witnessed. And if he was dead, there was no reason to worry about hurting him or anyone else who might cross their path. There would never be a cure. They would never return to normal. There was only one thing to do. Kill them again.

But if death didn't stop them the first time, what would?

"You should close this place and go be with your family," Dani said to Ravi as he stood looking overwhelmed.

"That was my family. Now I have only my brothers and a promised wife in Kolkata," he said, returning to the register out of habit just as Olivia took out her card to pay him for all of the items she had piled up on the counter. "Put your money away. Take whatever you need."

"Come with us," Olivia offered. "You'll be safer with a group."

Ravi looked around and sighed. He had no reason to stay now that his parents were gone, and he felt a strong compulsion to take Olivia's offer. Suddenly mission oriented, he pulled out a grocery bag and started stuffing it with cigarettes, encouraging the others to fill bags as well.

"If society is falling, these will be valuable," he said. "Get the wine too. Don't bother with the beer. It takes up too much space."

"Yes, sir," Olivia said with a smile, impressed. Ravi was younger than her and her friends, maybe in his early twenties, but seeing how he dealt with this situation, she felt like he would be a good addition to their group, especially considering she was beginning to fear that they would be building a long term solution. It was bad enough when they thought this plague could only be transmitted by some sort of contact, but Ravi's father hadn't come in contact with anyone infected. He had died of a heart attack, then he woke up and bit his wife. This was going to be much harder to contain that they had originally hoped. Ravi scrawled a warning on a piece of paper and taped it to the storage room door, then he grabbed his bags of cigarettes and left without locking up the store.

"Why are you bringing him with us?" June hissed under her breath as she and Olivia walked to the limo. "He's a Muslim."

"He's..." She started to say he's probably Hindu based on the statue of Ganesha behind the counter in the store, but she stopped herself. That wasn't the part that mattered. She turned to June with a scowl on her face and daggers in her eyes. "He's a human being who just watched his mother die horribly. We're taking him with us, and if I hear one more bigoted comment out of your mouth, I swear to Yahweh, Shiva, Allah, and Aphro-fucking-dite, I'll feed you to the next hungry corpse I see. Are we clear?"

June narrowed her eyes and got in the back of the car without saying anything. Yes, she understood, but she didn't agree. She also didn't vote for

Olivia to be in charge, and as soon as the car was rolling, she started whispering in Liana's ear.

Ravi rode up front with Olivia and Alek, and the back of the limo was getting cramped with all the bags. In order to put the gas cans in the trunk, they moved Dani's suitcases and the extra guns and ammo into the back, creating an unintentional barrier between the long side seat and the very back seat where she and Jax sat together. The whole world had gone to shit all around them, but they were lost in an intense connection that would have drawn them back into each other's arms even if the plague hadn't happened.

It would have driven Jax mad to have waited until Indianapolis to see her again, and from the moment he first made eye contact from the stage, all other women had become invisible. Penny, a young redhead with large breasts and a very liberated sexual attitude had been passed around by nearly the entire band since they picked her up in Syracuse, but earlier tonight, when she practically bent over and presented to him like an animal in heat, all he could think about was what happened with Dani in the bar. Though good in bed - all the groupie websites said so - Jax had never had a woman whose body responded to his touch quite like Dani. Lots of women pretended he could do that to them. There were even some who claimed he could give them an orgasm with a look, but he could tell it was just an act to get him to pick one groupie over the next. It was tired and boring. Dani was anything but.

What he did to her in that bar made his heart race, and even through the worst of tonight's events, his thoughts always drifted back to that moment. He tried to feel guilty for it, but something about the horror that surrounded them made it even more important to free himself from the negativity and dive headfirst into his infatuation. He looked into her eyes and knew she was his, and Dani saw the same reflected as he laid her back on the seat behind the wall of Army-Navy Surplus shopping bags.

He brushed her hair behind her ear and kissed her softly at first, but as their intensity escalated, Dani's mind toggled between being acutely aware of the other passengers very nearby and forgetting that anyone in the world existed other than Jax and her. He was unaffected. He had spent the entirety of his adult life in a world where it was not out of the ordinary to see his friends or have them see him having sex, and besides, except for Alek and Ravi, who were in the front with Olivia, there were only women in the back, two of which he'd seen blow his band mates on the tour bus earlier tonight.

Moving his lips to her neck, he slid his hand between her legs, touching her through her jeans as he lamented the loss of the skirt that would have offered him such easy access, and Dani locked her jaw to keep the sound inside as he traced his fingernails over the denim, finding her clit and awakening it even through two layers of fabric. She wrapped her leg around him, pulling him into her, and when she felt him hard as a rock against the crotch of her jeans, it took every bit of will power she had not to tear his clothes off right then and there.

Dry humping wasn't going to get it for her this time. She needed more. As she contemplated what she and Jax could get away with back there, Alek sat closer to Olivia on the front seat now that Ravi had joined them, and when she looked in the rearview and saw Dani and Jax reflected in the back window, she felt an intense flash of jealousy.

You've got to be fucking kidding me! she thought, irritated with the entire situation. She was experiencing the same urge to feel alive amid the death they had witnessed, to find escape in the rush of endorphins a quick fuck could provide, but she didn't have that luxury. She had a husband and a child, and that child was not with her at the onset of one of her worst case scenarios. She had to get home to Savannah.

"Where's the sat phone?" she asked Alek.

"Back in the glove box," he said. He had put it there for safe keeping when they stopped. She wanted it with her from now on in case Savannah needed her, but it was more of an excuse because as she reached across Alek and opened the glove box, the car swerved quickly into the other lane and back, causing part of Dani and Jax's barrier to fall over, putting a damper on their plans.

Embarrassed, Dani sat up abruptly as her friends in the back giggled, and even in the darkness with her deep, rich skin tone, Olivia could have sworn she saw a blush on Dani's cheeks. Jax, of course, handled it with his usual finesse, winking and pursing his lips at June, chasing her eyes away, and as Olivia watched in the rearview with amusement, her mind taken off their dire circumstances if only for a moment, the satellite phone rang. It was Savannah, interrupting the light moment with crucial information her mother had yet to discover out in the dark, terrible world.

In the panic room, Savannah and Rey had set the boys up to play video games to distract them while they watched the news, but there was nothing new other than the fact that more cities were reporting incidents involving similar outbreaks. Their parents knew now that the infected people were not actually alive, but no one had told the kids that and the news seemed reticent when it came to specific details. Maybe the government was making them hold back in an attempt to keep order in areas not already descended into chaos like Pittsburgh, or maybe they didn't want to scare the populous into committing mass suicide because there were a lot of people out there who wouldn't want to live in a world where the dead rose up against the living. Regardless, for Savannah, Rey, and the boys, ignorance should have been bliss because on their mountaintop, they should not have had to worry about it until their parents came home. Unfortunately, the worst of humanity has a way of spreading its disease to even the most secluded paradise.

Behind Savannah's head, on the monitor fed by the camera aimed at the front yard of the lodge, June's six-year-old son Elijah noticed someone walking toward the porch.

"The bad man is back," he said, and Savannah and Rey followed his gaze to see that the intruder they thought Evil had killed earlier was up and staggering around.

"What do we do?" she asked Rey.

"Can't we just ignore him? I mean, look at him. His throat is torn out. I don't think he can do much."

"Maybe you're right."

"Let's just keep track of him on the monitors," he said. "We'll let your mom know about him, and if he's still alive when they get here, they can deal with him."

It seemed like a sound plan, but they were scared none-the-less. With their eyes glued to the screen, they watched him so they would be able to tell their mothers where he was before they came through the gate. He staggered forward, stumbling at the bottom of the stairs, then climbing them clumsily. Now he was on the camera at the front door. They couldn't see his face as he held his head awkwardly, and Savannah grabbed the toggle to move the camera in for a better look. His eyes were cloudy and vacant, he was covered in his own blood, and most disconcertingly, the entire right side of his throat was gone. He shouldn't have been alive, let alone walking around, yet he was walking, seeing and listening, honing in on the faint sound of the camera moving. It seemed to excite or enrage him. He started banging on the door, clawing as he reached for the camera.

"What's he doing?" Noah asked.

"I don't know," Savannah said. "Maybe he's afraid of us recording him?"

"Wouldn't it be better to just move out of range?" Rey asked.

"Is he going to get in here?" Isaiah wondered, his eyes wide and terrified.

"No, sweetie," Savannah said. "That door is strong. He can't break it down."

"But maybe *they* can," Rey said, and Savannah looked up at the monitor fed by the night vision camera aimed at the front gate. This was the inner gate, the third and last, and there were three men and a woman standing there. Actually they weren't standing. They were more like lackadaisically crashing into the gate with their bodies as if they expected it to yield to them, but it didn't and wouldn't no matter how hard they rammed it. All three gates were extremely sturdy, and without a straight shot of road to pick up speed, a car wouldn't even be able to take the inner gate down from the outside.

Savannah pointed to the microphone button by the monitor and asked Rey to speak in a "deep, grown-up" voice to tell the people they were trespassing, hoping to scare them off, and Rey did a good job of sounding authoritative as he threatened to shoot them if they weren't gone in thirty seconds, but while they all reacted to his voice, lunging at the speaker, they didn't seem to understand.

"Tell them you'll turn on the electricity," Savannah said.

"What?"

"I can flip a switch and electrify the gate. Tell them!" she urged, and though he delivered her threat, when it fell on deaf ears, Savannah hit the juice. On the monitor, they could see the bodies twitching as they leaned against the gate, yet it did not seem to *consciously* faze them. She turned it up higher, and though their limbs jerked and jolted, they made no attempt to move away, even when they began smoldering.

"Oh, fuck!" Rey said because he realized something that Savannah hadn't figured out yet...or maybe her mind just wouldn't let her process it.

"What?" she asked, and Rey came close and whispered in her ear.

"They're dead," he said. "They're fucking dead and they're coming for the living."

"That's impossible," she protested, but it was hard to argue while they watched four people completely undeterred as they were fried by an electric gate on one monitor and a man with his throat ripped out banging against the front door on another. Then as Savannah turned off the current, afraid it might overload the system, they saw a fifth stranger approach the gate.

"Shit," she sighed because she realized they had to do something. The noise was attracting more of them. "We need to take out the one at the door."

Rey agreed, and they decided the best way to do that would be to slip out the side of the lodge and sneak up on him since opening the front door would put them in hand to hand combat.

They closed the boys in, leaving Evil right outside to guard them, made sure their guns were not on safety, and crept downstairs and across the lobby floor to the side door. They opened it as quietly as possible, and they were able to get around to the front without drawing the attention of an intruder, whose own banging drowned out the sound of their footsteps as fall leaves crunched beneath them. They walked up the stairs on the side of the porch, and Rey raised his gun, aiming for the intruder's midsection.

He pulled the trigger, and the first bullet hit the man in the side of his ribcage. It should have taken him down, but it didn't. Rey fired again and again, each shot causing him to stammer as he walked toward them.

"What the fuck?" Rey cried, panicked. Though the porch was long, the intruder full of bullet holes was closing the gap when Savannah raised her gun. She'd been an expert at target practice since she was ten, but she had never killed anything in her life and whether taking down this dead man was indeed killing or not, it felt like it. Terrified, she aimed, took a deep breath, and squeezed the trigger, putting her bullet right through his open, groaning mouth. He fell to the ground.

"Nice!" Rey said.

"Is he really dead this time?" she asked as they approached with caution, first kicking at him before Rey knelt and touched him to confirm that the body was utterly lifeless.

"We should get him on the other side of the fence just in case he might come back again," Rey suggested, but while Savannah was willing to drag him over there, she was scared of trying to lift him, afraid he might wake up while in the process and grab them.

"I have a safer idea," she said, and with Rey's help, she pulled him by his legs off the porch to a spot where there would be a camera aimed at him. Then she took out her pocket knife and sliced his Achilles tendons.

"Now," she said, "if he comes back, he won't be able to walk."

"Damn, girl," Rey said with a dropped jaw. He was impressed with her resourcefulness and a little freaked out as Savannah opened the door to go back inside, but she stopped dead when she realized she could hear the crowd at the gate. It sounded like it was growing.

Frustrated, they knew they had to do something about it, and they quickly walked down the gravel drive until they could see that it had, indeed, grown. There were seven of them now, and though they surmised that it was probably the gunshots that had lured the last two, they really had no choice but to use the guns to put them down. If they didn't, it could pose a problem for their parents when they returned or for vacation home owners coming to the middle ring.

The upper ring was near the mountaintop with the lodge and the cabins her parents owned and rented out. The middle ring was for vacation cabins with private owners that the Anders family rented for them, but they had only begun selling those units a little over a year ago. There were a few cabins that were already in use along with another ten in various states of completion. The same was true of the lower ring, which was to be occupied by residents who lived full time in their green, solar powered structures. So far only two families lived there, but the entire acreage had been parceled out into forty home sites with more than a dozen in progress.

Savannah guessed that it had to be someone heading for the middle ring who inadvertently helped the dead through the outer gates. Either that or they could have fallen over the fences because the middle and lower rings were so large that in some areas, there was just a series of wires held in place by existing trees. Though all of the gates were thick, heavy-duty steel, only the upper ring was protected by an eight foot chain link fence that would eventually be replaced by a stone wall, the foundation of which had already been poured, but as it stood now, the gate didn't seem as safe as it once had.

As Savannah and Rey came closer, the dead grew more and more excited, thrusting their bodies against the steel as they reached through gaps between the slats, and Savannah wondered how long it would take before they figured out how to get over or under it. Then she recognized two of them - the Wootens from the lower ring. They were an older couple who lived on the edge of Anders property and made an agreement with Reid for their ranch to become a part of the lower ring when the fences and gates were installed. They owned several acres with an apple orchard, and this was the time of year when they should have been at this gate with a basket full of homemade apple butter to sell in the lodge, not...like this.

As Rey reloaded his gun, Savannah raised hers and shot the people she didn't recognize, but when it came to the Wootens, even though the old woman snarled and hissed at her like a rabid animal, she couldn't pull the trigger.

"Close your eyes," Rey said softly. She heard two gun shots, and when she opened them, the Wootens, like the other five, lay motionless in front of the gate.

"Thank you," she said, smiling a sad smile, and relieved, they began to walk up the gravel path toward the lodge when Savannah heard her name whispered from the other side of the fence. She looked back to see her friends Sally and Bella running toward the gate from the woods on the side of the drive.

"Can we come in?" Bella asked, and Savannah entered the code to disarm the gate. Olivia had banned them this weekend, but given the circumstances, she didn't think her mother would mind.

"Is everything okay?" Olivia asked when she answered Savannah's phone call.

"Well, there's a pile of dead bodies at the gate, but otherwise, sure," she said, and then she had some explaining to do. Once she, Rey, Sally, and Bella were safely in the panic room, the first thing she had done was call the Vincents, the only other family who lived in the lower ring now that the Wootens were gone, to tell them the gate was open. All of the gates had surveillance, but with fewer monitors than cameras in their system, they had to be toggled to see everything on the property. Tonight, Savannah had them set to prioritize the upper ring, which made her feel guilty as she called the Vincents.

She didn't have any problem getting through to their landline because not too many people were up at that hour in Summers County. In fact, the Vincents were not even aware that anything was happening, and when she told him, John Vincent immediately made it his mission to patrol the road between the lower and middle gates as more owners could be arriving.

That already accounted for two of the seven corpses at the gate. Sally and Bella had seen it happen. They had sneaked out of Bella's house to meet a couple of boys, but instead, they ran into three men in an older model, red pick-up truck who had already equated the news stories they were seeing from the cities with an open invitation to anarchy. Though the girls assumed it was just a truckload of drunk, young rednecks at first, once they pulled up close and started making threats, they realized they were dealing with grown men. Frightened, they ran through the woods toward unfamiliar side roads, hiding behind houses and changing their routes to confuse the men, who continued to pursue them.

When they finally made it back to the main road, they found that they were closer to Savannah's house than Bella's and decided to take refuge there. As they hurried toward the private drive, the lower gate was open and they could see taillights ahead, but just as they began to feel safe, the truck appeared again, barreling up the road and past the gate before it closed.

The driveway wound through the woods, turning a distance of less than a half mile into more than a mile of road. While the girls ran in a straight path through the trees, the truck took the curves as fast as possible, knocking over the signs on the sides of the road and slinging gravel. At the middle gate, the girls saw a couple in an SUV, the driver's side door ajar as the man entered his code to open the gate, but before they could even warn him, the truck came around a curve and slammed right into the car.

As the terrified girls hid behind a tree, they could hear the driver gurgling blood, and the woman's soul-crushing wails echoed through the forest. They expected the men in the truck to straighten up and help or at least call an ambulance, but as they peeked around the sides of the tree, they saw the three men rush toward the woman, trapping her against the vehicle. As her husband lay dying, they slammed her on the hood of the car, and two of them held her down while the biggest one tried to rape her. As the girls listened to the cries of the poor woman who had befallen the fate they had spent their night trying to escape, they didn't notice the husband getting up until he was right behind the big guy.

He was covered in blood, his broken body seeming to stand by sheer force of will alone as he attacked, grabbing the rapist from behind and biting through his shirt, and the man howled in pain. Furious, he turned toward his attacker, and unaware that he was already dead, he didn't fear the smaller man like he should have. He wrapped his hand around his throat and swiftly put him on the ground on his back. Then he got on his knees, pinning him down.

"You want me to fuck you, too, son?" he asked as he tried to turn him over, but the husband struggled. To his opponent, he seemed to be trying to get free, but he was actually trying to find an opportunity to take another bite of him. With his pants around his knees, the big guy was at a disadvantage, and in the struggle, a set of hungry teeth found his inner thigh, tearing into his femoral artery.

"Motherfucker!" he cried as he punched the man in the face, not immediately realizing how bad he was injured, but it only took seconds for him to collapse, his blood covering the white rocks of the gravel drive. The other two men hurried to help their friend, but he was as good as dead already. So was the woman, who rushed to her husband's side, unwittingly offering herself up to him, and he took a savage bite out of her neck. It didn't take long for the other two men to fall as well, and Sally and Bella realized they needed to get the hell out of there.

It was just so quiet, the forest full of dead leaves to noisily crush beneath their shoes, but with no choice if they wanted to survive, they had to make a run for it. The husband was the first to follow them. With a severely damaged leg, he wasn't moving fast, and the girls began to feel relief as they approached the inner gate of Savannah's property. Then suddenly the same three men who had pursued them all night were chasing them through the woods just a few yards behind, only this time instead of catcalling, they were groaning and grinding their teeth. The girls hid behind trees and tried to be silent as the men moved closer. They could hear their noses sniffing the air, and from behind a trunk barely wide enough to cover her, Bella fought back the tears as she heard the leaves rustle just a few feet away.

Don't breathe, she told herself as she stood like a statue, not sure if she should wait it out or run. These guys were fast, and she didn't know if she could make it to the gate and climb over before they caught her as sound of the leaves got closer. Then she heard the same noise on the other side.

Oh, God. Oh, God, Oh, God.

About to be surrounded, it was now or never. If she couldn't make her legs move to carry her to the gate, she was going to meet a worse fate than when these men were just bent on rape. She opened her mouth to suck in a deep breath before beginning the sprint when a loud banging sound caught the attention of her pursuers, drawing them to the gate like moths to a flame.

Once they moved on, she looked around for Sally, finding her behind a nearby tree, pointing to the road where the woman was now walking toward the gate as well. But that's not what Sally wanted her to see. Back at the second gate was a third set of headlights where someone had stopped to check out the accident, but instead they had met the dead woman. Now there were two more bodies lying on the ground - two more bodies that soon stood up and began to wander through the woods toward the sounds inside the inner gate where the other five had already congregated.

It was the Wootens. A church deacon, Mr. Wooten had been awakened by a call from the pastor asking him to unlock the sanctuary for those seeking refuge. On the way home, he and his wife saw the cars at the middle gate, and thinking someone might need help, they drove to their deaths.

As the two elderly corpses meandered through the woods, Sally & Bella had to remain quiet, but once all the dead were congregated at the gate, the girls felt the first true glimmer of hope they'd had all night when a voice came out of the speaker. They couldn't tell who it was or make out the words, but it was coming from Savannah's house. Someone was home. Thank. God.

Later, once Sally and Bella were safely inside the panic room with everyone else, Savannah relayed their story and her own to her mother over the phone, and Olivia was proud and relieved to know that her daughter was handling things so well in her absence. It gave her hope, and it gave her insight because the kids had discovered something their parents hadn't yet. The only way to kill the dead was to take out the brain. They didn't know why it worked, but it didn't really matter as long as put them down for good.

Olivia and Savannah said their I love yous, and after they hung up the phone, Olivia continued to drive in an eerie silence. Even though there were people all over the country dealing with this plague, the roads were still surprisingly clear, most Americans sleeping right through it. They would see the occasional wrecked or abandoned car and when they passed busy exits, sometimes there were people running, but all in all, if they put it out of their minds, they could pretend it was just a regular night on a trip to a compound in a limousine packed with wine, cigarettes, rifles, and a diverse group of mostly strangers.

The remainder of the drive down Interstate 79 was uneventful. Olivia pulled the limo onto route 19 toward Beckley, and for miles, it seemed they were going to have a clear shot to the compound. It was just after 4:00 am when she saw an opportunity up ahead on a long stretch of deserted highway. A tractor trailer from Right Way Pharmacy sat unattended on a frontage road, the driver's side door open with no one around. She hit the brakes and pulled onto the shoulder.

"What's going on?" Liana demanded from the back.

"Can anyone drive an eighteen wheeler?" Olivia asked.

"I can," Ravi said. "I worked my way through college driving one of those. Why?"

"'Cause we're taking the Right Way truck home with us," she said.

"Wait just a minute!" Dani shouted from the very back. "You want to steal a pharmacy truck? Have you lost your fucking mind, Oblivia?"

Olivia laughed, but the name wasn't really applicable in this moment. She'd gone over a thousand scenarios since she and Reid started setting up to survive a catastrophe, and there was little out there more valuable than what could be in that trailer.

"Reid used to work for Right Way. There's a locked area in the back that could have hundreds of thousands of prescription pills that are about to be worth more than gold. We're going to look around, make sure we're not stranding the driver, then we're going to steal that truck."

"Jesus! You're nuts!" Dani protested, but no one else was willing to stand up to Olivia. Most of them were so scared, they were just glad someone had taken responsibility for them, and then there was Alek, who was thoroughly in awe of her. She was thinking so far ahead, he had no fear as long as he was with her.

"Let's do it," he said, grabbing a rifle and passing Olivia the handgun. Ravi pulled out the gun he had taken from behind the counter at his family's

61

store, but he had no clue how to use it. Alek gave him a brief tutorial, then Olivia told everyone else to sit tight as they got out.

"So nobody's going to put a stop to this bullshit?" Dani demanded once the doors had been stealthily closed.

"No," Jax whispered, "and baby girl, neither are you." She opened her mouth to argue, but his lips found her ear and silenced her with a promise. "Look at the size of the cab on that semi. Do you know what that means? There's a sleeping compartment in it. That kid from the gas station is going to drive it, and you and I are going to volunteer to ride with him."

A smile spread across Dani's face as she forgot all about caring that Olivia was committing grand larceny. She didn't even care that they were trusting that some twenty-something kid they'd just met could actually drive the thing.

Through the windows, they watched as Olivia, Alek, and Ravi crept around the truck. They looked under it. Clear. Olivia looked in the cab. Clear. Keys in the ignition. They could hop in and take off right now if their attention had not been drawn by a shadow moving in the truck's headlights, and when they peeked around the front of the rig, they saw the driver lying on the ground, bleeding and missing chunks of flesh. He was weak, but he still had the foresight to warn his would-be saviors what they were walking into. Shaking, he brought his finger to his lips to shush them, then with a nod of his head, he directed their attention to a black limousine on the side of the frontage road, hidden from view by the semi. One tire was off, and there was a jack in the middle of the road. The doors were open, and inside the driver and a woman were being eaten alive...or at least they had been alive. They weren't moving or making any sounds anymore. Also silent was the man atop the limo. He was sitting by a partially opened sunroof, curled up in a ball with his head hidden, but they could tell he was alive from his shaking.

"I stopped to help change the tire," the Right Way driver whispered with ragged breaths as Olivia crouched beside him. "They just came out of nowhere..." Every word was labored, and it was clear that he didn't have long. He had lost too much blood.

"We'll take care of them. Then we'll help you. You're going to be okay," Alek softly lied.

"I'm going to turn into one of those things," the man said. "I can feel it. Please don't let it happen. I'm begging you."

Olivia looked him in the eye and agreed. Then she counted the number of corpses feasting in the limo and realized they couldn't shoot the trucker first because it would draw the dead to them.

"If you can get the two in the front, I'll take the three in the back," she said to Alek, and he nodded. "Ravi, I want you to watch. If Alek and I don't make it, get in the driver's seat of the limo and get everyone the hell out of here. Okay?"

"Yes, ma'am," he said, and she turned back to Alek.

"You have to shoot them in the brain. Otherwise, they'll just keep coming," she said, and he gritted his teeth at the thought of it.

"Let's get this over with," he said as he cocked the rifle. Olivia checked her safety, then they moved in close enough to get a good shot, aimed, and took out the first two. The remaining three jumped up and turned toward them, bloody muscle and skin hanging from their teeth as they growled and came running. Terrified, Olivia and Alek aimed and fired again. She got hers right in the forehead, but Alek's shot only grazed its target on the side of the head. The dead man kept coming, moving so fast Alek barely had time to cock the rifle and get it in position again before the corpse was on him, the tip of the gun driving straight into his hungry mouth as he pulled the trigger. The bullet drove upward into the brain, smattering the pavement all around with grey matter and pieces of skin and hair. The last one, a teenage girl slipped on it and slid into Olivia, knocking her feet out from under her. She dropped the gun, and the dead girl clutched her jeans, pulling on them to climb up Olivia's body and get a good bite on her. While Olivia struggled to reach the gun, Alek hit her attacker in the head with the butt of the rifle, knocking her off before he cocked it and shot her between the eyes.

Olivia's heart was beating so hard, it felt like it was going to pop out of her chest as she exhaled long-held breath before thanking him. Then she picked up her gun and got to her feet just in time to hear the man on the roof of the black limo shout, "More are coming!"

Olivia and Alek looked up, and barreling down a steep embankment just a dozen yards away were more dead, some sliding, others rolling down the hill. She looked back for Ravi to tell him to get help, but he was gone. And the dead were almost upon them.

"How many bullets do you have left?" she asked Alek.

"Ten maybe?" he said. "I have eight in the extra magazine and a couple left in this one.

"I have five," she said. "Let's get the fuck out of here."

But it was too late. When they turned to run back to the limo, they crashed straight into the Right Way driver and Olivia had to use the first bullet on him. She pointed her gun upward under his chin and pulled the trigger, and the dead from the hill caught up to them before he hit the ground. They opened fire, Olivia planting each of her four remaining bullets in heads as Alek managed to succeed five out of nine times, switching out his magazine in the midst, and when he went to fire his tenth and final bullet at a corpse that was less than five feet away, there was no tenth bullet.

"Run!" he commanded Olivia with a guttural scream, planning to hold them off so she could get away, but the dead man changed course, going for her instead. As Alek reached out to try to pull her out of his grasp, they were both knocked to the ground. Scrambling to get away, they clawed at the blacktop on their bellies, kicking their attacker when Olivia suddenly remembered the knife from the army surplus store that she'd strapped to her belt loop when they rescued Jax. It wasn't a machete, but the blade extended long enough to reach the brain if she could jam it into the right place. She yanked it out of its sheath, twisting her body just enough to take aim, and it seemed to work as the dead man on top them fell in a heap as soon as the knife made contact.

Of course, the unsharpened blade never actually penetrated his skull. It was the bullet from Dani's rifle, and while Olivia and Alek lay catching their breath, they had to cover their ears to protect them from all the gunfire as the rest of the dead were put down. Ravi hadn't abandoned them. He had gone to the limo for backup.

"Come on," he said as he reached for Olivia's hand to help her to her feet. "From the looks of these corpses, I would say there's a bar up on that hill, and more could follow."

Ravi, Dani, and Jax got in the cab of the tractor trailer, and everyone else got back in the Hummer, including the man from the top of the other limo. Wearing a black three-piece suit, Jobe Stricklan unscrewed the lid on a flask and took a big swig while he sat comfortably in the backseat as Olivia pulled onto the road with Ravi following in the semi.

Leary, Olivia listened to him explain to everyone how he came to be cowering atop his own limousine as his wife and driver were eaten alive. His wife was from the area, and her grandmother had been in hospice for months. They got the call last evening that she would likely not make it until morning, and they had rushed to West Virginia so his wife could say goodbye before she passed. They had landed his jet at a nearby private airfield, and they were en route to Mount Nebo when the car got a flat.

"The driver pulled over and I got out to help him," he said in a southern accent that sounded almost forced. "Then all these drug-crazed maniacs just came out of nowhere, attacking us. We got back in the car, but we couldn't get the doors closed in time, and they just came in on us. I noticed that the sunroof was still half open from when my wife wanted some fresh air earlier, so I climbed through it. I was just about to pull her up when I realized they had a hold of her. What was I supposed to do? I could sit up there quietly until they went away and maybe live or I could die trying to save her when she was already gone." As he said it, he held his hands up like he was weighing the options, and something about him made Olivia feel sick as she remembered the Bible verses June had been quoting since the trip began. Olivia knew those verses too.

"Behold," she said sarcastically as she looked directly into June's eyes in the rearview. "A black horse, and he who sat upon it held scales and foretold great suffering."

"Excuse me?" Jobe demanded, taking the comment as personally as it was intended, but in a very different way.

"A joke," June said dismissively. "She thinks this is the apocalypse."

Suddenly, Olivia was fuming at the hypocrisy. It was all "thou shalt not suffer a witch to live" when she perceived that their time with the gypsy has resulted in Alek and Jax being in their midst, but *now that Jobe Stricklan was there, it was just a joke?* To Olivia, it wasn't one damn bit funny, and Jobe was clearly an asshole. From the things he had already said, it was evident that he didn't even know that the people who had attacked them were dead, and he didn't know that their bite was going to kill his wife and make her one of them. All he knew was that his wife had been bitten by some "drug-crazed maniacs", and when he had weighed his options, he decided to save his own skin rather than trying to help her. Olivia made a mental note never to allow him any role of responsibility when it came to anyone's life but his own.

The mood in the Right Way semi was very different from the limo. The cab had a bed in the back just like Jax had hoped, and he wasted no time ushering Dani into it, suggesting with a wink that she get some rest while he kept Ravi company. He sat in the passenger seat and watched for a few minutes to see how the young, quiet man handled the big rig, and impressed, he stretched and yawned.

"I've been up for more than twenty-four hours," he lied. "Will you be okay alone if I lie down in the back for a while."

"No problem," Ravi said with an amused grin. He knew who Jax was, and he knew what he was up to. Jax Bonham was the one person in this entire party who would not surprise him with this behavior. He was well known for his womanizing, and Ravi had met more than a couple girls in college who were as taken with the older man as they would have been if he was still in his twenties. Jax was a sex god, but Ravi wasn't jealous. Of course, sex was on his mind. At his age, it always was, and it was certainly something he would have been doing if the opportunity presented itself given the fact that the whole damn world appeared to be ending, but his priority right now was getting this truck to the refuge Olivia had promised. It was the only thing that mattered because he felt like he owed it to his parents to survive. If this plague was happening in Kolkata, he believed it was a safe bet that he was already the last of that particular branch of the Chatterjee family. Kolkata was one of the most densely populated places on the planet, and if the plague hit, his brothers and his beautiful, promised bride were on borrowed time if they still lived at all.

Ravi turned on the radio to drown out any sounds that might come from his "sleeping" companions. Many stations had switched to an all news format, reporting on the plague, and he skipped past a couple with preachers shouting about the end times to find that there were still at least a few channels on autopilot, playing the same twelve popular songs every hour over and over again. He kept tuning until he found a song on a classic rock station that made him laugh. It was ParraJax's *In My Arms*. He heard Dani giggle from behind the curtain, and he turned it up.

Dani's Journal
The Absolute, Most Fucking Amazing Sex Anybody Ever Had

The first thing Jax said was, "Finally," as he lay down with me. The rig's bed wasn't even as wide as a twin mattress, and there was only a curtain separating us from Ravi, but we didn't care.

"Finally," I repeated, our eyes gradually closing as our lips met. Then, even though I think we both had intended to take it slow and savor it, we had to laugh when we immediately began pulling off each other's clothes like a couple of teenagers with only ten minutes to get it on before mom came back from the store. It took about thirty seconds for us both to be completely naked, and...

Damn! Jax's body was the most amazing I'd ever seen!

I knew he had a well-toned chest and core because I'd seen him shirtless on stage, but now I knew every part of him was perfect, including 7" of steely, pink perfection that I couldn't wait to feel inside me - everywhere inside me. I pushed him onto his back and kissed my way down his body, running my tongue along the outline of his six pack, and he flinched and laughed as I came to his navel.

"Ticklish?" I teased, and up front, Ravi turned up the music a little more, which made us both laugh but not for long. I had serious work to do. I moved downward, wetting my lips and slipping the head of his dick between them. I felt myself shudder at the idea of finally having this nearly twenty year fantasy come to life, and he shuddered when I sucked him all the way into my mouth, swishing my tongue from side to side as I went. His hands found my head, sliding into my hair, but when I thought he was going to push me down, he lifted me up.

"Come here," he whispered, and though I didn't want to let go of his dick, I couldn't refuse him any request. I moved on top of him, and as he kissed me deeply, he rolled us over.

"Ladies first," he said as his lips made a path to my neck, sending chills all over my body. It was surreal. I was having sex with Jax Bonham. I mean, an army of the dead had risen up outside to eat us and all, which was also pretty surreal, *but I was having sex with Jax fucking Bonham, y'all!*

He was kissing my neck. Then *he* moved to my breasts, his sensual, pink lips closing around my nipple, and *oh, my God!* I was suddenly so wet, I felt it pouring out of me, and all I could think about was feeling him inside.

"Fuck the foreplay," I whispered, pulling him back up and wrapping my legs around his hips, prodding him with my heels.

"Dani, I don't have a condom," he said, looking into my eyes apologetically, and I was confused.

"Word on the street is; you had a vasectomy," I said, sure I read that somewhere.

"I did, but aren't you concerned about..." he paused, looking down at me sheepishly "...my past?"

"Should I be?" I asked. Maybe if things were different, if I had met him backstage at a show, it would have crossed my mind, but after the time we'd spent together tonight, I felt, perhaps naively, like I could trust him.

"I swear I've never been with a groupie without a condom, and I get tested all the...."

"Shut up and fuck me, Jax," I said.

"Fuck you, Dani? No, I'm not going to fuck you," he insisted, confusing me yet again, but when he kissed me softly and eased his dick inside me, I understood what he meant. Slowly and gently, he made love to me, looking into my eyes in the dim moonlight shining through the windows, and even though I began this with visions of back-clawing, teeth-gnashing fucking, those ideas became alien to me as the intensity between us began to grow on an emotional level, the orgasms building inside us giving life to a connection deeper than I'd ever experienced in ten years of marriage .

He took my hands in his, our fingers laced together tightly, and my lips began to quiver at the raw power of the moment. My body was on the verge of a cataclysmic explosion as I felt him gliding over my clit with each thrust, and my mind was completely overtaken by emotion with his eyes never leaving mine for a second. Then it happened. I felt the subtle shift as Jax stiffened inside me just before he was about to come, and that tiny detail struck my clit like lightning, taking me with him so suddenly, I forgot everything for one brief, devastating moment as a forceful cry began deep in my throat. Quickly, Jax silenced me with his mouth over mine, and as we breathed our ecstasy into each other, a tear escaped, streaming down the side of my face into my hairline.

"You're so beautiful, Dani," he whispered in a long, satisfied exhale as he looked down at me, wiping the water away with his thumb.

"You're beautiful," I said back to him, and he grinned modestly.

But he knows it's true.

He's beautiful. He's amazing. He's absolutely fucking perfect.

Route 19

From Route 19, Olivia took the limo onto Interstate 77 South - the West Virginia Turnpike. Route 19 dropped them off past two of the three toll booths on the turnpike, but as they made their way toward the last one heading south, Olivia started to feel anxious. There could be dozens of people congregated here - employees, police, all of the motorists who had to come to a stop in order to pay. The toll plaza was always more congested than the roads, and with no headlights in the rearview and no taillights up ahead, the last mile before they arrived was surreal. Then they came out of a slight curve and saw it glowing in the darkness up ahead, and everyone was seized by a feeling of impending doom. Without even thinking, Alek reached for Olivia's hand as it rested on the seat between them, and when he squeezed tightly, she felt a sense of comfort that was quickly eradicated by the scene ahead.

There were cars everywhere. Unattended. Ignitions running. Doors open. Crashed into guardrails. Flashers flashing. Headlights illuminating hellish scenes. A bus on its side. A dozen abandoned motorcycles. Some knocked over. Some wrecked into one of the booths.

Then there were the dead. Groups of them voraciously dining on human flesh as the limo rolled past at a glacial pace, the headlights killed beneath the bright plaza. The sound lured a few corpses away from their feast, but nowhere was there evidence that anyone remained alive. Even the attendants in the toll booths were dead and banging against the glass, unable to figure out how to get through the half open windows despite that it's how most of them were bitten in the first place when they were rapidly overtaken after a motorcycle wreck that initially resulted in a single death.

Olivia drove to the far left lane, the one with the fewest cars blocking it because there wasn't any route that would allow them to continue. She looked up at Alek with a defeated sigh, knowing they would have to clear the path. She was toying with the idea of taking route 19 all the way home when they noticed something that made the decision for her. There *were* living people here. They were hidden in cars, and now with hope that the limo and semi might be their rescue, they were starting to pop their heads up.

"Well, fuck," Olivia said, knowing they had no other option even as a small group of walking corpses meandered around the limo, unable to see what was inside the tinted windows.

"You're not thinking of going out there, are you?" Jobe asked.

"What choice do we have?" she countered.

"Maybe we could find a path through the median," he suggested. "Or we could turn around and use another road."

"The only other option is to go back and take Route 19 right through Beckley, which could be crawling with infected. I think this is still the safest route."

"You know what else is going to keep us safe?" Liana asked. "Numbers. The more people we have with us, the more people we can count on to protect us. Look at that bus. If any passengers survived, how many are so far away from home they just need a safe place to go?"

"Yeah, and how many of them are dead and just want to eat us? How many bullets do you have, lady?" Jobe scowled at her.

"Enough that we won't abandon the living if we can save them," Olivia hissed before Liana could respond, then she reached across Alek and opened the glove box to see that there was half a box of bullets for the hand gun. She knew they were set for bullets for the rifles, most of which were stacked up on the floor in the back of the limo, which Liana pointed to, smirking at Jobe as Olivia started barking out orders.

"Alright, we need to load every gun we have. Jobe, you and June can stay in the limo with the girls, and crack the window so you can hand us fresh guns when we need them," she said as Alek rolled his down about half an inch and aimed his rifle at the head of a dead woman standing there. He fired, and down she went.

"Let's get the ones we can from here," he said, and after they all lowered their windows just enough to slip the barrels out, Olivia turned off the engine and put the keys in her pocket. Until now, she had been leaving them in the ignition for the safety of the group, but she had an uneasy feeling this time.

The first shot had drawn more dead, but Alek's plan worked well. Penny and Brittani had terrible aim, so June taught them how to do the reloads, and that became their contribution while the rest fired from the safety of the limo. Through the driver's side window, Olivia could see a group of people heading north fighting the dead with sticks and tire irons as they tried to move vehicles to clear a path, and behind them she could see Jax and Dani climbing on top of the rig with their rifles. While Jax shot at the immediate threat on the southbound side, Dani was helping to cover the group headed north as Ravi shot from the passenger side window.

A small mountain of bodies grew outside the limo, and the dead on the southbound side began to lose interest in the limousine, drawn instead to the food sources they could actually see - the group on the opposite side of the road and the shooters atop the rig, which gave Olivia and Alek the opportunity to try to clear their path ahead. Olivia asked Liana to come with them, and she climbed over the seat into the front so they could all sneak out through one door - less sound, less eye candy for the hungry dead.

"Cover us," Olivia said with a stern look, and June nodded, knowing exactly what she was implying. Olivia didn't trust Jobe, but June didn't believe he was as bad as she thought. He was shell shocked. He had just lost his wife and been told that those crazed people who killed her were actually reanimated corpses. That would make anyone act out of character, and she was certain that he was not the coward Olivia was mistaking him for. *Why would a preacher fear death?* Heaven sounded like a much better place than Earth, especially now.

After Olivia, Alek, and Liana slipped out the door, they closed it as quietly as possible then hunkered down so the dead wouldn't notice them, and they practically crawled to the front car in the blockade. When they found the four door sedan empty, Olivia put it in neutral, and they went to the second car - a compact convertible where a woman sat motionless in the driver's seat beneath a shredded ragtop. She had so many bites on her, they were sure she was completely dead, but when Alek grabbed her arm to drag her out of the vehicle, her eyes flew open and she groaned, lunging at him. Olivia pulled her back by the hair, holding her while he released the seat belt, then they dragged her to the ground. She was thrashing and fighting against them, but she was much weaker than the others they'd encountered, many of her muscles not even working with so much of their flesh now in the bellies of the dead. As Alek held her face to the pavement, Olivia took out the dull knife from her waistband and shoved it in at the base of the skull, and the struggle was over. Liana knocked the car's stick shift out of gear, and they moved on to the third and last obstacle.

It was a van, and the driver's side was locked.

"Shit!" Olivia hissed, knowing they'd either have to sneak around to the try the other side or break a window. Either way, they would attract attention. The dead man in the nearest toll booth had already become wound up when he noticed them at the convertible, and behind them on the berm, a man and woman sandwiched between two crashed cars were growling and struggling as they reached toward the living. It was the only thing that seemed to excite them, and there was a clear line of sight between the congregation around the rig and limo and the passenger side of the van where the door could easily be locked as well.

"I have an idea," Liana said, and she turned to Alek. "Watch Dani. If you hit the window with the butt of your rifle at the same time she fires, the noise of the gunshot might keep their attention away from the sound of breaking glass." He nodded, and with his gun in position, he waited for Dani to fire then brought it down hard. The glass shattered, and as the women looked around, it seemed they had gotten away with it. Alek opened the door, and slipped inside. The plan was for him to use the van to push the two cars out of the way while Olivia and Liana got back in the limo to follow and pick him up on the other side of the toll booth.

But there was a problem.

Cowering in the back of the van were three little girls, their long hair tangled, their eyelashes stuck together with tears. The oldest of them couldn't have been more than nine, but she tried to be brave.

"You better get out of here, mister," she said. "My mommy and daddy will be back in a minute, and he's a policeman."

"Where did your mommy and daddy go, sweetheart?" he asked.

"To see why the cars weren't moving," she said. "They're coming back, so you better go because Daddy has a gun."

But Alek knew they weren't coming back. The man trapped by the wreck that prevented them from using the shoulder to get through was wearing a cop's uniform.

"Was your daddy dressed like a police officer?" he asked, and the little girl nodded. "He had an emergency, and your mommy had to help. They asked us to take you somewhere safe until they come for you." He lied because he didn't know what else to do.

"My daddy would never do that," she said firmly.

"Let me try," Liana suggested, trading places with him and leaning into the van. "I'm going to be honest with you girls. Some really bad things are happening right now, and we're in the middle of it. We could all die if we're not careful, and I know your parents have told you not to trust strangers. They were right about that, but in this situation, you have to just use your best judgment. Do you think I want to hurt you?" The girls shook their heads. "Of course I don't. I want to help you. Now, I need you to be big girls and come with us so we can keep you safe for your mommy and daddy, okay?"

"Okay," the oldest said after a few seconds of deliberation, then she stood up and led her younger sisters to the front of the van. When the three of them were in the driver's seat, Liana paused.

"Now I need you to be very quiet, and do exactly as we say. It's dangerous out here, and if we make too much noise, bad things will happen, okay?" When the girls nodded, she started helping them out of the van one by one, but when she set the youngest on her feet, through Liana's legs, the little girl saw her parents crushed between two cars, covered in blood, and groaning.

She let out a loud, blood-curdling scream, and for a moment, everyone froze as the attention of the dead from both sides of the interstate was drawn directly to the source of the sound. Then suddenly they were coming!

"Pick the girls up," Liana commanded Alek as her military training took control of her. "Olivia, we'll cover him. You take the left, I'll take the right. Go! Go!"

Alek scooped up the two smaller girls, ordering the eldest to follow him, then they made a run for the limo as Olivia and Liana shot in both directions, taking down as many of the dead as they could. They made it to the car and found Jobe sitting in the driver's seat. He rolled the window down, and Alek passed the girls through as the dead converged upon them. Dani, Jax, and Ravi were shooting from the rig, June was still shooting out of the limo's window, and Alek got his rifle up as soon as the girls were safe, but it wasn't enough. The scream had drawn every last corpse in the area. Several crawled out a broken window of the overturned bus, those across the road abandoned the northbound group, and more came from the buildings in the median.

"Give me the keys!" Jobe shouted, his fingers creeping through the crack in the window to tap Olivia's shoulder.

"What?" she demanded.

"Don't make us die with you!" he begged. "Give me the keys!"

It made her angry, but she knew he was right. They were fucked.

"Give me another gun!" she cried, out of bullets and desperate for a fighting chance.

"The keys!" he demanded as she resorted to using the butt of her gun in the faces of the dead, praying her friends atop the semi would shoot them, but they were running low on bullets too. Ravi had no more, Jax and Dani had just emptied their last box into the rifles, and all of the others were in the back of the limo with June.

"Guns!" Liana shouted at June, and as Penny and Brittani sat frozen in fear, she finally thrust a rifle through the crack in her window. Olivia passed it to Alek with one hand as she pushed a corpse's head away with other, then Alek fired, taking him down.

"If she keeps giving us fresh guns, we can do this," Olivia said.

"Cover me," Alek shouted. "We're getting on the roof." Being the tallest, he quickly climbed atop the Hummer, the bars of the luggage rack making it easier, and once he was up there, he dangled his legs over for Olivia to climb up while he covered her. They did the same for Liana, but even when they were all safely aloft, they looked out over the teeming crowd and were filled with desperation.

"How are there so fucking many of them?" Olivia asked, feeling numb and defeated as she sat down on the roof. "How can we beat an enemy that adds to its numbers each time it kills?" If not for her daughter, she might have turned the gun on herself right then and there. She was just so tired. They all were, but the enemy didn't tire. They didn't sleep. They didn't stop.

"On your feet, soldier!" Liana shouted, using her best drill sergeant voice as she tried to inspire Olivia to continue fighting in spite of their impossible situation, but as she offered Olivia her hand to help her up, they were startled by a sudden gunshot from inside the car. Liana turned toward the sound and saw June looking up at her through a now-busted run roof.

"I couldn't get it to open without the keys," she said apologetically, and Liana's relief and joy came out in a hail of laughter. They broke out the remaining glass, climbed through, and slid the interior sunroof cover closed, and June spread some of the Kevlar vests out on the floor to cover the shards. Olivia, Liana, and Alek were just thrilled to be alive, but they weren't out of the woods yet. They were still surrounded, and now the dead were right up against the car, rocking it side to side.

"Oh! Dear, God! What are we going to do?" Jobe asked nervously.

"The first thing you're going to do is get the hell out of my spot, asshole," Olivia hissed, and though he scowled at her as he climbed over the front seat to trade places, he knew better than to say a word. She was furious with him because not only did he want to take the limo and leave them for dead, he, of all the people in that vehicle, should have realized the sunroof was the answer since one had saved his own, miserable life earlier tonight.

Once Olivia and Alek were back in the front, they asked Liana to pass them several boxes of bullets and half of the extra rifles. They were just going to sit there and pick the corpses off one at a time. Beyond that, they didn't have a plan.

But someone did. Suddenly the van in front of them started up and began pushing the cars out of the way, and to their right, the sound of motorcycles roared. They looked out the window and saw six men on the bikes, revving the engines and making circles as they taunted the dead, drawing them away from the limo. Dani, Jax, and Ravi got back in the rig, and soon the way was clear. The limo followed the van, and the rig followed the limo as they rolled down I-77 South, leaving the horror behind. Olivia's group was saved, but they had only managed to rescue three little girls.

We have to go back, Olivia thought. She couldn't just leave those people she saw hiding in cars there to die. She looked in the rearview mirror at the toll plaza, wondering how hard it would be for the limo to make a U-turn now that the road was only two lanes again, when she suddenly saw the motorcycles catching up to them. As they drove past the limo, she could see that there were passengers on the backs of most of the bikes now, and she breathed a sigh of relief knowing they could continue on.

A few miles later, the van led them to pull over on a stretch of deserted highway, and when the door opened, and out stepped a certain, tall, dark-haired French-Canadian in tight jeans. His chin shadowed by the beginnings of a beard, he looked rugged and disheveled, and as he stalked toward the limousine in a Greyhawks t-shirt, everyone could see his well-defined muscles moving beneath his clothes. He was an absolute work of art sculpted from women's fantasies and men's nightmares as he carried a blood-drenched hockey stick he had been using to fight the dead. He had removed the blade from his skate, duct taped it to the end of the stick, and honed it to razor-sharp edge that had become stained deep red wit the blood of the freshly resurrected.

His name was Aiden LaCroix, and he was everything Liana had ever wanted.

"King of Staves," she breathed with an overtly erotic excitement in her voice, and despite that her friend had been alone for so long it was depressing to think about, June still went directly to her Four Horsemen spiel.

"Behold," she said, "A pale horse, and he who sat upon it was death."

Then in unison, Liana joined Olivia in her automated response.

"Shut the fuck up, June," they said, and everyone but June and Jobe laughed. She didn't appreciate it, and he didn't get it, but before he could ask for an explanation, Aiden LaCroix opened the door of the limo.

"Can I catch a ride?" he asked with a subtle French-Canadian accent that made Liana's heart skip a beat. "The van's almost out of gas." Liana took her feet down from the seat beside her and patted it as he got in. Penny and Brittani were sitting on the other end with two little, blonde girls sniffling in their laps, and June and Jobe were sitting in the very back, the barrier of suitcases and shopping bags now crumbled on the floor. The nine-year-old sat between them, taking everything in with a terrified look on her face.

"Thanks for helping us," Olivia said to Aiden as they pulled back onto the road. "I don't know what we would have done if you hadn't."

"It was the right thing to do. We'd be dead if your people hadn't been shooting at the zombies on our side." He was the first to use the Z word, and with his accent, it made Liana giggle.

"So where are you headed?" Olivia asked, noticing that the motorcycles were still following along.

"Anywhere safe," he said with a shrug of his shoulders. "We were trying to make it home to Canada, but we can't do another thousand miles of this. We're going to find a place to get our bearings, then decide what to do from there."

"What were you doing in West Virginia?" Liana asked.

"We were actually in Charlotte, North Carolina to see a very sick little boy whose wish was to meet the Greyhawks. The whole team went, but we're all that's left." He nodded his head backward to indicate his teammates on the motorcycles. "So where are you going?"

"We're going to Olivia's place," Liana said. "She's a doomsday prepper, so she has a compound in the mountains not too far from here."

"You're welcome to come with us," Olivia said. "As long as everyone pulls their weight, we should have enough to keep us all comfortable." She was already planning ten steps ahead, contemplating reinforcing the fence around the inner ring and wondering how to get more supplies. Some of their companions might have considered it overkill, but after what they saw at the toll booth, she didn't expect to hear anyone arguing with her. Liana wasn't going to argue. She was completely enthralled by the newest member of their group, and though she should have probably been more worried about their situation, she wasn't anymore. The other aspects of the spell had come true, so she expected that just as Dani had demanded, there would be no monkey paw bullshit. She, her friends, their children, and their chosen men were going to survive this. That didn't exactly bode well for the others they had picked up along the way, but no one was going to tell them about the spell anyway because even though individually it had crossed each of their minds that they were responsible for this plague, none of them wanted to find out how the others would take it.

Most would probably think they were nuts...and that was probably the best response they could hope for.

It was almost 7:00 AM when Olivia finally pulled the limo onto the private drive that led to her compound near the top of the mountain. The remainder of their trip had been uneventful, and thankfully, today was a holiday so there weren't thousands of people hitting I-77 on their morning commute. Or maybe people had seen the news first and decided not to leave their houses. At the compound, the kids had been watching, and the news outlets had finally discovered and started reporting on what Savannah and Rey had figured out hours before. It was surreal, and though they should have been sleeping like the boys were, there was no way any of them could get a moment's rest until there was an adult here to make them feel protected.

Olivia drove up the winding road, through the middle gate and past the blood-stained gravel and wrecked vehicles that the Vincents, who had been patrolling since last night, had moved out of the way. Growing numb to the horrors already, Olivia pressed on, and when Savannah and Rey saw the limo approaching the upper gate on the monitor, they cheered like they had won the super bowl, waking the boys.

Once the gate closed behind the Right Way truck and motorcycles, the door to the lodge swung open, and the children came rushing out to greet their parents, relieved to find that they had all made it home safely. As Olivia held onto Savannah as if her life depended on it, Evil came running out the front door toward her mother, and suddenly half a dozen rifles clicked.

"No! She's not dangerous!" Savannah shouted, protectively blocking the cat as she stood up on her hind legs and hugged Olivia, nuzzling against her face.

"I've missed you, Evie," she whispered, then she directed her gaze toward her human daughter, "but what is my sweet kitty doing roaming free?"

"Long story," Savannah said.

"Well, why don't you take her to her room and give her a treat, then you can tell me about it after we all get some sleep?"

"Yes, ma'am," she said. "Come on, Evie."

The cat followed her into the lodge, and once she had disappeared down the hall, Olivia led everyone inside. There was so much to do, but what they all really needed right now was rest. The lodge had only seven guest suites with an additional guest room in the Anders' private residence, and while the inner ring had several cabins, they decided it was safest to keep the group together for now. Olivia started pulling guns and bullets out of the safe beneath the counter, handing them out along with keycards for the rooms. She gave Dani and Jax a king room and a hand gun, then did the same for Liana and Aiden after her son expressed that he had no interest in rooming with his mother. There weren't really enough suites for her friends to have that sort of privacy since they had picked up the Greyhawks and the other new people from the toll plaza, but there were plenty of rollaway beds and places to put them.

Jobe volunteered to protect June, and Olivia set them up with June's sons, not even mentioning to Jobe that the sofa he'd be sleeping on pulled out into a bed. Then as they left with their keys, she slipped a gun in Noah's hand and told him to protect his mother.

When everyone else had a place to sleep, Olivia agreed to take first watch at the monitors.

"I love you, Mom," Savannah said, hugging her. Olivia repeated her words, and her daughter, Sally, and Bella headed off, leaving her alone in the lodge. She picked up the satellite phone and dialed Reid's number. This time, he answered.

"Where are you?" she asked.

"Hiding out in a hardware store on the West Side," he said. "It's a fucking mess here, babe. Are you okay? Where are you?"

"I made it home. I'm okay. Savannah's okay. Evie's okay."

"Thank God," he breathed.

"I'm worried about you," she said.

"You worry about keeping our daughter safe," he insisted. "It's just going to take me a little longer to get home, but I'm with a group of people, and we're going to modify one of the store's delivery trucks to drive out of here. It may take a couple of days because this place is surrounded, but I promise I won't do anything stupid. I'll make it back to you, babe. I swear, I will."

"You'd better," she said.

"Tell Savvy I love her, okay?"

"I will. I love you, Reid," she whispered, choking up as she fought back tears.

"Don't cry, baby. Everything's going to be alright. I love you."

Olivia slipped the phone into her pocket and walked across the floor, heading toward the hallway to her private residence when the front door opened, startling her. Alek stepped inside, and realizing she had assigned all of the rooms without giving him a place to sleep, Olivia wondered if her subconscious wasn't somehow to blame.

In truth, Alek was to blame. He had deliberately stayed outside because there was only one bed he wanted to sleep in.

"Where have you been?" she asked.

"I wanted to walk the perimeter just to make sure there weren't any weak spots in the fence," he said. It wasn't a total lie. He did walk the perimeter, and he did think it needed to be done.

"And?" Olivia asked.

"And it all looks good," he said.

"Thank you," she said. "Are you tired? I'm going to take the first watch at the security monitors, but I can find you a bed first if..."

"I'll keep you company," he said, and she smiled, motioning for him to follow her. There were three spots in the lodge where security cameras could be viewed - the panic room attached to her bedroom, a small security room behind the main desk, and a larger room underground that she wasn't ready to tell anyone about.

She led Alek down the hall to her suite where they spent the next hour watching the monitors in her private room and talking about plans going forward. They found that they shared a lot of the same ideas about what they should do in the short term, and though they were impatient to get started fortifying their defenses, as their shift wore on, both spoke slower with heavier eyelids.

At the end of the hour, they were eager to hand the job off to Dani and Jax, and Alek stayed behind as Olivia went to the second story of the lodge where she knocked on the door of the first guest room. Dani answered in one of the robes with the lodge logo, grinning ear to ear, and Olivia could see Jax lying on the bed in the matching robe. Having hit the mini bar for snacks, they both looked like they thought this was just a weekend in Vegas.

"You do realize this is still the end of civilization, right?" Olivia asked with a laugh. "You should probably get dressed. I'll bet Reid has something you could wear, Jax."

"That's okay," he said, standing up and shedding his robe. Reflexively, Olivia put her hand over her eyes as he pulled his jeans back on.

"My luggage is in the limo," Dani said. "I'll grab something out of there."

Olivia led them downstairs to the security room and showed them how everything worked, explaining that they should not use the electric fence function on the dead for fear it might overload the system based on what Savannah and Rey told her. Of course, if any living people with bad intent tried to get in, they were fair game.

Sensing Olivia's exhaustion, they assured her that they could handle it, and they promised to pass the instructions on to Liana and Aiden in room #2 when their hour was up.

"You look like you're about to drop, Liv," Dani said. "Go get some sleep. We've got this."

"Okay," she said, and as she walked back toward her private residence with the sun shining through the tall windows of the lodge, she looked forward to getting some sleep in her glorious, windowless room. It slipped her tired mind that there was a tall, blonde, beautiful man without a bed assignment waiting there for her, and when she came back and saw Alek, she was torn. She didn't want to do anything that might hurt Reid, but she didn't want to be alone.

"There's a pull out bed in my office next door," she said. "Or you could stay in here with me if you don't mind sleeping on the couch." Hers and Reid's room was set up like one of the lodge suites with a sitting area, and he had noticed the couch when they left the panic room. He had also noticed that it wasn't long enough for a man of his height, but if the cramped couch was as close as he could get to Olivia's bed, he was willing to take it.

She pulled out the drawer under the television armoire and got him a set of sheets, then she went to pull the extra blanket off the end of the bed. As she picked up the hand-stitched quilt, she remembered opening it for Christmas last year. Reid had taken all of the small scraps of embroidery they found in her grandmother's house after she died and had it made into a quilt for her.

He was the most thoughtful husband in the world, and now because of her selfishness, he might never make it home. She didn't think about that when they were casting the spell. Dani said they couldn't die as a result. Olivia said their children couldn't, then Dani included that the men they loved couldn't. But nobody thought to say that the men they loved had to make it home.

That's how it's going to work, isn't it? she thought. *I can be with Alek, and it won't affect my marriage because my husband's never coming home.* Olivia sat on the edge of the bed and broke down, sobbing.

"Hey, it's going to be okay," Alek whispered as he sat down beside her, putting his arm around her shoulders. She leaned her head against his chest.

"No, it isn't," she cried weakly.

"It is. I promise," he assured her. "Let's get some sleep, and when we wake up, we'll figure out what to do next. If the government isn't getting a handle on it, we'll reinforce the fence around this place. Hell, we can build a fucking twelve foot wall on all of the groundwork you've already laid. We're going to survive this, Olivia. Your daughter is going to survive this."

"But what about..." *...my husband?* She couldn't bring herself to say it. Alek was here taking care of her, comforting her when inside he was probably just as afraid as she was, and the last thing she needed to do was draw his attention to the fact that she was another man's wife.

She looked up into his eyes. "Would you hold me tonight?" she asked. "I'm not coming onto you. I just need..."

"Shhh...I understand," he whispered, resting the side of his face against the top of her head as he fought the urge to kiss her there, and when they got under the covers, he wrapped her in his arms, holding her close until they both fell into a deep, much-needed sleep.

No one woke well-rested. Most everyone dropped quickly from exhaustion then suffered fitful dreams. It was almost noon when Olivia opened her eyes to find herself wound around Alek. She was instantly racked with guilt, but she didn't want to move. She didn't want to let go. Reid would just have to understand. In a few minutes, she had to go out there and be strong for everyone, but in here with Alek, she could just be a woman terrified that the whole world had gone to Hell.

"You up?" he asked suddenly, startling her, and she sighed, knowing she had to pull away now.

"Yeah," she said as she sat up and ran her fingers through her hair.

"It's okay," he said, putting his hand on her shoulder. "I know you're married."

"I'm sorry," she whispered, her eyes cast downward, unwilling to turn her head to look at him. "I should have told you the first time we met."

"I get it. You thought we'd never see each other again."

"Yeah," she said, finally meeting his gaze, but feeling embarrassed, she quickly got up and started to make the bed. Alek got up to help, determined to continue the conversation as they tucked the flat sheet and spread the comforter taut, and when he pulled the covers over his pillow, he felt something silky against his foot under the edge of the bed. Using his toe, he dragged it out, glancing down to see the sheer black nightie that had been dropped the last night Olivia and Reid had made love. Though tempted to pick it up, he left it peeking out from under the edge of the comforter so she could find it and deal with it when he wasn't in the room.

"Where is he now?" he asked her about her husband.

"Charleston," she said. "It's only about a two hour drive from here, but he's stuck there for now."

"Do you love him?" he asked. It may have seemed like a silly question, but it was a legitimate one. When Alek moved to the U.S. from his small hometown outside of Stockholm, Sweden, he had learned that marriage and love could often be mutually exclusive. He'd learned a lot of things in Hollywood that were vastly different from how he grew up, but even though he'd lost his Swedish accent, he'd never lost the person he was. Even after he became famous and women began to throw themselves at him, he never looked at them as objects, and he still dated with the goal of finding a perfect mate to start a life with rather than just looking to get laid. That didn't mean he didn't want to fuck Olivia. He had wanted her since he saw her across the bar at the Kemp Hotel on Saturday night, but today when she nodded yes to answer his question, he knew he was not going to allow himself to push the issue with her. She loved her husband, and he couldn't build any kind of healthy relationship with her on the foundation of a loving marriage he deliberately destroyed.

But he couldn't stay away from her either.

"I'd like to sleep here again tonight, Olivia," he began. "I promise I'll respect your marriage, and when your husband comes back, I'll find somewhere else to sleep. I just really need a human connection right now."

She thought about it for a moment, and though she knew it was the wrong decision, there was never really any chance of her giving him an answer other than yes. She needed the connection too, and she realized that she was going to be guilt-ridden whether Alek held her at night or not. Either she would indulge in the fantasy that she could actually be with him in a perfect world where Reid wouldn't be hurt by it, or she would lay in that bed alone night after night waiting for her husband to come home to her while tormenting herself for casting a spell that prevented it from happening. Though skeptical of the reality of it, she couldn't escape the prospect, however remote, that she was never going to see Reid again and Savannah was never going to see her father again because of a thoughtless choice made in a moment of uncharacteristic self indulgence.

And she was in the midst of yet another such moment when she nodded her head to Alek and said, "okay."

"Are you sure?" he asked.

"Yeah," she said, "but I can't cheat on my husband, Alek. I hope you understand that."

"I won't even try," he said, and it suddenly occurred to him that if she found the nightgown beneath the bed at some point, she might think he was responsible and kick him out of her room. He bent down and picked it up.

"Of course, it would be a lot easier if you didn't leave these laying around," he said as he offered her the silky, black garment. Smiling bashfully, she snatched it from his hand and took it to her lingerie drawer, and when she held it up to fold it, an image of her wearing it popped into his head. His reaction was involuntary, but he knew he needed to get away before she saw it.

"Alek," she called out as he walked toward the master bath, and he looked back over his shoulder, unwilling to turn his body to face her. "I don't think anyone else needs to know where you're sleeping, okay?"

"It will be our secret," he promised.

Liana's Journal
First Night in the Arms of Aiden La Croix

I didn't believe in magic, not totally. My abuela, who lived with us when I was a kid, was always telling me and my brothers stories about growing up Catholic in a small village in Argentina where they believed in witchcraft and spells, but to us it mostly seemed like the superstitions of an old woman. I guess over time, it did become a part of me, though, because when Dani wanted to take us into that palm reading shop, I felt uneasy. I got past it, but it came back later when the civilized world ended. As a Catholic, I was obligated to be a little scared of going to Hell for summoning demons.

Then Aiden LaCroix walked up to the limo on the roadside of the WV Turnpike, and I forgot all about demons and Hell and everything else.

I can't explain it, but ever since I laid eyes on him the first time, I've felt drawn to him in a way I've never felt in my life. I'm not the kind of person to get all gaga over a hockey player or rock star or whatever. It's not like that. It's something deeper. Of course, I could never have done anything about it in real life. I would have been too insecure to even try to talk to him, but when fate - or Madam Levinia - put us together, he seemed just as into me as I was him. I'd blame that on Levinia too if I hadn't specifically insisted that she not cast a love spell. If he falls in love with me, I want to know it's real.

And I think it will be. Aiden and I really clicked last night, or I guess it was actually super early this morning. We talked all the way to Olivia's doomsday compound, and I couldn't wait to get there so we could be alone. She gave us our key, and we hurried upstairs pretending to be in a rush to get to sleep. Then as soon as the door was closed behind us, he kissed me. It was the most perfect kiss of my life. His dark brown eyes met mine, and they slowly closed as he leaned in and parted my lips, slipping his smooth tongue between them. Goosebumps broke out all over my body, and between my legs was an absolute flood. I had wanted him for so long, but we were covered in blood and guts and filth from the fight to get here.

Aiden took the first shower. He started undressing on his way in, and when he took off his shirt, I thought I'd die of a heart attack, finally being alone with him after years of fantasizing about him. His body is incredible, his pecks, his abs, his every muscle beautifully defined, and I just sat in a chair watching him like it was a private strip show, hoping he'd drop the pants as well. I didn't get so lucky, but the whole time he was in the shower, all I could think about was what might happen once we were both freshly bathed.

Then he came out, and I went in. That's when it hit me like a ton of bricks. The spell that brought us together didn't change the reason I haven't been with a man in years. It didn't take away my secret shame. I lifted my leg and looked down at my inner thigh and burst into tears. It wasn't fair.

It *isn't* fair.

It's not that I'm vain. I know I wouldn't be perfect without these flaws, but there would be balance. I have thighs that are a little thick, an ass that is a little wider than I would prefer, and according to my exes, beautiful lady parts. I don't have one of those armoire vaginas like Olivia has where you know there's a kick ass entertainment center in there if you can just pry the doors open, but it's a nice shade of pink with everything petite and symmetrical. I get wet so easy, and my taste, I'm told, is subtle and sexy. My college boyfriend used to call it the "Taj Mahal of pussies". Unfortunately, my Taj Mahal was built in the middle of a rundown trailer park.

I've had a problem with acne on my inner thighs since puberty. I know that doesn't seem like a big deal, but it's not just a few little zits and a blackhead here or there. I get cysts and boils, and depending on the time of the month, my inner thighs can look like a three-dimensional topographical map of a volcano belt. They hurt, they're gross, and they scar.

They only show up during one week of my cycle, and when I was a teenager, my skin would bounce right back except for some discoloration, so as long as I avoided taking my pants off during that week, I could enjoy a relatively normal sex life without ever having my boyfriend know how hideous I really was down there. But as I got older and the same skin suffered eruption after eruption, it didn't heal so quickly and perfectly anymore. It started to scar, and then the boils would form on the thick scar tissue and make it even worse. I'm thirty five now, and even when I'm not having a breakout, it looks like I am. The skin is all twisted and uneven, and there's nothing I can do about it.

I've been to doctors since it started, and while some had the misguided notion that they could help me, they couldn't. They gave me antibiotics, but the predisposition of that skin to form cysts wasn't about bacteria or cleanliness. I've always been obsessed with keeping myself clean because of it. It made me feel dirty, so I would bathe constantly, but when all was said and done, it didn't matter if I showered five times a day or didn't shower for five days at a time, the cysts were going to be there every month like clockwork. Hormones didn't help. Acne treatments didn't help. The only real option I ever had was a surgery where that area of skin would be completely removed and replaced kind of like a tummy tuck on the inner thigh, but my insurance wouldn't cover it, so it was really never an option at all.

And now that the civilized world is coming to an end? I guess I'll just do what I've always done. Restrict myself and work around it. Sometimes it isn't so bad. I've really become pretty clever about it.

By my late twenties, I had discovered BDSM. I wasn't honestly all that into being a Dominant, but having control over my partners gave me a freedom I hadn't experienced since the scarring began. As a Domme, I could blindfold my boyfriends and tie their hands behind their backs so I could guide their dicks or their tongues just where I wanted them...and *only* where I wanted them. It was the closest I'd ever come to having a normal sex life, but the problem with that was I had to find true submissives, which aren't the kind of men I'm into. The kind of men I'm into get bored with my BDSM games pretty fast because they want to be in control. It was a no win situation for me, and though I used to get depressed about it, it got easier on my heart once I just gave up men altogether.

That's when I started my five year relationship with Bob. Though there's nothing in this world that feels as amazing to a clitoris as a tongue that wants to please it, at least Bob got the job done. But now he was in a suitcase in a hotel in Pittsburgh while I was in West Virginia with the man of my dreams waiting to fuck me on the other side of the bathroom door. *God!* How I wish I could just walk out there, fall into his arms, and learn what it was like to have sex that wasn't planned out in detail to hide my shame. I wanted to know what it was like to let a man take control and make love to me...fuck me...use me like a toy...but I was a thirty-five-year-old woman who had never even had sex with the lights on, so what did I do?

I rejected him. I asked him to hold me instead. We were wearing nothing but the robes we found in the bathroom because we didn't have any clean clothes, and he politely turned his back so I could get under the blankets first. I shed my robe, and when I was covered, I watched from behind as his robe slid over his shoulders then came completely off. His ass was so tight and muscular, I wanted to just take a bite of out it, but what I wanted even more was to see the front. That didn't happen. When he turned back around, he was holding an extra sheet blocking my view. He switched off the light and crawled into the bed, covering up with the new sheet, leaving me the other, which separated us beneath the comforter, and he made the joke that it was to protect my virtue. Of course, then he pulled me into his arms, holding me tightly, the thin fabric of the sheets no barrier at all as I felt every peek and valley of his firm, naked muscles. Intrepidly, I slipped my leg over his to get closer, feeling him begin to grow hard as my thigh passed over his groin, and *ay, dios mio!* The thought of being that close to Aiden LaCroix's erection made me so wet, I could feel it on my thighs. But all I could do was give him a squeeze and whisper goodnight.

I fucking hate my life.

This isn't fair.

Day 4

Over the course of several days, life in the Anders compound settled into a pattern. The news continued to broadcast as the government tried to come up with a means of battling the disease that caused the dead to rise and feast on the flesh of the living, which included bombing several major cities like Pittsburgh, and when it was clear that the military effort would yield no useful results, the group on the mountaintop worked to fortify their position.

The roads in Summers County were relatively clear, and it was easy for them to "borrow" the things they needed to begin building a wall around the inner ring. They brought in a bobcat to dig trenches along the perimeter, and inside the chain link fence, they started the wall using stone stolen from a construction project not far from the compound. The sound drew the occasional corpse, but in such a sparsely populated area, it was only a minor inconvenience to have to stop and put a bullet through its head.

There were a few in the group who thought they were overreacting by shoring up their defenses so quickly, but they were overruled. Olivia, for one, knew what to expect because the compound itself existed for the sake of surviving a societal catastrophe, and even though she was basing her expectations on research of governmental breakdowns in other countries, she was able to appeal to the others by referencing end-of-the-world-type disaster films, which nearly everyone had seen. She reminded them that if the government was unable to protect the citizens, it wasn't going to be the peacemakers who rose up and took charge. If history and cinema had shown them anything, it was that the sort of warlords who rose to power from disaster were never overflowing with compassion for humanity.

They were going to need more than just walls to protect them. They needed weapons and ammunition. Though Olivia and her husband had been preparing for a long time with plenty of guns and bullets already stockpiled, she knew it wasn't enough. The compound had been built with two things in mind - profitability until the polar ice caps melted and protection and sustainability thereafter. They had chosen a place with fairly easy interstate access to large metro areas like Charlotte and DC for the revenue it would bring, but this catastrophe was not the one they had prepared for. They were going to need a lot more ammunition if all of those people from the large metro areas began heading into the hills looking for refuge because wherever their food source went, the dead were sure to follow.

"I noticed a gun shop on the side of the road when we went on the last run," Aiden said as he sat down at the dining room table in Olivia's residence to discuss plans with the others. There were seven of them - Olivia, Dani, Liana, Alek, Jax, Aiden, and Damon, the Greyhawks ' goalie who had already proven invaluable on their scavenging missions. They had excluded June because Olivia didn't want Jobe to be a part of the community oversight. She didn't trust him before he tried to take the limo and abandon them, and she damn sure didn't trust him now. No one did but June, so no one expected anything from him. His only job had become keeping June and her kids safe, though every day Olivia spent time honing the boys' shooting skills because they were likely going to have to be their own protectors. Of course practice meant they needed more bullets, so in his cool, aloof manner, Aiden suggested they loot the gun shop. Piece of cake.

"If a gun shop hasn't already been looted by now, it probably means there's someone in there shooting the looters," Alek rationalized.

"I don't know, man," Damon said, running thick, strong fingers through his brown hair. He wasn't from French-speaking Canada like Aiden, and he barely had an accent unless he said words with the *ou* sound. "The place was surrounded by dead. If there was someone protecting it, wouldn't they be shooting them in the head? Maybe the parking lot is full because many have tried, but nobody's been able to clear it enough to get in there."

"I don't know if we should risk it," Dani said, reaching for Jax's hand under the table. Jax went on some of these missions, and the idea of him battling a parking lot full of corpses was more than she could bear.

"Are you talking about Sylas Gun and Pawn down on Route 20?" Olivia asked, and Alek nodded. "What were you doing all the way down there?"

"I remembered passing a brickyard on the way in from interstate. It's where we got the last load of stone for the new wall," he said.

"We should probably start keeping a log of scavenging locations so we know where to look if you don't come back," she said.

"If we don't come back, you probably don't want us back," Alek pointed out.

"Is it that bad out there?" she asked, realizing that she was sitting safely on her mountain while others risked their lives for that safety. That wasn't going to happen anymore.

"Yes," Aiden said sadly. Yesterday, they had lost one of his teammates on a mission to clear a small, local pharmacy, and he knew that wouldn't be the last. "I had hoped that here in the middle of nowhere it would take longer for it all to collapse, but everything is overrun now. Everything."

"Then we need those guns," Liana insisted.

"Agreed," Olivia said, and she gave the group a little background on the guy who owned the shop. Randy Sylas, was a paraplegic Vietnam vet in his sixties who was confined to a wheel chair, but he was still a crack shot. If he was holed up in his shop, he could definitely take out looters, but he should be able to take out the dead as well. He should have also figured out that he had to shoot them in the head by now, so if his place was surrounded, they surmised that Randy was either dead or not there.

They decided they were going in. Liana was going to lead the mission, and they were taking Olivia, Alek, Damon, Aiden, and Ravi to drive the Right Way truck. They'd stolen so many rigs to bring stone up the mountain at this point that several of them had figured out how to drive tractor trailers, but somebody was going to have to maneuver it to back up to the gun store just right. Ravi was the only one with that kind of experience.

With everyone suited up in Kevlar and armed to the teeth, Alek, Olivia, and Liana climbed into the cab of the rig with Ravi while Damon and Aiden followed on motorcycles. One of the first things they did was modify the mufflers to cut down on the sound, but even as quiet as they were now, in the unnatural stillness of the new world, they may as well have been honking their horns as they rolled through the first gate. At the bottom of the mountain, Olivia had Ravi stop the truck so she could talk to John Vincent, whose family was the only one living in the lower ring now. He knew Randy better than she did, and she was hoping he could give her some insight in case he was in the shop.

He did one better. He offered to accompany them.

Leaving his unhappy wife and children, John climbed into the cab, and they made their way down the roads toward Pipestem on Route 20. Olivia watched in horror as they passed so much death and destruction, and though part of her wished she had never left the mountaintop, she knew she was not capable of sitting idly again while others did the dirty work. She needed to get out there and see what it was like because she was the one ultimately making the decisions that affected them all. She never asked to be their leader, but they all looked to her for answers.

Liana, on the other hand, was excited as they headed toward danger. Once her military training had kicked in, the urge she once had to be a general had resurfaced, and she was ready to reclaim the entire world from the dead one mission at a time. Her orders were for Ravi to pull the rig off the road before they reached the shabby, outdated mini plaza with the gun shop so Aiden and Damon could use the motorcycles to lure as many of the dead away from the parking lot as possible, and when they were sitting on the shoulder watching the Greyhawks lead the horde of corpses down Route 20 like Pied Pipers, it seemed brilliant.

As Aiden and Damon slowly drove, the dead came from other parking lots and joined them, and they were soon leading a march of about fifty in an area neither of them were terribly familiar with. By the time they disappeared from sight, the mini plaza was clear except for a few random corpses with wounded legs that prevented them from walking, and as Ravi navigated the parked cars, the others got out of the rig to put them down, noticing that they all had two things in common. Their leg wounds were caused by gunshots, and they had been bitten multiple times. This, along with the haphazard way the cars were parked, made it obvious that someone was inside the gun shop taking out potential looters.

It had been the middle of the night when the plague began. The parking lot should have been empty, but the looters set their sights on Sylas Gun and Pawn early on. It was probably the most valuable asset within twenty miles for those who didn't realize the worth of pharmacies at that point. The shop was full of expensive jewelry and weaponry. Only one of those things had any value today, but three days earlier, looters may not have seen it that way.

Olivia and Alek shot the rest of the dead using silencers one of Aiden's teammates had made from the barrels of flashlights. He had managed to look it up online before the internet went down, and they were able to fire without drawing the attention of the crowd following the cycles. Aiden and Damon had filled their gas tanks before leaving the compound, but they were at a complete loss of what to do with the herd they now led. No one had envisioned it working so well, assuming that they would be followed more casually and be able to just turn around and zip past the dead to get back to the gun shop once they'd led them a few miles off, but as more joined the group, they took up the entire road. Then before Aiden and Damon even had time to come up with a plan, the herd's attention was abruptly drawn back to the mini plaza as a hail of gunfire erupted.

"Oh, shit!" Aiden cried, worried for Liana. He didn't know which end of the bullets his friends were on, but he was certain that fifty walking corpses weren't going to help matters. He and Damon hurried back to the herd, revving their engines and trying to get the focus back on them, but it only attracted a dozen or so stragglers who hadn't rushed off to the new stimuli.

The majority of the dead were running a three mile marathon back toward the gun shop where an AR-15 was spraying bullets into the parking lot from the mail slot in the steel door. Most of them were hitting the rig as Ravi had done a perfect job backing it up, and while the shooter was focused on the front of the shop, Liana, Alek, and Olivia crept around to the backdoor, hoping to break in and sneak up on him. Meanwhile, John Vincent stood by the front waiting for a lull in the gunfire so he could be heard. If it was Randy, he thought he might have a chance.

"Randy!" John shouted when the shooter finally stopped to reload. "It's John Vincent! Hold your fire!"

"Get the fuck out of here, John! I don't want to have to kill you," Randy yelled back.

"I'm your friend, man. Let me in."

"I don't have any friends anymore. Now, go the fuck away!"

"I can help you, Randy. What's the matter? Are you having a flashback?" he asked, confused about why his friend wouldn't be willing to let him in.

"No, I'm not having a fucking flashback, you jackass! You show up here with a bunch of armed strangers in the middle of the goddamn zombie apocalypse, back a semi tractor trailer up to my front door, and you think my problem with you is a flashback from a war I fought fifty fucking years ago? Fuck. You," he spat, and John laughed, realizing how ignorant it was for him to make that assumption.

"I'm sorry, brother. I can see how this must seem, but I swear it's not like that. We're here to help you," he insisted.

"Help yourself, John. Get the fuck away from my store!" Randy shouted, then John heard a click and jumped back from the door just before the AR started spraying the back of the rig with bullets. John threw his hands up in the air in exasperation, but behind the building, Alek had been waiting for gunfire to use as cover. He shot the knob off of the backdoor, and he, Olivia, and Liana were able to slip inside.

Quietly, they stole through the backroom of the shop. There was a short hallway that led to the main store where Randy was shooting out of the mail slot, and off to one side was an office. Liana and Olivia peeked in and saw two young girls hiding under a table in the corner, terrified, but as one of them took a breath in to scream, Liana and Olivia dove under the table and put their hands over the girls' mouths, holding firm.

"We're not here to hurt you. We're here to help you," Liana repeated the words she'd said a hundred times to Afghani children in similar situations, and she meant it just as much now as she did then. "Are you here against your will?"

The older girl shook her head no.

"I have a daughter your age," Olivia said. "Savannah Anders. Do you know her from school?" The girl nodded. "She's at my house right now with Sally Chambers and Bella Fugate. We came to get you out of here and take you to my house where you'll be safe."

"I'm going to remove my hand now, but if you scream, you'll be putting yourselves and Randy in danger, do you understand me?" Liana asked, and they both nodded. She looked at Olivia, and they nervously released the girls. They stood up and backed toward the door as Liana put a finger to her lips to remind them to be quiet, but as soon as the women turned away from them, the girls started screaming, "Grandpa! Help!"

"Goddamn it!" Olivia cursed, expecting the worst, not even realizing yet that the gunfire had stopped.

"It's okay," Alek called out. "I've disarmed him."

Randy hadn't heard his granddaughter's cries over the sound of his own gunfire, nor did he hear Alek sneaking up behind him until he had a gun pointed at his head. With Randy's gun now on the ground out of reach, Alek ordered him to turn around and face him.

"Well, fuck me running!" the old man with the grey ponytail grumbled as he glared at Alek. "Every armed wannabe badass in Summers County died trying to steal from me, and I get taken out by a fucking Hollywood pretty boy!" Olivia smiled as she approached them. Yes, he was pretty...and delightfully resourceful.

Olivia wheeled Randy out of the way so John could get in and they could start loading the trailer, but when Liana opened the door and shouted to John, who was standing at the side of the truck, he looked back and shook his head.

"We've got a bigger problem now," he said, and she took a peek through his binoculars to see the horde of the dead in the distance. She estimated that they had about three or four minutes before they hit the parking lot.

"Okay, Alek, get Ravi, and the two of you need to start moving vehicles to block off the front of the store while we load the truck. Olivia, tie Randy up if you have to because we need to get started now. John, get the girls out here and put them to work."

"Yes, sir, General Navarro," Olivia teased, and while Alek continued to hold his gun on Randy, she looked around for something to tie him up with. She found a rack of rope bracelets, and when she pulled one down, trying to figure out how to untangle it, Alek looked down at Randy impatiently.

"Is this going to be necessary?" he asked. "We came here to rescue you and take you somewhere safe. I'm not going to lie. We need your guns, but we weren't going to just steal them and leave you here."

"And I'm supposed to just take the word of some Hollywood actor?" Randy balked.

"If that's not good enough, take my word, Randy," John said, irritated as he walked by carrying an armload of weapons headed for the back of the truck. "I left my family alone to come down here because I didn't want this to end with a bullet in your stubborn head."

"Come on, Randy," Olivia said. "How many times has Reid bought guns from you? Have we ever lied to you or tried to rip you off?"

"Fine. I surrender," he relented with a scowl, but Olivia hesitated.

"What do you think, John?" she asked, not sure if they could trust Randy.

"I think he's a good man, and we can take him at his word," he said, glaring at Randy as he spoke to emphasize that he had better not prove him wrong.

"What am I gonna fucking do?" Randy asked. "Run over you with my wheelchair?"

They laughed awkwardly, deciding to take the chance on trusting the older man, and now that Alek was no longer stuck holding a gun on him, he went outside to start blocking the coming herd. It wasn't hard. Most of the cars had keys in them because they had come with the intent of robbing the gun shop. Alek and Ravi moved as many as possible to create a perimeter around the entrance so they could keep loading the truck while leaving the rig a clear, yet narrow, path to drive out of there. With seconds to spare, Alek climbed over the cars and went inside to help as Ravi got back in the driver's seat and prepared to make their getaway, and when the dead finally made it back to the lot en masse, they surrounded the front of the truck.

Inside the shop, it took about fifteen minutes to load the rig with every weapon and bullet in the showroom. Since Randy was in a wheelchair, he had various ramps and carts, making it easier, and a lot of items in the back were already stacked up on dollies. They took bows and arrows, knives, bullet proof armor, and even the jewelry, anything they thought they might find a use for, leaving only the guitars and other pawned instruments that Jax might have

90

been inclined to take if he had come on the mission. It went quicker than expected, but by the time they were all packed up and ready to head back to the compound, there was no way Ravi was going to be able to drive through the teeming sea of the dead blocking the rig.

"That looks like half the population of Summers County," Olivia exaggerated.

"How the fuck are there so many of them already?" Liana complained. Her training did not extend to clearing areas of dead people who didn't respond to being threatened with a gun.

"I'll tell you how," Randy said. "Looting assholes! Bunch of crazy pricks from up these hollers hear there's civil unrest, and they see opportunity. They're as bad as the goddamn gangs in the city, but they're not as fucking smart. I've sold weapons to damn near every motherfucker in this county, and they'll protect what's theirs just like I did."

Olivia realized he was right. There were far more good people than bad, but in this situation, good people - like her and her group for instance - had resorted to looting just like the bad people, and like Randy said, a lot of motherfuckers in this county were armed.

"So what do we do?" she asked.

"I have an idea if one of you can shoot a bow," Randy said.

"Can you?" Olivia asked Alek, thinking about the bow his demon character on TV used.

"I can," he said because although he had trained with expert archers so he would look like he was doing it right on the show, he didn't feel like an expert himself. "But if there's anyone more experienced..."

"Not unless you want to carry my ass onto the roof," Randy said with a chuckle as he wheeled himself back toward the rig, and as Alek pushed him up the ramp, he explained that he watched a group get away from the dead at the gas station across the street a few nights ago by setting a fire. He grabbed a bow and a box of arrows, then he rolled himself back down the ramp and into the office where he gathered sterno, cheesecloth, sparklers, and duct tape. He shaved the sparklers into several packets of sterno dipped cheesecloth, and prepared five arrows, which he handed to John.

While Olivia collected the rest of the supplies he had used, John and Alek followed Randy's directions to get to the roof. Once up there, they could see their target - an old shack that was falling down in the middle of a field to the right of the mini plaza. It was about two hundred yards away.

"You've got to be joking," Alek said when he realized the distance.

"Can you hit it?" John asked.

"Guess we'll find out," he said, gritting his teeth. John struck the lighter beneath the arrow as Alek held it in place until the sterno caught fire. It took him three shots to finally land one on his target, and the dry grass around the first two arrows seemed to be burning better than the shack. He shot the remaining two arrows, one hitting the roof, the other landing in front, and after a minute, they could see that the shack had caught fire. In the dry, fall air, it took only minutes for it to spread, and when the flames began to put off a cloud of black smoke, it finally drew the attention of the dead.

"They're clearing out," John said as he and Alek came back downstairs. "Let's go ahead and get in the back of the truck so Ravi can take off as soon as they're gone."

They couldn't use the walkie talkies to communicate with Ravi yet because the sound might draw attention, but they had rigged a communication system in the truck using technology not much more sophisticated than two cans on a string.

"Remind me to loot Radio Shack next," Olivia whispered as the others quietly climbed in, and while Alek pushed Randy up the ramp, he realized that Liana and his granddaughters were missing only seconds before one of the girls let out a blood-curdling scream. It came from the office. Liana had been helping them pack up, and since the backdoor no longer latched after Alek shot off the knob, some of the dead had wandered inside when the wind blew it partially open. Now Liana and the girls were trapped in the office by three corpses, and Liana did not have a weapon.

With the silencers in the cab of the rig, they were afraid that gunfire would draw the entire herd, most of whom were in the field next door now, so Randy handed Alek and John two large, sharp hunting knives. They hurried toward the office, but when they reached the hallway, they were met with problems of their own as the scream had drawn even more corpses through the open door.

They began driving the knives into eye sockets as the dead were bottlenecked in the hallway, and though effective, the dead just kept coming. Realizing they were going to have to use the guns, Alek was reaching for his when they heard the sound of a motorcycle, and it was coming down the hall so fast, they barely had time to jump out of its path. It was Damon, he had made his way back to the parking lot and had been leading stragglers toward the fire when he saw a group going through the door. He knocked them down as he drove into the shop, then made a u-turn and another pass through the hall, planning to leave the bike in a position to hold the back door closed, but first he had to drive back through a group of five who had come in after him. One grabbed his jacket, causing him to cut the wheel, and the bike skidded out of from under him, slamming the door shut.

With the dead now blocked from entering, even though Damon's leg was injured in the fall, he quickly got his bearings, jumped up, and started fighting, and when John and Alek joined in, they took out the rest of the dead. With Liana and the girls, they ran for the rig, slammed the doors shut, and told

Ravi to hit the gas, and finally, they made it out of there with a truck full of weapons and no casualties.

No *known* casualties anyway.

"Where is he?" Liana fretted as the semi turned onto the main road.

"I don't know," Damon said. "We got separated."

"We have to go back for him!" she cried.

"We will," Alek said. "Let's get the rig back home, and I'll lead a search party."

"I'll show you where I last saw him on the map before you go," Damon offered.

"Oh, my God, Damon! You're losing a lot of blood," Olivia suddenly shouted out as she noticed it pooling beneath his leg.

"It's nothing. It's just a cut," he said, but he knew better. When he crashed the bike, he had been bitten in the few seconds he spent on the ground disoriented, and though he knew he wasn't going to make it, he didn't want the others to know for fear that they would shoot him or put him out of the truck. Holding his hand over the wound to hide it, he was hoping to hold out at least until they returned to the compound, but he was already beginning to feel sick and weak.

Liana felt weak too, and heartbroken. All she could think about was how selfish she had been with Aiden, so focused on her own issues, she'd denied them both something they desperately wanted, and now he might be gone forever.

"He's dead. I just know it," she whispered, and Olivia came close, speaking directly into her ear so no one else would hear.

"Do you love Aiden?" she asked.

"Yes," Liana said without hesitation, surprising even herself.

"Then he can't die. It was part of the spell."

"You don't believe that," Liana bemoaned with a tear in her eye, and Olivia smiled a sad smile because it was true. She didn't. Even after everything that happened and all of the weak moments when she thought she was personally responsible for everything, deep down Olivia believed it was all a coincidence. And Aiden was probably dead.

Liana walked to the back of the rig where Randy's chair was parked by the door. He had been watching the road behind them through one of the bullet holes he was responsible for, and he looked up when he noticed her staring at him.

"Sorry about all this," he said, pointing at the holes letting in rays of light.

"Man, you were gonna shoot me," John complained.

"Damn straight I was," Randy shouted, "but I'm sorry. It's just that..." He paused and sighed. "I served in Vietnam for two years, and that never fucked me up as bad as the past four days."

Just like Bella and Sally, Randy had found out within hours of the first broadcast that there were people in this world who were just itching for a societal breakdown. His daughter and son-in-law had come to the shop to take him to their house, and as they and their two young daughters tried to persuade the stubborn old man that abandoning his shop was the safest measure, there was a knock at the front door. It was four young men, brothers and cousins, who were among Randy's best customers.

He knew at the start that he had to lock things down because a gun shop was a target during any sort of disaster situation, but when a truckload of men he knew showed up, he hadn't yet learned that people he considered friends before the dead came back to life weren't necessarily his friends anymore.

"I knew these guys, John. I'd been hunting with them, drank with them. I mean, they were a little anti-government...hell, so am I, but when the dead get up and start eating people, I'd vote Democrat if they had a good plan to stop this shit. These guys, though? They were getting off on it.

"At first they said they were just there to buy some ammo, which I rang up for them, but then one of them got a look at my granddaughters. He went over and started to touch..." he stopped abruptly when he saw his oldest granddaughter begin to twitch as she stared at the ground. "She's twelve-years-old, goddamn it! And those fuckers wanted to..." He couldn't even say it out loud, skipping over it as he continued his story. "Things got out of hand pretty quick, and we ended up in a shootout. One of them got away, but I killed the other three assholes! I didn't know I had to shoot them in the head, though I didn't figure that out until they came back and bit my daughter and her husband. I had to put them both down, and I had to have the girls help me drag their parents bodies outside.

"I protected those girls for four days, and by the time you all came around, there had been at least a dozen more groups just like them. I sat at the mail slot until I had the best shot, then I'd kill the fuckers. At first, I was shooting them in the kneecaps to make them suffer, then I realized they'd be more use to me if they could get back up and protect the parking lot from the next group, and I started shooting them in the chest. So, I am sorry, John, but I'm a crippled old man and the only defense these girls have against a world of sick motherfuckers. I'd have killed you and not thought twice about it," Randy said. "But I'm glad I didn't."

"I am too," John said with a subtle laugh, and as everyone rode in silence, feeling uneasy at the thought of what the girls had been through, Randy turned away and went back to staring through the bullet holes.

The trip was quiet and morale low until they hit a long, straight section of the road where he noticed something moving behind them in the distance.

"What's that?" he wondered aloud, and hopeful, Liana rushed to find her own bullet hole. Slowly, the image grew larger until she realized they were being followed by a motorcycle.

"It's Aiden!" she cried. "Oh, my God! He's alive!"

Instantly, a sense of joy spread throughout the trailer as everyone realized they had all made it back from their most dangerous mission to date, and even Damon cheered with what little energy he had left, happy to know that at least his friend was going to survive this.

When the rig finally pulled through the inner gate to their sanctuary, the doors were opened, and Liana flew out, tackling Aiden with an enthusiastic hug. Alek told Damon to sit tight as he went to find help to lift the larger man out of the truck while Olivia went searching for June to take a look at his injuries, but before either of them returned, Damon breathed his last as John was setting up the ramp to get Randy out of the rig.

Seconds later, Damon's eyes opened again. Blocked by Randy's wheelchair, no one noticed, not even Randy until he felt a tugging on his jeans and looked down to find Damon biting into his calf. Paralyzed, he didn't even feel it, but when he saw it, he screamed, pulling his gun out of its holster and unloading it in Damon's head.

John rushed into the rig and pushed Randy's chair down the ramp, picking him up and lying him on the ground.

"Someone please take the girls to the lodge!" he shouted. "Then somebody get me an axe and some alcohol! And I'll need something hot to cauterize the wound!"

As Liana led Randy's granddaughters away, Alek grabbed the axe from the woodpile on the side of the lodge, and Ravi pulled out a flask, all while Randy lay there confused, unable to hear what they were planning because the sound of the gunfire in the back of the trailer had temporarily deafened him. Then he saw John pour the alcohol on the blade.

"No!" he begged as he began to thrash, but with gritted teeth, Alek came to hold him still while John brought the axe down, taking off his leg just above the bite site. Randy howled in agony. He couldn't actually feel it, but he had never had a stronger phantom limb sensation than in that moment. Then Aiden drove his motor cycle over, and John used the hot muffler to cauterize the wound, filling the air with the stench of melting human flesh.

"What the fuck are you doing?" Olivia demanded suddenly as she returned with June, who immediately rushed over to care for Randy. While she and the other men helped him back in his chair Alek apprised Olivia of the situation.

"Thanks for 'rescuing' me, assholes!" Randy hissed, making air quotes as June wheeled him toward the lodge. They set him up with a cot in the office behind the reception desk because the upstairs was not handicapped accessible, and they wanted to keep him sequestered until they were sure that cutting off his leg would stop him from dying.

They were only sure of two things at that point. Everyone who died would rise again regardless of whether or not they had been bitten, and a bite from the dead was a guaranteed death sentence. John surmised that since the cause was somehow present in everyone, the bite either killed through extremely aggressive bacteria or a concentrated dose of the reanimation virus, and therefore he believed that immediately cutting off the limb above the bite site might stop the killing agent from getting into the bloodstream. While June agreed that it was a medically sound possibility, Olivia thought it was completely absurd given the speed at which the heart pumped blood through the body because she knew how quickly she felt pain medication move through her veins when she was in the hospital, but since they would never have a better guinea pig than Randy for this experiment, she was curious to see the outcome on the condition that he be observed under constant armed guard. John volunteered for the first shift, asking that his family be moved to the inner ring in the meantime. Olivia had been urging him to do that since the beginning, but it took Randy's story about his granddaughter's rape to finally scare the stubborn independence out of him.

It was going to be hard to find them a safe, comfortable place because everyone continued to sleep in the main lodge until the trenches were finished, and it was starting to get cramped with even the private guest room in Olivia's residence taken. She gave the Vincent family her living room, and though it didn't have a door, it was more private than adding their cots to those already spread throughout the lodge since she insisted on keeping the office connected to her bedroom as Alek's room. When Reid got back, she would be honest with him, but he didn't need the rest of the group looking at him and wondering how he felt about the fact that his wife had had another man in her bed while she awaited his return.

Things were going to get a lot easier once they could start moving people into the cabins, but for now they all sat empty, which was convenient for Olivia's friends who knew where to find the master keys.

"Come with me," Liana said to Aiden after sneaking away with one. She gave him a sly smile, and his eyes flashed, knowing they were finally going to sate the desire ignited the first moment he had seen her across the median at the toll plaza and decided to abandon his plans to return to Quebec. He had been instantly taken in by her beauty and bravery, selfishly convincing his teammates to follow him into the unknown, and he was certain it had been the right decision. He figured he would probably already be dead somewhere on road by now, but instead he was about to get naked with a hot brunette who had amazing tits, gorgeous bronze skin, and the most delightfully wicked gleam in her amber eyes.

Liana's Journal
Day 4

Aiden and I stole one of Liv's master keys, and we snuck up the hill to the cabin farthest away from everything. It was a little one bedroom unit, but it could have been a tent for all I cared. I just wanted to get Aiden alone...and naked. First, I had to make sure there were blackout curtains in the bedroom because there was no way I was going to take off my clothes in the middle of the day without them, and once I closed them, I could barely see anything.

"Come here," I said to Aiden as I stood by the bed unbuttoning my shirt, and he was quickly on me, his fingers taking over the task, his lips finding mine in the near-darkness. I felt like my body was on fire, every part of me begging for his touch, and I shuddered when he grasped my shoulders, pushing my shirt down my arms as our vision adjusted to the low light, the excitement in his eyes reflecting my own.

My top fell to the ground, and he ran his hands around to the back, working on my bra strap. Just the sensation of his fingers against my skin was electric, and I wished I wasn't going to have to tell him that he couldn't use them south of the equator. As he unhooked my bra, I opened my mouth, but he silenced me, grabbing my full breasts in his hands, his breath audible as he stared at them.

"Damn, Liana, you're beautiful," he whispered, his mouth barely finishing the words as it sought my nipple. He sucked it in, swirling his tongue over it, and I felt the sensation between my thighs as if it were somehow linked. I never even knew I had that sort of connection before, but as he continued to worship my breasts, I could feel a direct line, my nether regions flooding with desire for him, my clitoris erect against the course denim fabric.

God! I wanted to put my hands on his head and push him down...

And Aiden had the same idea. He began to kneel before me, his hand running downward to find the snap on my jeans, and it damn near killed me to do what I had to do next.

"Aiden," I whispered, my voice airy and desperate for the complete opposite of what I was going to say.

"What is it, mon cœur?" he asked, not even looking up as he kissed my navel, unsnapping my pants with nimble fingers, making it even harder to stop him, but I had no choice.

"Aiden," I repeated, taking his hands in mine to get his full attention. "I don't like...I don't want you to touch me below the waist."

"What are you saying?" he asked.

"Let's get in bed," I say, and though I could tell he was confused as hell, he didn't argue, pulling off his shirt as I turned away from him to remove my pants. I looked over my shoulder and caught him watching me, and since my shame can't be seen from behind, I bent at the waist as I slipped off my panties, giving him a bit of a peep show as a distraction. When I was naked, I motioned for him to look away while I spun back around and slid beneath the sheet, then I lay propped up on one elbow to watch him as he took off his pants.

"Uh-uh," he said, shaking his head and instructing me to cover my eyes.

"Oh, come on," I protested, dying to see his beautiful body in its full naked glory. From what I'd seen so far, Aiden was an absolute masterpiece, his chest and abs deliciously defined, a dark pathway of hair disappearing into his jeans, but he was stubbornly refusing to let me see where it led.

"Quid pro quo," he whispered with a smirk, and I rolled my eyes as I gave in and covered them, trying to peek through the spaces between my fingers. He noticed, and though he faced the wall, I still got to see his nice, muscular ass as he took everything off. Then, I suppose just to spite me, he backed into the bed, getting under the sheet before he turned toward me.

"Stop being stubborn," I teased.

"Tell me why I can't touch you," he said, and I decided to make up an excuse in the moment because dealing with this was seriously starting to fuck with the level of excitement that had brought me here in the first place.

"I got all sweaty on the mission," I lied.

"I don't care about that," he said, brushing my hair out of my face.

"Well, I do, so can we just...will you just...you know..."

"Fuck you?" he asked. "Is that what you want?"

"Uh-huh," I said, shyly biting my lip, and he grinned a wicked grin then flipped me over onto my stomach.

"You want me to fuck you?" he repeated as he grabbed my hips and forced me up onto all fours.

"Yes."

"Then say it," he commanded, and I could feel him hard and sliding against my clitoris from behind. He was so...big.

Oh, God!

"Say it, Liana. Tell me you want to be fucked."

"I want to be fucked," I said.

"Hard?" he asked as he began swirling his cock over the tiny bundle of nerves, using it instead of the fingers I'd refused.

"Hard. I want to be fucked hard," I admitted.

"Beg me," he demanded. "Beg for my cock."

"Please, Aiden," I complied, ruled entirely by my lust now, and there was no way it was going to let me screw this up. "Please fuck me. Please shove your cock inside me."

And he did, slowly filling me with every bit of what had to be at least eight inches.

"Oh, Aiden," I moaned as he thrust in again.

"You want it faster?" he asked.

"Oh, yes!" I begged, and with his hand on my hips, pulling me back into him, he sped up. I had come here with visions of making love in my head, but this..*oh, my God, this is what I needed!* This, but a little something more...

"Harder!" I urged him, and he clutched my hips tighter, his nails digging into my skin as he pounded me fiercely, keeping up the pace and intensity so much longer than I would have expected before I could tell he had reached the pinnacle. His whole body tensed, and I felt his excitement coursing through me, beckoning me to join him in ecstasy. As he grew closer and closer, I cried out, bucking against him, aching for the satisfaction of his release, and finally, he called my name in a tortured voice as I whispered his into the darkness. Then suddenly, he pulled out.

"Oh, my God, Liana," he groaned as I felt his orgasm raining down on the back of my legs, and I fell forward on the bed, collapsing from the weight of a terrifying, stressful morning topped off with the immense satisfaction of finally fucking the man who had been the star of every encounter I had with Bob in the past five years.

"God, I needed that," Aiden breathed as Liana lay in his arms beneath the sheets.

"Me too," she cooed, and he kissed her atop the head. Then she turned and looked up at him. "You didn't have to pull out, you know."

"No?" he asked. "I didn't want to risk getting you pregnant."

"I can't get pregnant. Well, at least not for five years. I had a new IUD put in just a few months ago," she said. It was something she kept up to date even without a relationship because it made her periods go away. She had about five years before she was going to have to figure out how to use a menstrual cup like the unfortunate women in the compound who didn't have an IUD.

"I wish you'd told me. You don't know how hard it was to leave you," he said, gazing into her eyes intently.

"Next time, you won't have to."

"Next time, I want so much more," he growled as their lips met, and when he kissed her, he swirled his tongue over the tip of hers, clearly indicating what he wanted next time. Liana shuddered at the delicious thought of Aiden La Croix mouth on her clit, but the reality of her situation quickly overtook the fantasy. She knew it wasn't going to happen.

"Aiden, there's something I have to tell you," she said, her voice small and apologetic as she pulled away from him. "When I said I didn't want you to touch me below the waist...it wasn't really about me being sweaty."

"I don't understand."

"This is going to sound crazy, but I'm really shy about sex," she explained, and he gave her an incredulous look because she had just let him fuck her from behind the first time out of the gate. That didn't seem like a woman who was shy to him. She smiled and sighed. "It's not about everything. I just don't like hands down there."

"I wasn't offering you my hand," he said, licking his lips, and the sight of it was absolute torture. She swallowed hard before spouting her next, agonizing lie.

"I don't like that either," she said, hating herself for having to do this, and now she just wanted the conversation to end because she had ruined the moment as she lay in the arms of this gorgeous, sated man.

"Are you sure?" he asked. "I'm pretty good at it."

"I'm sure," she said, interpreting his determination as a need for reassurance that her dislike for oral didn't extend to blowjobs. "But that doesn't mean I won't go down on you."

"Of course it does. If I can't do you, you can't do me. It's only fair."

"And how long are you going to put up with that?" she asked, irritated by his stubbornness, but instead of arguing, he gave her a long, intense kiss.

"You'd be surprised at what I'd put up with when the pussy is this good," he whispered, offending and praising her in the same breath. It was a heady mix that set off an unexpected rush of excitement between her thighs. She didn't like it when men used the "P" word, but she found herself surprised by what she'd put up with for Aiden LaCroix. And besides, somehow it sounded sexy coming out of his mouth.

Day 5

The fifth day of the apocalypse began with a burial. Randy had died in the night, and when he came back, John, who had been standing watch, put a bullet in his head. As Liana comforted his granddaughters, promising that they would be kept safe by the community, several men carried Randy's body to the other side of the fence to dig a grave while Olivia and June cleaned the blood and brains out of the office.

"I didn't think that would work anyway," Olivia said as she rolled the bedding into a bundle and placed it outside the door to be taken to the laundry room. The entire compound was run on solar and wind power with its own water filtration system and no reliance on utility companies, which made this mess much easier to clean than it would have been if they were among the millions of people who were without utilities as the grids had gone down all over the country.

"We don't know that it didn't work," June argued. "He could have developed an infection from John cutting off his leg with an old axe from a woodpile." This seemed more reasonable to her because Randy had developed a fever last night, which she attributed to infection. She gave him some of the antibiotics that were in the Right Way truck, but she surmised that either they weren't the right ones for the bacteria or the dose wasn't strong enough.

"Should that infection really have killed him so quickly?" Olivia asked. "I give John credit for trying. It would have been great if we could have discovered a way to save people who've been bitten, but honestly, even if he had a sanitized axe in his hand at the very second the bite occurred, I don't see how it could've been fast enough to keep whatever it is that causes this out of the blood stream."

"Your problem is, you're trying to find the science behind this, and I don't think there is any. It's all a product of the witchcraft we dabbled in, and that transcends science."

"June, we didn't cause this, okay? If you want to believe the spell worked to bring us together with the guys, then fine, knock yourself out, but we didn't do anything to raise the dead."

"Didn't we? By turning to the witch, we turned away from God and set these wheels in motion. It was an egregious sin, Olivia, and this is our punishment," she said doggedly.

"Jesus Christ, Tituba! Did I sleep through the part where we danced with the devil and wrote our names in his book?"

"I just think if everyone in the community worked together to help us atone for our mistake..."

"There is absolutely no way I'm going to tell the entire camp that this is all happening because God is pissed off that we played a game with a gypsy so Dani could get laid after her divorce. Do you realize how asinine that sounds?"

"Sure, if you put it that way."

"It sounds pretty, damn asinine your way too," Olivia said with a roll of her eyes.

"How can you be so arrogant to think you're somehow above divine punishment?" June indicted her.

"If this is divine punishment, it's not meant for us, June. You didn't see how many corpses there were at the gun shop yesterday, and that's just a drop in the bucket at some random, little town in the middle of nowhere. I can't imagine what it must be like in the cities. Do you really think the creator of the universe would destroy the entire human race just to teach you a lesson?"

"I have a close, personal relationship with God," was June's canned answer, and even though Olivia knew she was talking to a brick wall, she couldn't stop herself.

"You know what I find hilarious? You go on and on about how arrogant everyone else is. Scientists are arrogant. Atheists are arrogant. But the truth is that you're the most arrogant motherfucker I've ever known if you honestly believe that you're individually that much more important than the other seven billion souls who once lived on this planet! What about all the other people from your church? What about their close, personal relationship with God?"

"Not everybody who calls themselves godly really is," June snapped back at her with an accusatory glare.

"You don't say," Olivia hissed, then she had to walk away before something really nasty came out of her mouth. She didn't understand June, and she never would because they had grown into polar opposites. With age, Olivia had become certain that she wasn't an authority on anything, and June seemed to think she was an authority on the one thing that trumped everything. What Olivia didn't realize was how uncertain June really was. The only thing she was sure of in this world was that she was probably going to die, and she was terrified of going to Hell for starting the apocalypse.

June's Journal
Day 5

When Dani gave this thing back to me, I probably should have just burned it. I was embarrassed that I wrote it in the first place and embarrassed for Dani to read it because she was going to find just what Olivia said she'd find. But there's a reason for that. There are a couple of them actually. For one thing, my husband is a selfish man. I don't think it's his fault. I don't think he knows any better. I have a background outside of the closed-off world my parents took me and my brother into when our old church became too progressive. My husband spent his entire life sheltered.

When I met Jimbo in college, he'd never even been kissed. I pretended I hadn't either because I didn't want him to think I was a slut. I'd done things when I was younger but not too much. Most of my experience came from playing husband and wife with Olivia, Liana, and Dani when we were kids. I was still allowed to hang out with them even after my parents moved me to our church's school in the seventh grade, but they had become interested in real boys and didn't want to practice kissing or anything else anymore. Then came high school, and they started having s-e-x. I remember listening to them talk about it, and I was jealous, but I kept telling myself at least I had something they didn't. I had my virtue.

I was still a virgin on my wedding night, and so was Jimbo. I figured that's why I wasn't experiencing what the girls always talked about, but it also scared me because I had always been taught that if I was a good girl, married relations would be amazing. It was a confusing time for me, and I didn't have anyone to talk to. I couldn't admit that I wasn't enjoying it to any of my church friends because they'd say it was my fault, and I couldn't admit it to my old friends because they'd never understand. I just kept thinking about how they said things got better with their boyfriends as they learned more about each other, so for a while, I was still hopeful. But it never got any better with Jimbo. All we ever did was straight, missionary position lovemaking anyway because that's all we were supposed to do, and even if I didn't enjoy it, it was my duty as a wife to endure it when he wanted it because men have biological needs that women don't experience. It's not like it took all that long anyway, so I usually just held still and let him do what he wanted.

The fact that Jimbo couldn't please me wasn't what made me stop loving him. I could have easily gone the rest of my life without good s-e-x. I loved my children. I had a lot of close friends. I had a good life...as long as Jimbo wasn't around. When he was around, that whole "submitting to your husband whenever he wanted it" thing had gotten out of control. If I had been honest in this diary before, I would have mentioned that all that "lovemaking" I talked about wasn't lovemaking at all. Most of the time, I wasn't even a willing participant.

It all started one night when I told Jimbo no. I had a headache. It was a real headache - a bad one, like a migraine, and it had taken every last bit of energy in me just to get the boys fed and tucked in, but my husband didn't care. When I told him no, he threw me down on the bed and had s-e-x with me anyway. He must have really liked that because a pattern developed - a pattern of him just taking what he wanted. I could be washing dishes, and he would walk into the kitchen, grab me by the arm, drag me into the bedroom, and use my body. Sometimes, he would just push me down on the kitchen floor and do it right there where the kids could come in and see, and sometimes, I would wake up in the middle of the night and find him on top of me.

It got to the point that he was doing it as many as five times a day, and he didn't care if I was ready for it. He would just cram it into me, and sometimes it hurt. I cried once when I was so dry he broke the skin, but he just held a pillow over my head, pressing down so hard, I couldn't breathe. And one time he didn't like the look on my face while he was on top of me, and he pulled my hair on both sides of my head so hard trying to force me to smile that some of it came out by the roots. He didn't care. He didn't care if I was bleeding. He didn't care if I had an infection. He didn't even care that the doctors said it wasn't safe for me to have sex until six weeks after giving birth. He let me wait four after Noah was born. By the time Elijah came around, he gave me five days. He was just sticking it in a swollen, bloody mess, but he did it anyway.

I cannot even begin to express how relieved I was when I couldn't get back to him after we went to Pittsburgh, especially when I couldn't get a hold of him by phone. I didn't realize how bad this was going to be at first, and I expected that when I finally did make it home, things were going to get ugly, but at least for a little while I'd be free.

I couldn't believe he let me come here in the first place, but I did do a very crafty job when making the arrangements. We planned it on the same weekend that he was hosting a retreat with our church so he wouldn't be able to get out of it, then I told him Liana was getting married and asked me to be a bridesmaid. I still didn't think he'd go for it, but by some miracle, he did. Of course, I had to lie to the kids, which I hated. I suspected that Noah knew something was up, but if he did, he didn't say anything to me about it. He's such a good kid. At least my prayers have been answered when it comes to my boys. I used to pray every day that they didn't grow up to be like their father. The best thing for them would have been to get them away from him, but I knew if I tried to leave Jimbo, the entire community would rally around him and I'd lose those boys.

Now I just hope Jimbo's dead.

I know that sounds awful, but when I heard Dani tell the gypsy that the men we loved couldn't die, it made me smile inside. I haven't loved Jimbo in a long, long time, and since I had already set the condition that anything I did with Jobe would not be cheating, I thought, *wouldn't it be wonderful if Jimbo just died?* He isn't a godly man anyway. He can't possibly be.

Then there's Jobe. I know the others don't think too highly of him, but they don't know anything about him. I've watched his ministry for ten years, and I know he's a good man. I didn't pick him because I really wanted to be with him. I don't have fantasies about him or anything. I don't have those kind of fantasies at all. I just thought he'd be safe. He'd respect me, and he seems like the kind of man who would want me to be pleased if we did make love.

I can't do it though. I don't know that Jimbo's dead, and as long as he's alive, I'm a married woman. Jobe says he understands, but I know his biological needs are making it hard on him. I have to be careful around him. I watch how I dress so as not to tempt him even though it's hard to do since we're all borrowing clothes from Olivia. Thank God it's fall because all of her shorts are way too short, and her summer blouses show too much skin. The same is true of the clothing her daughter and the other girls wear. I see how the boys look at them, and well, it makes me glad I have sons and not daughters. Olivia doesn't seem to notice, but I know if I open my mouth, she'll say the same thing she always says. Shut the f-u-c-k up, June.

I pray for her soul.

Day 12

While continuing to loot the surrounding area for stone to add to their wall, back at the compound, every day they worked on digging a deep trench around the five acre inner ring on the other side of the chain link fence. They were building the stone wall inside the fence, but since the community was growing as the teams they sent out found other survivors in need of a safe place, the lodge had become too full. Now the trench was finally complete, and they felt safe assigning cabins. June and Jobe were given the largest so they could keep her four boys with them and give her a separate bed from Jobe since she, as a married woman, was more afraid of Hell than cannibal corpses. Though Olivia considered it a waste of available space, she had learned to pick her battles with June, and at the moment, while she was handing out the keys to the cabins, it was more important for her to put her foot down on a different issue.

"Jobe just wants a place to minister to the group and comfort people," June pleaded her case as she tried to persuade Olivia to let her and Jobe start a church inside the compound.

"I don't think that's a good idea right now," Olivia said.

"What's so wrong with it?"

"What's wrong with it is that we need every able body working for our protection," Olivia said because right now they didn't need a preacher. They needed him to roll up his sleeves and help build the wall.

"He can do it in the evenings after the work is finished," June argued.

"No," Olivia said flatly, then she sighed, compelled to clarify her position. "Look, June, we're a small community, and we all depend on each other for survival. We can't start a club that automatically excludes some of our people."

"So you're going to deny a church to forty people for one Muslim?" June demanded, referring to Ravi. It infuriated Olivia, but she refused to set her straight. June's opinion of Ravi needed to change because he was a good person not because she learned he practiced a different religion than the one she misguidedly considered inherently evil.

"It's not about Muslims, June. Do you know what everyone's religion is? Liana is Catholic. You know that. And the little girls from the toll plaza? The oldest told me their parents weren't raising them in any particular religion so they could make their own decisions when they were old enough. Do we have the right to change that when we know their parents' wishes? Then there's John and his family. They're agnostic, and Penny is a Wiccan. I know your heart's in the right place, but at this early stage, we can't focus on anything that divides us. Surely you can understand that."

"I understand, alright. It's religious persecution!" June charged, and Olivia groaned as her palm met her forehead, slowly dragging its way down her face.

"No, June. What you're asking for is called preferential treatment," she explained. "My decision is to treat everyone with the same consideration. It doesn't matter if 99.9% of us worship the Flying Spaghetti Monster. The one guy standing there without a colander on his head still deserves to feel like he belongs here just as much as anyone else."

June narrowed her eyes at Olivia. "May God have mercy on your soul, Olivia Anders," she snapped, grabbing her key off the counter and storming out the door.

"R'amen!" Olivia called after her in frustration. There was no way she was ever going to place June in any position of religious authority because she was terrified of June's convoluted ideas about sex seeping into Savannah's consciousness. June was a victim of purity culture, and Olivia found it repugnant that girls raised like her ended up tying their entire self worth to their virginity. She wanted her daughter to have sex. Not today; she was only fourteen, but when she was emotionally ready to handle it, Olivia wanted her to experiment, to find out what she liked and what she didn't, so someday when she was ready to settle down and get married, she'd know if she and her future husband were compatible before committing to each other for a lifetime. She wanted Savannah to have a marriage like hers and Reid's...or at least like it was before they got separated by a hundred miles of hungry corpses.

The very thought made her anxious because she hadn't talked to Reid in two days. They had agreed that he would turn on his satellite phone and call her for two minutes every morning then turn it back off to save the charge. When she talked to him last, he still had 72% battery life, but her phone hadn't rung yesterday or today. She was terrified that it meant he was dead, and she hated herself because she turned to Alek for comfort, lying in his arms last night as she fought back the tears. If it hadn't been for that stupid spell, she wouldn't feel so guilty about it. Her need for a connection was human nature, and though it didn't mean she didn't love Reid with every fiber of her being, the fact that she had wanted Alek before all this happened was threatening to tear her apart at the seams.

"Oblivia!" Liana shouted, snapping her fingers in her face. "Are you okay?"

"Huh? Yeah, I'm fine. Sorry. Do you and Aiden want to move to a cabin?" she asked, forcing a smile as she tried to push the anxiety of out her mind, but   Liana was about to chase it away for her with a surprising distraction.

"Yeah...and I heard through the grapevine that there are cabins that have..." she leaned in close and dropped her voice low "...certain BDSM accoutrements?"

"Really?" Olivia asked, not sure which she was more curious about: How Liana knew about the BDSM cabins or why she wanted one.

"Really," she confirmed, biting her lip. According to the internet research she had done when she found out that her friend owned these vacation rentals, there were only two that had been outfitted thusly, and she wanted to make sure she got one of them. She had not yet brought up the idea with Aiden, but she was ready to move their sexual relationship to the next level. And BDSM was the way she traditionally did that.

Olivia keyed the cards, then she led her up the hill to the cabin to show her the secret room that was only made available to guests who wanted the option. To others, it was dismissed as a storage closet, but the locked door in the bedroom actually led to a small, secret chamber in the center of the cabin with a bondage table, a St. Andrew's Cross, and a few other fun surprises - whips, cuffs, and chains not included.

"So do you have something you want to tell me?" Olivia asked Liana with a raised eyebrow.

"Actually, since you're the one with the BDSM cabins, I was wondering if you had something you might want to tell me," she countered.

"Nah," Olivia said. "Reid and I tried it out and thought it would be a nice option to offer guests who are into it, but it's not our thing. What about you?"

"It's just something I dabble in." It was all Liana was willing to admit.

"Well, if you need anything to go along with it," she said, pointing to a drawer built into the wall, "There's a catalog in there of the items we kept on hand in case guests forgot something. I have a small stockroom in the lodge."

"Really?" Liana asked, grinning. She thanked her friend as she headed toward the door, but then called out to her before she could leave. "Hey! One more thing. Please don't tell anyone about this. I don't want Dani to tease me or June to shame me."

"You got it," she said with a laugh, but as soon as she closed the door behind her, she ran into Dani, who had no intention of teasing Liana. She had been scouting out the cabins when she saw them go into this one, and spying through the bedroom window, she got a slight glimpse of the secret room.

"Got anymore of those?" she asked.

"I may have one," Olivia said with a smirk. "But who's chaining who to the wall?"

"Girl, I don't even care. Jax is just all I want to do all the time any way possible," she said, and Olivia realized it had to be true because she'd hardly seen either of them since they got there. They would come out of their room, do whatever work was assigned to them, then disappear.

"I'm happy for you," she said.

"What about you? Are you and Alek..."

"Reid's still out there, Dani. He's coming home to me."

"I hope he does, but what about Alek then?"

"He promised me he'd step aside," she said with a sad smile, and Dani winced. "I know it's wrong. I should just stay the hell away from him for everyone's sake, but I can't. I keep thinking what if Reid's dead? What if I push Alek away, he finds someone else, then Reid never comes home?"

"I feel you, but you can't just keep him on a back burner. It's not fair. He's out there every day risking his life for this community. He should at least be getting laid."

"Well, you're welcome to try," Olivia said with a snide glare.

"I don't think Jax would like that very much. He's really possessive."

"That's funny for a guy who used to fuck a different woman every night."

Olivia just blurted it out. She knew it was a shitty thing to say, but she felt like Dani was judging her. Dani had no business judging her. None of them did. They didn't know what it was like to love someone like she loved Reid, and being without him was torture, not knowing where he was, what was happening to him, if he was even alive. As for Alek, she needed him, and besides, he was a grown man. If he didn't like their arrangement, he was perfectly capable of saying so. Of course none of that gave Olivia the right to be cruel to Dani, and even though, as a therapist, she understood, it still stung.

"People change, Olivia," she said. "Jax has changed."

"Yeah, maybe he just needed the right woman," Olivia said rather than reminding her that Jax already found the right woman. Her name was Mrs. Bonham, and she was probably safely at home in their Redondo Beach mansion at that very moment. Jax's open marriage was common knowledge, but even though Olivia was pissed and looking for someone to lash out at, she couldn't bring herself to do it. Dani had suffered in a bad marriage for so long. She deserved some happiness.

Olivia gave her the other "couples only" cabin, then she spent the afternoon assigning the rest of them and trying to keep herself distracted from thinking about Reid or Alek. Both were in danger today. Reid would be in danger in her mind every day until she saw him again, and Alek had gone to Princeton this morning with a half a dozen others. He had decided they needed electric cars because they were quiet and would eliminate the need to find gas.

Many of the stations in the area had already been sucked dry. There was another group that might have been bigger and more organized than Olivia's, and two days ago, Alek had been out scavenging and watched them pull a tanker up and completely empty an entire gas station. If Olivia's group didn't do something soon, they would be forced to go car to car siphoning, and they needed to conserve what gas they could find to move the stone for the wall and operate the equipment.

The problem was that the closest electric car lot was more than twenty miles away in Princeton. Not only was there the distance issue, Princeton's population was six times that of the small town of Pipestem, and it was right off interstate 77. But Alek insisted, so Olivia spent all day worrying about him and kicking herself for not insisting that they wait until they had some means of long range communication. They used to have the spare satellite phone, but now that was in the pocket of a dead man in the parking lot of a brickyard. Only Olivia's remained as far as she knew. Savannah claimed hers was missing, but it wasn't the truth. She was afraid Olivia would take it away from her to send on scavenging missions, and she just knew that if her dad was going to call her, it would happen while the phone was out of her possession. At least her lie kept Olivia from having to make the decision because the same concern would have tormented her like not being able to contact Alek was tormenting her now.

With no sign of him, day turned into evening and evening into night. Around 1:00 AM when everyone was already in bed - and comfortably so now that they didn't have to sleep on cots in the lodge - the only people awake other than Olivia were on watch. She sat in her panic room with Evil at her side staring at the monitor fed by the camera at the first gate, aching to see headlights. Alek should have been back by now.

At 2:00 AM, she could no longer sit still.

"You want to go for a walk, Evie?" she asked, and the cat, who had been stretched out on the floor, perked up immediately. With so many people around, she didn't have the opportunity to even roam the private residence like she used to, and she was eager to go outside and walk with the human she thought gave birth to her. Olivia put on a jacket, checked the guns in her ankle and shoulder holsters to make sure they were full, slung a loaded AR-15 across her back, and led Evil out the door. When they came to the inner ring gate, Jax and Dani were on watch.

"Uh-uh," Dani said when she saw Olivia headed for the door beside the gate. She stepped in front of it.

"Funny. Now get out of my way," Olivia demanded.

"You're fucking nuts if you think I'm letting you go out there alone," she protested.

"I need to do something, Dani. I'm just pacing the floor, driving myself crazy," Olivia said.

"So you're going to go prowl around in a forest full of crunchy, fallen leaves in the middle of the damn night when there's nothing for the dead to do but listen for shit like crunchy, fallen leaves?" Dani argued.

"Let me use the door, or I'll open the gate," Olivia threatened, indicating the remote control on her belt loop. She was being good-natured about it, but she wasn't going to take no for an answer.

"Damn it!" Dani complained as she stepped out of the way and let Olivia and Evil pass. On the other side, they headed toward the wooden planks over the trench, which would eventually retract like a drawbridge. For now, it had to be raised and lowered manually, but it was already in place tonight anticipating the return of the scavenging party.

"Thank you," Olivia called back, and Dani shouted at her through the open window of the guard station.

"You know, we take this watch because nothing ever happens at 2:00 am, but now we have to sit up here and worry about your dumb ass getting eaten out there. I hope you're happy."

"Thrilled," Olivia said with a laugh as she and Evil walked over the bridge. On the way down the mountain, she stuck to the road to avoid all those crunchy, fallen leaves, and the cat stayed right by her side. At the middle gate, which was eight feet high now with the intent to later build up the fence to match, Olivia climbed over while Evil reached the top in a single jump.

"Show off," she said as the cat leapt to the ground on the other side. When they made it to the lower gate, it was easier to scale because it was still the same one as always. Until the upper and middle rings were better protected, they didn't want the lower gate to give anyone on the main road the impression that there was anything interesting up this gravel drive.

Right now, it just looked like a dozen other gates along that stretch of road. With trees growing right beside the posts on either side, Olivia grabbed a thick limb, hoisting herself up and climbing about ten feet off the ground where she found a vantage point to watch the main road. Facing toward Princeton, she made herself comfortable, then Evil dug her claws into the trunk and followed her up. With her head in Olivia's lap, she issued the low, rumbling purr-like sound she made to show her contentment as she urged Olivia to relax and scratch her behind the ears like she liked.

Olivia had never set out to make such a domesticated pet of the great cat. They took her in because they were able to provide the good, safe home she deserved, but even though they knew they could never return her to the wild, they had not expected to have such a deep, familial bond. They thought when she grew up, she would be a beauty to look at but not necessarily to cuddle with. Maybe it would have been like that if someone else had raised her, but Olivia had a way with animals. She had rehabbed and released dozens of local species on this mountaintop from birds to raccoons to a pair of abandoned black bear cubs, and even though she did her best to prepare them for life in the wild rather than making pets of them, many maintained the attachment they had to her when they were handfed babies. She had birds who came to see her every spring when they returned from the south, squirrels who nested in the inner ring that would eat right out of her hand, and a raccoon who would knock on her door in the winter months looking for food and sometimes spend a few minutes inside the lodge by the fire.

There were *no hunting* signs posted all over the property, and all guests were made aware of the potential of the animals within the fence to have no fear of humans. They always did their best to protect all wildlife on their property, and no one had been a greater challenge to this approach than Evil. Luckily, she eventually accepted that all animals were off limits. She even learned not to try to eat the livestock in the barn, though it didn't preclude her from terrorizing the chickens. She always enjoyed climbing the henhouse fence and watching them freak out and scatter, but the worst she ever did was steal a few eggs for herself. Aside from that and fishing in the stocked pond, the cat really had been no trouble, and even though she had to spend much of her time sequestered in the private residence with only her enclosure exposing her to the outside world, she never ran wild when Olivia let her out. She was just a member of the Anders family, who was sitting in a tree snuggling like a kitten in Olivia's lap until her ears suddenly started twitching. She raised her head, sniffing the air, then she let out a soft, low rumbling deep in her throat.

"What is it, Evie?" Olivia asked in a whisper as she looked around, and though the road below them was hard to make out in the dark through the tree branches, after a few seconds, she saw movement. There was a dead man ambling up the private drive from the main road. She grabbed her knife, planning to climb down and take it out, but first she wanted to watch and make sure more weren't coming. Evil didn't share her patience, and the cat's superior hearing had already told her that this was a loner.

She jumped down out of the tree, tore out his throat, then turned to climb back up, unaware that the tactic she had used to protect Savannah from her attacker weeks earlier would not be effective on the dead. The corpse stood back up and grabbed at her hind leg as she dug her claws into the tree, and Olivia felt a jolt of anxiety. While there was no evidence to suggest that animals could succumb to whatever was causing the dead to resurrect, there was also no evidence to suggest that the cat could survive a bite.

"Come on, Evie," she urged, trying to get her to climb back up, but Evil would not accept defeat, she whipped her head around, growling at the dead-eyed corpse that gnashed its teeth and tried to get a hold on her. Then Evil gnashed her own teeth, pouncing and knocking it to the ground. She took a bite, ripping the entire face off, but it just kept struggling, trying to bite back. She sank her teeth in again, deeper this time, and she only grew more frustrated as the foul smelling interloper continued to fight her. Finally, she opened her mouth wide and came down for a kill bite, her fangs sinking into the brain, and all movement ceased.

Satisfied, Evil dismounted her kill, shook her head vigorously, and climbed back up the tree beside Olivia where she sat cleaning herself, and as Olivia looked down on her handiwork, she saw that the cat didn't eat the flesh she tore away as it was all piled beside the ruined head. She wondered if it was because of the stench of death on it, but considering that she didn't eat the man she killed to protect Savannah, Olivia surmised that she knew what she was doing. She was protecting her family, which was good. The last thing they needed was a jungle cat with a taste for human flesh.

"Good job, Evie," she said as she stroked her fur, staring longingly at the road, praying for headlights. She checked her watch, which she did frequently over the course of the next hour, and though she was inclined to give up when she saw that it was already 3:30 AM, she kept telling herself *just a few more minutes*. Besides, the cat had drifted off with her head in Olivia's lap, and even though her legs were falling asleep as they dangled from the tree, she didn't want to disturb Evie.

For another fifteen minutes, Olivia sat in silence, the cat sleeping peacefully until she was suddenly jolted awake. She sat upright on the tree limb and stared in the direction of the main road, her ears perked, but Olivia heard nothing. She still didn't hear anything when she started to see lights in the distance, lights that got closer until she could tell that they were in pairs - headlights! But there was no sound.

Then it hit her!

Electric cars. There was an entire caravan of them coming up the main road, and she and Evil hurried down out of the tree to open the gate as she desperately hoped that Alek would be in one of them. When the first car turned onto the gravel, she watched it drive past her with the passenger and back seats filled with looted items, which might have explained why they took so long, but Alek was all she cared about in that moment. Then in the fifth car, she saw his blue eyes reflecting the lights from the dashboard, and a tidal wave of relief washed over her.

He slowed down as he passed her, but with no room for her in the car, she gave him a wink then ran through the woods to the top of the mountain. Though she wasn't able to beat him, she wasn't too far behind when the last car drove through the gate. As Olivia entered the compound, Alek was already out of his car and rushing toward her, and when he threw his arms around her, she held him tight, never wanting to let go. But she had to because a jealous 157-pound jaguar was trying to worm her way in between them. When they parted, Evil stood up on her hind legs and licked Alek's face. It was the first time she'd ever shown him affection, and though it scared him a little, he understood what high praise it was. She didn't accept just anyone into her family.

"Well," he said once she had gone back down on all fours, "at least the cat wants to kiss me."

"Don't start," Olivia said. "I've spent my whole evening freaking out, thinking you were dead."

"All the more reason to kiss me," he teased, and when she narrowed her eyes, he asked, "Would it make it all better if I told you I brought you a gift?"

"That depends on what it is."

"It's two gifts actually. We looted an entire Radio Shack for you, so maybe the next time I'm away, we'll be able to communicate. We also have drones now, and more surveillance equipment. I know you like surveillance equipment," he said.

"I do," she agreed.

"And what if I said I brought you someone who knows what to do with all this technology?" he asked, and Olivia's eyes lit up because they needed someone like that almost as much as a doctor in her mind. Alek motioned for the person in the passenger seat of his car to join them, and a girl in her early twenties dressed all in black with blue hair stepped out. "This is Rena."

"Hi," Olivia said, surprised as Rena fearlessly reached out to pet Evil. The other new people had all frozen the second they saw the great cat, but Rena recognized a kindred spirit.

"Yo," she said to Olivia with a crooked smile as the cat rubbed up against her. She was awkward around people, but she had a way with animals and was an absolute genius with technology. Near the beginning, she and her friends had broken into the Radio Shack to loot the place themselves only to get trapped by a herd of the dead. When they ran out of food and water, they tried to fight their way out, and she was the only one who survived, forced back inside by the cannibalistic throng. By the time Alek's group found her, she had been working on using the technology in the shop to plan her own escape, but she was so depleted, her plan B had been suicide.

Deciding to leave the unloading for the morning, Alek took Evil to her room while Olivia worked out sleeping arrangements for Rena and other new members who had been picked up along the way. When she finally made it to her bedroom, she found Alek and Evil in bed, the cat sprawled out in the middle.

"She wouldn't take no for an answer," he explained.

"I think she missed you," Olivia said with a smile, wondering if Evil was doing the same thing she was; clinging to the small victory of Alek coming back alive, which allowed her to temporarily suppress her anxiety about Reid. If she allowed herself to think about him for more than a few seconds at a time, she feared she'd lose all semblance of sanity. Her mind kept going back to the gypsy's spell and telling her that she was responsible for whatever was happening to Reid. It wasn't really the spell itself that caused the guilt though. It was the way her body had reacted to Alek on the street in front of the Kemp Hotel in Pittsburgh. It was the fact that she never told him she was married when they were drinking together in the bar the night the world went to shit. It was how much she wanted him in this moment while her husband was probably fighting for his life to get back to her.

She thought she was a horrible person undeserving of the comfort Alek could bring, and though the cat didn't smell the best after chewing on the face of a corpse earlier, Olivia didn't run her out of the bed, instead letting her sleep between them as penance for her selfishness.

Day 14

It had been two weeks since the dead rose. At Olivia's compound, they were still able to pick up the occasional broadcast on the satellite dish, but very few bothered watching it because all it served to do was reinforce the hopelessness. Though only American journalists were openly reporting that the dead were eating the living so far, it appeared that there wasn't a corner of the globe that had not descended into utter chaos, and not a single government had managed to find a successful means of protecting their people. Everyone assumed that the U.S. federal and state governments were operating from underground bunkers, but the truth was that most of them had already fallen, having retreated to their safe havens at the very onset out of fear. Without understanding the plague, they took the wounded with them, and once the first person died in these facilities, it spread throughout as quickly as it did in any isolated population that hadn't figured out the pathology. The majority of governments were eliminated, and those that remained were in no position to govern. Even the largest military in the world was no match for the hungry dead as it spread through their ranks like wildfire.

In just two week's time, the population of the United States had been cut by more than 90%, and though June couldn't possibly know any statistics about the governments or the populace, it was the momentum of the total societal breakdown that she saw as proof positive that there were biblical forces at work. While she and Jobe both suffered through their share of the labor to make the compound a defensible fortress, they spent their evenings praying for an end to the curse. If the dead would just stop rising, they could ultimately clear the planet of the corpses and start building a new civilization. June was convinced that atoning with God would bring that end about.

Dani disagreed, and as she, June, Olivia, and Liana discussed the future plans for the compound in Olivia's office, she made it clear. She thought they should prioritize working on a cure. Of course, they didn't have anyone qualified to do so, and it frustrated her that June, the only one among them with any sort of medical background, was the one who also had a total disregard for science.

"So what do you suggest we do, Dani?" Olivia asked. "Start looting research facilities?"

"I don't know. Maybe."

"It's a waste of time," Liana argued. "Even if we found a lab and a how-to book, you really think any of us could figure that out? What we need to be doing is recruiting and training an army."

"An army?" Dani asked, incredulous.

"Yes! An army. Do you not realize what's going to happen next? Right now everyone is just trying to survive, but they'll start banding together. Look at all the people we've brought in already? There will be more and more groups, then they'll come after smaller groups because the more people you have, the more productive you'll be. We'll get power hungry assholes exploiting people's fears just like we did before this happened, and if we're not ready, we'll end up losing this place and everyone in it."

"We're preparing for that," Olivia said. "We're building up our defenses. Once the wall is finished, we'll be able to start developing defensive strategies, and we're already training everyone with guns."

"It's not enough. We need to teach them hand to hand combat. We need to teach them how to fight as a unit."

"So you think we're going to end up having to fight the living and the dead? I'll just die, thanks," Dani said, overwhelmed by the very idea of it.

"That's easy for you to say. You don't have any children," June said. "If you did, you'd know we have to fix this world for them."

"So how do you suggest we do that?" Olivia asked June, who gave her staple answer of prayer, infuriating Olivia.

They began to argue, and Jobe rolled his eyes as he waited outside the room for June. He wanted to be a part of the oversight of the compound, but he realized that being pushy with Olivia wouldn't get him anywhere. He knew how to read people, and he had learned what not to do by watching how June dealt with her. June was constantly pushing her buttons and getting nothing accomplished, and Jobe had things he needed to get done in order to find his place in this new world. He didn't care about the church June wanted to start because he gave a shit about having a church; he cared about it because he wanted the power he lost when the apocalypse came. He used to have hundreds of thousands of followers, and now he had one - June. Her kids didn't even seem to give him much credence.

Jobe was frustrated.

"What's going on?" Alek asked as he walked down the hallway toward the office, looking for Olivia to show her some of the things Rena was designing in the workshop they set up for her.

"Women," Jobe said, wincing.

"Is everything okay?"

"I'm sure it'll be fine. They're just arguing about all of our futures," he said. Then he added something that made Alek's skin crawl. "Things would be a lot more rational if we were in charge around here. Maybe you need to put a baby in that woman to keep her busy."

"You're joking right?" Alek asked, disgusted, but Jobe read something different in his expression.

"You're not getting any, are you?" he asked. "Yeah, I'm not getting any from June either...not yet anyway. Never had so much trouble sealing the deal before, especially with a woman with such itty bitty titties."

"If you aren't attracted to her, maybe you should move on," Alek said.

"Come on. You know why I'm with June. It's the same reason you're letting Olivia drag your dick through the dirt, my friend," Jobe said as he patted him on the back, and Alek cringed, assuming Jobe meant he was with June because she was as close as he could get to being in power in the compound. "Can't believe I've been reduced to this when I used to make women's morals *and* panties go right out the window at the mere snap of my fingers. But you're famous too. You know what it's like."

116

"What's it like?" Alek asked, suddenly curious to know just how much of a prick this guy really was.

"You know, the little sluts let you do anything you want," he said, his eyes flashing and his fists clenched with excitement as he reminisced. "I had to be more careful than someone like you because I had a public image to protect, but as long as the cameras weren't rolling? Shit. I could just walk up and grab their titties or shove my hand up their skirts. Goddamn, I miss it! Yesterday, I'm trying on vaginas like hats, but today, the pussy well's gone dry."

Suddenly Alek had had enough. When Jobe looked up at him, he could see that his blood had begun to boil, and he started to inch away as Alek began speaking, his voice dripping with disgust.

"If that's how you think about *pussy*, you don't deserve any," he said, looking down at the smaller man with repugnance. "In the future, if you want to swap stories about trying on vaginas like hats, maybe try Jax, but let me just make one thing clear to you right now; if I ever see you just walk up and grab a woman's breasts or stick your hand up her skirt, I'll remove the offending appendage. Do you understand me?"

"Hey, no offense, man. I didn't know you were like that."

"Like what exactly?" Alek demanded, then out of the corner of his eye, he saw Dani. She was standing in the office doorway staring at him with wide eyes, and he immediately backed off, not wanting to have to repeat this conversation in front of all four women. They deserved to know what an asshole Jobe was, but if he were to say anything right now, he felt like he'd look like the asshole wanting credit for putting him in his place. He'd tell Olivia later and let her decide what to pass along.

Dani's Journal
Day 14

Jax is going to cheat on me. I know it. I can feel it. It's only a matter of time. He's used to having a different woman every night, but now I'm the only woman he's had in two weeks. I see how he looks at other women, and I just don't know what to do. I don't want to lose him, but I could never be like his wife. I don't know how she handled the humiliation of knowing he was out on the road every night fucking around on her. The thought of it makes me sick.

It also makes me kind of sick to know he has a wife out there, but she's three thousand miles away. He's never going to try to get back to her, and she doesn't know where he is. When he tried to call her the night it all went down, she didn't answer, so maybe she's dead already. I'd say I hope so, but I don't know what difference it would make anyway. I feel like my time with him is going to be short.

Hell, he may be cheating on me already. This afternoon when I was coming out of a meeting with Olivia, Liana, and June, I overheard Alek telling Jobe that he needed to have a conversation with Jax about "trying on vaginas like hats." I don't know what he meant by that, but the look on his face when he saw me spoke volumes. He knows something.

Or maybe it's nothing. Maybe I'm just losing my fucking mind. I finally have the man I've always wanted, but it had to happen in a world I don't want to live in. Sometimes I wish we could build that stone wall ten feet thick and twenty feet high and just forget about everything outside. That's what I would do in Olivia's position. I would never go out on scavenging expeditions like she does, and I wouldn't make Jax work on the wall. We could both just live in our inner sanctum making all the plans and decisions, and I'd be sure that we were surrounded by only men and old women so I would never have to worry about him cheating on me.

Or maybe I need to suck it up and start offering him threesomes. I don't fucking know. I just don't fucking know.

Day 25

When the actual compound oversight meeting took place without June, they decided to consider everyone's strategy, and over the course of the next eleven days, they built up a good portion of the ten foot stone wall that would ultimately surround the five acre inner ring of the compound. They still had a lot of work to do, but with the entrances complete, two strong gates, and a deep trench around it all, they were beginning to feel secure from the dead and the living. Once finished, getting into the mountaintop compound against the will of the people inside would be like a castle siege, and when corpses strayed up the mountain, they were already falling into the pit where they were left as a deterrent for any potential intruders considering making the jump over it to scale the wall.

After enough stone had been collected, the scavenging groups began to loot doctor's and dentist's offices, looking for anyone or anything that could help in Dani's quest to find a cure while satisfying Olivia's desire to stockpile medications and medical equipment. Of course, Dani's interest had begun to wane as she became more and more convinced that Jax was cheating on her.

She had begged Olivia & Liana not to send him on any missions so he would not be out of her sight during the day, and she was now sleeping so lightly, if he got up to use the bathroom in the middle of the night, she would bolt upright and demand to know where he was sneaking off to. Able to blame that behavior on dreams since it only happened at night, she was careful not to let her intense jealousy and paranoia show during the day, but now that Alek's comment to Jobe had festered inside her mind for nearly two weeks, she decided she had to know what he meant regardless of how it made her look.

Early one morning while everyone was going about their daily chores, she asked Alek to help her move a dresser, but once they were walking together up the gravel road away from the lodge, she told him the real reason she wanted him to come to her cabin.

"I don't actually have anything to move," she confessed as they approached the driveway before hers, and Alek stopped, turning toward her with a sigh. He didn't know exactly what was coming, but he was sure it had to do with her suspicions about Jax.

"I know you think I'm crazy," she began, "but a couple of weeks ago, you were talking to Jobe about Jax, and I heard you say he was trying on vaginas like hats..."

"Dani," he said impatiently, rolling his eyes behind closed lids.

"I just need to know what you were talking about," she said. "That's all. I promise."

"I'll make you a deal. You tell me why I keep overhearing June say you guys caused the apocalypse, and I'll tell you about trying on vaginas like hats."

"Deal, but I asked first," she said, planning to make something up when her turn came because Olivia would kill her if she told him about the spell.

"Fine," he said, then he relayed the conversation he had with Jobe. "I was really just trying to tell him to fuck off. I don't have a lot of stories about one night stands, but being a rock star, I figured Jax would have plenty. That's all it was, I promise, and if you would just talk to Jax about how you're feeling..."

"I can't do that. He'll think I'm pathetic...or crazy."

"You're not pathetic," he said with a wink, "and I think you'll be surprised by what he has to say."

"Why? Do you know something?" she asked, and in fact, he did. He and Jax had had a long conversation while building the wall one day, but Alek wasn't going to be the one to tell Dani how he felt about her. She needed to hear it directly from the source.

"Just talk to him" he said. "Now, about you ladies causing the..."

Alek froze as he heard a scream coming from the direction of June's house. He grabbed his gun with one hand and Dani with the other, pulling her to stay close behind him as he ran up the driveway. Then they heard it again when they were standing right outside the cabin.

"That's June," Dani confirmed, and fearing that the dead had somehow found their way into her home, she and Alek hurried inside and down the hall, where they could now hear June's muffled cries along with other, softer sounds that made it clear that the dead had nothing to do with it at all.

Angered, Alek kicked open the bedroom door to find Jobe pinning June on the floor beside the bed. He saw Jobe's hand covering her mouth, the other hand pressed into her back, holding her down, and as soon as she was aware that others were in the room, June started begging for help behind Jobe's hand. In a rage, Alek rushed over to Jobe, picked him up, and threw him against the wall as Dani helped June to her feet. She pulled a blanket off the bed to cover her nakedness and held her head against her chest while Alek beat Jobe until his face was an unrecognizable, bloody mess.

"Alek!" Dani yelled as he continued even after he lost consciousness. "Alek. He's out cold!"

He stopped abruptly, standing up and looking at them apologetically, ashamed that his anger had taken him over.

"Did you...kill him?" June asked. She was shaking, but her expression was completely blank.

"He's not dead," Alek said. "Dani, can you take June to your cabin while I drag this piece of shit to the lodge?"

"What are you going to do to him?" June asked.

"I'm going to put him under guard and talk to Olivia about it," he said

Dani guided June up the hill to her cabin as Alek stayed behind to deal with Jobe. He wasn't sure what Olivia would decide to do with him, but he was sure of his own judgment. He wanted Jobe dead. There was no place in this world for a rapist.

In the small office behind the lodge desk, John Vincent stood guard. Inside, Jobe Stricklan lay, handcuffed to a cot, awaiting his sentence while the community leaders discussed his crime and punishment.

"We should kill him and be done with it," Alek said.

"I think he may be right," Jax agreed.

"What is it with Americans and the death penalty?" Aiden asked, earning dirty looks from everyone but Liana, who was torn between her faith saying that it was wrong to kill and her feminist inclination to jump on board with the executioners. Alek, though not American, didn't bother to correct him because it didn't matter anymore. Unless this plague was restricted to North American, there were probably no more countries anyway.

"This has nothing to do with the American legal system," he said. "It's about the safety of our community."

"Look, rape is a heinous act. I'm not saying otherwise, but June is alive, isn't she? He didn't kill her. Even if we're going back to an eye for an eye, a death sentence is not warranted."

"Fine, then," Dani said, infuriated. "You go take his eye for an eye. We'll wait right here."

"Raping Jobe isn't going to solve our problem," Olivia said. "If we don't kill him, what are our options?"

"We could build a jail cell," Aiden suggested.

"You want to waste the time and resources to build a cell, have guards watch it, and then feed and take care of a rapist when we're lucky to have enough food and water for the contributing members of this community?" Alek demanded.

"Then exile him!" Aiden said. "Throw him out of the community. Make him fend for himself." Liana nodded, and when it looked like Jax and Dani might be swayed as well, Olivia put her foot down.

"Absolutely not!" she snapped. "He knows we're here, and he knows what we have. No way in hell am I going to throw someone out of this community and risk having them bring back others to try to take it away from us."

"Does he even know where *here* is?" Liana asked, trying to make peace. "He was in the back of the limo on the way in, and he hasn't left on a single run since. What if we drove him like fifty miles away and dropped him off? Could he really find us again?"

"Perhaps that's something to consider," Olivia said.

"Is it?" Alek demanded. "So we're just going to let him rape a woman and then risk our lives to drive him fifty miles away to turn him loose?"

"You saw what a coward he is," Dani said. "He'll never survive on his own."

"Then why not just throw him in the trench?" Alek asked.

"Because at least he'll have a chance if we drive him somewhere," Aiden said.

"A chance at what? Raping someone else?" Alek snarled.

"Alek is right," Dani said. "If he's done it once, he'll do it again."

"You don't know that!" Aiden argued.

"Why are you defending a rapist?" Alek demanded, slamming his fist down on the table.

"I'm not!" he shouted, bolting up out of his seat, but realizing arguing would get him nowhere, he sighed and sat back down. "I'm not. It's just that this is the first crime we've had, and we need to do the right thing. We're building a society here, and we need a strong, humanitarian foundation. The death penalty is not the answer. If we're going to execute someone for rape, what do you think that says to the next rapist in our community? May as well silence your victim forever."

"No," Olivia said firmly. "What it says is don't rape anyone around here. We have a chance to build a world where women don't have to fear walking alone at night or crossing the path of a male stranger. If we take a strong stance on rape and make sure everyone understands it, maybe there won't be any more rape."

"And what is the community going to say?" Aiden asked. "Have you considered gathering them together and asking what they think?"

"Let's do it," Alek said. "Let's lay out the options for everyone to consider. We can either waste our man power and precious resources keeping a rapist in a cell, we can risk lives by driving him fifty miles away to basically get off scot-free, *or* we can kill him and make sure no women in this or any other community ever have to worry about being raped by him again. We should ask absolutely everyone!"

"No one asked me," June said, speaking up for the first time. She had been sitting in the corner of the room as everyone else was gathered around the dining table in Olivia's residence, and she had been so quiet, they had all nearly forgotten she was there.

"Then what do you think we should do to him, shug?" Dani asked.

"Well, I don't think we should kill him for something that's not his fault."

"What do you mean?" Olivia asked.

"I mean it's my fault too."

"June, did you say some variation on the words, 'Jobe, I have a rape fantasy, I want you to fulfill it, and by the way, here's the safe word?'" Alek demanded furiously.

"I don't have a rape fantasy," June hissed, insulted.

"Then it's not your fault," he said.

"But I tempted him. I was always tempting him," she said as Alek stared at her, incredulous.

"Her parents raised her in a world where men have biological needs that drive them to lose control if women are not careful about how they act and dress," Olivia explained.

"Are you fucking kidding me?" he asked, disgusted.

"I wish I were."

"June, that's complete bullshit," he said, then he looked down for a second and back up at her. "Listen. I promised Olivia no one would know about this, so I need everyone in this room to keep what I'm about to say to themselves, and Olivia, I hope you can forgive me." He gave her an apologetic smile, then he told their secret.

"Every night, I slip into Olivia's bedroom after all the lights go out. Every night, she falls asleep in my arms. Her skin is so soft, and her hair smells so good, and I want her like you couldn't possibly imagine." He spoke softly as he watched her with a wistful reverence that made her feel shy, then he looked back at June.

"I do have biological needs, and sometimes it gets to the point that I feel like my dick is going to burst, and you know what I do?" he asked, his tone suddenly brimming with anger for anyone who would raise a girl to believe that she was responsible for the actions of men. "I go in the fucking bathroom and take care of it myself because nothing Olivia could possibly say, wear, or do will ever give me a legitimate reason to rape her!"

Alek stood glaring at June, and his imposing, 6'3" frame intimidated her back into her seat, which could not have been further from his intent. Frustrated, he sat back down, and after a long, tense moment, Aiden broke the silence.

"Alek is right," he said, then he turned to Liana. "I wasn't able to put it in perspective because I had you in mind. You're too strong, Liana. If Jobe tried to attack you, you'd tear him apart, but June isn't like you. And we have a lot of young women and girls around here who couldn't fight him off. Their well being is more important than the life of a man we already know is rapist."

"You're right too," Alek said. "We should present it to the community as a whole. We can't just come out of this room and announce that we've made the decision to kill a man."

"I agree," Olivia said. "But first, I want to take a vote here. If we were going solely on our opinions alone, who thinks we should execute him?"

Dani, Jax, Aiden, Olivia, and Alek immediately raised their hands. Then Liana's slowly went up, her eyes cast downward, ashamed but knowing it was the right choice as June sat quietly, consumed by her guilt.

"Okay," Olivia said, wrapping up the meeting. "We'll keep everyone in the lodge after dinner tonight and take a vote, and if they vote to exile, I'll escort him out myself."

And he'll never, ever find his way back to my compound, she thought deviously.

Every night, the entire group gathered in the lodge for dinner. They hadn't grown too large to fit everyone in a single shift by using some extra, folding tables, and while they all worked during the day, fortifying their compound, scavenging, caring for the livestock, or pruning and harvesting in the greenhouse, a few members were usually on kitchen duty. Olivia had installed a large, restaurant-style kitchen off to the right of the reception area because a chef, who was moving into the first ring when her house was finished, was planning to operate it as a restaurant and offer room service. Olivia had hoped she would find her way to the compound after the world ended, but she never did.

On the way to dinner that night, June stopped Olivia, begging her to just let the whole thing go, but when she refused, June took her boys back to their cabin so they wouldn't hear anything about her being raped. In the lodge, Olivia asked everyone to stay after the dinner dishes were cleared, then she stood up with the two witnesses at her side and told them what Jobe had done, leaving June's name out of it, but for much of the community, the rumor mill had beaten her to it.

Once everyone knew what had happened, though many of the people were just as torn as their leaders had initially been, there were a few with some very clear ideas of what Jobe's fate should be. John and Sharon, for instance, didn't want a rapist anywhere near their teenage daughter nor did they want to take the risk that he could lead others back to them. Then there were others, like Rena, who couldn't stomach the idea of killing a man who wasn't a murderer.

"What if it wasn't a grown woman, then?" John asked. "What if it was my fifteen-year-old daughter? Or one of Randy's granddaughters?" When he said that, Randy's elder granddaughter looked down at her shoes sadly because she knew the answer, and she knew how her grandfather dealt with it. He killed every man who tried to break into their shop from that point on. Unfortunately, her actual rapist had gotten away. He was still out there somewhere, and because of that, even under the protection of the people in the compound, she lived in fear. She didn't want to feel that way anymore, so she decided to share her story, but before she could get the first word out, everyone's attention was drawn to the front door of the lodge as it flew open so hard, it slammed against the wall.

In walked Jimbo Connors dragging one of the two guards who had been at the gate tonight. The tall, imposing man with dark hair and angry eyes threw the much smaller man down on the ground as Olivia marched toward him, furious.

"What are you doing, Jim?" she demanded.

"No one tells me I can't come in to see my wife and kids," he spat at her, and since Alek was guarding Jobe in the makeshift jail they'd created out of a storage room on the other side of the greenhouse, Jax and Aiden stepped in front of her, blocking her from the intruder. But, unintimidated, she put her hands on their shoulders to gently guide them out of her way.

"The guards at the gate were protecting your wife and kids! They don't know who you are," she said, assuming that they had followed procedure and held him at gunpoint. Of course, the next step would have been to contact her on the walkie, but she had heard nothing. She turned to the guard, who was still visibly shaken. "Why didn't you call me?"

"He didn't give us a chance. He ambushed us!"

"Who was on guard with you tonight? Where's your partner?" Olivia asked.

"Phil. He's tied up in the guard station."

"What the hell, Jim?" Olivia shouted. "You can't just come in here and attack our guards. If you had just asked them..."

"I don't have to ask."

"Yes, you do. This is still my property."

"I want to see my wife!" Jimbo shouted in Olivia's face, and all over the room, guns clicked. Then Alek appeared in the entrance to the kitchen, armed and furious. Savannah had been at the monitors, but because of the toggling, she didn't see Jimbo until he was approaching the front porch. By that time, all she could do to help was call Alek to protect her mother.

"You don't come in here and make demands," he said, and as he approached Jimbo, he gave Olivia an apologetic look. He hated to have to take over when she was the one really in charge, but by all accounts, Jimbo was not the sort of man who was going to recognize Olivia's authority.

"You're not her husband," Jimbo said.

"No, I'm not, but I'm helping her take care of this place until he gets back home, so why don't you drop all your weapons, come with me, and I'll take you to your wife and children?" When Dani heard this, she quickly slipped away so she could run ahead to warn June. She wasn't going to be happy that her husband was here, but at least she'd have a heads-up.

"Everyone else has weapons," Jimbo argued.

"And if you become a trusted member of this community, you can carry weapons as well, but right now, you're some guy who crept in here and ambushed our guards," Alek said, giving him a look like he would an errant child, and true to his upbringing, which told him to respect male authority, Jimbo handed over three guns, two knives, and a knapsack full of bullets.

"We'll keep these safe for you," Liana said as she carried them off to be stored in the weapons locker, and once Alek led Jimbo away, Olivia brought the meeting back to order even though she knew they were not going to come to a resolution on Jobe's fate tonight. After seeing a stranger waltz into the main lodge, all anyone wanted to talk about was security, and with concerns of her own, Olivia realized that she could provide the community with the peace of mind they needed while occupying her friend who would otherwise be hassling her to let her train an army.

She told everyone they would pick up where they left off tomorrow then introduced Liana as the new head of security, turning it over to the general and to check on June while Randy's granddaughter slipped away to go back to her room and cry, hoping she would still have the courage to tell her story the next time it became relevant. The very idea of them allowing Jobe to live was more than she could bear.

Dani and Jax were scheduled at the front gate after midnight the night Jimbo broke into the compound, and though they usually spent their late night shifts completely ignoring everything but each other, they realized those days were about to be over. In the morning, they would begin drawing up designs and gathering stone to build towers at the front gate, the back gate, and every two hundred yards in between. They didn't have enough people to man all of these towers, but until they did, their new tech guru had a plan to make the unmanned towers appear to be staffed by using dummies rigged to looted technology to make them move around randomly. She had excitedly hurried off to her workshop with two blowup dolls from Olivia's x-rated stock room, and if their circumstances that night had been better, Dani would still be laughing at the idea of June learning that they were being protected by sex dolls.

"Hey," Jax said, recognizing the distant look in her eyes. "She's going to be okay. Her husband is back now, so she won't have to be afraid after what Jobe did to her."

"I'm not sure her husband is an improvement," Dani said. She had read through June's diary in Pittsburgh, and she had noticed a pattern other than the fact that every entry was practically identical to the last. June was lying. It was obvious, but she could not quite put her finger on the reason for it. One thing she was certain of was that June was not having all of the orgasms she claimed to be having. The way she wrote about them, it seemed like she didn't even understand how the female orgasm worked, and Jimbo had never struck her as the good lover sort. There was something about him she couldn't put her finger on either.

"If it will make you feel better, I'll try to get to know the guy," Jax offered.

"That might help," she said.

"You know what else always makes you feel better?" he asked.

"Jax, we can't. What if Jimbo didn't come alone and has friends just waiting to come in and take over?"

"What if I bend you over so we can both watch while we fuck?" he countered, and while his lascivious smile would normally have melted all of her defenses, it wasn't working tonight. It was partially because she was worried about June, but she also still had the nagging suspicion that he was cheating on her.

"What's wrong, baby?" he asked, lifting her chin as she stared at her feet and shook her head, not ready to discuss it. "Come on, Dani. Talk to me."

"It's nothing, really," she insisted.

"Then fuck me," he said with a smirk, and she laughed as she buried her face in her hands.

"I didn't want to do this yet," she said.

"Do what? Are you breaking up with me?" he said, and the hint of panic in his voice made her smile.

"No, nothing like that. I've just been worried because..." she stopped and sighed. "It's just that you used to have a different woman every night, and now..."

"Are you fucking kidding me?" he snapped, incredulous. "Goddamn it, Dani! I haven't been that guy in ten years, and I thought you, of all people, would know that about me!"

"You were locked in a bathroom with two twenty-year-olds when we rescued you!" she argued.

"And the only motivation I had to save them from getting killed by my band mates is that I was fucking them? They weren't even with me. You seemed to understand that at the time. Do you really think I could have gone straight from being with you in that bar to fucking those two little girls? Because that's what they are to me, Dani - little girls! If my daughter had lived, she'd be their age right now!"

"Your daughter?" she asked. She didn't know he had ever had any children.

"Yeah, my daughter!" he snapped, then his face fell into sadness as he stared into the distance for a long moment before he spoke again.

"Linzie got pregnant while we were still in high school in New York," he began. "It was just as the band was starting to take off. We spent the summer on the west coast recording our first album, but Linzie stayed home so she could be near her mom and her doctor. I was in the recording studio when she went into labor at thirty-two weeks, and by the time I got back to New York, it was too late. The baby didn't make it."

"I'm so sorry," Dani said, squeezing his hand as Jax's eyes grew misty.

"I didn't want to be a father at seventeen," he said, wiping his face. "My friends thought I'd be relieved. I know that sounds awful. But we were just kids, you know? The thought even crossed my mind before it actually happened, but when I got to the hospital and saw her lying in Linzie's arms as if she was just asleep, it hit me like a ton of bricks. That was my baby, and she was gone.

"She even had a name already - a name that was just going to go on a tombstone now. We'd been calling her Hope, but it didn't feel right anymore, so we named her Faith because that was the day I lost mine. After that, Linzie and I decided we weren't going to have any more children, and as soon as I made enough money to pay for it, we both got sterilized.

"You wouldn't believe how hard it is to find doctors who will perform those surgeries on eighteen-year-olds. I got so fucking sick of assholes who thought they knew everything telling us that we didn't know what we wanted because we were just kids, but I knew I was never having children. I'm almost forty now, and I still feel that way," he said, then he looked Dani squarely in the eye. "But if you want children, baby girl, I understand."

"You understand what?" she asked, her heart suddenly in her throat as her paranoia told her that Jax had gone into the entire story with the express purpose of breaking up with her for the greater good because his vasectomy would leave her childless in the long run.

"I understand that we'll have to find a sperm donor, and since we've been flung back to the medical Dark Ages, that means in vitro is not an option," he said very matter-of-factly, taking Dani's breath away. "Of course, we'll still try it with a turkey baster because I don't like to share."

"What are you saying?" she asked coyly, desperate to hear him confirm what she thought he meant.

"I'm saying I'm crazy about you, beautiful, and even if everything returns to normal tomorrow, you're the only woman I want to be with."

"Oh, Jax!" she cried, throwing her arms around him. "I'm crazy about you, too." She had tears in her eyes because even though he didn't say he loved her, she could feel it emanating from him, and it had been so long since she believed someone actually loved her, she could barely remember what that was like. Her ex-husband, Bill, had never really loved her, and though she thought she loved him once upon a time, as soon as she found out why he married her, that love - or whatever it was - simply ceased to exist.

When she met Bill, he was still living like a frat boy in his late twenties on his rich parents' dime, and apparently he had been given an ultimatum by his mother, a state senator in Indiana. She had been threatening to cut him off for years if he didn't do something to earn his keep, and when she set her sights on the governorship and needed to win urban areas like Indianapolis, she made a deal with her son. He needed to find a nice, educated, respectable woman of color to marry, and with Dani's doctorate and need to put as much distance between herself and her West Virginia upbringing as possible, she fit the mold perfectly.

Of course, she knew nothing about that arrangement until two years ago when, during an argument about his drinking, Bill blurted out the truth. Afterward, he tried to convince her that he just made it up to hurt her, but the damage was done. She went to her mother-in-law, and they made an arrangement for a no-fault divorce to take place after the election that would leave Dani with a very expensive condo in Indianapolis and enough money that she wouldn't have had to work if she hadn't loved her career. It also left her with a broken heart because Bill's family was the closest thing she'd had to a support system since her own mother died when she was five, leaving her to grow up with an aunt and uncle who didn't really want to be parents. She had never felt loved before Bill, and when she found out that it wasn't real, she hit the lowest point in her life.

Jax's situation was not dissimilar, but he wasn't ready to share that part of his past just yet. He wasn't even ready to admit that he was in love with her even though he had felt it growing since the first moment he saw her. Looking down from the stage in Pittsburgh, his eyes met hers, and suddenly he found himself drawn toward her by some primal force he couldn't fight. It wasn't just sexual. It was spiritual, almost scary, and during the last encore, after he held her hand from the stage, he gave Gino a signal to take backstage passes out to her and her friends. But Gino got waylaid en route, and by the time he reached their seats, the show was over and they were gone. He wanted to tell Dani all of this, but he was afraid. The last woman he had been so open and honest with had used him for years. He didn't think Dani would do that, but he never thought Linzie would either.

Completely unaware of how much she needed to hear them, Jax withheld those three, magic words, breathing in her ear again that he was crazy about her, and when he kissed her, what began as sweet quickly turned passionate.

"You'd say anything to get your way, wouldn't you?" she teased as his hand slid between her legs.

"Bend over and face the window," he demanded with a growl, and unable to resist him, she leaned forward on the counter of the guard house, trying to stay coherent enough to keep an eye on the road as he slowly slid her jeans off her hips, chasing the waistband with his mouth.

Then she felt his breath as he knelt behind her. She froze.

"Jax!" she complained.

"What's the matter?"

"I haven't had a shower since this afternoon," she protested, worried that she might be sweaty from being in the lodge by the fire, but to Jax, she smelled inviting, arousing, irresistible.

"Shut up, Dani," he breathed with a soft laugh as he pushed her thighs apart and buried his face between them, his tongue snaking forward to find her clit, and any self-consciousness she may have had was driven from her mind along with all other thought as she struggled not to forget she was on watch.

When Olivia finally put Liana in charge of security, it was a rush for her. She'd been dying to whip the camp into shape so they could better protect themselves, and now that June's husband broke in and showed Olivia their weakness, she was going to get her wish. She knew that didn't mean she could wake everyone up for drills at 5:00 am tomorrow morning, but that time would come once they had enough soldiers to build an army.

When she dismissed everyone from the lodge, she was so pumped up, she couldn't wait to get her hands on Aiden, and when he called her General Navarro on the walk home, it gave her the idea that tonight might be the night to reveal the secret room of their cabin.

When she used BDSM in the past, she always just had her submissives call her Mistress Liana, but the idea of being called General had a certain appeal. As she and Aiden walked back to the cabin, she really believed it was going to end with him using those words. With her eyes full of promise and her grin devilish, she told him she had a surprise for him when she sat him down on the bed and entered the secret code to the locked door, and when it opened to reveal the dungeon, the smile was not chased away from his face.

"How did you know?" he asked.

"You're into it?" Her eyes flashed with excitement.

"Why do you think I've never been attracted to puck bunnies?" he asked as he walked forward and began inspecting the equipment.

"This is amazing. I was afraid it was going to be something I'd have to talk you into," she said with a relieved giggle as I followed him in, and he laughed too.

"I thought the exact same thing."

"So, you ready to give it a try?" she asked.

130

"Absolutely," he said, and he moved close to her, nuzzling his face against hers as his lips found her ear. "Why don't you get in the shower while I acquaint myself with everything, and we can talk about your hard and soft limits when you come out?"

"You mean we can talk about your limits?" she corrected him, and he stopped for a moment, looking down at his feet while she stared at him, struggling with the realization that they had a problem. Finally, Aiden sighed and looked her in the eye.

"I'm not a submissive, Liana," he said unapologetically.

"Not yet," she said.

"Not ever," he refused.

"Fine," she hissed as she turned away from him, feeling defeated. There was no way she could submit to him, and if he didn't submit to her, there was no way they were ever going to experience anything more together than they had already.

"Liana, please. Can we talk about this later?"

"Whatever," she scoffed.

"Hey," he whispered as he came up behind her and put his hands gently on her shoulders. "I'm sorry I've disappointed you, but it doesn't need to spoil everything we have. We can still make love."

"No. We can't," she said sadly as she walked out of the room to avoid escalating things. All she wanted right now was to be left alone, so she climbed up into the loft, planning to sleep there tonight, but Aiden followed. He stood on a rung near the top of the ladder as she lay on the small bed, facing the wall.

"Come on, don't be like that," he begged.

"Like what?"

"Don't shut me out just because we've had a disagreement. We're not always going to be 100% copasetic on everything."

"I get it. It's fine," she said, wishing he would just go away.

"If it were fine," he said, walking on his knees across the floor because the ceiling of the loft was too low for him to stand, "we'd be making love right now."

His words made her furious. She turned over and sat up, looking him in the eye as she let her rage out.

"No, we wouldn't be making love because we never make love! We fuck! You bend me over like a goddamn animal, and we fuck! So, sure, Aiden. If that's what you need to do to make you feel better, bend me over and saddle up!"

He looked at her, wounded as he sat down on the edge of the bed. Sure, he liked to do it from behind, but that didn't mean he wasn't making love to her. Though he didn't understand how she could think that when he was always so conscious of her feelings, the fact remained that it was exactly what she thought. It never crossed her mind that she wasn't the only one with something to hide.

"It would be easier to make love to you if you would let me touch you," he said.

"Back at you," she sniped.

"You started it, Liana," he said. "You want to touch me? Let me touch you."

"You're being stubborn. I don't like to be touched, okay? I don't like the way it feels, but that doesn't mean I don't want to touch you. I'd love to touch you."

"And I'd do anything to touch you," he said sorrowfully.

"Anything except bondage apparently," she grumbled.

"Is it really important to you?" he asked, and embarrassed, Liana looked down as she answered.

"Yeah," she whispered.

"Then let me think about it, okay? I can't make any promises, but I don't ever want to disappoint you, mon cœur. I want to share everything with you."

Liana's eyes lit up.

"I want to share everything with you, too," she breathed, but even though she meant every word of it, she knew she couldn't follow through. There would always be things she felt like she had to hide because she was so ashamed, and no matter how understanding and wonderful Aiden was, she'd never be able to lie before him naked and let him freely explore her body.

She felt weak and uncertain, the rush from earlier that made her want to tear his clothes off and tie him to the cross completely obliterated, leaving her with a need for comfort and tenderness. Aiden sensed it as he brushed her hair out of her face and kissed her softly. He took her hands in his and wove their fingers together as he pinned them by her head on the pillow, then he whispered in her ear.

"I'm going to roll you over," he said, "but don't you dare try to tell me I am not making love to you."

Liana's Journal
Day 25

On the small bed in the loft of our cabin, Aiden began unbuttoning my shirt and unzipping my jeans. It made me nervous at first, but when the zipper was down, he left my pants on, lying me on the bed flat on my stomach.

I felt him climb atop me, straddling my hips, and he leaned forward and pushed my hair out of his way, softly kissing the back of my neck. It gave me goosebumps all over, and I began to get excited as I felt his cock growing hard against me. Then his lips found my ear, teasing the lobe with his tongue, tracing it over the cartilage, gently thrusting it inside. When it was wet, his breath felt cool against it as he spoke to me in a gentle whisper.

"Don't you *dare* tell me I'm not making love to you," he repeated, gripping my shoulders and pressing his erection against my ass.

He started to slide down my body, his hands pulling my shirt off my shoulders and his mouth trailing kisses as he moved toward the foot of the bed, taking his time and savoring my body. When he reached my bra strap, he popped it open with one, skillful move, then he kept going until he came to my waistband. He slipped his fingers inside and began to shimmy my jeans over my hips, taking my panties with them.

Then he bit my ass check. It startled me, making me giggle, but as he grabbed my ass in both hands and continued to nibble gently, it was killing me. I wanted him to go down on me so bad, I could almost feel it, but instead, he mounted me from behind. But then his hand slipped around and under my belly, stealing toward the small knot of nerves from above.

Yes! Yes! Yes! My body cried, but my mind said *absolutely not*, forcing my muscles to tense. Now I had to remind him that it was off limits even though stopping him was like pulling my teeth out with pliers.

"Aiden..." I began, my voice small and crestfallen.

"Shhh, baby," he murmured in my ear. "Just give me a chance. If you don't like it, I'll stop."

Realizing that if he just kept his hand where it was, he wouldn't come into contact with any of my blemishes, I tried to relax.

"Okay," I whispered nervously, and when his fingers made the first, tentative swipe, I heard my breath catch loudly.

"That didn't sound like someone who doesn't like to be touched," he growled in my ear, punctuating it by pressing down and making a slow circle over me.

Oh, God! I thought, moaning involuntarily as he massaged my clit with masterful precision, his fingers wet and slick with my own lubrication, and I could feel his big, beautiful cock twitching inside me, desperate for more action as he held still and focused only on pleasing me with his fingers.

"F..." I began to beg him to fuck me, but then I remember what he had said and changed my words.

"Make love to me, Aiden," I whispered, and with a soft, pleasured hum, he began to move so gradually it was a form of torture - delicious, heavenly torture. It had been so long since I'd been able to relax and just enjoy the sensation as someone else did the work, and Aiden was so good at it, like his mind had a direct line to my body, knowing just when to increase the speed and pressure. He matched his fingers' actions with his thrusts, wrapped around me from behind as I lay on the bed with him leaned over me, his hot breath at the back of my neck, and I couldn't control myself. The closer I got, the louder and more enthusiastic my praise grew, and when he finally had me on edge, I was spouting out a long, inarticulate soliloquy of pure joy. And Aiden had me just where he wanted me, suddenly whispering in my ear.

"Come for me, Liana," he issued his command only to see it followed instantly, fervently...*violently*.

"Oh, myyy gaaaaaawd!" I cried in a rush of ecstasy that came in waves, each more powerful than the last, crashing down upon me until I was utterly devastated. I trembled and bucked against him, urging him to join me, and before my own orgasm faded into afterglow, I felt him surge inside me, reaching his limit as he abruptly called my name.

"Yes! Oh, Aiden, Yes!" I moaned as he erupted, both hands gripping my shoulders now so hard I could feel his nails digging into me as he began thrusting slowly and sporadically until he finally exhaled a deep, long breath. Amid the airy, wraith-like sound, I could've sworn he said he loved me, but that was probably just wishful thinking because I felt desperate to tell him in that moment that I was hopelessly in love with him.

June's Journal
Day 26

Yesterday afternoon, Jobe forced himself on me, then last night my husband did the same. I'm sitting in Olivia's office now where Alek pretends to sleep so I can write this. I was keeping my diary in the guest safe in my cabin because if Jobe caught me writing in it, I could just throw it in there real quick, and that would be that, but now that Jimbo's back, I can't take the risk. I shouldn't be doing this at all, but I guess I'm hoping that someday my story might help others, so I'm hiding it in Olivia's office.

I really hoped I'd never see Jimbo again. I wanted him to be dead because then I could move on and marry someone else, someone who loves me and is gentle with me, someone who cares how I feel and if I'm hurting. I don't know who that could possibly be, but I know there are men like that out there, men like Alek. He seems absolutely perfect, and because of him, I'm so confused right now. Since I was twelve, I've been told that men cannot control their biological needs, but yesterday, after what he said in the private meeting about Jobe, I just don't know what to think. I knew I needed to ask him to tell me more, and it seemed especially important to me after what my husband did last night.

When the whole community was gathered in the lodge at dinner time, Olivia was supposed to talk to them about what happened between Jobe and me while I stayed in the cabin with the boys. I didn't know Jimbo had shown up and interrupted everything, so when Dani suddenly started banging on my front door, I thought she was coming to tell me the verdict. It was worse. She was only about three minutes ahead of Jimbo. Alek escorted him to my cabin, and as they stood there on the porch together, I stared at my husband and this other man who seemed so perfect, and I felt sick. I want a man like Alek. When I picked Jobe, I never even knew men like Alek existed, but I've known plenty of men like Jimbo.

"Oh, Lord above, I missed you," he said as he walked into the cabin without an invitation, and while he hugged me, I looked at Alek over his shoulder. I could tell he was watching me for signs that I was afraid, so I faked a big smile like I always do to hide how I really feel about my husband, and after talking to us for a bit, he and Dani left us alone. It took Jimbo less than ten minutes to tell the boys they needed to get to bed, and even though he'd been out on the road fighting with the dead for three weeks to get here, he stuck his tongue in my mouth and pushed me into the bedroom. I don't think he'd even brushed his teeth the whole time.

I tried to tell him I didn't feel like it, then he accused me of cheating on him, and I thought, *oh sweet Jesus, what's going to happen when he finds out Jobe was living here?* Dani was already making the rounds telling everyone to keep Jobe and me a secret because I know Jimbo's going to believe I wanted to have s-e-x with Jobe no matter what I say. I hate my life, and it's not even because of the dead people trying to kill us all the time. It's because I always mess everything up. I can't even make a pact with the devil right. Back in Pittsburgh, when Alek and Jax came into the bar that night, I had really started to believe that the gypsy's spell was going to set me free, and that was almost worth selling my soul for. But as it turns out, I sold it for nothing.

Just like it was back at home, Jimbo held me down, and hunched over me like a dog on a leg. Afterward, I waited for him to fall asleep, stinking and snoring in my bed so I could go shower his filth off me. I saw blood in my panties after I took them off, but I wasn't surprised. I was still sore from Jobe, and even though Jimbo's privates are a lot smaller, it still felt like I had rug burns inside me. When I detached the showerhead to wash down there, even the water hurt. I guess it's what I deserve for being unfaithful.

I just don't understand it. I'm the one who tries to do everything right. Dani's a divorcee, Liana's a single mom who never even tried to find a new father for that boy when her husband died, and Olivia's sleeping with a man while her devoted husband is out there trying to make it home to her. At least two out of three of them are having premarital relations, and they're all just fine, but look what happens to me!

It isn't fair, and I'm so confused right now. I thought once Jobe started, he couldn't stop, but then Alek told me it wasn't true. I asked him about it when I ran into him this morning after Jimbo took the boys up to the pond to fish. I came to Olivia's office to write in this journal and found him in here folding up the pull out couch he still pretends to sleep on, and when I brought it up, and he swore that he was telling the truth.

"Men *can* control themselves, June," he insisted. "And if it starts to get difficult, they can take care of themselves."

Just like the first time he said it in the meeting about Jobe, the image of Alek touching himself popped into my head, and I started to feel weak and warm. I knew I should have ended the conversation there, but I let him go on because I think I'd let him do about anything he wanted. Besides, he was just trying to help me understand in his unashamed, liberated way.

"Maybe this will put it in perspective for you," he said. "Have you ever heard of the withdrawal method?"

I shook my head.

"It's a means of birth control where the man is inside the woman until the point of orgasm, then at the last minute, he pulls out and finishes on her stomach or back using his hand," he explained. "It's a shitty idea that will probably get you pregnant sooner or later, but lots of people do it."

He gave me a serious stare as I listened intently to him make his point.

"*Lots* of people," he emphasized, "and if a man in the throes of orgasm can manage to pull his penis out of a vagina, do you really think a man with a hard-on can't manage to stop himself from forcing it into one?"

Wow! I thought as I looked at him, totally dumbfounded. My mother, my father, my husband, and everyone in any position of authority in my life had always told me that men couldn't control this urge once it begins, and I had watched so many women and girls stand up in front of our congregation and apologize to the wives of men they tempted beyond their limits of control. So I believed it too, even when my secular friends - Olivia, Dani, and Liana - insisted that it was wrong.

I was lucky I even got to remain friends with them anyway. I had to assure my parents that I knew they weren't being raised right just to continue to hang out with them occasionally. One of Olivia's grandfathers was still pastor in the old church we used to go to and the other was a deacon, so I was allowed to stay over at her house once in a while because even though my parents considered their church too progressive, they still respected religious authority. Plus her mother never remarried after her dad died. With only her and her mom living there, I would be safe, unlike at Liana's house with all of her brothers or Dani's with her uncle. Funny thing was, Olivia's mom was the least religious of them all, and I always thought there was way more to her relationship with the woman who rented the apartment over her garage, but I never dared to say anything or I'd lose all access to my best friends.

I wish I could just go back to when we were kids. It's the last time I remember being truly happy. I miss playing house because everything was always perfect, and even though Liana and I usually got stuck being the husbands, I didn't mind. At night, sometimes we'd kiss and do other things, really just pretend to do other things because we didn't know exactly what husbands and wives did, but I was always a much better husband than Jimbo ever was to me. I was the kind of husband I wanted to have some day, and right now, I kind of wish I could just curl up in Dani's arms and fall asleep like we did back then. I could never do that with Jimbo because I don't love him and he doesn't love me. He owns me, and now that he's found me, I realize Olivia's right. There's no such thing as magic.

Day 27

It was early in the morning before the sun came up, and Olivia, Liana, and Dani were wide awake, sitting in Olivia's bedroom after Alek had gone to take care of the animals in the barn. Tonight at dinner, Jobe's fate would be decided, and Olivia was frustrated with the whole situation. June had been raped, and nothing about that was her fault. Of course, Jimbo Connors wouldn't see it that way. He would see it just like they did in some of the authoritarian Islamic theocracies where a rape victim might be killed for bringing shame on her family. It was shocking to Olivia how the people she knew who had the biggest problem with Islam had so much in common with their fundamentalists. The only significant difference as far as she could tell were the holy books, and based on everything she knew about both, neither was doing a very good job of interpreting them.

Olivia had never departed from the religion she was raised in, but now that the dead were eating the living, she was beginning to question everything. *How could God let a man like Jimbo Connors find his family in the apocalypse while a loving husband and father like Reid was still out there somewhere unable to make his way home?*

"I know what you're thinking," Dani said when she noticed that Olivia had gone silent as the three were discussing the potential outcome of tonight's vote.

"You do?"

"Well, I don't know exactly, but I'm sure it's about Jimbo, and I'm sure it isn't nice," she said with a laugh.

"It doesn't take a psychologist to figure that out," Olivia said.

"No doubt. I wish we were voting on whether to kill or exile his ass tonight instead," Liana said. "You wouldn't believe how bad he treats her."

"Did she tell you that?" Dani asked.

"I read her journal," Liana admitted. "I know I shouldn't have. I just wanted to be sure about Jobe before casting a vote that could take his life."

"What did she say about him?" Olivia asked.

"She said he forced himself on her, but she never used the word rape, and honestly, her journal gave me more questions than answers," she said, then she looked at Dani. "I know what you and Alek saw when you found them, but I can't stop thinking that maybe June needed it to look like rape so she wouldn't *technically* be cheating on her husband."

"Do you realize what you're saying?" Olivia asked, taken aback.

"Unfortunately," she said, then she sighed. "Look, you guys don't know her as well as I do these days. She talks to me more, and she's so scared of going to Hell, she can't even think straight. Their church is a cult. I went to it. They're fucking crazy, and they've really messed her up. I'm worried that maybe she told Jobe the only way he could have her was to just take it without asking so she wouldn't go to Hell for it, and let's face it. Jobe isn't really a preacher. He's a con man, so he wouldn't give a shit about Hell, and then when I think about how she needed us to literally twist her arm before she would even drink in Pittsburgh...." She looked down and put her head in her hands. "I know that sounds awful."

"Yeah, but if it's true, we kind of need to know that," Dani balked. "What if we vote to kill him?"

"Exactly," Liana agreed, then she looked up at Olivia. "Has anyone questioned Jobe? What does he have to say for himself?"

"I did," Olivia said, "and he just kept saying 'she wanted it', like when a rapist thinks he's doing his victim a favor..." But as she said the last part, she realized something. Just because that's how she took it didn't mean that's how he intended it. As she went back over the conversation in her mind, she scanned the memory of his face for a smirk or any other body language to indicate that he was guilty, but it wasn't there. He had looked at her with glazed eyes and said, 'she wanted it'.

"I have to talk to Jobe," Olivia said.

"Wait! Why?" Dani asked.

"What if Liana's right? What if her journal and her screams really are her way of spiritually covering her ass?"

"Does it matter?" Dani demanded. "What kind of man would do that?"

"If you had a rape fantasy, would Jax refuse you? What about Alek? What would he say?" Liana asked. She wasn't sure about Aiden because neither of them were sure about anything when it came to the other yet, but as Dani contemplated what Jax might say, Olivia was certain of Alek's answer - a firm, resounding "hell no!"

"I honestly don't know what Jax would say," Dani admitted, "but I get your point. It isn't fair to judge people's fantasies, not even the hardcore shit."

Liana agreed, and though she didn't fantasize about being raped, she was drawn to what she had been denied by her secret shame. She understood the desire to have a man take control of her, and she couldn't judge anyone else if they took that desire to an extreme level.

"But this fantasy could get a man killed," Olivia said, and because of that, she left immediately to talk to Jobe while Dani agreed to read June's diary to see if she took it the same way Liana did. As they went to the office to get the journal, Olivia hurried down the hall, through the lodge, and toward the storage shed where they were keeping Jobe. It was on the other side of the greenhouse, which was connected to the lodge kitchen, and it had originally contained soil and plant food, all of which had been moved out to create their makeshift jail. When she got there, she was instantly unnerved because there was supposed to be a guard. She didn't know who was on duty, but whoever it was had clearly abandoned the post. She pulled her gun out of its holster and turned off the safety.

"Hello?" she called out as she approached the door to the holding cell. No one answered. She turned the knob. It wasn't locked.

Fuck, she thought, knowing that no matter what, this meant a huge pain in her ass. Then she pushed the door open and inched inside, letting her gun lead the way. There was someone on the cot, curled up under the blanket, but when she flipped the light on, he didn't move.

"Jobe?" she asked as she poked at the body, keeping her gun trained on him just in case. He remained motionless, even when she reached out and pulled the blanket off to reveal that it was not Jobe at all. It was a man named Aaron who had been part of a smaller group that joined them after a scavenging mission.

"Aaron, are you okay?" she asked, but when he didn't respond, she put her gun away and tried to rouse him by shaking him. Gradually, he began to come to, and once he rolled over, she noticed his empty gun holster. "Aaron, what happened?"

"Huh?" he asked, disoriented as his hand went directly to the top of his head where he had a huge knot. Olivia pulled out her walkie talkie.

"Alek, I'm at the cell. The guard was incapacitated, and Jobe appears to be on the loose."

"Are you fucking kidding me?" he asked, furious.

"No. I'll explain more later, but for now, we need to find him."

"I'll lock everything down and start a sweep. Are you okay?"

"I'm fine," she said. "I don't know about Aaron, though. Could you get June to come take a look at him? I think he may have been hit over the head."

"Yes, ma'am," Alek said, and after they signed off, Aaron got his bearings and began to recount what little he could. He had heard a noise over by the pear trees in the greenhouse and when he walked away from the door to investigate, someone came up from behind and struck him hard on the head. The next thing he knew, Olivia was waking him up. He had no idea who it could have been.

Olivia waited with Aaron until June arrived to check on him, and they helped him back to the room he shared in the lodge with instructions not to fall asleep again because June was afraid he had a concussion. Once he was given some analgesics and turned over to the care of his roommates, Olivia looked down from the railing and saw that Alek and Liana were heading out with teams to start the search for Jobe, so she decided to use the opportunity to question June about the rape.

"Can we talk for a minute?" she asked.

"I should probably get back to my husband," June said.

"He can wait. You can't be outside until they finish the sweep of the inner ring anyway. Jimbo will just have to understand." Olivia led her down the stairs and into her private residence, but instead of going through the office where Dani might still be reading June's journal, she took her into her bedroom from the hallway.

"You know where that goes?" Olivia asked, pointing to one of several doors in her bedroom. June shook her head. "It leads to my office. In my office is a bed..."

"...where Alek pretends to sleep at night," June said.

"Yes. He does that because I can't stand the idea of people knowing that I'm in here sleeping with a man who isn't my husband," she admitted. "I know Reid is probably never coming back. He hasn't called me in weeks, and considering the state of the world right now, I don't think anyone would even care what Alek and I do. I'm just not ready to take that step. I'm telling you because I want you to know that I understand what it's like to feel like you're not free to follow your heart. Do you get what I'm saying?"

"I have no idea what you're saying," June insisted.

"I want to talk about Jobe and what happened to you, and I don't want you to think that I'm judging you in any way. I just need to know one thing. Did you ask him to do it?"

"I'm a married woman! *I* would never willingly cheat on my husband!" she hissed with a judgmental glare, but Olivia completely ignored her dig.

"Which is exactly why I'm asking the question," she said. "Listen, this is a hard conversation for me too. The idea of even suggesting that you were complicit in your own rape goes against everything I believe in, but this could end with a man being executed. We can't get this wrong.

"I'll be honest with you, June. I don't like Jobe. I think he's a disgusting human being who preyed on the weakness of others to get rich. I think he cowered up on top of his limo and let his wife die, and maybe he doesn't deserve to live for that, but that's not what he's on trial for. He's on trial for rape, and if they vote to execute, he'll die."

"He doesn't deserve to die for it," June said.

"Perhaps not, but I'll let you in on a little secret. If the community voted to exile him, do you know what I was going to do? The plan was for Alek and me to blindfold him and take him fifty miles out so he couldn't find his way back, but the truth is, I don't even trust that fifty miles would keep us safe. I'm sure he's heard enough about routes and nearby towns to find us if he wanted to. Exiling was never really an option." As Olivia said this, June's eyes grew large.

"You were going to kill him either way?" she asked, and Olivia nodded. "Why? Why would you do that?"

"For every man, woman, and child living here," she said unapologetically, and Dani, who had been listening through the office door, stealthily cracked it to hear better. "We have a great set up, and there are plenty of people out there who will want what we have if they find out about it - evil people who will kill us to take it. I can't have anyone out there who might be inclined to sell us out because they have a grudge. I'm talking about our safety, June. Our safety and our lives. Noah's life. Isaiah's life. Savannah's life. I would kill any man, woman, or child on this planet to keep her safe, so you can bet Jobe Stricklan doesn't have a prayer. Now what I need to know from you is would you really make a murderer of me? Because if Jobe raped you, I would feel no guilt about his execution, but if he didn't...if he didn't, I don't know if I could live with myself. So you need to tell me right fucking now if I'm planning to murder an innocent man."

As June stared into Olivia's face, her eyes rapidly tracking back and forth, she tried to come up with a scenario that would absolve her of guilt, but quickly realizing that telling the truth was the only option she had, she burst into tears.

"Oh, God!" Olivia cried as Dani pushed the office door open and entered the bedroom.

"June, how could you?" she asked, her face twisted in anguish.

On the couch, June drew her knees to her chest, trying to hide her shame behind her hands as Olivia furiously paced, and Dani shot her a look, begging her not to start yelling. Frustrated, Olivia held her tongue.

"Come here, shug," Dani said in a motherly fashion, putting her arm around June and pulling her close. "Tell me what happened."

"I...I can't," she muttered between deep sobs, and Dani looked up at Olivia, motioning to the door with her eyes, suggesting that she leave.

"Oh, hell no!" Olivia snapped. "I'm not going anywhere. I was going to kill that man for you, June! I have more right to hear this than anyone, so you're going to start talking or I'm going to beat your ass until you do!"

"Not helpful!" Dani shouted, but she was wrong. June wasn't raised like the rest of them. She responded to authority. Her dictatorial stance is how Olivia got her to crack in the first place, and though Dani was an excellent psychologist with a doctorate, she had trouble applying her academic knowledge to June because in her mind June was still her best friend from grade school. Perhaps that girl was still in there somewhere, but she had been pushed deep inside by all of the expectations of her parents, her husband, and her cult. She was so compressed at this point, if she could ever break through the layers of stone and sediment, she would emerge as a beautiful, sparkling diamond, and Olivia was determined to see that happen.

"Talk, June," she said as she squatted in front of her. "Tell us everything, and we'll fix this."

"Everybody's gonna hate me," she whimpered, terrified.

"Don't worry about that right now. Just tell us the truth, shug," Dani said, kissing her on the side of the head, and June took a deep breath and stared into space as she recounted the events up until the point that Dani and Alek caught her with Jobe.

She and Jobe had talked about a lot of things that had long been considered taboo in her world. As a preacher, she valued his opinion, but when it came to sex, his opinions did not coincide with what she had been taught all of her life. For starters, he didn't seem to care that she was still a married woman, so sex with Jobe would be cheating, and even if Jimbo *was* dead, it was still wrong because she wasn't married to Jobe.

June had been taught that it was an egregious sin that could buy her an eternity of damnation, but she wanted to have sex with Jobe because through their conversations, she had become convinced that he would be the lover she had always longed for. She wanted desperately to know what her friends loved so much about sex. What she didn't want was to have to deal with the guilt that would accompany it, and despite what she told Alek, she had many times hinted to Jobe that perhaps it would be best if he just took what he wanted.

They had had another conversation about it right before it actually happened. No one used the term rape fantasy, but the offer was clearly on the table. It was a sort of unspoken agreement that none of her friends could ever fully understand, but one thing she was sure of was that Jobe thought he had permission.

"Then why were you screaming?" Dani asked. "That's why Alek and I came into your cabin in the first place."

"It hurt," she said. "I didn't realize there would be that much difference between one man's privates and the next, but I guess Jobe's is really big."

"You guess?" Olivia asked, incredulous.

"I didn't actually see it. He was behind me, and when he put it in, I screamed." Jobe had shushed her and paused for a second, then when he started moving again, she had the same reaction.

"If it hurt so bad, why didn't you tell him to stop, June?" Dani asked.

"I didn't think I could," she said, and the looks on her friends' faces showed her that what she had said was as foreign a concept to them as the idea of asking him to stop had been to her. She sincerely believed she had set the wheels in motion and had to endure it until it was over, which she expected would only take a couple of minutes anyway based on her experience with her husband.

As Olivia and Dani listened, they realized that the situation was not as black and white as it should have been because of June's complete lack of sex education coupled with all of the misinformation she had been fed all of her life. They weren't even sure if they could lay the blame on Jobe because they had made assumptions about June's understanding of the world themselves, not even realizing it could be so different from their own.

Jobe probably thought the same thing. Perhaps he should have been more considerate. Perhaps he should have asked her if she wanted him to stop when she was screaming, but when he instead chose to put his hand over her mouth to muffle the sound, he may have thought it was part of the bargain. June admitted that she gave him no indication that anything was wrong beyond those initial cries until Dani and Alek burst in.

"Wait. I'm confused," Dani said. "If he wasn't really raping you, why did you cry for help when we got there?"

"Because I had to! I didn't want to be a whore. Whores go to..." she paused, the word *Hell* lodged in her throat until finally, it came out in a shaky whisper, and she completely broke down, sobbing in Dani's arms. As Olivia watched, her pity and anger jockeying for control, she didn't even allow herself to be offended by the fact that June had basically just called all of her friends whores because she was more worried about how Alek was going to cope when he learned that he had beaten Jobe bloody just for having consensual sex. Then there was the mess they were going to have to clean up with the community because they couldn't very well exile or kill Jobe now. Of course before they did anything, they had to find him.

Leaving Dani to comfort June, Olivia went in search of Alek. She called him on the walkie talkie then went to catch up with him where his group was sweeping the partially constructed vacation cabins in the middle ring. He and

Olivia sat down on the porch of one of the cabins so she could tell him what June had done, but his reaction was not what she expected.

"If you're hurting a woman, you don't cover her mouth to silence her cries," he said. "You stop."

"I know. I agree, but she didn't tell him to stop. She didn't struggle. She didn't say no. And then she admitted that she only started calling for help when you all came in out of shame."

"Let's forget about that part for a minute and look at what happened before. You're putting June in your shoes. You need to put yourself in hers. If I just walked up behind you, pushed you over, and stuck my dick in you, what would you do?"

Come instantly, she thought, but knowing what Alek meant and how seriously he was talking this situation, she forced herself to approach it with that in mind, glad her jacket hid what the thought had done to her nipples.

"I guess I'd scream and fight," she said.

"What would June do?" he asked, and she sighed.

"Okay, I get it. She'd probably just submit, but how can you expect Jobe to know that?"

"I expect him to know to stop when a woman screams in pain," he said.

"They didn't want anyone to know what they were doing, so he put his hand over her mouth to keep her quiet. Maybe he couldn't tell pleasure from pain."

Alek shook his head. "I understand that sometimes people falsely report rapes, and I get that June's story sounds exactly like one of those cases - she got caught, regretted it, said it was rape. But are you sure there's not more to this?"

"Maybe, but as much of an asshole of a human being as Jobe is, we can't hold him responsible for not knowing that June has some seriously convoluted ideas about sex."

"So, you're comfortable with him being loose in the community? You'd be comfortable with him being around Savannah?" he asked, and she couldn't answer the question. There were plenty of reasons she wouldn't want her daughter around Jobe, but on this particular issue, she just didn't know. Alek was certain he did. "You didn't see him, Olivia. He wasn't just covering her mouth, he had one hand on her back pinning her down."

"I know what it looked like, but if June hadn't called for help when she saw you, could it also have just looked like rough sex?" she asked.

"I don't know. I guess," he said, and though she knew it wasn't right, she saw an opportunity to end the conversation. She wanted to ask Jobe some questions before she delved any deeper, so she took the low road.

"Lots of people like rough sex, Alek," she said, then she smiled. "Like me, for instance."

He laughed and shook his head. "You don't get to do that, Olivia," he complained.

"Do what?" she asked, feigning innocence as she noticed a stray corpse wandering toward them from across the field. Alek glanced at it then back at her, staring into her eyes with a smirk.

"One of these days, woman," he began, leaning in until his lips were so close to her ear she could feel his words as he spoke. "I'm going to fuck you, and no matter how rough you like it, there will be no question that you wanted it because you'll be screaming my praises so fucking loud, every corpse within a hundred miles will be standing outside the gates when I'm finished with you."

He sat back in his chair and watched the visceral response as her eyes flashed and her cheeks turned rosy. Desperate to escape, when the intruder in the field caught her eye again, she decided to go take care of it lest she drag Alek inside the cabin and break her vows this minute.

"You're killing me," she said with a smile as she backed away from him then turned and hurried toward the corpse.

"*You're* killing *me*," he whispered sadly as soon as she was out of earshot.

Alek held his gun aloft, covering Olivia until she safely took the zombie in the field down, and while she stood wiping the rancid blood from her blade, Liana's voice came over her walkie talkie.

"Hey Olivia, can you meet me at the lower gate when you have a chance?" she asked, trying to sound breezy, but Olivia knew her well enough to realize that it was something serious.

"Be there in a minute," she said as she stared at the cabin porch, and having heard the conversation on his own walkie, Alek gave her a smile before going inside.

As Olivia walked down the road toward the main entrance, she radioed for a body removal in the field because they had begun burning them, and the crew put on their homemade hazmat suits and jumped on their four wheelers. Then Olivia arrived at the lower gate and found Liana frantically pacing back and forth.

"What's the matter?" she asked as she approached, and Liana pointed in the direction of the main road. Olivia couldn't quite see it until she climbed over the gate, but when it came into view, it stopped her in her tracks. Liana's team had found Jobe. He had been crucified, and now he was reanimated.

He thrashed and jerked, his hands and feet nailed to a pair of trees, one stripped of its branches though still rooted to the ground, and the other cut down and tied with rope to form a cross. There was a cropped branch beneath his crotch, holding him aloft so the nails didn't rip through from his weight, and the sign around his neck said one word: Adulterer.

"Take him out," Olivia commanded with a look of disgust on her face, and one of Liana's men raised his weapon and put a bullet in Jobe's brain. His body slumped over.

"I think it's fairly obvious who did this," Liana hissed.

"Jimbo," Olivia sighed. "Wonder how he found out?"

"I have no idea," Liana said. "Everyone knew not to tell him."

"I think I might know the answer," Ravi offered, approaching them with Noah, June's eldest child. As Liana's team cut through the ropes that held Jobe's body to the cross, Noah had shown up, walking toward the entrance to the compound on the main road. His hair was a mess, and both of his eyes were black and puffy.

"Oh, my God!" Liana cried, reaching out and hugging him. "Are you okay? What happened?"

"My dad happened," Noah scowled, then he told them how he came to be wandering the main road and how Jobe came to be crucified alongside it.

"We were eating dinner last night, and my little brother, Jeremiah, started talking about how Pastor Jobe didn't like it when mom cooked greens because he hated the smell. We all tried to cover it up. I said he was the minister who came to check up on us and have dinner sometimes, but our dad didn't believe me.

After everyone went to sleep, he took me out in the woods to make me confess. I didn't want to tell him, but he just kept hitting me over and over until I did. I didn't mean to get anybody hurt. I just wanted it to stop," he said as tears started streaming down his face, and Olivia put her arm around him while Liana wiped them away with the sleeve of her shirt. Noah winced when she touched the bruises, but he pressed on with his story, wanting everyone to know what his father had done.

"I swore Pastor Jobe never slept with mom. I told him I'd swear it on the Bible, but he didn't care about that. He said it made a fool of him in front of the whole world, and then he said he was going to kill Pastor Jobe for trying to take what was his."

"Why didn't you tell someone last night?" Liana asked.

"He hit me over the head with a rock, and I was out cold until right before the sun came up. I've been trying to find my way back home all morning with dead people following me around."

"Come on, let's get you something to eat and have your mom take a look at your injuries," Olivia said.

"Can't I just hide out in the lodge and you tell my mom you can't find me?"

"Sweetie, we can't let your mom think you're missing. She'll worry herself sick," Liana said.

"Better than my dad knowing where I am," he protested.

"He's right," Olivia said. "He can stay in my office for now. Does anyone know where Jimbo is?"

"No idea," Liana said.

"Dani," Olivia spoke into her walkie. "Dani, are you with June?"

"No, she went home a little while ago," she replied. "Is everything okay?"

"Everything's fine. Just wanted her to take a look at a rash," Olivia lied because she didn't know if Jimbo was within earshot of any of the walkie talkies. She made a mental note to speak with Rena about setting up a more private communication system, then as she and Liana began walking back up the drive toward the compound, she asked her to have her men have Jobe burned separately from the dead.

"Why?" Liana asked.

"Because we don't burn community members with zombies," Olivia said, and Liana nodded in agreement, looking back over her shoulder to give the order when she saw a small herd of corpses approaching from a driveway across the main road. There were at least twenty of them, and the men carrying Jobe's body were completely unaware.

"Behind you!" she cried, and though they immediately dropped Jobe to protect themselves, one fresh, faster-moving corpse outran the herd and bit Brent, a twenty-year-old kid they picked up in Princeton. As another man took the attacker down, Blood squirted into the air from Brent's arm, riling up the other corpses, and the group raised their weapons. But realizing that gunfire was probably what drew them in the first place, Olivia pushed Liana's weapon down.

"No," she said. "I have an idea."

She opened the gate and ushered everyone through. Brent was the first, holding himself at the bite site, and the others followed as quickly as they could while trying to hack away at the dead with razor-sharp machetes and long, thin swords. When they were all on the other side, Liana started to push the gate closed, but Olivia stopped her.

"We want them to follow us," she explained, then she turned her attention to the youngest member of Liana's team. "Hey kid, run through the woods to the second gate and open it, then tell whoever's on duty at the inner gate what we're doing."

"What are we doing?" Liana asked.

"Stocking the pit," Olivia said, and though Liana questioned the timing, she didn't argue. She had six people with her, one already sent as messenger, and she asked two more to hurry ahead with Noah and Brent.

"Make sure they're inside the inner gate and close the door before we get there," she instructed. "I'll have Dani meet Brent and take care of him."

They ran ahead as she, Olivia, Ravi, and Phil, who had been with them since the I-77 toll plaza, made noises to keep the horde focused on them so they wouldn't wander off into the woods after the runners. Except for the one who bit Brent, this group of corpses looked like they had been dead for a while, and though they weren't as slow as Olivia would have liked, they weren't sprinters either. As long as they kept up their pace, they could stay ahead by a comfortable distance, making it a safer option than standing and fighting at the entrance to their compound, which could draw unwanted attention from the dead or the living.

Olivia made an announcement over her walkie talkie that everyone was to stay away from the entrance road and surrounding area until the herd was safely in the pit, and as soon as she finished, Liana took over, speaking directly to Dani.

"Brent got bit," she said. "I need you to execute plan X-ray Tango Charlie. He'll meet you at the inner gate."

"I'm on it," she replied. "Over and out."

"What's X-ray Tango Charlie?" Olivia asked Liana.

"X-T-C. Ecstasy? We got a shitload of Demerol vials when they started hitting doctor's offices. She's going to shoot a hundred milligrams into him, and once he drifts away, she'll have someone put him down."

Olivia was a little pissed that they'd made the plan without consulting her, realizing they needed to keep tighter security on the medicine cabinet, but she had to admit it was a good idea. Brent was going to die either way. At least his last memory would be extremely pleasant. There was just one thing.

"Dani, you're going to want to add twenty-five milligrams of Phenergan to that cocktail so he doesn't vomit," Olivia said, and Liana gave her a surprised look.

"Why?"

"Demerol makes a lot of people puke. If you'd told me about X-ray Tango Charlie, I could have told you that," she said. "And if you're shooting it into his veins, Phenergan burns."

"Dani doesn't know how to do the veins. She'll put it in his hip. That's why we're doing a hundred instead of fifty," Liana clarified. "How do you know so much about drugs?"

"Maybe some time when we're not leading a herd of cannibal cadavers up the mountain, I'll show you my appendix scar...or my gall bladder scar...or my salpingo-oophorectomy scar..."

Liana laughed. She didn't even know what the last one meant, but she was thankful for Olivia's scars. Without the benefit of her experience, she would not have known about the vomiting, and the last thing she wanted X-ray Tango Charlie to do was make Brent start throwing up on top of an injury that he already knew meant certain death. She was starting to understand why Dani was prioritizing a cure, though it would be much easier to train an army to make sure that what led to Brent's death never happened again. They needed more people. If they had more people, Jimbo Connors would never have been able to kidnap Jobe, his son would not have been lost in the woods to unintentionally lead a herd of corpses back to their home, and Brent would never have been in the position to get bitten. As soon as they got these corpses in the pit and caught Jimbo, she was going to start working on a recruitment plan.

When Olivia's group was nearing the top of the mountain, Alek radioed her to say that they still hadn't found Jobe, and though she wanted to tell him to call off the search, she was afraid of putting that information out on the open airwaves where Jimbo might overhear it. But he wasn't even listening because he had no intention of paying for his crime. Although he may not have been known for being the smartest of men, he had carried out Jobe's crucifixion at the end of the drive for a reason. He knew that once they discovered the pastor missing, everyone would be scattered as they searched, but he figured the main road would be the last place they looked, giving him the opportunity he needed to take his wife and kids and get far away from the heathens of Olivia's compound. He had seen how they were corrupting his family, enticing them with the sins of the secular life, giving his wife a sense of self outside of being Mrs. Jimbo Connors, and he knew he had to get them back to North Carolina where their church had set up a safe zone of their own. It didn't have electricity or running water yet like this one, but he thought it would be a much better place for his children's immortal souls.

He was packed and ready to take them there while Olivia and the others led a herd of corpses up the road he had walked the night before, chopping down trees that only he knew how to dodge to make it difficult for anyone to follow him when he and his family escaped. Today, Olivia was furious as she saw the devastation to the beautiful forest around her road.

"What happened here?" she wondered aloud.

"I don't know," Liana said, "but we cleared three different piles of trees and brush off the road on the way down. When I first saw the way they were set up, I thought they might be traps, but they were just roadblocks."

"Jimbo," Olivia growled.

"How would they be traps?" Ravi asked.

"Deadfall traps where you dig a hole then cover it with brush so the prey falls in when they walk over it."

"Deadfall. I like that word. It would be a good name for the compound," Ravi said.

"Nobody's trapped here, Ravi," Phil said. "We're a community."

"Yes, but we can't very well call it Sunshine and Rainbow City. We want it to sound like a terrible place to scare off terrible people," Ravi said. "Hell, we probably should have left Jobe hanging down there as a warning to anyone thinking of breaking in."

"The Deadfall," Olivia said. "I like it. I like your idea of a deterrent at the gates too, just maybe not at the main gate."

"I like the name," Liana said, making it clear that it was the only part she liked, but as the gates of the Deadfall came into view, the conversation died when one of the guards' voices was heard over the walkie talkie, bringing ill tidings.

Just inside, Jimbo sat with his family in a stolen truck, demanding that the gate be opened so they could leave. The guards asked Olivia for authorization, and knowing that Jimbo would hear her, she responded by saying that no one was a prisoner here and that residents were free to leave whenever they wanted.

"But, we're herding corpses into the pit right now, so you can't open the gates until they're all in," she added. "Please ask them to wait patiently."

"Yes, ma'am," the guard said, and then he asked Jimbo to sit tight.

"I don't have time to sit tight. Every second I waste here is a second of daylight I'm losing," he argued. "Do you want my family to die out there because we couldn't get where we're going by nightfall?"

"I understand, sir," the smaller, younger man said, and Jimbo could see that he was intimidated. "I just cannot open that gate until they finish on the other side. It would put everyone at risk."

"I don't give a crap about anyone in this place who isn't in that truck right there, so I'm going to give you a choice, son. You can open the gate, or you can end up in that pit yourself," he threatened, pulling out a pistol and holding it against the man's chest. The other guard pulled his gun, aiming it at Jimbo, but he was shaking so badly, Jimbo just reached out with his free hand and snatched it away from him.

"Now what're you gonna do?" he taunted them, and when they didn't answer, he said, "Yeah, that's what I thought. Open the dadgum gate!"

The guards looked at each other and realized they had no other choice. They firmly believed that this man would shoot them if they didn't, and they weren't entirely sure that he wasn't going to shoot them anyway once they gave him what he wanted. The one closest to the panel sighed and entered the code.

"Good boy," Jimbo said as the gate slowly began to open.

Outside, tethered to posts designed to keep them from falling in, Olivia, Liana, Ravi, and Phil stood on the bridge luring the dead to them then pushing them into the pit, and when they noticed the gate moving, the dead noticed it too. Drawn off course by the motion and the sound of the gears turning, they rushed toward the opening.

"What the fuck?" Olivia demanded loudly as she reached for the remote on her belt loop that controlled the gate. She pressed the button to make it close again, but it wasn't moving quick enough to stop some of the corpses from slipping through. Four made it inside with a fifth one caught between the doors, and without a safety feature, it just kept trying to close until it crushed the bones and splattered filthy, black blood all over the front of the compound.

"We have to get in there!" Liana called out to Olivia as she pushed a corpse into the pit. "He's trying to kidnap June and the kids."

"You go on inside," she said to Liana, planning to follow when they were finished, but Ravi stepped up.

"We can handle the rest. You go do what you need to do," he said, wiping off his brow, sweating even in the chilly fall temperatures from working so hard putting more corpses in the pit than anyone else. He had already taken off his coat, and Olivia was worried about him being exposed while fighting the dead.

"Are you sure?" she asked, and when he insisted, she nodded and thanked him before unclipping her tether and hurrying into the alcove in the stone where they had built a door for foot traffic. Liana caught up to her, and while she entered the code, they both gasped as they watched Ravi struggling with a particularly tenacious corpse. He was bathed in sweat, his surprisingly ripped muscles flexing through his damp, white shirt as he fought to escape the strong grip the corpse had on his shoulders, and even when he pushed its legs over the edge, it continued to chomp at him. As it dangled unwilling to let go, Ravi finally head-butted it to get its mouth away just long enough to use his hands to pry himself free. Then he threw it down into the trench with the others.

"Oh, my God!" Liana gasped as she stared back at him, anxious.

"Go!" he shouted at them when he felt their eyes on him. "Don't worry about me!"

"Be safe," Olivia said, and she and Liana went inside where they were greeted by a nightmare. The guards had been bitten, and one was already up again, so there were now five corpses surrounding Jimbo's truck. He hit the gas, backing up, and when he saw Olivia, he rolled down the window.

"You better open up the gate, or I'm going to ram it!" he yelled at her.

"I can't open the gate! It's jammed!" she lied, hoping to buy some time as she and Liana started shooting at the dead. Even with their silencers, the commotion drew more people, and since most of their best fighters were out looking for Jobe, it was the younger residents who came, like Savannah and her friends.

"Get back in the lodge!" Olivia shouted at her daughter, then she turned to Dani. "Radio Alek and ask him to get everyone back up here!"

Dani nodded, ushering Savannah, Bella, and Sally inside, but some of the others picked up weapons and tried to help. It was a mistake because even though Liana had trained them in hand to hand combat with the dead, she hadn't covered every eventuality, and one young woman, who walked by what she thought was a thoroughly dead guard and got bitten on the ankle before she knew what was happening.

It had become complete chaos on both sides of the wall. Outside, the men struggling to get the remaining corpses into the pit had to remove their tethers to chase after them once they became distracted by the noise coming from inside where Jimbo revved his engine, threatening Olivia as he tried to force her to open the gate. Alek, Jax, Aiden, and the others who had been in the outer rings were running up the mountain, but they still had a long way to go when Jimbo hit the gas.

The truck tires spun on the gravel, slinging it as the vehicle picked up speed. He ran over the dead, then he hit one of the living, and he just kept going until someone unexpected got in his way.

Noah.

He jumped between the truck and gate, and when June saw her eldest son in her husband's direct path, she reached out and grabbed the wheel, forcing him to hit the brakes or run directly into the stone wall. The truck skidded to a stop, tearing up the grass to the left of the gate, and furious, Jimbo threw the truck into park, backhanded his wife, and jumped out to deal with his son. As the first group came home, Alek stepped through the door from the middle ring just in time to see Jimbo approaching Noah, and his immediate response was to rush to protect the boy. Olivia stopped him.

"I've got this," she said, asking him instead to take his group to find and put down the rest of the dead who were wandering through the compound.

"Yes, ma'am," he said, wishing he could kiss her because it would have felt so right, but instead, he rushed off to do her bidding while she kept her gun trained on Jimbo as he threatened his son.

"What do you think you're doing?" he demanded.

"Stopping you," Noah said firmly as his father strode toward him with an ominous glare, but the boy refused to be intimidated by him anymore.

"You think you can stop me? Get your little, sissy butt in the truck before I beat it!"

"I'm not going anywhere with you," Noah said, looking at his father bravely through his swollen eyes, "and you're not taking my mom or my brothers either."

"Oh, is that what you think?" Jimbo said, his expression irritated but amused.

"It's what I know," he said, pulling his gun out from behind his back. Then he started shouting so everyone could hear. "Last night, this man drug me out in the woods and beat me until I passed out!"

"That's a lie," Jimbo growled, and he took a step toward the boy, raising his fist to threaten him long before he was close enough to make contact. Without hesitation, Noah squinted his eyes, zoned in on Jimbo's kneecap, and fired his gun, and the much larger, stronger man fell to the ground, screaming in pain.

"It's not a lie," Noah hissed, "and you're never going to raise a hand to me again. You're never going to hit my brothers again. You're never going to rape our mother again. You're never going to kill anybody else like you did Pastor Jobe." Then he raised his voice once more. "Last night after he left me in the woods to freeze to death, this man kidnapped Jobe Stricklan and murdered him! Thou shalt not kill, father." He stared him down. "Thou shalt not kill."

"You calling me a sinner, boy? Your mother's the one who broke a commandment!" Jimbo cried out as he got to his feet, taking one clumsy hop toward his son with his wounded leg dragging, his eyes issuing a warning.

"You really believe that, don't you? And you think that because Pastor Jobe's an adulterer, you had the right to put him to death," Noah said, and as his father inched closer to him, he turned to the gathering crowd. "That's what the sign around the Pastor's neck said when they found him crucified. Adulterer! Not rapist. Adulterer! Who else but you would put that sign around his neck?"

"Honor thy father, boy!" Jimbo roared as he limped forward.

"Stay away from me or I'll shoot out your other knee. I swear I will," he said, and when his father kept coming, Noah fired a second shot, hitting him just where he said he would. Jimbo howled as he fell to the ground and lost control of his mouth.

"Goddamn you to Hell, you little, fucking bastard!" he spat, and June gasped as she stood by the truck protecting her younger boys.

"And finally the real Jimbo Connors shows himself," Noah said with pure hatred in his eyes.

"Watch your mouth or I'll fucking kill you!" Jimbo roared.

"And I'll bet you already picked out the verse you're going to use to make yourself feel righteous when you do it!" Noah shouted. "You're nothing but a cruel and selfish excuse for a man, and there is no place in this world for your kind of hate anymore!" He aimed the gun at his father's head.

"You'll burn in Hell for this! You'll all burn in Hell for this!" Jimbo threatened, glaring back at June, but this time she didn't let him chase her eyes away as the words of her first-born chilled her to the bone.

"I'm your son," Noah said. "I was born in Hell, and I lived there for twelve years, but not anymore." Then he calmly unloaded his gun into his father. Every bullet made contact, and as Jimbo's blood spurted and splashed, nearly the entire community looked on. Some were unsure what they were witnessing, but those who knew the situation had decided to let it unfold. Aiden and Jax had returned, both standing with their guns trained on Jimbo to protect Noah if necessary, and though neither of them even knew half of the story, they only lowered them when they saw a bullet enter Jimbo's head.

Feeling safe at last, June ran to the side of her eldest son, wrapping her arms around him and crying as Alek came back after clearing the property of the last of the dead, tears in his eyes, a small, blonde child limp in his arms. Because of Jimbo's selfish decisions, they had lost six members of their community today, including the little girl who was bitten as she fed the chickens at the barn. She should have been safe there. Everyone should have been safe within the walls, and though Olivia still believed that leading the herd to the pit was the best decision at the time she made it, she would always wonder if they would have suffered fewer casualties if they had just shot them all at the lower gate.

That night, after burning their dead, the community gathered in the lodge to pay their last respects. With no bodies or pictures, everyone shared stories about the two women, three men, and the little girl they lost. Jimbo's body was burned with the rotting corpses, and no one had any kind words for him, not even his children. The same was true of Jobe, though Olivia insisted that his remains be treated with dignity like the other community members. After the ceremony, the time came for a moment of silence so those who chose to pray could, but only a few said a quiet prayer for him. If there was a heaven, maybe he didn't deserve it, but at least his fate was no longer in their hands.

That was one of the worst parts of leadership for Olivia. None of them had expected that it would be such a difficult task, but it was especially hard for the reclusive woman who had moved up on top of a mountain to get away from people. She had been doing fine so far with her friends and Alek, but she was starting to remember why she and Reid preferred the company of animals to humans.

She also preferred the quiet of their mountaintop, and as everyone in the lodge went silent in that moment, it was suddenly clear just how loud the ringing in their ears from all of the gunfire had become. She and Liana had discussed possible damage when Randy discharged his weapon in the back of the Right Way truck, but now that she was experiencing it firsthand, she realized they couldn't wait any longer to do something about it.

After the solemn funeral service, while Dani wheeled out a cart with a keg of beer and several bottles of wine, turning the dining room into a mead hall so they could drink to their dead, Olivia took Rena aside to discuss solutions to their dilemma. They had a large stash of noise cancelling ear muffs from Randy's shop that were supposed to block out anything over 80 decibels to allow the wearer to hear ambient sound, and Olivia realized they needed to begin wearing them on away missions if nothing else.

"I've been working on a short range comm system we can use out in the field," Rena told her. "I could probably modify it to work with the gun muffs."

"As long as the comm system won't affect their ability to hear ambient noise in both ears," Olivia said. They had to be able to hear if anyone or any*thing* was sneaking up on them.

"I'll make it work," she promised, excited to get back to her shop and get started.

"I can't wait to see what you come up with," Olivia said.

"Me either!" Rena chirped as she grabbed the cell phone she'd been tinkering with all evening and headed out of the lodge. She was one person who had really found her niche in the apocalypse, and Olivia was so glad Alek's group had been the one to save her. Her talents would have been wasted if she was still stuck out there struggling to survive on her own or if she had crossed paths with some other group, like the ones Randy had killed through the mail slot of his shop. The cannibalistic dead were scary, but Olivia was more afraid of what humanity was becoming outside her walls. She wanted to get as many good people inside as she could while making sure that she and the community leaders remained among the good people.

And good people don't lie to stay in power. That night, she found herself wrestling with her conscience over the decisions her friends seemed to have made easily - letting a lie about a dead man stand. Jobe, for all of his flaws, did not deserve to go down in their history as a rapist, but it wasn't even about Jobe at this point...or June. It was about covering her own ass.

How could she lie to all of those people who trusted and depended on her? Worse yet, *how could she tell them that she had been advocating killing an innocent man without a trial?*

This scenario was a prime example of why she and Reid had basically dropped out of society.

Day 28

Last night, after everyone cleared out of the lodge and went to bed, Olivia sat alone by the fire, unable to sleep. Alek sat down beside her to comfort her because he suspected he knew what was bothering her. It was bothering him too. He understood that they needed to protect June, but he wasn't sure that covering up her role in the events that happened that day was the best way to do that. If June needed to be protected from anyone, it was herself.

Olivia was torn between her loyalty to her old friend and her need to be open and honest. She was having the same issue when it came to Alek sneaking into her room at night. She hated lies, and it was probably because she seldom did anything she felt like she needed to lie about.

She and Alek decided to sleep on it, but she was restless and woke long before he did. Evil had stayed in bed with them, and as soon as she heard Olivia stir, her eyes were glowing in the darkness. Olivia quietly got dressed, then she and the cat slipped out the door. The sun hadn't even begun to rise yet, and she could see her breath as she headed toward the back exit of the inner ring. She wanted to walk in the woods and think, and she couldn't do that inside the wall. Besides, she was armed with three guns and a jaguar. The guards at the gate didn't even argue with her when they saw her enter the code to open the door.

"Be careful out there, Ma'am," one of them said as she and Evil started up the mountain. The very top stood several hundred yards higher than the spot where they built the compound, and as they climbed, they passed the two hunting cabins and came to the spring that provided their water and fed the stock pond. She made a mental note to be sure that they protected their water. The next wall was going to encompass the entire middle ring, which included the spring, but she felt like it should have its own barricade at this point as it was their most precious resource.

As she knelt down to cup her hands and take a drink beside the cat, in the distance, she noticed a light that shouldn't have been there. She wondered if she should go back. It could be anyone or anything, and even though she trusted that Evil would try to protect her, she was also afraid for the cat, who would be no match for a bullet.

She took out her binoculars for a better look and found that the light was a flickering flame in the window of a small shack built against the mountainside. The entire structure was not even as big as her master bathroom, but even so, she was sure it hadn't been there before. She had walked this property hundreds of times and never seen it, yet from the weathered boards, it looked like it had stood for a century.

With her gun at the ready, she walked toward it cautiously, watching her every step, trying to keep the sound to a minimum even though the forest floor was blanketed with dead leaves. Not even the stealthy cat could avoid them, and though Olivia knew this was probably a bad decision, she couldn't stop herself. Evil followed her lead, pausing when she paused, walking when she walked, and it took them a good ten minutes at their creeping pace get close enough to look in the window with the binoculars.

She saw a stone fireplace inside and dried herbs hanging on the walls around it. Then a face suddenly popped up, dominating the entire field of vision. Olivia froze as an old woman looked in her direction, but thinking the crone couldn't possibly see her through the window in the dark, she didn't look away until she heard Evil growl. She turned to the cat to shush her then quickly looked back up and was startled to find that the face was not in the window at all. The woman was standing in the path, blocking her view of the shack altogether.

Olivia abruptly dropped the binoculars, letting them hang around her neck as she raised her gun, but the woman just laughed.

"Shoot me if you must, but I mean you no harm," she said, and Olivia was taken aback. The look of the shack and location made her expect the old mountain woman to have a hillbilly accent, but she barely had any accent at all.

"Who are you?" she asked.

"Who are you?"

"My name's Olivia Anders. This is my property."

"I see," the woman muttered with a disapproving glare.

"Are you all alone up here?" Olivia asked.

"There are no people with me if that's what you mean," she said cryptically. "Would you like a cup of tea? I just boiled the water before you surprised me."

"Sure," Olivia said, apprehensive but curious to see the inside of the mysterious shack. She followed the woman to the door, and when Evil came along with her, she whispered, "Wait here, Evie." The cat usually listened well, but she stood in the doorway and would not let Olivia pass.

"She's welcome to come in," the woman said, "as long as she won't bother my bird."

Olivia conceded and let the stubborn cat enter ahead of her, startled as a rooster took flight and landed on the back of one of two Adirondack-style chairs woven out of twigs and vines. Olivia tensed, knowing how much Evil liked to torment chickens, but the cat didn't even seem to notice the bird. She sniffed the air for a moment, then positioned herself protectively in front of the other chair, which the woman offered to Olivia.

Sitting at the fire now, when her eyes adjusted to the light inside the shack, she looked around. This place was like a small, rustic library with stacks upon stacks of old tomes gathering dust on weathered shelves, but perhaps most curious was the woman herself. She looked ancient, the wrinkles on her face deeply etched as they wound around petite features, her lips so thin and washed out, they barely appeared as lips at all, and her eyes so pale and cloudy, it was hard to distinguish where she was really looking. Tied around her worn, muslin dress, was a tattered apron that she wiped her hands on as she made tea in two cups fashioned out of scorched wood, adding a pinch of dripping honeycomb into each.

"Here you are," she said, handing Olivia hers, and a little afraid to drink it given the weird circumstances, she brought it to her mouth and pretended. But the taste against her lips was so sweet and enticing, as they began to talk, she found herself absentmindedly sipping it anyway, a hundred questions swirling through her mind, including the most simple and obvious.

What was her name, and how long had she been living there?

Of course, the woman didn't want to bother with those things.

"Are there not more important matters in the world today?" she asked. "Why are you out wandering the woods in the middle of the night?"

"I have some difficult decisions to make," Olivia admitted.

"Heavy is the head that wears the crown," she said and as she looked Olivia directly in the eye, her face seemed so familiar, Olivia was frustrated that she couldn't figure out why.

"It's not like that. I'm nobody's ruler."

"You are a queen. It's your destiny," she said, "and the queen does not concern herself with the opinions of peasants."

"Are you mocking me?" Olivia asked, confused and offended as that last statement flew in the face of everything she believed.

"You didn't run away to a mountaintop because you wanted to rule over others, but it's the role that has been thrust upon you. I've seen the wall go up. I've seen people come to join you. I am not mocking you. I am trying to ease your burden. A queen must do what she thinks is right for her people, and if your leadership is keeping them alive, that's all you owe them. Let them survive outside your walls if they don't like it."

She had a harsh way of looking at things, but Olivia understood her point. She was never going to be able to please all of the people, but she could keep them safe and alive. That was her priority.

"What about you?" Olivia asked. "You'd be welcome inside the wall. No one would bother you if you don't want to be bothered, but you'd be safe."

"I'm safe here," she said.

"You do know about the dead, right?"

"I've seen the dead walk on this mountain. I've walked amongst them. I have no fear," she said.

"You've walked amongst them?" Olivia asked, feeling hopeful that this woman possessed some ancient wisdom that could help the people of the Deadfall, but her response instantly extinguished that likelihood.

"A protection spell," she explained, and Olivia did a terrible job hiding her disappointment. "I can see you don't believe me. Perhaps you should try it for yourself."

She opened an old book with yellowed pages and leafed through it until she found the spell she wanted, ripped it out, and handed it to Olivia. "Here. I've used it so many times, I know it by heart. Try it, and you'll see." Olivia folded the paper with the ornately handwritten words on it and zipped it up in the inside pocket of her jacket with no real intention of ever looking at it again, but useless or not, it was the thought that counted.

"Thank you," she said. "Is there anything I can offer you in return? If not our protection, do you need supplies?"

"The forest provides for me, but I could use a laying hen if you can spare one."

"I'll bring it myself," Olivia promised. "It may take a day or two."

"I will be in your debt," she said, then with a slight smirk, she added, "my Queen."

As the sun rose, Olivia made her way back down to the compound contemplating the advice of the strange woman living on her property. Perhaps the time would come when keeping information secret from the community was the right choice, but for now, she decided it was not the best course of action. She did, however, take the advice about not concerning herself with the opinions of others, starting with her friends who were convinced that it would be best to let June's false accusation against Jobe stand. Olivia could not do that.

And, technically, Olivia *was* queen.

At breakfast, once everyone gathered in the lodge, she stood up in front, clanging her glass with a fork to get their attention, and nobody knew what was coming.

"I need to talk to you all about yesterday," she began once their eyes were on her. "There are things you don't know, and I've realized that we cannot build a healthy society if you're asked to vote without being given the whole story."

June felt her heart leap into her throat as Olivia spoke, and though she wanted to slink out the door, she was too afraid to move.

"The first thing you need to understand is that Jim Connors would have killed Jobe regardless of what I'm about to say. He didn't kill Jobe because he thought Jobe raped his wife. Jim Connors killed Jobe because he was a violent man involved in a religious cult. The reason I'm telling you this is because I need you all to forgive June for what I'm going to tell you next. I also need you to forgive me." Olivia swallowed hard, nervous as hell about what she was about to admit, but with all eyes on her, she couldn't stop now.

"Jobe Stricklan did not rape anyone to the best of my knowledge," she said finally, and though she had expected gasps from the room, she was taken aback by the sheer volume as she anxiously forced herself to go on.

"It was a misunderstanding," she began, pausing until they quieted down. "It was a misunderstanding, and I did not handle it properly. I believed the stories of the eye witnesses because they believed in what they saw, and what they saw was an image of rape that was perpetuated by Jobe's rough handling and June's brainwashing from the cult she's been a part of since she was a little girl."

As briefly as she could, Olivia explained what June was raised to believe about sex and rape, and she told them about the irrationally intense fear of Hell that had compelled her to scream for help when she was caught with Jobe.

"June Connors should be in a cell!" one man called out, and as others expressed their agreement, June burst into tears. Dani put her arms around her, staring furiously at Olivia for making this decision without consulting anyone, but Olivia pressed on, shouting down the crowd.

"Everyone! Please!" she demanded their attention. "Let me remind you that her husband killed Jobe for adultery, not rape. She never told him she was raped. She never actually told anyone she was raped, and yesterday she confessed everything to us. I assure you, she would not have let us murder an innocent man." As the crowd began to roar again, Dani stepped in.

"Hey! Listen up, y'all!" she cried from the back of the room. "June doesn't deserve this! You don't know what she and her children have been through! They've been in a cult, cut off from the world we all used to live in, and abused by that son-of-a-bitch for more than thirteen years! She doesn't need or deserve your condemnation! What she needs from us is help...understanding...guidance. She and those poor, little boys have been to hell and back."

Olivia looked at Dani and smiled before she reclaimed the floor.

"Dani's right," she said. "June has been in a situation most of us only read about or see in movies, and she made a mistake that she's deeply sorry for. But her mistake wasn't the one that could have cost Jobe his life. That was on me. Jobe Stricklan was a con man, and it was easy for me to believe he could be a rapist as well. I was wrong not to consider all of the possibilities before bringing this issue before you, and I swear it will never happen again. I am truly sorry for my part, and I hope you can find a way to forgive me."

With that, Olivia left the room, and though Alek's first inclination was to follow her, he realized it was more important to stay and hear what the people were saying about her. He listened quietly, trying to be as unobtrusive as possible so no one would censor themselves on his account, and he was surprised by the reception. Although there were a few men who used it as an opportunity to say Olivia should not be in charge, they were quickly shut down as most everyone else was praising her for her honesty and claiming that her ability to admit mistakes made her a great leader.

Liana found herself feeling jealous. No one thought of "General Navarro" like that. She was the mean bitch who wanted to make them do drills and march in formation. No one looked at Dani as a leader either, though perhaps more than anything else, it had to do with the fact that she was the only one running around the apocalypse in full, flawless makeup. As for June, she was glad the focus was on Olivia because she just wanted to make a quick, unnoticed exit, but that was not going to happen.

The first person to see her heading toward the door was Rena, and though she was generally their resident socially awkward nerd, she wanted to make sure June knew that she understood. She rushed over to her and wrapped her arms around her, hugging her tightly. Next Penny joined in, then Brittani, and soon, June was surrounded as every woman in the community and many of the men lined up to hug her and offer their support. Alek smiled. He wanted to be pissed at Olivia for making the choice without him, but he was so thoroughly enamored of how she brought everyone together on the heels of yesterday's tragedy, he couldn't maintain any anger. He went looking for her and found her sitting at her desk in the office.

"The people love you," he said, moving to stand behind her chair. He reached over her shoulder for her hand, and she wove her fingers around his, holding on tightly.

"I never wanted this," she admitted. "I never wanted to be in charge of anyone."

"That's why you're perfect for the job," he whispered, resting his chin atop her head. He meant every word because he had come to believe that those who actively seek power are inherently unfit to wield it, and Olivia could not possibly want it less.

June's Journal
Day 19

I haven't been able to sleep. My son killed his father, and he seems no worse for it. He feels no guilt, and my other sons feel no sense of loss. I've talked to them, and I'm making them all talk to Dani because I fear that this could cause psychological damage down the line, but my children believe that he got what he deserved. Elijah - my precious, innocent, little six-year-old baby - told me that he was so scared when Jimbo loaded us into that truck to leave that he planned to sneak off and try to find his way back to Olivia's the first chance he got. He said living here is the only time in his life he's felt safe. There are corpses trying to eat us, and that feels safer to my child than being with his father.

I didn't know how bad the abuse had gotten, and even now, I'm not sure they've told me everything. I knew Jimbo was hard on them, but I didn't realize he was beating them as much as they say. Then I saw poor Noah's face after what his father did to him in the forest.

"He usually just hits us in places where it won't show," Noah explained, "but last night, it didn't matter anymore because he planned for me to die in the woods." Jimbo blamed him for allowing Jobe to live in our cabin because Noah was supposed to be the man of the house in his absence. He's a twelve-year-old boy, and Jobe treated him better than his father ever did. I just can't believe I was so caught up in my own pain that I failed to see that my children were suffering...or maybe I didn't want to see it. I've spent so much of my life so afraid - afraid of Jimbo, afraid of the devil, afraid of God.

And then there's Jobe. I feel horrible about what I did to him. I've been praying on it, but I can't make peace with it. I understand why I did it, and I understand that it's why the community seems to forgive me. I just don't know how I can ever forgive myself. Everything was wrong about what I did.

Everything was selfish. I should have just been satisfied that Jimbo wasn't here to rape me, but I couldn't stop myself from wanting to be with Jobe.

I'm not a bad person. I just wanted to know what every woman in the world but me seems to know. Just once. I wanted to feel beautiful, desirable...sexy. But I was so stupid. I thought if it looked like Jobe wasn't giving me a choice, then I could trick God. Then when Dani and Alek busted in, I knew if I didn't react like he was forcing me, God would know. But God knew already. He knows everything. I just wish I knew what I did to deserve the life I've lived. It would have been so much easier to be a heathen, but I did everything by the book, and the one time I stumbled, people ended up dead.

I'm so sorry, Jobe. You may not have been a perfect man, but you were just trying to make me happy, and look what I did to you. I hope if you can see me from Heaven, you read this and know how I feel. If I could do it over again knowing what I know now, I would do it differently. I would never have let Alek beat you up, and when Jimbo showed up at our cabin, I would have figured something out so things would have ended up better.

And now I'd do anything just to be forgiven - by Jobe, by my sons, by God. I never meant for any of this to happen. I've made terrible mistakes, and I'm so, so very sorry.

Day 30

Early in the morning, everyone at the compound was going about their regular daily routines, and Olivia was in the henhouse collecting eggs for breakfast. As their leader, she could have found someone else to take on that task, but it was important to her to maintain her connection to the animals. She never wanted to lose who she was and become the queen the strange lady in the woods said she was destined to be. Later today, she would deliver the hen to the old woman as promised, then after that, she intended to forget all about that shack and the disturbing predictions she heard there. Since she still had moments when she believed that the spell they cast in Pittsburgh had come to pass, on the off chance that those were actually her moments of clarity, she didn't want to expose herself to the temptation of casting more spells.

But Dani did.

After Noah killed his father, the community decided that everyone should have a session or two with their resident PhD in psychology, and she found herself relieved of the manual labor she so hated. Around noon, with a little free time between appointments, she had set out to spy on Jax when she saw Olivia heading up the hill from the barn carrying a box with a hole in it. She rushed to catch up because, although Olivia had only mentioned the strange woman in the woods to Alek, Dani had overheard the conversation, lingering just outside the room as she often did, trying to feed her paranoia about Jax.

"What's in the box?" she asked.

"Nothing special," Olivia said. Then the box clucked, and Dani raised an eyebrow. "It's a chicken."

"And where are you taking the chicken?"

Olivia sighed. She hadn't really rehearsed what she would say if anyone questioned her because usually no one did.

"There's a woman squatting on the property," she finally said. "I asked her to join us. She doesn't want to, but she asked if we could spare a chicken. I've been letting four hens clutch their eggs, and we'll have dozens of chicks in a few weeks, so I felt like we could spare one."

"I'm sure you know what you're doing," she said. "Want some company?"

"It's a long hike," Olivia said as she looked at Dani's boots. Though not her trademark spiked heels, they certainly were not made for hiking.

"I can walk five miles uphill on concrete in stilettos. I think I can handle this."

"By all means," Olivia said as she handed Dani the box of chicken and started off up the hill. Dani narrowed her eyes and followed.

Along the way, Olivia pointed out the well so Dani would know where it was if something happened to her, and a five minute trek thereafter, they came upon the shack to find that the woman was not home. Olivia opened the door, which had no lock, stepped inside, and let the chicken out of the box to stretch her legs. The rooster immediately came down from the windowsill to inspect his new companion, and while Olivia watched to make sure they were going to get along, she asked Dani to look for a pen so she could leave a note. Dani didn't find a pen, but she did notice a lot of things that reminded her of Madam Levinia's parlor, including tarot cards, a crystal ball, and perhaps most interesting, a spell book. She picked it up and began to leaf through it.

"Put that away," Olivia hissed.

"I thought there might be a pen inside," she lied as she continued to examine the grimoire until Olivia snatched it from her hands and placed it back on the shelf.

"Forget the pen," Olivia said. "When she comes home and finds the hen, she'll know where it came from."

"If the rooster doesn't kill it first," Dani said as she watched him jump onto the hen's back, pecking at her neck. Olivia laughed.

"She'll be more likely to find a fertilized hen than a dead one." She winked at her confused city friend.

"Oh," Dani said, gritting her teeth.

Dani's Journal
Day 30

Today Olivia took me up to cottage of the Witch of the Wellspring. She didn't call her that. She didn't even call her a witch, but come on, Olivia! Her cabin was full of witchy shit. Animal parts in jars. A book of spells. Herbs and dried flowers hanging all over the walls. The whole, damn shack was creepy and amazing, and I can't wait to go back and actually meet her. I paid close attention, and I think I can find it again on my own. I don't really want to cast any more spells. I just want her to look into her crystal ball or something and promise me Jax can be faithful to me.

It's not that I don't trust him. I don't trust other women. It doesn't matter that the world has ended and he isn't in a band anymore. Every time a new woman joins us, she knows who Jax Bonham is, and most of them want a piece of him. Olivia and Liana wouldn't understand. No one has recognized Liana's obscure, Canadian hockey player, and even though a lot of women recognize Alek, Olivia has nothing to worry about. He's completely obsessed with her for one thing, and for another, it's not like actors are all that used to women flashing their tits and handing them a sharpie, you know? I mean, no one in the compound has actually done that to Jax, but there are a lot of *fuck me* stares because that's just expected of a rock star. Part of his job was whoring it up. So even if he's trying to be faithful, when they have their breasts pushed up or they find some bullshit excuse to bend over in front of him in tight jeans, how long will it be before he falls back into that old habit?

God! I realize what I must sound like, and if anyone ever reads this and assumes that I think like June, let me make one thing perfectly clear. I am not blaming men's sexual behavior on women. If Jax cheats on me, it will be because he's a fucking pig, not because some temptress turned him into an animal who couldn't control himself. It's just that I know he is easily tempted, and it makes me utterly batshit, fucking crazy. It's because I love him so much, losing him would kill me. I need a little insurance. That's all. I just need to know he's not going anywhere. Then I can relax.

Dani's Journal
Day 30, Second Entry

Jax was on patrol tonight. I didn't know who he was working with as he walked the interior perimeter for six hours, but even though there are only five acres inside the wall, there are plenty of quiet, secluded spots along the path. Most of the new trailers they brought in are in the same area because Olivia had been planning to add more cabins there before the apocalypse, so the plumbing was already in place, and since the original layout included a lot of trees to give the cabins privacy, there are lots of wooded areas.

Around midnight, I decided to go check up on Jax. I had to be extra stealthy because his entire job tonight was listening for anything out of the ordinary. I finally found him near the corner of the property on the side opposite the back gate, and he was alone. On the way there, I had passed his partner, and while it made me happy to know that he wasn't on patrol with a woman, the fact that they had split up made me suspicious. But I found Jax all by himself, looking sexy and bored as hell.

As I watched him from behind a tree, I accidentally stepped on a dried twig, snapping it loudly, and Jax whipped around, raising his gun. The light from a solar, landscape fixture cast his silhouette on the wall behind him, tall and still, as he scanned the patch of woods and listened for another sound. There was plenty of ambient noise. The last dead leaves clinging to their trees in the cold wind. The night animals foraging on the forest floor just outside the fence. A lone owl hooting in the distance. But I was silent. I could have made the game more fun. I could have sneaked up on him or lured him into the woods with more suspicious sounds, but even though Jax wasn't a coward who would shoot first and ask questions later, he was armed, it was dark, and things that go bump in the night were no longer restricted to children's nightmares. I decided it would be best to announce myself.

"Is that an AR-15 in your shadow or are you just happy to see me?" I asked as I sauntered out of the tree line into view.

"Dani," he said, a smile spreading across his face as he lowered his rifle. "You scared me."

"Did you think I was a zombie?"

"You never know these days."

"Well, I do plan to bite you," I teased as I got close enough to lean in and nip at his neck.

"What are you doing?" he asked.

"I think you know what I'm doing," I said as I went for the button on his jeans, slowly walking backward and pulling him toward the trees.

166

"I'm on watch," he protested.

"We'll be quick and quiet," I assured him, and he sighed, looking both ways for his partner because he knew he was going to give in.

"If anything happens, it's all on you," he warned me. "You know I can't tell you no."

He followed me into the small patch of forest, unzipping his pants for me as we walked toward a large tree where he stopped me, pushing my back up against it. He took my hands in his and wrapped my arms around the trunk behind me, and they were just long enough for him to interlock my fingers behind it.

It was cold out, and we were both wearing coats. Jax unzipped mine and unbuttoned my shirt beneath. When he found that my bra wasn't a front closure, he folded the cups down to release my breasts, and my already hard nipples tightened painfully in the frigid air. He grinned as he took one in his mouth, biting down in an exquisite combination of pain and pleasure that made my breath catch loudly. Nervous because his partner could be within earshot, I sucked the sound back in, but Jax just laughed.

"To hell with quick and quiet," he said with a heated stare, then he grabbed my breasts, soothing away the sting of his teeth with a swirl of his smooth, warm tongue. I tried to keep my hands locked together, but as he began to make a trail of kisses down my belly, I couldn't maintain it, my fingers winding through his hair, gently urging him to go lower. He unzipped my jeans and pulled them down over my hips, and when faced with my panties, he pressed against me, breathing me in through his nose and exhaling warm air back through the thin, slinky fabric. I shuddered, gripping his hair tighter as he slipped his fingers inside, pulling the crotch out of his way.

With my jeans impeding me, I couldn't spread my legs at all, but he gently held me open with his fingers. And when his tongue made contact with my clit, it was like fireworks going off head to toe. He's so amazing. People think it's because he's had all this practice constantly getting laid as a rock star, but it wasn't practice on other women that taught him to control my body like he was born to do it. The fact is that he *was* born to do it. He has instinctively known just how to please me from the first orgasm he gave me through my jeans in the middle of a crowded bar, and tonight as he knelt before me against that tree, he knew exactly what to do to make me forget everything else in the world around us.

He slithered his tongue over me, teasing me gently, and once I was fully aroused he used his thumbs to spread my lips further, pulling my skin taut like it would be if I was lying on my back with my legs wide apart. Then he started going faster, flickering rapidly over my swollen clit as I held him there with my hands on his head, and I could feel my fingers clinching, my nails making impressions in his scalp as the orgasm began to overtake me. It excited him. He moaned against me, bearing into me and intensifying his attack until suddenly, I exploded!

"Oh, Jax!" I cried loudly, forgetting where we were as he swiftly grabbed my hips, pulling me against him to tap every last bit of pleasure my clit had to give, and when I started to feel the sensitivity coming on, he slowed down, softly teasing as I weakly breathed his name over and over again.

"Did I please you, my queen?" he asked, looking up at me as I leaned against the tree for strength.

"Oh, God, yes," I moaned, weakly reaching out for him to stand. I was going to switch places with him and return the favor, but he had other plans. He spun me around to face the tree, pulling my ass back several feet to bend me over, and with my jeans still around my knees, he slid his dick inside me. I held my hands in front of my face so I didn't accidentally scrape it against the bark, but as Jax started thrusting, he reached around and cupped my breasts, pulling me upright. Then one hand meandered toward my clit.

"It's too soon," I whispered, but he ignored me, teasing around it without making direct contact. I didn't fight it. I stood upright, one hand against the tree for balance as he tried to reawaken my spent clit, and with his dick slowly thrusting into me and his tongue my ear, I began to feel like it might be possible. Jax felt it too. I heard a pleasured hum escape his lips. Then I heard another noise - the sound of a limb cracking beneath a shoe. I froze.

"Someone's watching us," I whispered.

"Then let's give them something to watch," he growled in my ear, and an unexpected flash of excitement radiated outward from my clit as his warm breath against my neck and his magic fingers brought it back to life. Then Jax began thrusting into me again, amplifying the sensation.

"I think someone likes the idea of being watched," he accused me, and when I instantly grew wetter at his words, I couldn't deny it. I was being fucked by the hottest man on Earth. Of course, I liked the idea of being watched, and as I imagined who it might be, Jax knew just what I was thinking.

"It's probably my partner," he said meekly. "He wants you, Dani. Everybody wants you. All the men in this camp jack off just thinking about what it must be like to kiss your beautiful lips, touch your perfect tits, taste your sweet, sweet pussy. Should we let him see it, Dani? Should we give him a little peek at the most luscious pussy in the whole fucking world?"

He didn't let me answer. He slowly began to turn me sideways to face the direction the sounds had come from, holding me upright so my breasts were exposed. He pinched my nipple in one hand as his other sped up the assault on my clit, his dick resting inside me as I leaned my head back on his shoulder.

"Give him a show, beautiful," he commanded. "Let him see how fucking hot you are when I make that pussy come."

"Oh, gooooood!" I cried as his fingers instantly drove me over the edge again, a pleasure more intense than the first tearing me apart as I shook and convulsed against him, shocked that he was able to do what I thought was impossible as the rush of endorphins devastated my body and mind.

"That's it, Dani," he breathed as he teased me through the aftershocks, and when I finally started to come down, he switched hands, gently massaging my clit with one as he shoved the other in my mouth.

"Suck," he demanded, and as I did, I could feel his dick twitching inside me. He was so close, I couldn't stand it. Abruptly, I pulled forward, spinning around and falling to my knees so I could finish him.

"You said to suck," I reminded him, staring into his eyes seductively as I grabbed his shaft and slipped the head between my warm, wet lips.

"Oh, God, Dani," he groaned as I swirled my tongue around, drawing him into me deeply then spitting him out again. His hands went to my head, and I sped up, one hand teasing his balls as the other matched time with my bobbing head.

"Oh, fuck. Oh, yeah," he growled, his hips thrusting into me as his legs began to shake, his praise constant until he suddenly erupted with a loud growl of my name. I kept going, giving him as much as he could take, and when he withdrew from me, panting and weak, the only other sound we could hear were the faint crunching of leaves beneath sneaking shoes. Jax laughed as he called out to his partner.

"Hey, Phil, come back, man! The show's not over 'til I take a bow," he shouted, and the footsteps became louder and faster until they fell off our radar entirely.

Day 36

June started therapy with Dani shortly after her son shot her husband, but she wasn't there to work through the stages of grief. She had reached acceptance years before Jimbo was actually dead since the man she had fallen in love with in college and planned to be with in this world and the next died a long time ago, and whatever evil it was that had begun to inhabit his shell after that was not someone June felt like she had any reason to mourn.

She needed her sessions with Dani because she was plagued by guilt. She had taken on all the blame for Jimbo's death, and even though both she and her children were better off for it, she expected to be the one who paid with her immortal soul. And then there was Jobe. Even though her false accusation was not what got him killed, she still felt as much guilt as if it had.

"I wish I could just tell him I'm sorry," June sighed.

"He knows, June," Dani assured her friend.

"Does he?"

"Jimbo put a sign around his neck that said adulterer. You think he didn't explain exactly what his issue was to Jobe?"

"I just can't shake the feeling that I'm going to be the one held accountable for it all in the end," June lamented.

"By the community?"

"When I stand before the throne of judgment," she said, and though Dani's inclination was to tell her she was being ridiculous, she was not having this conversation in the capacity of a friend who had had her absolute fill of June's hellfire and damnation. As an objective therapist, she saw a broken woman who had been so psychologically abused, her fears of Hell were as real and terrifying as if she were staring down the barrel of a gun 24/7, and this gun would fire over and over for all eternity.

Hell was something that Dani had stopped believing in a long time ago, at least in the context that June understood it. She agreed that there were souls who deserved punishment in the afterlife, but she could never wrap her brain around a just and loving God sentencing someone to be tortured *for all eternity* for the acts committed in a single, finite human lifetime. She had tried more than once to explain this to June, and every time she got the same response as today.

"But according to Pastor Weiland..." June insisted, and Dani began to wonder if Pastor Weiland had read the same Bible she had because Pastor Weiland seemed to have some specific, fucked up ideas that did not jibe with what Dani knew to be in there.

After their session, June went directly to work a shift in the kitchen, and since her sons were at target practice with Liana, Dani knew the cabin would be empty but probably unlocked for the boys. She hurried down the hill and slipped inside to look for clues about Labor of Faith Ministries and Pastor Weiland. Though June's luggage had been left in Pittsburgh, her sons' suitcases were there, and Dani found that each of them had a Bible and a book called *Pastor Weiland's Bible Companion*. She took a copy.

Back at her place with a couple of hours of free time before her next session, Dani sat down and leafed through the companion, and the insanity immediately began to jump off the pages, including lists of unforgiveable actions that would lead to an eternity in Hell. It was no wonder June was scared of everything.

Disgusted yet fascinated by the revelations about her friend this book brought to light, Dani skipped to the interpretation of verses about marriage, and she instantly understood why June put up with Jimbo's abuses. She found a terrifying litany of eternal tortures a woman would suffer for disobeying a husband or denying him sex.

"Un-fucking-believable!" she spat as she came to a realization that could have been the cornerstone of the sex study she was working on before the world went to shit. Like June, there could have been millions of people out there exposed as children to abusive misogyny disguised as spirituality, and Dani could have made an entire practice out of guiding them back. Right now, there were five people in their compound who needed her help, and it would have to begin with June.

She picked up her cell phone. After the issues they had with the walkie talkies the day Jimbo was shot, Olivia had asked Rena to come up with a solution, and from a stash of looted cellular equipment, she had created a short range system to allow them to communicate with each other using Wi-Fi boosted by the compound's existing cell tower. She had neither the supplies nor the time for everyone to have their own yet, but all of the community founders had one and there were units mounted at the gates, in the security room, and at other strategic places around the property. Dani had her own line, and she called Liana first, then Olivia.

That afternoon, the three of them convened in Dani's cabin to prepare for an intervention with June, and they knew what they had to say would not be well-received because June had been raised in a branch of Pastor Weiland's Labor of Faith Ministries since she was ten-years-old.

"This companion book is horrifying," Dani insisted. "There's even a caveat that says premarital and extramarital sex is sanctioned by God if the church elders say so."

"That's like carte blanche to sexually abuse members!" Olivia shouted, furious.

"Yeah, and listen to what it says about orgasms," she said, flipping to a page she had dog-eared. "'When a women marries, she must never have been with a man outside of the sanction of the church, and if she is pure and true in her faith, she will achieve ecstasy through her union with her husband. If the union does not bring ecstasy, she must reaffirm her faith through confession and acts of service to her husband and church. The same is true of her husband. His wife will bring him ecstasy if he is pure and true in his faith, yet if he is not, he will receive no pleasure.' How much you wanna bet no man was ever accused of not being true in his faith?"

"No shit!" Liana added. "A man who's a virgin on his wedding night? That would take like, what? Thirty seconds? What chance does the wife even have?"

"I could get off in thirty seconds," Olivia grumbled.

"And we're all jealous as fuck. Get over yourself, Olivia," Dani said with an eye roll.

"I don't think she was bragging," Liana disputed. "I think she's so sexually frustrated at this point, her brain isn't working. Would you please just fuck Alek already?"

"I can't," she sighed.

"Want me to get Pastor Weiland to sanction it?" Liana joked.

"Seriously, Liv. You can, and as your psychologist, I'm prescribing it," Dani said.

"How can I do that when Reid could be out there somewhere fighting for his life to get back to me? What kind of person would that make me?"

"Oh, come on, Olivia! The odds that Reid is alive are..." Liana stopped abruptly, covering her mouth as Olivia's eyes began to fill with tears. "I'm so sorry. I shouldn't have..."

"No, you're right," Olivia said. "He's probably been dead since the first day he didn't call me, but that doesn't mean I'm free to do whatever I please. My husband dies on a Tuesday, and I'm already fucking another man by Wednesday afternoon?"

"Darlin', this is not normal life," Dani said, sitting down beside her on the couch and putting her arm around her shoulders. "Let me ask you. If Reid is still alive out there but can't get back to you, what would you want him to do in a world where he could die at any minute?"

"I'd want him to find comfort wherever he could," she said. "I get it. Okay?"

"But you think he wouldn't want the same for you?" she asked. "Just because you're inside these walls doesn't mean you're not in danger every moment of every day. Someone could die of a heart attack in their sleep, and twenty minutes later, the whole damn compound is full of zombies. You deserve to take comfort where you can find it."

"And what about Alek?" Liana asked. "Doesn't he deserve...*comfort*? Is that what we're calling sex?"

"He does," Olivia muttered, covering her face with her hands. She appreciated what they were trying to do because she needed absolution, but she could find none because her desire for Alek didn't begin after Reid stopped calling. He had been sleeping in her bed since the first night, and she hated herself for it. She hated herself for wanting him, and she hated herself for knowing that sooner or later she was going to have him. If only she could be certain that Reid would want her to move on at the accelerated rate their current circumstances necessitated, maybe then she could forgive herself.

"Look," she said finally as she wiped her eyes with the backs of her hands. "I know what I'm doing right now isn't fair to Reid or Alek. I don't know how to deal with this, but I'm trying, so can we please move on?"

"Okay," Dani said reluctantly, "but maybe it wouldn't be a bad idea if you started sessions with me once a week."

"I'll think about it."

"In other words, no," Liana said with a laugh.

"You either agree to therapy with me or with Alek," Dani said. "Your choice."

"I believe we came here to talk about June," Olivia insisted, refusing to consent to either. She didn't need anyone inside her head. She'd spent enough time there herself, and it wasn't a fun place to be lately.

"You're the most stubborn motherfucker I've ever known," Dani balked, then she grabbed her cell and punched in June's code.

"Hello?" June answered.

"Hey shug, it's Dani. Can you come over for a few minutes?"

"Be right there," she said, and when Dani disconnected, she gave Olivia a satisfied glare.

"She'll be right here...and *that's* what you do when your shrink says you need therapy."

"Fuck you, Freud," Olivia said, making them both laugh.

June did come running when Dani called, but as soon as she stepped through the door and saw the others there, her face fell. Though she didn't know exactly what they had in mind, this gathering had intervention written all over it.

"What's going on?" she asked hesitantly.

"Everything's okay. Have a seat," Dani said in her soothing, therapist voice, which only made June more defensive. Then Dani laid a Bible down on the table, and her curiosity was piqued. She had become convinced her friends were all godless heathens, and she was fairly certain Olivia was a Satanist based on the teachings of Labor of Faith Ministries. In truth, she had no idea what that meant, picturing the cannibalistic orgies she was warned about by her cult leaders because her friends were absolutely right in their assessment. The Labor of Faith Ministries was a cult. They used fear along with brainwashing and mind control techniques to make Pastor Weiland and the other leaders rich and powerful while keeping the flock subservient, and before the internet went dark, there were hundreds of articles about all five branches between North Carolina and Ohio, including the local assembly that was less than thirty miles from the compound, being under investigation for everything from tax fraud to sexual abuse.

But none of June's friends knew these things. Olivia didn't even know she lived so close to a Labor of Faith branch. She didn't need to know anything beyond what she had learned from spot reading Weiland's Companion. That had shown them all what the ministry really was, and now it was time for June to see the light.

They approached her cautiously with nothing but gentleness and understanding, Olivia letting the others lead the way lest her own impatience and cynicism taint what could be the awakening June so desperately needed, and her self control paid off as she quietly watched June's face when Dani started reading the comments about sex and marriage from the companion book and showing her where there was nothing corresponding in the Bible. Her expression betrayed the intelligent mind working behind the scenes, but her mouth toed the line.

"Pastor Weiland said that the English versions weren't accurate, so his notes in the companion come directly from the original texts," she protested.

"The original texts are under guard in the Vatican," Liana said, "and even if they let some small-time, protestant preacher come in to see them, could Pastor Weiland read and translate Ancient Hebrew and Aramaic?"

"June," Dani began with an impatient sigh as she saw her resisting Liana's facts. "Let's focus on what I read to you instead. Were you blessed with ecstasy from your union with Jimbo?"

June looked down at her feet for a moment before answering in a small, grudging voice. "No."

"And what happened when you went to confess?"

"I didn't confess," she said. "I knew it was my fault."

"How could it be your fault?" Liana asked.

"Because I wasn't pure!" she shouted, then she burst into tears. Olivia rolled her eyes as Dani scooted in close, pushing her to continue.

"What do you mean, shug?" she asked.

"I fooled around with my boyfriend before Jimbo," she admitted.

"Well, holy fuck me!" Olivia exclaimed almost joyfully. "Sister Christian wasn't a virgin on her wedding night!"

"You take that back!" June snapped. "It's not true. I didn't have sex with him."

"What was it then? Oral?" Olivia asked, her perverse pleasure in June's discomfort earning her harsh glares from the others.

"No! Never! We always had our clothes on!" she defended herself as if she were on trial for her life...*or her immortal soul.*

"Then what did you do that was so bad?" Dani asked.

"We would kiss and rub up against each other," she said meekly, then to everyone's surprise, she elaborated. "It felt so good, and I remember every last detail of what it was like to be excited...*down there*...to want something so much but not even know what it was that I wanted. I should've married him so I could have found out. I should've just..."

"Wait," Liana stopped her. "What are you saying? Because it sounds like you're saying you haven't felt that way since."

Ashamed, June looked up at Liana's face, opening her mouth several times as if she might speak, but no words came out.

"Are you saying you've never had an orgasm?" Olivia asked, the amusement on her face replaced by pity.

June sucked her lips into her mouth as they began to tremble, and her eyes welled with tears. Her chest heaved as she tried to hold the emotion inside, and she couldn't make eye contact with any of them.

"Oh, June," Olivia said, bumping Dani right out of her way as she sat down beside her on the couch, putting her arms around her old friend, who collapsed against her. Olivia felt horrible. She knew sex with Jimbo was probably lame and missionary only, but she never dreamed June wasn't being taken care of in some capacity. Suddenly, she wished she could take back all of the shitty things she had said. Sure, June perpetually tried to make the others feel like sluts for their sexuality, but now she knew that it went beyond self-righteousness. It was driven by envy.

"Do you know what it was that felt so good when you were rubbing against your old boyfriend?" she asked, and June shook her head shyly. She had no idea because she hadn't felt the sensation in over fifteen years. "It was your clitoris. Not every woman can have an orgasm from penetration alone."

"Really?" she asked, curious yet ashamed of her curiosity.

"I can't. The first time Aiden and I had sex, I faked it," Liana confessed, the words slipping out of her mouth before she even thought about their potential ramifications. She never intended to admit that to Aiden. She didn't even admit it to her own journal. "Shit! You all can't tell anyone that - not ever!"

"I won't say a word, but what the fuck, Lilo?" Olivia asked, saddened because living vicariously through her friends was all she had at this point.

"It wasn't his fault. I can't come from penetration. He didn't know that."

"He's going to figure it out sooner or later, or do you plan to just keep faking it?" Dani asked.

"Or you could figure out how to do it, then it will be a nonissue," Olivia said. "You know it isn't the same kind of orgasm, right?"

"Wait! What?" Dani asked, confused. For her it was exactly the same.

"The orgasm from penetration is a different kind of orgasm than the one you get from oral," Olivia said.

"No, it isn't," Dani argued.

"Yes," Olivia said. "It is. It's completely different, and you can do it over and over without any down time."

"Huh?" Dani wondered.

"And also how?" Liana added, thrusting Olivia into an unfamiliar position. Liana and Dani had always been the experienced ones while she was utterly clueless, and now the tables were turned thanks to Reid.

"I'm not sure how. It just happens," she admitted. "I feel it somewhere inside, and...I don't even know how to describe it. It just feels overpowering and incredible, and it's not final like the other one. Reid can make me come like again and again and..." She trailed off with a giggle as she realized she'd become lost in her thoughts of her husband while the others looked at her incredulously.

"So you're saying it's completely disconnected from your clit?" Dani asked.

"Yeah...well, no, but yeah. It's disconnected in the sense that I can just fuck without anything else and get off, but when Reid fucks me right after he goes down on me, I come even faster, and it's more intense," she said, still speaking of Reid in the present tense. No one mentioned it.

"Okay," Dani said. "I have to admit when I skimmed your journal, I thought you were completely full of shit saying you could come twenty times in a row, but I didn't realize you were talking about something different because it doesn't work that way for me. I'm one and done...or at least that was the case before I met Jax." Just the thought brought an impish grin to her lips.

"Well, I'm glad you know what she's talking about because I'm still lost," Liana said.

"*You're* lost? I don't have the slightest clue what any of you are talking about," June suddenly interjected, and they realized they had completely forgotten why they were there in the first place.

"We're talking about the meaning of life, June," Olivia said.

"Orgasms," she whispered under her breath, shy about even saying the word, "are not the meaning of life."

"I challenge you to say that again once you've had one," Dani said, and the others laughed.

"I don't even know how," June protested, "especially after all of this."

"Maybe you need a Bob of your own. I have several brand new ones to choose from," Olivia said, speaking of the secret sex toy shop she had to go with the BDSM cabins. There were plenty of vibrators in there.

"Are you suggesting I...masturbate?" she asked, whispering the last word.

"Consider it a prescription from your therapist," Dani said.

"Masturbation is a sin."

"Masturbation is not a sin, June," Olivia said. "Orgasms are a basic human right."

"A basic human *need*," Dani added.

"What's the point?" June asked. "Apparently, I can't have orgasms from penetration anyway." The "dirty" words, again, were barely audible as she spoke.

"A vibrator may look phallic, but you don't have to stick it inside yourself," Liana said with a roll of her eyes, thinking June was just being stubborn at this point.

"Using the...c....the cl...."

"Clit," Olivia said impatiently.

"That's a bigger sin," June whispered, and Olivia growled in disapproval.

"June, honey, how can that be a sin?" Liana asked.

"Because it isn't part of natural, normal sex."

"Oh, my God! I can't even!" Olivia jumped to her feet, throwing her hands up in the air. She wanted to help, but she just had no tolerance for this level of ignorance.

"June," Dani began, sitting close on the couch and looking into her eyes. "You've been given a bunch of misinformation by men who wanted to control you. You have every right to enjoy sex as much as a man, and I'm sorry, shug, but you just can't do that without your clit."

"It's true, Junie-bug," Liana said, nodding her head. "Except for Liv, who apparently hit the female orgasm lottery, a huge percentage of women can't come at all without involving their clits. Like me for instance."

"Me too," Dani said. "So, how can it be a sin? How is that fair?"

Before June could come up with an answer, Olivia grabbed a kitchen chair, flipped it around backwards, and sat down facing her with a look that said: *I got this.*

"When babies start out in the womb, you can't tell what sex they are. They all look the same. Then as the sex organs start to form, the nerves that become the penis in a male become the clitoris in the female. So how could it possibly be wrong for a woman to use those nerves when it isn't wrong for a man?"

June didn't know what to say. She'd never heard it put that way before, but now that she had, she was having trouble reconciling what she had been taught about her body with what she was coming to see as reality.

"So, you're saying that even if I can't have an orgasm from regular sex like Olivia, I could still have one from regular sex however Dani does?" she asked finally.

"Not necessarily," Olivia said. "I don't know if I'm atypical, but I couldn't possibly have a clitoral orgasm from just fucking."

"And I need direct clitoral stimulation to come while fucking," Liana added.

"Then what are you saying?"

"We're saying there's no single answer. You need to figure out what works for you," Dani explained.

"How?"

"Touch yourself," Dani said. "It's your clit, your labia, your vagina. Go home, spread it out in the mirror, and get to know it."

"I can't do that," June insisted, looking down as a blush came over her.

"Of course you can," Olivia argued.

"Will you promise me that you'll at least think about it?" Dani urged her. "Maybe later tonight when you're in bed, just let your mind wander over everything we've talked about today, then we can discuss it more in your next session, okay?"

"Okay. I'll *think* about it," June acquiesced grudgingly, but she still meant it. Even before this conversation, she was starting to see that their ideas of a normal, healthy life did have merit because her sons were thriving here like they never had under the rule of the Labor of Faith Ministries, and she really wanted to take their sex advice as well.

"Good enough," Dani said.

"So is the intervention over?" June asked, and when the other women nodded, she got up, thanking them sarcastically as she hurried toward the door.

That night at dinner, Olivia, Liana, and Dani were on kitchen duty with June, and they couldn't help but notice that there appeared to be a change in her. She seemed happier, lighter. Liana was as well because after their conversation earlier, Olivia had decided to bring her an unmarked brown paper bag with a lovely new Bob. Liana had followed Olivia after she left Dani's cabin wanting to know more about this elusive, interior orgasm of which she spoke, and during their conversation, Liana admitted that she wouldn't allow Aiden to perform oral sex on her. It was driving Olivia crazy that she refused to say why, but Liana was not ready to tell anyone about her blemishes.

Though aggravated with her friend's stubbornness because she couldn't imagine why anyone would ever turn down oral sex, it was still important to Olivia to help Liana, so she went straight to the locked, walk-in closet that served as her private stockroom to find a solution. And there it was staring her in the face.

Lilo needs a Lelo, she thought as she picked up the black Lelo oral sex simulator.

When she handed it over, Liana peeked in the bag and let out an excited squeal. This had been on her wish list for a while, but it was so expensive. Now she couldn't wait to get home and try it out with Aiden. June was really curious about the package at first, but when Dani told her it was a sex toy, she rolled her eyes.

"You guys are deviants," she said as she headed out into the lodge dining room with a tray of clean silverware.

"So," Liana began after she was gone. "You think we actually got through to her today?"

"I think it's a start," Dani said. "If we all continue to be supportive and open minded, we can probably deprogram her."

"I think an orgasm would help her more than anything," Olivia suggested. "I also have a purple Lelo in stock. Maybe I should leave it on her doorstep."

"That, or you could just let her fuck Alek," Liana teased. "I mean, since no one else is."

"I already told you once," Olivia said. "If I can't fuck Alek Hellström, none of you bitches can."

And as they laughed, June, who was listening through the door, felt the wheels inside her head begin to turn.

Liana's Journal
Day 37

"What's in the bag?" Aiden asked as I came home carrying the gift Olivia brought me. I was so excited to try this thing, I couldn't stand it, and I swear if Aiden reacted to it like he did when I showed him the BDSM shit in the secret room, the Lelo and I would have slept in the loft for a week!

"It's a surprise," I said with a mischievous grin on my face.

"Can I see it?"

"Are you ready for bed?" I asked.

"Oh, it's that kind of surprise, is it?" he asked as he walked over to me and put his arms around me. He kissed me like he does every night when we see each other at home. He had an early evening and has been here since dinner ended, but I had to stay behind and work on the plans we have in a couple of days to bring more solar cells up the mountain.

"I missed you," he said.

"Show me how much," I challenged him, and with my bag in hand, he scooped me up into his arms and carried me into our room. He laid me down in the middle of the bed and stood at the foot, methodically unlacing my boots and removing them. He took off my socks, then he unzipped my jeans and pulled them off. I lay there with my legs held tightly together as he took off his shirt and got in bed with me.

"Can I see it now?" he asked, eyeing the plain, brown bag, and I opened it, pulling out the Lelo in its neat, stylish box. "What is it?"

"It's an oral sex simulator," I admitted shyly.

"And why do we need a simulator?" Aiden asked as he opened the box.

"Because someone won't let me suck his cock," I said, suddenly realizing that it might not be charged, but when he picked up the toy, a little note fell out from Olivia.

Charged and sanitized, it read.

"This doesn't look like it was made to suck cock, Liana," he said suspiciously as he examined the toy.

"But it could lick your balls while you fuck me," I informed him.

"Or it could lick your pussy," he suggested.

"Well, if that's what you think we should do," I said, and he laughed.

"Drop your panties," he ordered as he switched off the lamp, and when we were left in near darkness but for the moonlight shining through the gaps in the blinds, I relaxed and did as he had commanded. He positioned me on my knees. I felt him naked behind me, his cock already hard, and as he began rubbing it against me, I flooded with desire for him. He slid it forward, using it like a finger on my clit, and with my own, slick lubrication, it glided over me, making me yearn for more. Then he turned on the toy.

As Aiden continued to gently rub himself against my clit, I heard him going through the settings. I wasn't sure what they were, but some of them sounded like a vibrator and some didn't. It made me wonder which I would need. I knew that using Bob as often as I did made me less sensitive to natural touch, but it had been almost two months since I'd felt anything vibrating down there and Aiden's fingers had been doing the job spectacularly. I almost spoke up to tell him not to use it, but when he finally settled on a function, I didn't hear the tell-tale hum, just the low, industrial noise of the motor inside working the tongue-like apparatus. Though louder than I expected, the sound wasn't off-putting. It was almost like an audio rendition of the pleasures it would offer, and I felt my clit throbbing in anticipation at the thought of it. Whatever it was that he picked, I was ready.

180

But first, he slid his cock inside me. I moaned at the delicious sensation, and as he slowly began to make love to me, he reached around my body with the toy in hand. Then it made contact with my clit, and *ay, dios mio!* Maybe it was because it had been five years since I'd had the real thing, but it felt so much like it, I was stunned. As it lazily swished up and down, Aiden leaned over me, kissing the back of my neck, and chills began rolling down my spine as my clit was set on fire. Then he rotated it, and it began to flicker side to side.

"You like that?" he asked, his breath in my ear, his warm chest against my back. My entire body was on edge, and each subtle point of contact between us sent electricity shooting through me.

"Yes," I murmured, lowering myself on the bed as I spread my legs wider for him.

"You want more?"

"Yes! Please!" I begged, and when he pressed the button, it suddenly began to make circles over me. I heard my breath catch as my knees grew weak and my thighs shook, and I was so close so fast, I couldn't believe it. This wasn't the deep, demanding work of a vibrator. It was gentle yet powerful, and I wanted to say something to Aiden, to tell him what he was doing to me. But I was rendered utterly speechless, and the only thing that could have made this moment any better was if it were Aiden's face beneath me on the bed. But at least he was with me.

He lifted me up, urging me to walk forward on my knees until I could grip the headboard, and with one hand holding the toy firm against my clit and the other grasping my breast, he started moving again, faster now. My mind toggled back and forth between imagining that it was his tongue swirling over me and knowing he was fucking me, his cock so close to erupting, we could have come together if the intensity of it all didn't push me over the edge so unexpectedly that I must have sounded like I was having a seizure.

I couldn't form words or even moans, the noise coming out of my throat more like the clicking of dolphins as I felt my clit explode. Shockwaves of pleasure radiated outward, taking me over, causing my entire body to tense and twitch as he held the toy against me until I collapsed, leaning on the headboard. Nearly there himself, Aiden kept up his pace, and with my last ounce of energy, I reached down between my legs and grabbed the toy, pushing it back against his balls. It was still wet from my orgasm as it gently licked him in places he wouldn't let me touch.

"Oh, Christ, Liana," he groaned as both of his hands went to my hips, pulling me into him as he chased the pleasure toward his own end.

"Come for me, Aiden," I urged him, pushing back hard as I held the toy in place, and he called my name out in an anguished growl just before I felt his orgasm burst inside me, filling me with his hot, wet desire in one final thrust so deep, it bordered on painful.

"Oh, my God, Liana," he breathed as his body crumpled over mine, and he gently kissed my shoulder before I let my legs give way, landing us both flat on the bed.

Bless you, Olivia, you delightful deviant, I thought as I lay there lost in ecstasy thanks to her secret stash of sex toys...and Aiden knowing just how to please me with the one she chose.

Dani's Journal
Day 38

Today I decided I was finally ready to meet the Witch of the Wellspring. After my morning sessions, I packed a bag with some fresh fruit from the greenhouse so I could pay her for her services, then I went to the back gate. Ravi and Phil were on duty, and they didn't want to let me go. It really pisses me off. Olivia or Liana want to go strolling in the zombie-infested woods? No problem, Lady Bad-asses! But Dani wants to go out, and even the AR-15 strapped across my back isn't enough to make them think I can't handle myself. The thing is not only can I handle myself, I can do it looking like I just stepped off the cover of Vogue, thank you very much.

Ignoring them, I entered the code to open the door, and Phil actually stood in my path and tried to stop me. So I reached out and grabbed his collar while I hooked my leg around his ankle and put his ass on the ground before he knew what hit him.

"I can take care of myself," I said as I stood over him while Ravi laughed his ass off. They didn't argue with me after that.

It took me about a half hour to climb the mountain, and I was starting to think I was lost just before I noticed the wellspring in the distance. After Olivia was up here last, she initiated the construction of the gated fence around the area where the spring surfaces into a little, clear pond before going underground again and connecting to the compound's water system. The cottage wasn't too far beyond the well, so I was getting excited until I started to hear rustling leaves like people walking through the woods.

I looked all around, but I couldn't see anyone. It was a sunny fall day, and more leaves were on the ground than the trees. I should have been able to see everything clearly, but the woods were thick, the sun was brilliant, and the shadows made a disorienting geometric labyrinth on the forest floor. I started to panic because the sounds were growing louder and closer, and though I couldn't tell where they were coming from, I took off running in the direction of the cabin, hoping to get inside before whatever it was found me. It could have been the dead. It could have been a damn mountain lion. I had no idea, but I wasn't going to stick around to find out either.

Okay! I admit it! Coming out in the woods alone was stupid! I thought as I ran, stumbling over roots and dodging low hanging limbs. The sound of leaves crunching beneath feet was right behind me now, and I was terrified to look back and see what was making it. It wasn't just a single pair. There were enough feet that it was practically white noise, then I heard the tell-tale moaning.

Oh, fuck!

The dead were coming for me. Not just a couple of stray corpses, which I had been prepared for. There were many, their groans like a roll call - one, two, three, four...there must have been at least eight distinct "voices" calling out to me, urging me to trip, to fall, to succumb. I could see the cabin ahead, but it was dilapidated and built into the side of the mountain. If I went through that door, there would be no way out.

I had to make a stand.

I pulled the gun off my back as I ran, made sure the safety was off, then I stopped, turned toward them, and fired. I missed. I fired again, hitting one in the head, but the others just kept coming. There were so many of them. Ten. Maybe a dozen. I fired again, taking down a second one, then I had to run because they were getting too close.

I spun around and sprinted off to the right, heading back down the mountain because running uphill was exhausting. They followed, but they were clumsy and slow going downhill. I was relieved when I looked over my shoulder to see that I had managed to get a lead on them, then I turned my head back around in time to see myself crash straight into a tree. I hit it so hard, it knocked me to the ground, and I rolled down the hill.

I landed on a soft bed of moss, and everything got quiet. I could hear the birds singing. They sounded like seagulls. There was a warm breeze as the sun shone down on me, and I could smell the salt air. Then I saw Jax, his face over mine. I heard moaning, and when he grabbed my hands, interlacing our fingers, I thought maybe we were making love. No. That wasn't right. He was pulling, trying to lift me or drag me somewhere.

"Come on!" he shouted. "Hurry!" Only his voice didn't sound right. It wasn't his. It was a woman's, and she was leaned over me, urging me to get up.

What the fuck? I wondered, then it hit me. I wasn't on the beach! I was on the forest floor surrounded by the dead. She must've been trying to save me. I let her pull me to my feet, and I realized that one of the corpses had a hold of my leg. I kicked at him, but he wouldn't let go, so I grabbed my gun and shot him in the face.

The woman yanked on my arm, impatiently warning me that the gunfire would bring more even though the dead all around us didn't seem to be aware of her. At her insistence, we began to run through the woods, up the hill, and to the witch's cottage, and once we were right outside the door, I looked back to find that the dead weren't following us. As I stood catching my breath on the patch of dirt that served as the welcome mat, I began to feel safe because I realized that my savior was the witch herself.

Once inside, she offered me a seat, asking if I was bitten. It was a miracle, but I wasn't. I thanked her for saving me, and then I wanted to know why the dead didn't seem to want to bite her. She shrugged off the question. In fact, she wouldn't tell me anything, not even her name, instead keeping the focus all on me. She asked me what I was doing in the woods all by myself, and I told her I was coming to see her. I pulled the apples and pears out of my backpack, some of which had been bruised in my fall, but she was still appreciative, saying she wouldn't otherwise have had any fresh fruit until spring. Then she wanted to know specifically what I expected in return.

I was ashamed to admit it after what had just happened. I could have died because I was afraid that my boyfriend might cheat on me. It sounded so ridiculous, I couldn't bring myself to tell her, but it didn't matter. She already knew.

"So what do you want me to do about it?" the Witch asked Dani as she sat down in the chair of knots and vines opposite her. Her accent sounded Slavic, reminding Dani of Madam Levinia, but she seemed kinder, more grandmotherly. "Do you want to know the future or shall I cast a spell to make sure the man you love remains faithful?"

"I've had enough of spells. The last one we cast destroyed the world," Dani said, half joking. She was like Olivia in many ways, and she didn't want to believe that their spell had any effect on reality whatsoever. Yet here she was, seeking out magic at the first opportunity.

"Let's look at your future then," the witch said as she reached onto a shelf behind her and pulled down a mason jar that contained a bird's skeleton. It was perfectly reconstructed inside the jar as if it had been wired together, and when she took off the lid and placed it in front of Dani, she told her to turn it upside down and dump it onto the small table between them. Dani did as she was bid, and the skeleton stayed perfectly intact until the rim of the jar made contact with the table. Then the bones fell into a pile all at once.

The witch removed the jar and started examining them with a long, yellowish fingernail. Without directly touching the bones, she carefully studied the position of each one, and as Dani watched her intently trying to glean her prophecy from her expression, her face was utterly blank, offering no hint until she was ready to reveal her findings.

"You worry too much," she said. "You'll line that pretty face of yours."

"What are you saying?" Dani asked, hopeful.

"The bones don't lie. The man you love will never cheat on the woman he loves."

"So he won't cheat on me? Or he won't cheat on me as long as he loves me? Will he stop loving? Is that what's going to happen?"

"See? Too much worry. If you smother him with your worries, you'll drive him away," she said, but Dani already knew that. That was Psych 101. She wanted more reassurance. She wanted a little magic. Luckily, the witch knew what Dani was too afraid to admit.

"You want me to cast a spell," she said. "You just don't want the responsibility of asking me for it."

"What makes you say that?"

"It's what everyone wants deep down, even your hardheaded friend, Olivia. She tucked her spell in her pocket, telling herself she'd never use it, but she didn't throw it away because magic is irresistible."

Dani thought about it for a moment. She knew it wasn't right to use a spell to keep Jax faithful to her, but there was a community of people down there who needed her to help them get through the psychological trauma of living past the end of the world, which she could not do to the best of her abilities if she was constantly worried about infidelity. So, she rationalized that a spell would be for the greater good. However...if she used magic to keep him faithful, she would technically be using it to make him love her, and if he only loved her because he was under a spell, then the love wasn't real. She needed the love to be real.

"I'm sorry. I can't," she said as she stood up to leave. "But thank you...for rescuing me earlier and for your advice."

"You'll be back," the witch whispered as Dani closed the door to her shack. "They always come back."

Day 40

"Do you really need Jax on this mission?" Dani asked Liana as she drew up plans to transport an entire solar farm to the mountaintop. About fifteen minutes away by car was a massive field full of solar panels that Olivia had had her eye on since they first started looting. They'd sent out scouts several times and were pleased to find that the farm appeared to be abandoned...by humans at least. There were about fifty corpses wandering around within the property's fences.

"How the hell did so many end up in there?" Olivia had asked suspiciously in the last meeting.

"There are several abandoned vehicles outside the fence," Liana had explained. "It seems to me that there was a group living there, and they ended up overtaken when somebody died."

"Hmmm," Olivia had groaned, uncertain. "Did anyone check for bullet holes in the dead? You need to be sure there isn't another Randy Sylas hunkered down inside."

"Duly noted," Liana said, but she didn't believe that would be an issue. She was confident in her assessment, and she expected to have no problem taking out corpses so they could come back to the compound with enough solar panels to power the middle and lower rings and then some. It was why she was taking only the men on this mission despite Dani's protests. Today was not about competence or marksmanship. It was mostly about heavy lifting.

"Yes, Dani, I need him," Liana said with an irritated tone because she knew what Dani was getting at. "But if you're worried about him, you're welcome to tag along."

"No, thank you."

"That's what I thought," Liana said, and Dani snarled as she left the cabin, planning to see if Olivia would override General Navarro.

Liana locked the door behind Dani, then she looked at her watch and smiled. It was dark outside already, and Aiden would be home from his shift at the gate soon. With plans for him, she grabbed her robe and headed into the bathroom for a shower, stopping to watch herself undress in front of the mirror. With her top and bra off, she liked what she saw. Her breasts sat high and round with petite, peach-colored dots when she was excited or cold, and her bronze skin was flawless, not a single blemish or even a mole or freckle. From the waist up, Liana looked like a curvaceous centerfold whose pictures wouldn't even need retouching, and as long as she kept her pants on, she could pretend that she was the perfect woman that Aiden deserved.

She turned sideways, then she spun around and bent down, looking back over her shoulder to see her ass in her jeans. There was so much she would do if she had nothing to hide, but she couldn't shower or have sex with her jeans on. Eventually, the illusion would dissolve, and she would have to acknowledge the flaws that stood between her and her desires.

But tonight she wasn't going to let it make her sad. Tonight she was hoping to bring up BDSM again with Aiden. She probably wouldn't be able to talk him into trying it immediately, but she needed to know he was at least considering it. Ever since that new toy made contact with her clit, all she could think about was him on his knees before her, and she was suddenly lost in the moment, imagining what it would be like to look down and see his beautiful face between her legs, his eyes blindfolded, his mouth pressed into her, swirling his smooth, wet tongue over her most sensitive flesh. She caught a glimpse of her face in the mirror, her cheeks flushed, and she realized if she didn't get into a cold shower quick, she was going to end up taking care of herself before Aiden even had a chance.

Or I could just make the water warm and pull down that detachable showerhead, she thought, knowing no matter what happened tonight, it wouldn't be what she really wanted. It was times like these when she missed being in an exclusive relationship with Bob. He didn't care that she wasn't perfect, and he worshipped her clit on demand.

"What are you doing up there?" Alek demanded as he yanked Noah down from his perch atop the trash bin outside Liana's back window. It was a long, narrow pane high on the bathroom wall designed to let in light without anyone seeing through it...unless, of course, they dragged a garbage can around the side of the cabin.

"I thought I heard something inside. I wanted to make sure she was alright," Noah insisted, but when Alek recognized the sound of the water turning on in the shower inside, he knew exactly what was going on.

"You little, fucking liar! You were peeping," he said as he smacked him in the back of the head.

"I'm sorry! Please don't tell my mom," he begged.

"What I should do is kick your ass," Alek said as he dragged him by the arm down Liana's driveway. "Women aren't objects. You don't get to look in their windows and watch them undress."

"I know. You're right. I'm sorry," Noah said, and when Alek saw how ashamed he was, the reality of the situation dawned on him. Noah wasn't ashamed of what he did for the right reasons. He was ashamed because all of his life, it had been drilled into his head that his natural, sexual impulses made him a bad person. Alek sighed.

"Come with me," he ordered the boy, leading him toward the lodge.

"What are you going to do to me?"

"Set your ass straight," Alek said, and though Noah was terrified of what that meant, his training not to resist authority compelled him to follow even when Alek let go of his arm. All the way down the hill, through the lodge, and into Olivia's office, he felt like he might piss himself, then when Alek told him to sit and wait, he spent that time trying to come up with a good excuse rather than risk having to face the shame of his behavior.

But Alek didn't plan to shame him. He actually went into Olivia's bedroom looking for something he thought would help. He went through Reid's drawers and his side of the closet, and he finally found a small stack of magazines under a pile of blankets on the top shelf. They were pretty dated, but after Alek leafed through and found that they contained only tasteful nudes with no gynecological shots, he decided they would do. On the way back to the office, he went to the nightstand, hoping to find a new bottle of lube, and when he opened the drawer, he saw Olivia's journal laying there. He paused, his curiosity overwhelming him, but he forced himself to grab the lube instead, hurrying back into the office as he tried to put the journal out of his mind.

"Here," he said to Noah as he handed him the magazines.

"What the..." the boy trailed off, completely confused.

"Let's be clear. I'm not rewarding your behavior. What you did was wrong, and I don't ever want to hear of you doing that again," Alek said, sitting down in the chair opposite him. "*However...* It's normal and natural to be curious about women's bodies, and after you look at these, it's normal and natural to take care of yourself if you need to. And use this, not your mother's moisturizer." He placed the lube atop the stack of magazines, and Noah blushed, staring at the ground as Alek continued.

"There's nothing wrong with wanting to see naked women, but you only get to look at naked women who want you to look at them. The women in these magazines posed for these pictures. Ms. Navarro was having a private moment in her bathroom. Watching her through her window was completely unacceptable, and you will be in serious trouble if there's a next time. Do you understand me?"

"Yes, sir," Noah said.

"Good," he said, then he softened his approach. "Look, Noah, you're going through puberty, and the urges you're feeling are not a sin, no matter what anyone has told you. What would be a sin is letting those urges hurt other people, and if Ms. Navarro knew what you had done, she'd be hurt and embarrassed. I'm not going to tell her, but I need to know that you've learned your lesson."

"I have, sir. I swear. I'll never do it again."

"You're a good kid, Noah," Alek said. "You just need some guidance, so if you have any questions about women or sex or anything at all, you come to me, okay?"

"Really?"

"Really."

"Thank you, Mr. Hellström."

"Alek," he corrected him as he emptied a box that was sitting on the bookshelf with old mail in it, placing the magazines inside, then he grabbed a few gardening catalogs from Olivia's desk and put them on the top as cover.

"Thanks, Alek," Noah said, trying to mask the excitement in his voice.

"Do not let your mother find these," Alek instructed as he handed Noah the box. "Or your little brothers."

"Yes, sir," he said with a sincere nod of his head, and Alek smiled, amazed by how resilient the kid was after what he had been through less than two weeks earlier. As Noah left, trying to figure out where he should hide his new treasure, Alek returned to the bedroom with his mind on his own idea of treasure - Olivia's journal. It hadn't left his thoughts for second after he saw it, and Olivia and Evil were at the back gate tonight and shouldn't be home for at least an hour. He knew it was wrong, but once he flipped it open and the word cock jumped right off the page at him, the temptation to read it was too great.

Olivia's Journal
July 27

The new strap-on I ordered came in today. Reid would kill me if he knew I was telling you about this. That's the one thing we do that freaks him out, even though he loves it. He's so afraid of what someone might think of him because of it, which is silly. If they've ever experienced it themselves, they'd completely understand, and if they haven't, I feel sorry for them. I feel sorry for the woman they're with too. I don't like being the only one to come out of the bedroom fucked utterly stupid. It doesn't seem fair that I get orgasms in the double digits to every one Reid gets, but toys like this little, latex baby level the playing field.

Last night when Reid got out of the shower, I was waiting for him with my new acquisition on the nightstand. It was a red, jelly cock that pops onto a knob on the front of the harness using a powder lubricant, which makes it so much easier to switch out toys than the kind I used to have with a pouch, not that I switch much. He seems to prefer the smallest cocks I can find, but that's something I think this new harness will help with. What I really want is to make a mold of Reid's own cock and fuck him with it. He's afraid it will be too much, but he's wrong because it's perfect.

This little red dick is smaller than the real thing though a bit larger than the last toy I used on him. I didn't think he would notice, but when he walked in the room with his towel around his hips, it was the first thing on his mind.

"You're not using that on me!" he said, his eyes wide.

"What's the problem?" I taunted him.

"It's way the fuck bigger than the purple one."

"Half an inch, princess," I said, rolling my eyes.

"Don't call me that," he growled as he climbed onto the bed and pinned me beneath him.

"Then don't be a pussy," I accused him.

"Pussies aren't weak, Olivia," he said, reaching between my legs and taking hold of mine. Wet already as I lay here thinking about what was to come, he easily slipped two fingers inside me to the hilt, curving them toward the front and pressing against my mound with his thumb. "This one isn't weak. It can take everything I give it."

He pulled back, and thrust into me, and I moaned as his thumb slipped lower and began massaging my clit. His mouth closed over mine, attacking me with his tongue and his hand at the same time. When he finally pulled back and released his grip on me, I took in a breath to speak, to push the issue of the new, red dick, yet nothing came out, and a satisfied smile spread across his face.

"That's what I thought," he said, and he grabbed my hands, pinning them beside my head and shoving his cock inside me, so hard he needed no help to guide him.

"Oh, God!" I cried as his smooth, steely flesh glided over hyper-sensitive nerve endings, building rapidly on what he had started with his fingers. Knowing what I like, he sped up quickly, and with my legs wrapped around his and my fingernails digging into the back of his hands, he effortlessly drove me to the first of many exquisite releases.

I called his name. I shuddered and tensed. I sank my teeth into his neck. And he fucked me, over and over, slowing down when he made me come, pulling out and teasing me so he could last. I had planned to be in control and use my new toy tonight, but I wasn't in control of anything as I lay there drowning in my own endorphins. And Reid wasn't even close to finished with me.

190

He stood up, wrapped his hands around my ankles, and dragged me to the foot of the bed. I breathed the word yes, knowing what was coming. I just didn't know exactly how he planned to do it. He fell to his knees, and when he had me on the edge, he put my legs on his shoulders and leaned back, pulling me to the floor to straddle his face.

"Oh, fuck," I moaned as I felt the first, delicate swish of his warm, wet tongue on my clit. He had been a master of this act before we met, but in the last fifteen years, he had learned to play my body like a fucking virtuoso, starting slow and soft before attacking me with a force that seemed unsustainable. Yet he could keep it up as long as I needed, flickering rapidly over me as my body began to quiver. Weak, I leaned back, resting one hand against his knee as he worshipped me, his eyes closed, his lips hiding the extraordinary skill that was threatening to tear me apart, and as the impending release began to announce itself in waves of pleasure rolling over me, my hands began to clench into fists with nothing to hold onto at the sudden, delicious moment when the orgasm seized upon me.

"Oh...my...God!!!!!" I screamed, out of my mind in ecstasy and writhing against his beautiful face, and Reid held me in place, his hands on my hips as he bore into me, forcing me beyond the first release, through a sensation that felt like it was just too much until I came again. It was even more intense, and as I cried out, he kept pushing me onward, and...

"Alek!" Olivia shouted as she opened the bedroom door, and he jumped, immediately trying to hide the journal. "What the fuck are you doing?"

"Nothing!" he lied, but he quickly realized he had been caught red-handed. He hung his head and apologized.

"Give me that," she demanded, snatching it out of his hand. She went to her side of the bed, took the other two volumes out of the nightstand, then she opened the wall safe and shoved them all three inside.

"Oh, come on!" he protested, realizing his best option at this point was to try to make her laugh. "Now, I'll never know how it ended!"

"With a money shot, Alek. The same way all good sex ends," she sniped, irritated because he had at least succeeded in bringing a smile to her lips, a smile that quickly faded when she looked him in the eye and asked him why he did it. He sighed and began to explain.

"I caught Noah peeping through Liana's bathroom window this afternoon, and after I set him straight, I came in here and looked through the drawers trying to find some Playboys or something to satisfy the little pervert's curiosity when I came across the journal. I didn't mean to read it; I just couldn't help myself." He looked down, ashamed, and she realized he was already beating himself up about it more than she would have. "I'm really sorry, Olivia. I violated you, and that's not who I am. Please don't be angry."

"It's actually pretty funny," she said as she sat down on the end of the bed and smiled. "You came in here and basically did the same thing you just jumped Noah's shit for. Remind me, who's the little pervert?"

"I'm not little," he said with a grin, hoping to distract her. It worked.

"No, you are not," she replied with a crinkle of her nose. She'd felt him against her leg so many times, she could probably have picked his cock out of a line up even though she'd never seen it, and each time, she found it harder to stop herself from just reaching out and grabbing it.

"Come here," Alek said, patting the bed beside him, and she crawled from the foot to lie facing him with her head on the pillow. He reached out and brushed his hand down the side of her face, his eyes staring wistfully into hers.

"You don't have to lock them up. I'll never do that again," he assured her.

"I don't really mind that you did," she said. "I'm not ashamed of anything in there. I just don't want you to..."

"...compare my skills to your husband?" he asked.

"Well...yeah."

"It's kind of hard not to," he said, then he looked away, not making eye contact as he confessed his specific concern. "Olivia, I have to be honest with you. I don't think I can do everything I read."

Suddenly her heart was in her throat. She had just assumed all along that they would be sexually compatible, but now she realized maybe they should have been talking about it before becoming so emotionally connected.

"What do you mean?" she asked, and he paused, not knowing how to say it. He was embarrassed, but he also felt like they needed to have this conversation because he was daunted by the fact that her husband was apparently some sort of sex god.

"Were you...exaggerating?" he asked finally. It took a moment, but when it dawned on her what he meant, she giggled in her relief.

"I was afraid you were going to say you don't do oral," she admitted, and Alek's eyes instantly became fixed on hers, chasing the laughter from her mouth.

"Going down on you is all I think about," he said, and she blushed as she felt her body suddenly set ablaze. She wanted him so badly, but unwilling to let herself succumb, she continued the conversation, pretending that all of the blood in her body wasn't draining southward.

"Good," she said, "because that's my deal breaker."

"And not being able to make you come a million times isn't?" he asked.

"Alek," she sighed, pushing him onto his back. She sat up, and leaned over him as she looked into his eyes. "Don't worry. You're perfect."

"*You're* perfect," he insisted, mesmerized as she held her position, her face just inches from his. "You're perfect, and there's nothing I won't do for you, Olivia. Absolutely nothing."

As the words danced in her ears, all she wanted in the world was to shove her tongue in his mouth, and forcing herself to break the spell was one of the hardest things she'd ever done. But she knew she'd never be able to forgive herself if they made love. Selfishly, she let herself linger for just a few seconds more before she slid back down onto the bed, lying on her side. Alek rolled over to face her, his cock still hard between them, and she shuddered as it grazed against her. It made him smile.

"So, you have no hang ups at all?" she asked, and he shook his head. "No deal breakers?"

"Same as yours," he said.

"I assume from my journal, you already know where I stand on that," she said.

"I didn't get that far," he admitted, glad of it because he couldn't stand the thought of her with another man's cock in her mouth.

"Well, you may as well know," she said, her gaze rolling leisurely down his body then back up to his face. "I really, *really* enjoy doing it."

"You do?"

"I do," she confirmed, her eyelids heavy with desire, and it made him smile to know what he was doing to her. There was just one thing...

"There's something I need to tell you about myself," he began.

"Okay," she said, the serious shift in his tone making her a little nervous.

"I wasn't born in the U.S."

"I know that," she said with a giggle.

"Well, in Sweden, circumcision isn't as common as it is over here."

"You're uncircumcised?" she asked, suddenly fascinated. "Can I see it?"

"Not unless you plan to use it," he said, and she thought about it for a second.

"I could use my hand," she offered, biting her lip.

"Uh-uh," he refused playfully.

Olivia twisted her mouth into a pout.

"Do I get to reciprocate?" Alek asked.

"That's not part of the deal," she said sullenly.

"Then I'll wait until it is."

"God, you make me feel guilty!"

"You should feel guilty," he teased, but Olivia wasn't laughing, her expression showing him just how terrible she felt about their situation. He didn't want her to feel that way because he understood where she was coming from, and as much of a disservice as it was to himself, he was compelled to assuage her guilt. He pulled her to him, resting her head on his chest as he stroked her hair. "It's okay. You're in a difficult position, and I don't mean to pressure you."

"You're too good to me," she sighed.

He *was* too good to her, and she didn't feel like she had been good enough to him or to Reid. She believed the right thing to do would have been to kick him out so he could find someone else and be happy while she mourned her husband properly, but that was because she didn't understand that he was already happy. She was everything he had ever wanted, and though each minute of their lives seemed so much more significant since the world ended, they had really only known each other about six weeks. Alek didn't see anything wrong with waiting six weeks, or even longer, for a relationship to grow intimate. Of course, it would have been a lot easier if she wasn't sleeping by his side every night. But he wouldn't have changed that either.

"You have nothing to feel guilty about, baby," he breathed, and he almost kissed her atop the head before he realized what he was doing and stopped himself, nuzzling his cheek against her silken hair instead. To Olivia, it all felt so good and so right, she could feel her resistance beginning to drain away, and it made her hate herself so much more.

Liana's Journal
Day 40

Aiden came home from work pissed off at Olivia. He'd been frustrated with her for a while, and I understood it because I wanted to do things differently around here after the whole Jimbo/Jobe disaster. I just didn't want to talk about it tonight because I was hoping to bring up BDSM with him again, but that wasn't going to happen while he was worried about the future of our community.

Olivia and Aiden were always going to butt heads on these issues. The funny thing is they're a lot alike politically. They both want to protect everyone while giving them as much freedom as possible in this new reality. In the pre-apocalypse world, they both had very progressive leanings, though I had no idea there were any progressives as armed as Olivia, but now that society has drastically changed, their ideals are so much more divergent than I would have ever expected.

We all agree we need to grow our community. There's safety in numbers, and I want to train a militia because once all the dust settles, there are going to be the modern equivalent of warlords that we are going to have to defend ourselves against. Olivia doesn't necessarily disagree with that, but before we can dedicate any members of our group to any one task, we have to have enough members to man all of the posts along the wall, to patrol the lower rings, and to scavenge the things she insists that we need.

I can even agree with that, and so does Aiden. The thing they can't agree on is how to increase our numbers. Aiden and I think that unless someone is obviously unfit, we should take whoever we can get. That's what we do in the military, and most of them come out as good soldiers. It's the ones who don't that Olivia worries about. She's afraid that anyone we kick out is going to come back with a force and try to take this place from us, but that's just crazy. If someone is out there on their own before we find them, *how are they suddenly going to be capable of putting together an army and coming after us?*

She says they might go out and join another group, tell that group about everything we have up here, and then that group will come to take it. By the time someone could accomplish that, if we keep taking people in, I'll have my own army to defend us, but that's not good enough for Olivia. Though she's willing to do things my way, it's only on the condition that nobody gets out alive - her words - and she literally means that the only way out of the Deadfall is with a bullet to the head.

When Aiden found out that's what she was planning to do with Jobe if everyone voted to exile him, he was furious. Behind her back, he calls this place the Hotel California, and he calls her Countess Báthory. I didn't really think of her that way, but after the conversation he had with her today, I'm having a hard time not seeing his point. Apparently, she actually intends to take Ravi's suggestion after Jobe was murdered - to crucify some corpses to make it look like they were executed, then hang signs around their necks so anyone approaching the compound will know that we take punishment seriously here. She wants to put out a murderer and a rapist, which I can almost get behind, but he said she also wants one to say traitor.

Traitor.

That's the one that scares me.

It sounds kind of crazy, and it makes me wonder if Olivia's starting to get paranoid. I asked Aiden what he thought we should do, and thankfully he just wants to keep an eye on her for now. Meanwhile, he pointed out that if I train an army, they'll be loyal to me. That thought scares me even more. I know he's not planning a coup; he just wants to have options if we get to a point that Olivia has to be brought under control. I get that, but thinking ahead to who the army will follow seems uncomfortably devious.

I'm so torn, and all I really want is peace between them. But if I have to choose, I'll choose Aiden. I'd do anything for him. I just wish he felt the same way. He says he does, but it seems that every time he comes home to find me freshly showered and waiting to talk about our relationship, he has something more global on his mind. I'm starting to wonder if it's deliberate. Maybe there is no good time to bring up BDSM with him again, and *if that's the case, suddenly any time is a good time, right?*

I'll let it slide tonight, but this is the last time.

Day 45

The day of the mission to the solar farm had come, and Dani woke early, nervous and upset. She didn't want Jax to go, and it wasn't because she was worried about him cheating on her this time. There were not going to be too many options as far as that was concerned since Liana was the only woman going. Though the women of the Deadfall were just as capable as the men when it came to defense, this trip was mostly about lifting and carrying. They were going to disassemble and move an entire solar farm, and though the individual panels were not particularly heavy, there were a lot of them. And based on their surveillance of the farm, there were also a lot of corpses "guarding" them.

The plan was to go in and take the dead out without firing a shot so they didn't attract others, and they expected it to be fairly easy, which did not explain the feeling of impending dread that overwhelmed Dani. She tried once more to convince Liana to leave Jax behind, but all it did was succeed in making her feel like an asshole.

"If you're so afraid that something bad is going to happen, don't you think it's fucked up to try to get your man out of the mission without worrying about the twenty other people involved?" Liana demanded, shutting Dani up in one, well-crafted sentence. She was right, and when called out for it, Dani was unable to rationalize her selfishness. She just couldn't help it. She finally had someone who loved her, and she was terrified of losing him.

She went to talk to Olivia instead. Olivia always made her feel better because Olivia tended to give her a free pass. Dani was the beauty queen, and Olivia never really expected her to break a nail even though Olivia herself would get down and dig in the dirt with a freshly painted French manicure...if they still had such things. Now all they had were press-ons, and Dani had taken all of the kits from the Right Way truck as her personal inventory. Today she was wearing rhinestone tips, which she was biting at as she tried to convince Olivia to help her keep Jax home.

196

"Would you stop worrying?" Olivia urged her as she sat in the lodge with a group that was sharpening the blades and loading the guns for the mission.

"I can't help myself," Dani lamented. "Every time he goes out there, it kills me just a little."

"Well, this should make you happy," Olivia said as she picked up a pair of headphones with Rena's comm system wired to them. She had used a variation on the cell phone system inside the compound. Each member had a headset and a wristwatch, and the entire team could communicate on an open channel or individually.

It wasn't a perfect system. It had a range of less than five hundred feet and required a Wi-Fi router hooked to batteries, but Rena was still pretty proud of her accomplishment. She had barely slept since she came up with the idea, working day and night and cannibalizing parts of various electronics until she had managed to get a set ready for each member of today's mission. This morning, once she gave everyone a tutorial and made sure they were working properly, she was going to crash.

"So, you see," Olivia said to Dani," Jax is going to be in constant communication with the entire team. They'll all have each others' backs. He'll be fine."

"And besides," June added as she sat down at the table to help. "He can't be killed. You sold your soul for that one."

Olivia gave her a dirty look and sucked in a breath to speak, but June beat her to the punch.

"I know. Shut the fuck up, June," she said as she rolled her eyes, but what really surprised her friends was the fact that she didn't censor the curse word.

"Are you okay?" Dani asked.

"I'm better than okay," June said. "I've made some decisions. I think I'm going to try things your way for a while."

"What does that mean?" Olivia asked.

"I think she might be looking for a boyfriend," Dani suggested.

"Not a boyfriend," June said. "Just a... What's it called? A friend with benefits?"

"I'm sorry, what?" Olivia was having trouble processing it. She had not been privy to June's sessions with Dani since the intervention, so this seemed surreal to her, and she was waiting for the punch line.

"You heard me right. I've spent too much of my life not knowing what it was like to enjoy anything, so I'm going to try to...you know...have an orgasm with somebody."

"So you're just looking for a guy who will come in and get you off with no strings?" Olivia asked skeptically.

"No strings," June said, "but I want someone experienced who can teach me things."

Then she noticed Ravi staring at her from the next table. As their eyes met, a smirk spread across his face, and she was almost certain he had overhead the conversation.

"What's the matter?" Dani asked.

"I think that nosy perv was listening," she said, indicating Ravi with a nod of her head.

"Have you ever seen him without a shirt?" Olivia whispered. "He has a really nice body."

"Fuck, yeah, he does. I saw him take it off when he was working on the wall one day," Dani added. "Maybe you should hit that, June."

She gave him a quick glance, trying to envision what lay beneath his clothes, but although she had to admit that there was something sexy about Ravi, she wasn't in any position to live out a Mrs. Robinson fantasy. And besides, she had other plans.

"He's not exactly what I had in mind," she said, but what she meant was Ravi wasn't exactly *who* she had in mind. She already knew who she wanted that no strings orgasm to happen with, and if events continued on their current trajectory, she felt like she stood a reasonably good chance at getting her way.

Still, she stole a peek at Ravi's ass as he walked out of the lodge carrying a load of rifles for today's mission, and just feeling free to think in those terms gave her an unexpected rush of excitement.

Lined up along the road between the lodge and the front gate, the caravan made up of several flatbed trucks and electric cars was ready to go. Liana, Aiden, Alek, and Jax were driving solo, leaving space in their cars for potential new members or to carry existing members back home in case they were to lose a vehicle. Liana and Olivia tried to prepare for every possibility, and between the two of them, they felt like they had done well. The cars and the cabs of the trucks were like fortresses on wheels with weapons systems and protective armor, and they had plenty of extra fire power.

Liana's car was in the lead with the others bringing up the rear, and Jax's was second to the last with Alek behind him. As Dani stood by the trunk, holding him possessively while she kissed him goodbye, Alek looked on, wrestling with his frustration. He knew Olivia wanted to be there with him doing the same, but he also knew that she couldn't. She hadn't even kissed him in private yet, so there was no way she was going to do it with the entire community gathered in the yard. But the sentiment was there.

She looked up at him with worry in her eyes as she kept a reasonable distance and whispered, "Come home to me."

Give me something to come home to, he sniped at her inside his head. It was getting really hard to be the good guy, but he forced a smile and promised to see her again soon. Then with a quick, platonic hug, she hurried away as he got in the driver's seat.

The gates opened, and though the caravan started to move, Alek was stuck waiting for Dani and Jax to let go of each other.

"Come on, motherfucker!" Alek yelled out his window as he tapped the horn. "Let's go!"

Jax flashed his sexy grin, the women on the porch swooned, then he flipped Alek off as he pulled away from Dani and swaggered to the car door. As she walked backward toward the lodge, he rolled down the passenger side window and blew her a kiss, winking at the other women and making them giggle, and Alek entered his number into the cellular watch on his wrist, Jax put on his headphones and answered.

"Why does the beginning of every mission with you feel like a scene out of *Bye, Bye Birdie*?" Alek complained.

"I don't know what the fuck that is, but I'm sure you're a dick for saying it," Jax fired back.

"Uh-huh, we're going to be fifteen minutes behind the rest of the group, but *I'm* the dick," Alek said, and they both laughed.

They might not have been fifteen minutes behind, but the caravan had already turned left onto the main road and disappeared from sight by the time Jax's car reached the lower gate. Alek hit the remote in his car to close it behind them, and they pulled out onto the blacktop, hitting the "gas" hard in the two, compact cars that had been modified to plow through zombies and painted to blend in with the fall scenery around them. The painting was one of Rey's jobs. He used to tag underpasses and interstate bridges, and now he was using his artistic talents to contribute rather than deface. He was good too. Once Jax's car picked up speed and got a few hundred feet ahead of Alek in the curves on Route 20, it was hard to spot through the naked trees lining both sides of the road.

"What's the matter, old man? Can't keep up?" Jax taunted on the comm system, and he responded by pressing the peddle to the floor.

"You're older than I am, bitch," Alek balked as he caught up to him. Then he honked his horn. "Is that as fast as you can go, grandpa?"

"Not even close," Jax said as he slammed his foot down. The car bolted forward with Alek right on his heels, and they were moving so fast now, they could finally see the caravan ahead. Then Alek's car started pulling hard to one side, and he couldn't control it. He slammed on the brakes and skidded off the road.

"What's the matter, man?" Jax asked as he looked back.

"I think I got a flat."

"Hold on. I'll turn around and help you."

"Nah, don't worry about me," Alek said. "I'll change it and catch up to you guys. I know where I'm going."

"You sure?" Jax asked, uncomfortable leaving him alone, but they weren't so far from the Deadfall that Alek couldn't make it back if something went wrong.

"Yeah. They don't need to take on that herd at the farm two men short," he said as he got out of the car and looked at the tire. It was completely flat.

"I'll let the general know you're running late. Hope she doesn't court marshal you," Jax joked, and Alek laughed, signing off and removing his headset as he knelt down to look more closely at the tire to see what caused it. There was a broken piece of aluminum sticking out of it, but he didn't realize that it looked like the shaft of an arrow until he went to the trunk to pull out the spare and another one just like it whizzed by his head. He quickly ducked, pulling his gun out of the holster and moving toward the other side of the car.

But he wasn't quick enough.

Two more arrows came at him, one missing him entirely, the other striking him in the head. He felt it piercing through his skin as it knocked him over the edge of the hill where his car was parked. Everything went black as his body rolled downward, scraping over rocks and stumps and crashing into trees, careening toward the bottom until he landed in a cold, narrow creek, his blood mingling with the fresh, clean water.

At the top of the hill, three men looked down on him, one whose crossbow was still aimed at Alek as he lay immobile in the water.

"He's fucking dead, you moron," the leader said. "Don't waste another arrow." He punched the younger, smaller man in his arm, and he lowered his weapon.

"Jesus, Monroe," he said, rubbing his arm.

"Quit your whining and get the tire changed, Davey boy, or I'll give you another one. Oz, you grab the jack," he ordered as he looked around on the ground. "Did you see where he dropped his gun?"

"Yeah," Oz said, looking over the hill and trying to avoid seeing Alek's body as he stood at the trunk unscrewing the nut that held the jack in place. "It's about half way down that hill."

"Fuck a duck," Monroe said.

"It don't make no difference," Dave said. "Look at the fire power in the backseat."

"Well, happy fucking birthday to me!" Monroe shouted as he opened the passenger side door and pulled out Alek's guns. There were two hand guns with silencers, an AR-15, and five boxes of bullets. These weapons were higher caliber than the guns they had in their backpacks, guns they didn't use on Alek because they didn't want to be heard.

While the other two changed the tire, Monroe made sure they were all loaded, then he slung the AR over his shoulder and filled his pockets with bullets. He pulled a blanket out of the emergency kit in the trunk, leaving it open, and when the car was ready, he gave a gun and bullets to each of his companions.

"You lay down under this blanket in the backseat," he said to Dave, then he tapped the trunk.

"I don't want to get in the trunk," Oz protested, but Monroe gave him a stern look that he dared not disobey. Oz, who was only fifteen, was terrified of him, and he wasn't even the worst guy back at camp.

Monroe closed the trunk on the boy and got in the driver's seat, turning the car around and driving it back where it came from. They'd been watching the compound for more than twenty-four hours, and though Monroe hadn't intended to invest so much time, this wasn't just some group camping in the woods with a makeshift fence protecting them. These people had a nearly-complete ten-foot, stone wall, but unfortunately for them, there was something inside the men really, really wanted.

He used the remote controls in Alek's car to get through the gates, and when they came to the last one, he was counting on the tinted windows to keep the guards from questioning him. It didn't work, and one of them walked up to the vehicle, tapping on the window.

"Well, fuck me running," Monroe muttered, then he turned to Dave in the back seat. "Gimme the handgun - the one with the silencer."

Dave slipped the gun out from under the blanket, and Monroe rolled down the window and grabbed the guard by her collar, shoving it in her face. To the other guard inside, it just looked like she was leaning into the car.

"Tell your friend to open the gate," he commanded, and when she shook her head to refuse, he punched her in the nose with the gun. "You know, it would be a real shame to waste a prime piece of pussy like you, but don't think I won't do it, bitch!"

She didn't move, but behind her back, she waved to the other guard for help. He stepped outside and approached the car, and as soon as Monroe noticed him out of the corner of his eye, he pulled down hard on the girl's shirt collar and shot the old man over her shoulder.

With barely a sound, he fell, but the bullet had struck him in the heart. Now they needed to get him in the head before he came back.

"Dave," Monroe shouted. "Get out and put this bitch in the trunk for me."

As Dave followed orders, letting Oz out and forcing the woman in, Monroe put a bullet in the old guard's brain before going inside the station and opening the gate. The three men got back in the car and drove up the hill toward the lodge where everyone who hadn't gone on today's mission was gathering for lunch.

Savannah and Bella were in Olivia's panic room watching the security cameras, and when the monitor toggled back to the front gate, they saw that it was open with one guard dead on the ground. They immediately went running down the hall to warn the others, calling Olivia on the comm system, but before they reached the lodge, they heard a hail of gunfire.

Monroe, Dave, and Oz had jumped out of the car, grabbed the first woman they saw, and fired into the air to draw everyone's attention. Olivia, Dani, and the other women and men who had stayed behind rushed outside to find June being held with a gun to her head.

"Ladies and Gentlemen!" Monroe shouted with a terrifyingly gleeful tone as the community continued to gather on the porch. "Don't do anything stupid, and you won't get hurt. My associates and I have just come to take a few things we need, then we'll leave in peace and nobody else has to die."

"What do you want?" Olivia demanded, moving to the front of the crowd as if to protect them all. She was armed, but she was afraid to use her gun. If she missed, June would die, and even if she hit the man holding her, the other two would probably open fire.

"We're just a few lonely bachelors looking for companionship, ma'am," Monroe said. "Send us on our way with a few ladies to keep us warm at night, and we'll go peacefully."

"That's not going to happen," Olivia said.

"Maybe I didn't make myself clear? This is not a negotiation, darlin'. We've come for women, and we're not leaving without them. We don't necessarily want this one," he said, indicating June, "so I got no problem putting her down to prove my point to you." Then he turned to his friends. "Which ones do you want, boys? As for me, I think I'll take the little chickie over there." He pointed to Penny, who was standing off to the side, trying to slip away.

"Mmmm-mmm-mmm. She sure is a pretty one," Dave said as he looked her over. "What about you, Ozzie boy?"

"I kinda like the black one," he said, looking at Dani with a bashful, country-boy grin that chilled her to the bone.

"You sure she ain't more woman than you can handle?" Monroe asked, glaring at Oz with eyes that said something entirely different, something no one else could read, but Oz understood. It made him nervous.

"Hey, man, I don't judge you," Oz said, making a ghoulish joke of it because Penny was actually older than Monroe's preference, but as she stood there frightened out of her wits with no makeup on, Monroe mistook her for younger than her eighteen years. As he glared at Oz, Dave butted in to diffuse the situation.

"It don't matter if he likes the dark meat just so long as he keeps his hands off the pretty, little piece I came here for," he said, then he turned his attention to the porch. "Kylie Vincent, come on down!" He shouted the name of John's young daughter like a game show host, and when she gasped, he zeroed in on her. "There's my girl."

"She's a hottie," Monroe said with a wink, and Olivia could stand no more.

"She's a fifteen-year-old child!" she shouted sternly.

"In case you didn't notice, the old rules don't apply no more," Monroe said. "I make the rules now, and I say if she's got titties, she's ripe for the pickin'."

"Take me," Olivia offered suddenly.

"Take you? What are you? Thirty? The kid over there might be into washed up, old hags, but there's too much nubile, virgin pussy up in here for me to waste my time with you," Monroe said, and though the very thought of her next move made her sick, Olivia was committed to doing whatever it took to save the girls.

"I may be a little older," she said as she began to slowly saunter toward the three men, "but I can't get pregnant. I don't bleed, so I'm never out of commission, and I know things these little girls haven't had time to learn. Of course, if you're just looking for something tight and wet to stick your dick in, I guess I mistook you for men when you're really just little boys."

"Nice try, bitch, but experience is not necessary for the job we got in mind," Dave said, and he laughed a creepy laugh. Monroe joined in, and when Dave elbowed Oz, the boy laughed too until Monroe brought it to an abrupt end.

"Now I've had about enough of this shit!" he shouted, pressing the barrel of his gun against June's face so hard it seemed to disappear into her jaw as she trembled with tears rolling down her cheeks. "Oz, get those three little whores in the fucking car so we can get out of here. I wanna be back at the camp by nightfall seeing if that little redhead's carpet matches the drapes." He gave Penny a look that made her flesh crawl, and when Oz walked over to her and grabbed her arm, she fell to the ground and started begging.

It was killing Olivia to watch it, but she had no idea what to do next. She thought about just letting them go. If she did, she could immediately get in her vehicle and pursue them. If she made a stand now, they could lose a lot more than just three members of their community, not counting the guard she didn't know was in the trunk, and she felt so helpless as she watched Oz try to pull Penny to her feet.

"Don't!" Olivia cried out, desperate. "Please! Let me show you! Just you. Come inside with me, and I'll prove to you that you want to take me and leave these girls behind."

"You seem to want me awful bad, Momma," Monroe said. "Is one of these *your* little girl?"

"They're all my little girls," she said.

"Well, I'll tell you what I'm gonna do then. I'm still gonna take them, but I'll take you, too, so you can keep right on mothering them. How's that sound?"

Olivia nodded, thinking she could somehow get them out of this if she went along, but before another word was spoken, a bullet hit Monroe's head, tearing straight through and blowing a hole out the other side before it finally lodged itself in Dave's cheek. Monroe fell dead, releasing June, who was soaked in blood and brain matter but otherwise unharmed as Dave clutched the side of his face with his right hand and began to fire his gun with his left. A quick burst of bullets sprayed into the air as Alek rushed out from behind the car and took aim, but when the fatal bullet was planted between Dave's eyes, it was not Alek's gun that fired it. It was Oz, who immediately dropped his weapon just before Alek tackled him, shoving his face into the ground.

"Oh, my God! Alek!" Olivia cried excitedly as June ran to Dani and collapsed in her arms. Alek pulled zip ties out of one of the many pockets on his fatigue pants and bound Oz's hands behind his back, then he stood up, six feet and three inches of absolute perfection, and locked Olivia in his sights. Immediately, he dropped his gun and stalked toward her, his muscles outlined by his shirt, his blonde hair only slightly marred by patches of dried blood on the sides, and his eyes brilliant blue as they peered into hers.

"He can't take you; you're mine," he growled as he cupped her face in his hands, and when their lips finally met, it took her breath away. They melded together as everything else in the world faded to nothingness, lost in the ecstasy of a connection they'd waited far too long to make, and in that moment, Alek felt weaker and more powerful than he'd ever felt in his life.

"You're mine, Olivia," he repeated with hooded eyes as he ended the kiss, and she nodded, softly breathing the word yes as a shy smile spread across her face.

She was his.

There would be no more denying it.

Olivia stood captivated after Alek released her, watching his every move with worshipful eyes as he turned back to Oz. He bent over, grabbing the boy by his arm and pulling him to his feet, and when Oz looked up and recognized Alek, he jumped backward, pure terror in his eyes.

"You're dead, man!" he cried. "I saw you! That arrow went clean through your head!"

"It just grazed me," Alek said dismissively.

"No, sir, it did not," Oz argued. He had the same local accent as his dead companions, but there was something different about the way he carried himself, particularly now that he was alone. "I was right there watching when Dave shot you, mister. I saw it go through your head!"

"Look, kid, I don't know what you think you saw, but clearly, I'm alive with no hole in my head," Alek said. "However...if you don't drop this shit and start answering some questions, I'm going to put a hole in yours."

"I killed Dave, man! I'm on your side," he insisted, falling to his knees before Alek. "Please, Mister. I didn't want to be here. I didn't want to try to hurt your wife or your daughter or anyone."

"My *wife*," Alek said, winking at Olivia, "is actually the leader of this community, and I have no doubt that if I hadn't come along, she would have found a way to kill you and your friends. But thanks to the bad aim of an incompetent murderer, I'm here. So this is what's going to happen, kid. I'm going to lock you up and discuss your fate with our leader, and you just better hope she's in a forgiving mood."

He recruited a pair of armed women to escort Oz to the holding cell and guard him, and as they led him away, Savannah and Bella were standing on the side of the porch, staring at him.

"Austin?" Savannah called out suddenly, and the boy hung his head in shame. "What the fuck, Austin? How could you do this?" Sally joined them, and the three girls continued shouting at him as he was forced around the outside of the lodge and past the greenhouse.

Austin was in the 9th grade with them. He had actually been a popular boy that Savannah had a crush on in middle school, but they hadn't recognized him when he came up with the other guys. His blonde hair was so dirty, it looked brown, and he had grown a patchy beard and mustache. Even his voice was different, though it could have dropped earlier in the school year, and the girls wouldn't have realized since they barely saw him unless it was on the football field. They were in the honors classes, and Austin wasn't. Still, they would never have guessed he'd become the kind of guy who would kidnap them just six weeks into the apocalypse, and they were not having it. They had a serious talk about it then went looking for Olivia, finding her in her office with Alek.

"Kill his ass, Mom!" Savannah demanded as she stormed in flanked by Sally and Bella.

"Excuse me?" Olivia asked.

"That boy? It's Austin Strayer. We went to school with him, and we may not have recognized him, but he sure as hell knew who Kylie was when that other guy picked her to be taken!"

"No shit!" Bella added. "Kylie was on the JV cheer team with us. He knew who we all were!"

"He wouldn't even make eye contact with me!" Savvy complained.

"Okay..." Olivia began, but Savannah cut her off.

"Okay, you'll kill him?"

"No. Okay, I'll take that under advisement, and don't you girls go doing anything crazy in the meantime, you hear me?"

"Whatever," Savvy said, rolling her eyes, annoyed that her mother seemed to know that it had crossed her mind to do the same thing Jimbo had done to Jobe, though she didn't think she would bother with a crucifixion. Getting past the guards and shooting him in the head would be sufficient.

"Listen, girls, I know you're pissed off," Alek said. "I'm pissed off too. Those men thought they could just come in here and take you, but you're not a commodity, and as long as I live, I will never let this world turn you into one. That being said, I want to know more about where those men came from, and if we kill Austin, we may not find out until the next group of them try to break in here, so we can't kill him yet no matter what we decide. Okay?"

"Yes, sir," she said grudgingly because she hated that he was right. If there was a chance that more men like Monroe and Dave could come to their compound, perhaps she shouldn't kill Austin...yet.

"Thank you," Alek said.

"Why do you have to be so fucking smart?" she sighed, a pout on her lips.

"Language!" Olivia snapped.

"Yeah, right," Savvy said with a deep laugh, and Olivia laughed too. Every once in a while she called Savannah out for cursing, but the truth was that she never really thought it was a big deal. Without someone to be offended by them, they were just words, and there weren't a whole lot of people out there to offend these days.

"Alright, ladies," Olivia said. "Why don't you a go find something fun to do to take you mind off it? Alek and I need to talk."

"Yes, ma'am," Savannah said, and her friends echoed her as they left the room. Olivia sighed and shook her head.

"Well, it seems my daughter is a sociopath," she said with an uncomfortable laugh as she went into the bathroom to grab the alcohol and some cotton balls.

"She's just adapting, Liv," he assured her. "And maybe she's right. If that boy is like those men he was with, there's no point in keeping him alive."

"But he's just a kid," she argued.

"A kid we may decide we have to try as an adult," Alek said as she began to dab the bloody area on the side of his head. He didn't even flinch, and as the blood was wiped away, she couldn't find a wound, only a faint scar.

"What the hell?" she wondered aloud, and when she checked the other side, she found the same. There wasn't a fresh scratch on him. "How did the blood get there?"

"I don't know," he said impatiently, taking the cotton ball from her hand and laying it down on the nightstand. "I didn't bring you in here to talk about that or Austin or the men he broke in with."

"What did you want to talk about?" she asked, biting her lip, hoping he was about to inform her that the claim he made earlier would extend into the bedroom, but she should have known better with Alek.

"I shouldn't have just grabbed you and kissed you like that," he said.

"What do you mean?"

"I should've asked. I should've given you a choice."

"You didn't do anything wrong, Alek," she insisted, walking closer to him as he leaned against her desk. "In fact, I think you should do it again."

"I'll kiss you again. I'll kiss you any time you'll let me, but that's as far as it's going."

"Are you saying you don't want to fuck me anymore?" she asked with a smirk as she realized what he was getting at.

"You know I want to fuck you, baby, but just because I kissed you doesn't mean that I expect you to start putting out."

"Alek," she sighed. "I've wanted you to kiss me since the moment we met. You know that, and you know why I'm holding back. What you did made it easy for me to let it happen, and that could possibly extend to other things..."

"What? You're June now? You expect me to just take you by force? That's not happening, Olivia."

"It's not the same."

"I deserve better," he said, standing up and looking down into her eyes as he towered over her. He gently grasped her shoulders. "If you want me to make love to you, you're going to ask me to do it. I will not take it from you, and if that means I have to wait for a fucking year, I'll wait for a fucking year." Then he smiled. "But let's be honest. I won't have to wait much longer."

He pulled her inside, leaning in as if he was about to kiss her, but he moved his head at the last second and went for her neck instead, her breath hitching as she felt his teeth nip at her, sending a shockwave down her body that set off a flood between her thighs. Her nipples tightened into hard dots that he could feel against his pecks through the layers of their clothing, her chest heaved, and she moaned involuntarily, quickly sucking the sound back into her mouth as Alek swirled his tongue in a tight circle that she yearned to feel elsewhere. When he pulled away, she could sense the satisfied grin on his lips before she saw it, and she was embarrassed, blushing as she stared at the floor, unable to make eye contact.

"It won't be long at all," he breathed, then he turned and walked out the door to check on their prisoner, leaving her overwhelmed and contemplating touching herself for the first time in as long as she could remember. It was something she seldom ever did, but now that Alek had turned up the heat, she needed something to help her continue to resist. At the moment, she was too busy wrestling with her conscience over her lust for him, and that level of guilt was manageable. But if they made love, the guilt could consume her.

"What are you girls doing here?" Alek asked as he found Savannah, Sally, Bella, and Kylie gathered near the shed they were using as a holding cell. The women standing guard had been keeping a close eye on them, afraid of what they had in mind as they whispered and watched the door.

"I want to talk to that asshole!" Savannah said. "Everybody at school knows I live here, and I want to know why he thought it would be okay to bring those old men up here shopping for child brides!"

"I want to know the same thing," Alek said, "but if you go in there yelling at him, it's not going to do anyone any good."

"It might make me feel better," she said, and when he saw the tears gathering in her eyes, he realized there had to be more to it. He held out his arms to offer her a hug, and she fell straight into them.

"What's really going on, Savvy?" he asked as she cried against his chest.

"He was like you. He was a good guy, and look what happened to him. Look what he turned into so fast. I don't want to live in a world like that. It's not fair."

"I know, sweetheart," he said, stroking her hair. "But not everyone has lost their humanity. We have a lot of good people in this community. We're going to have to deal with some assholes out there, but we're going to keep growing, and we'll get this world back on track."

"You promise?" she asked, looking up into his eyes

"I promise," he assured her, and she smiled a sad smile. He reminded her of her dad, kind and thoughtful, not authoritarian at all. "Let me talk to him, okay? Let me get to the bottom of this, and I swear to you that he will be held accountable for whatever he's done."

"Okay," she acquiesced, and Alek wiped a tear from her eye and gave her a smile before sending her and her friends away. He hoped that he'd done well at his first crack at being a father figure. Savannah was missing Reid as much as her mother was, and since life was more serious in this new world, if he was going to be Olivia's lover and help her run this place, then Reid's other responsibilities were his as well, including Savannah. He hoped she didn't see him as trying to replace her dad, but he did want to take care of Olivia's daughter as if she were his own. He was in love with Olivia, and keeping that secret was much harder on him than waiting for sex. He deserved to be able to say the words. He had just crawled up a mountain after being shot in the head with an arrow to save her, for fuck's sake.

And now it was time to deal with the last, living son-of-a-bitch responsible.

He went inside the shed and found Austin lying on the cot facing the wall, and when he cleared his throat and the kid turned over, a kid is exactly what he looked like. His eyes were red-rimmed and filled with tears, his cheeks were wet, and his mouth was twisted into a mask of tragedy.

"Are you going to kill me now?" he asked right off the bat.

"That depends, kid," Alek said.

"On what?" Austin's voice was thin and weak. He had been crying so hard, his nose was entirely closed off, and as he sniffled, trying to breathe through it, Alek handed him a box of tissues from a shelf on the wall.

"It depends on you being honest with me," he said.

"I'll tell you anything you want to know. I wasn't like those men. That's why I killed Dave. I'd been trying to find a way to kill them since we got on the road."

"Why were you with them?"

"I didn't have a choice," Austin said. "I didn't know what I was getting into when I joined them, but they don't let you leave because they don't want anybody knowing what they do."

"And what do they do?"

"They..." Austin began, his lip trembling as Alek watched him from his chair, trying to determine if the boy was being sincere or just trying to win his sympathy. "I can't. I just can't."

"Take your time," he said. "It's okay."

"No, man! It's not okay!" Austin shouted, looking up at Alek with wild eyes, his cheeks glistening in the dim light of the shed. "Look at me! I'm a fucking fifteen-year-old guy, and I can't get my dick up! It's not okay, and it's never going to be okay again!"

Taken aback, Alek was unsure of what to do as Austin broke down, sobbing hard, doubled over where he sat on the cot. Alek reached out to pat the boy on the shoulder, but he shrugged it off.

"Please don't," he begged without looking up. "I don't deserve it. I don't deserve to live. You should just take your gun out and kill me now."

Please, he thought. *Kill. Me. Now.*

The sun was about to set when the caravan from the solar farm returned to the compound, every vehicle heavy-laden with supplies. The flatbed semis carried the solar cells, and the cars carried food and medicine. They hadn't completed the mission without casualties, but because of the Kevlar Liana had collected, they were in much better shape when the farm turned out to be protected by more than just hungry corpses.

Dani rushed down the hill from her cabin when she received the signal that the gates were opening, and she watched as the last cars came through with no Jax. There were two vehicles missing. His and Liana's.

"Oh, God!" she cried as she rushed up to Aiden the second he stepped out of his car. "They're dead, aren't they? Jax is dead."

"No, no, Dani," he said. "They're fine. They stayed behind because there was a little more work to do. That's all."

As soon as she received confirmation that Jax was alive, she became suspicious that the one female who went on the mission was the only person who stayed behind with him, and when Aiden noticed the look in her eyes, he just shook his head and walked away, annoyed with her jealousy. He had just lost a friend at the solar farm, and Liana and Jax had promised to burn the body. They weren't going to betray him or Dani.

As everyone gathered in the lodge for dinner, Alek could see how worried she was. She claimed it was because Jax was still out there after dark, but he knew better. She needed a distraction, and he had one. He wanted her to meet with Austin because he had no idea what to do with him. Obviously, the kid had done something so horrible that he would rather die than face it, and Alek recognized that he was not equipped to be the one to help him.

But more important to him than helping a fifteen-year-old boy who was a party to attempting to abduct young women was learning more about the group he came from. Alek had become convinced that the men they killed today were not the only bad guys in that group, and if so, this compound would never be safe with them out there. He wanted to know who they were, what they were doing, and how many they numbered.

"Any information you can get out of him will help," he told Dani.

"I'll do what I can," she said, planning to take Austin a plate and talk to him after dinner. "Would he not tell you anything?"

"He was crying and begging me to shoot him, but he wouldn't say why," he explained, then he frowned and added, "There was one thing that might give you an angle. He said he couldn't get it up, and it seemed like he was implying that the people from his group are the reason for that."

"Or maybe he was confessing that he can't get it up unless he kidnaps and rapes," Savannah said with disgust as she sat down beside Alek. He had been speaking low because he didn't want to be overheard, but she had been paying close attention.

"You weren't supposed to hear that," he said.

"Well, I did, and it's just one more reason I think he needs to die."

"So does he," Alek said. "He asked me to kill him. Don't you think we need to know what's going on with his group if he came out of it with so much self-loathing?"

"I already admitted that you were right, goddamn it," she said grudgingly, making Dani giggle.

"Is there anything else you can tell me about him that might help?" she asked Savannah.

"Nothing useful," she said. "He was a freshman, captain of the JV football team, and by all accounts, he never used to have a problem getting it up."

"And you had a crush on him," Dani said.

"No," Savannah protested, but Dani had caught her, giving her an impatient glare. "Fine. Yes, but that was before I found out what a total slut he was. He had a different girlfriend every two weeks. Not my kind of guy."

"Your mother will be pleased," Alek said with a wink.

"Yeah, apparently celibacy runs in the family," she said, winking back as she picked up her plate to go sit with her friends, leaving Alek stunned.

"Don't let her get to you," Dani said. "If that's the worst thing she ever says to you, you're lucky." She laughed, drawing a smile out of Alek. "She misses her Dad, but she understands that what's going on between you and her mom is a symptom of the state of the world right now. She's actually coping with it a little too well if you ask me. Just treat her gently."

"I wouldn't dream of treating her any other way," he said, surprised at how well Dani was able to analyze everyone but herself, and like clockwork, her uncertainties came out.

"So, you really don't have any clue why Jax and Liana didn't come home with everybody else?"

"I don't know anything you don't know, but if they stayed behind, I guarantee you two things: There was a good reason for it, and Aiden would not have left them alone if he didn't feel it was safe. Okay?"

"You're probably right," she reluctantly admitted.

"Would you please tell Jax how you're feeling? I promise he'll understand."

"Would you? If your girlfriend was always thinking you were fucking someone else, would you understand or would you think she was just an insecure nutcase and dump her?"

"Well, if I was in love with her," he began, staring wistfully at Olivia as she stood talking to someone on the other side of the room. "I'd want to do whatever I could to make her feel confident that her faith in me was well-placed. Jax was a rock star, Dani. He knows you're going to feel insecure sometimes, but you need to understand that at some point you have to stop holding his past against him and give him the same trust you would any other man. Besides, Olivia has more cause to worry than you. Celibacy's starting to get real, fucking old." He laughed when he said it because he was teasing, but the joke would only be funny for so long.

"Make you a deal. I'll talk to Olivia if you'll talk to Jax," she offered just as June sat down with them. She was carrying a cup of tea, having already cleared her dinner dishes.

"I *have* talked to Jax," Alek said. "But if you want to know what he told me, you're going to have to ask him yourself. As for Olivia, my patience isn't quite spent...yet." He flashed his stunning smile and dipped his head as he stood to leave. "Goodnight, ladies."

"Goodnight," Dani said.

"Alek, wait!" June blurted out suddenly. "Can I talk to you for a minute? In private?"

"Sure," he said, then he led her out onto the front porch where no one was around. "What's up?"

"I just wanted to apologize to you. I've been meaning to do it for a long time. I've just been too embarrassed."

"It's okay, June. I understand."

"I hope so because I really am sorry. I didn't mean to mislead you, and I know how you must feel after what you did when you 'saved' me."

"Honestly, I'd been looking for an excuse to kick Jobe's ass anyway," he said with a wink. He was trying to help her feel better, but it was still true and had been since the 'trying on vaginas like hats' comment.

June giggled like a schoolgirl at his joke. She had spent the days since her husband's death thinking more and more about all the things she had missed out on because of the cult, and no one represented what she had been robbed of more perfectly than Alek.

"That makes me feel so much better," she said, looking up at him with doe eyes, and when they parted ways, she rushed back inside to find Dani.

"I need you to do me a favor," she said. "Would you talk to Olivia for me?"

"What about?" Dani asked, taking her last bite.

"I think I have an idea that could kill three birds with one stone," she said with a mischievous grin, and when Dani placed her napkin atop her plate, June pulled on her arm, urging her to go someplace private.

Dani's mind was a million miles away as June dragged her down the hallway, through the kitchen, and out into the greenhouse. Alek's words had been no more reassuring than the stories she had overheard in the lodge at dinner about what had happened at the solar farm.

If they had been so surprised by the militia they found there, what made them think there wouldn't be more surprises if they left Liana and Jax behind? What Dani didn't know yet was that they were certain, and she would understand when she heard the full story.

When the caravan arrived at the farm, they pulled onto a gravel road that ran behind the fence to the solar installation with the intention of taking out the dead through the chain links with swords, long knives, and other sharp, pointed weapons. They all lined up as soft music played through a directional speaker rigged to one of the trucks and aimed at the fence to draw the herd from inside without getting the attention of any that might be lingering nearby. Though they did have to take out a few strays here and there, Liana had planned for it, and their formation kept them from being ambushed by any corpses.

Estimates from the most recent surveillance mission had put the total number of dead within the fence at around fifty, but as more and more ambled toward their demise, it seemed that the count was off or something had happened in the past forty-eight hours that shored up their numbers. Liana was not concerned. They were making quick work of the corpses that had begun to pile up along the perimeter.

Then suddenly, they heard gunfire.

It came from inside the fence, and while several of the dead fell before their eyes, two members of their group were hit. John Vincent took a bullet in his upper left arm, and Neil, one of the few remaining Greyhawks, lay dead while everyone scattered, hiding behind the vehicles as they tried to figure out who was shooting at them.

Liana climbed onto one of the rigs, peeking through the window to survey their situation, and over the heads of the corpses left standing, she could see a small militia approaching - twelve men loaded down with Kevlar and weapons. She watched for a second, scanning the buildings inside the fence for snipers, and though these men appeared to be the only threat, they were fearless as they stalked toward the dead in a V formation. Then just as Liana raised her rifle, balancing it on the hood by the windshield to take aim at the man in the front, a bullet whizzed through the cab of the rig, shattering the window to her right. She fell backward, and Aiden caught her, leaving her with only a couple of superficial cuts on the side of her face.

"Oh, God!" she breathed, truly scared for the first time since they had gone through the toll booth the night the apocalypse began, but her military mind would never succumb again. She immediately began formulating a strategy. She drew her army to the spot where she was hunkered down behind the sturdiest truck and quickly laid out the plan, sending them left and right, high and low.

When everyone was in position, Aiden and Jax got in Liana's heavily armored car, and drove off toward the road they came in on to draw the attention of the shooters - Jax firing the semi automatic weapon Liana had rigged to shoot through a slot in the passenger window while Aiden drove in a serpentine pattern, and as part of the militia headed after them, another group of Liana's men used the cover of the tractor trailer to shoot down all of the corpses blocking them from their enemies. The remaining militia members, in body armor and helmets, felt invincible as they rushed the break in the herd along the fence, but that was just another distraction.

Crawling on their bellies, Liana joined her best snipers as they made their way to the end of the line of the dead, then they took aim at the unprotected legs of their attackers, mowing them down. The four men who had gone after Aiden and Jax came running back to meet the same fate, but while immobile, they were still heavily armed, most of them retaining the strength to continue the fight. That's when Aiden stopped the car, and having fallen completely off the militia's radar, he and Jax pulled the crown jewel of their arsenal out of the trunk, a wonderful surprise they'd found in a big, heavy box from Sylas Gun & Pawn that was labeled "random parts".

"God bless you, Randy, you crazy, fucking redneck," Aiden said as they set up the grenade launcher on the car's roof. Then Liana's voice came out of the loud speaker on the truck.

"You are surrounded," she said, interrupted by shots as the dead encroached upon the men they had been herded to protect. "You are crippled. Lay down your weapons, and we will let you live."

"Fuck you, bitch!" shouted the man who appeared to be the leader. He lifted his rifle, aiming at the speaker as Liana gave Jax the hand signal, and the first grenade deployed. The leader turned, trying to shoot it out of the air, but it landed, exploding right next to him and taking out four others.

The remaining men had their sights on the grenade launcher now, but they also had the dead to contend with. Jax and Aiden reloaded, and Liana gave the men another chance.

"You are surrounded," she repeated. "You are crippled. Lay down your weapons, and live."

"Okay! Okay!" one man yelled. He was young, he was terrified, and seconds later, he was dead as one of his own men put a bullet in his neck.

Liana gave the signal, and another group of three were obliterated.

"Last chance," she said, but the loud speaker was drown out by gunfire as the entire herd, including the one soldier they didn't have the sense to shoot in the head, converged upon the survivors.

"Well, that's that, then," she said, motioning for her team to gather. While Jax and Aiden locked up the grenade launcher, half of the group went through the gate and began taking out the rest of the zombies, but the other half had to stay out and deal with more than had been drawn by the sound of gunfire. Almost instantly, Jax and Aiden found themselves on the roof of the car having to use knives because they had left their guns in the cab.

"We're in the middle of goddamn nowhere. How are there so many of these bastards?" Jax complained, and then Aiden drew his attention to a barn up on a hill on the other side of the complex. There was someone peeking around the side of the structure as a few straggling corpses wandered out.

"Cover me," he said to Jax, and he took out his binoculars and saw a woman in chains with a thick collar around her neck. She was underdressed for the cold weather and cowering by the barn.

Aiden dropped his binoculars around his neck and picked up his knife, jumping down and quickly taking out the dead blocking the passenger side door. He reached in and grabbed their guns and some ammo, and as Jax followed, they fought their way past the corpses toward the barn, taking the long way to avoid the herd coming down the hill. Most of the dead were focused on the activity inside the fence, but Liana had already closed the gate. The corpses lined up along the perimeter as the group dispatched the ones on the inside, and Jax and Aiden caught up to the woman who released them.

"Please don't hurt me!" she cried as she fell to her knees, looking down as if afraid to make eye contact.

"We're not going to hurt you," Aiden said as Jax grabbed her arm and pulled her to her feet.

"Why did you do that? Why did you release the dead on us?" Jax demanded.

"I had no choice," she said, indicating the collar around her neck.

"What is that?" Jax asked.

"It looks like a shock collar," Aiden said. "For dogs."

"It is," she said. "Please let me go. Please don't make me say anymore. If he finds out I talked to you, he'll hurt me."

"No one's going to hurt you," Jax assured her. "Let's get this thing off you." He reached for the collar, and she jerked away.

"It will explode!" she cried.

"May I?" Aiden asked. "I won't take it off. I just want to look at it."

She let him, and though he realized pretty quickly what was going on, they were interrupted before he could say anything.

"Widow Six!" shouted an angry, male voice from a speaker attached to the woman's belt. "Widow Six! Where the fuck are you? Get your ass down to the gate and let the dead fucks take care of these assholes!"

"Who's that?" Jax asked.

"It's the boss. I have to go. He'll kill me!"

"Unless he's a sniper, he's not going to kill you," Aiden said. "There are no explosives attached to this collar."

"They're in the box," she insisted, pointing to a large, plastic cube on the back of it that had a small lock on the side.

"That's the battery pack that shocks you," he said. "I've seen plenty of these collars. Trust me." Jax looked at him curiously, wondering why he knew so much about shock collars, but Aiden just winked at him as if to say he was stretching the truth for the woman's sake.

"Are you sure?" Jax asked.

"I'm willing to cut it off myself," he said. "If there's a bomb in there, I'll lose my hands, so yeah, I'm sure."

"Do it," Jax said.

"Hold her steady," Aiden instructed.

"Widow Six!" the boss yelled through the speaker.

"Please be careful," Widow begged, and Jax put his arms around her from behind, holding her hands against her chest. He was so warm, and she was so cold. Then Aiden slipped his knife between her neck and the collar.

"Don't move," he warned her.

216

"Just relax," Jax whispered in her ear, and she leaned her head back on his shoulder and held her breath while Aiden removed the collar that had forced her to live like a slave for more than a month now.

"Done," Aiden said, and Widow let out a long exhale.

"Now do you want to tell us what's going on around here?" Jax asked.

"Widow Six!" the boss screamed.

"Who is he?" Aiden demanded.

"I don't know his name. Calls himself the Widowmaker, and he calls all us slaves Widows. He keeps our husbands tied up working in the drug rooms, and if we fuck up, he takes it out on us and them."

"How many people are inside that building?" Jax asked.

"Now that you killed the soldiers? Maybe twenty," she said, "but they're not dangerous. I mean, they will be because they think their collars are wired to kill them, but if you take out Widowmaker, none of the people down there will fight you."

"Can you get us inside?"

"Widow-Fucking-Six!!!" Widowmaker screeched on his end of the line.

"Yeah, but I have to answer him first or he'll send more of the slaves out here."

"Can all of the slaves hear him call you on that walkie?" Jax asked.

"No. Everyone of us has a different one."

"Well, that sucks," he said, then he paused for a moment, thinking of a new plan. "Okay. Tell the Widowmaker that his yelling drew the dead to you and you've been bitten. He'll send someone else up, right?"

"Yeah, but they'll probably be sent to kill me since the fake bomb couldn't."

"We'll protect you. Go ahead and tell him."

Widow pressed the button to speak, saying just what had been scripted for her, and the Widowmaker's response was swift and heartless.

"Rot in hell," he growled. Then her walkie talkie went dead, and she knew someone would be sent to kill her. Aiden dialed Liana to tell her what was going on, and since the group down the hill had already cleared the dead inside the fence, he asked her to get them to work on the dead on the outside instead of entering the building. Aiden didn't want Widowmaker to change his next move because at the moment, he was right where they wanted him.

"We're on it, babe," Liana said.

"Be safe, mon cœur."

"Y tu," she whispered, wishing she could say she loved him. She was just too scared to be the first, and the last thing she needed right now as they faced potential death was to have him hesitate. But he wouldn't have, not for a second.

A few minutes later, another woman in chains with a shock collar emerged from the barn, which contained an underground tunnel to the building on the solar farm. It wasn't a nice, well-lit, comfortable tunnel like those beneath Olivia's compound. It was cramped and dark, and the women had to crawl through it because its original purpose had been to allow the owners of the farm to escape in case of a drug raid. While Widowmaker may have been responsible for the meth lab, the grow rooms were preexisting.

When the woman Widowmaker sent to kill Widow Six stepped out into the daylight, it blinded her because she hadn't seen it in weeks, but as soon as her eyes focused, she came for her former comrade, who stood alone by the barn while Jax and Aiden hid around the side.

"I have to kill you," the new woman said, wielding a machete.

"No, you don't."

"If I don't bring him your head, he's going to activate my collar."

"You mean, this collar?" Widow Six asked, holding up what was left of hers. "There's no bomb. It's just a battery pack."

"Really?" she asked, her hand instinctively going straight for the box on the back of hers. Her designation was Widow Two, and she'd been a prisoner here since the first week of the apocalypse when Widowmaker and his friends killed the solar farm owners and took over. Her husband spent his life in the grow room tending the poppies and marijuana plants the original owners had started. Others worked in the meth lab, and all of the wives and girlfriends were forced to cook, clean, and service Widowmaker and the militia. The women used to be allowed to see their husbands for a few minutes each day, but it had been over a week since the last time. They had become convinced that some of the men were dead and that they were all being kept away so they wouldn't know which ones.

"I can cut off your collar," Six said to Two, "but first I need you to go back down there one more time."

"No! God, no!" she cried, ready to shed her collar and run for the hills.

"Please. Listen to me. Your husband is alive. I heard Widowmaker talking about him when he sent me up here," she lied. "You can't just run off and leave him. I need you to go open the gate like he asked you. Then go back downstairs and let everyone know that their collars can only shock them. You'll have three minutes, then I'm going to lead these two men down there to kill Widowmaker." Aiden and Jax stepped into view.

"Then we're free?" she asked.

"Then you're free," Jax said, and she immediately hurried toward the gate. There were dozens of dead in her path, but she had become proficient at dodging them because, like Widow Six, she was often sent out on the missions to collect them. She knew how they moved, how they "thought", and how to slip through their grasp because her life and her husband's life depended upon it.

She opened the gate to let the dead inside, and once she had returned to the barn and gone below, Widow Six led Aiden and Jax through the cramped, dank tunnel that exited into a basement room behind a bookshelf that swung open like a door.

"This is strange," Widow Six said as they emerged to silence. Widowmaker should have been shouting out orders, and the others should have been running around following them, but instead, everything was quiet. When she led them to the room where Widowmaker had been sitting in his command chair watching the video feed from the farm, it was clear why. Widow Two didn't want to wait for the men with the guns to take out her tormentor. She wanted to do it herself.

She had wrapped the chain he used to keep her tethered to the wall around his neck and strangled him, and when her shock collar wasn't enough to stop her, he used a taser on her, not realizing the chains would conduct the current into him as well. Now they were both corpses, bound together by metal links melted into the flesh of the short, stubby man who had controlled this place, and they were not alone. Down the hall a group of the dead feasted on one of the widows who was now too far gone to reanimate.

Aiden and Jax raised their rifles and mowed them all down.

"We only gave her a three minute head start," Widow Six said, shocked.

"I've seen it happen myself," Jax consoled her. "It spread through my tour bus so fast, I shouldn't even be alive."

"Oh, my God, you're Jax Bonham!" she cried.

"That was a different lifetime," he said dismissively. "Where are the rest of your people?"

"Down here," she said, motioning for them to follow her into the hallway, but as they checked room after room, they found only corpses. In the end, five men and two boys who had been locked up in the meth lab and the grow room had survived. Counting Widow Six, there were eight of them, and when her husband was not among them, she realized she had been right. He was already dead before this group even showed up.

Aiden called Liana to tell them they had taken the building, and outside, their group had finished off the dead. There was nothing to do now but break down and load the solar panels, and Liana asked Aiden to come up and oversee it while she joined Jax in the bowels of the drug operation. She knew Olivia would want every last drug in the place brought back to the Deadfall, but she also knew it had to be done secretly.

While Aiden salvaged the guns and tactical gear of the militia, Liana put the former slaves to work carrying up all of their food and water and loading it on the trucks, and once that was cleaned out, she turned all but Widow Six over to Aiden to help with the solar panels while she and Jax stayed below to "dispose of the drugs so they didn't fall into the wrong hands." That was a lie, and as soon as the caravan drove away with their haul, they began loading the two vehicles Aiden left for them. They harvested all of the pot they could and loaded up nearly everything else - the lights, the meth, a large stash of pills and IV narcotics, as well as a small crop of poppies and their yield.

"Widow Six," Liana called out to her as they stuffed the pot plants they couldn't transport into a massive incinerator the original owners had installed in case they needed to destroy evidence in a hurry.

"Just Widow now," she said, looking up from her work. "The others are all dead."

"Wouldn't you rather we use your real name?" Jax asked.

"Nothing matters anymore," she whispered sadly.

"I'm so sorry," he said, putting his hand on her shoulder, feeling partly responsible for the loss of her friends.

"None of this was your fault, any of you," she said. "It was the motherfuckers who made slaves of us in the first place."

"Widowmaker?" Liana asked.

"No. He just ran this place. My husband and I were brought here by the same group of assholes that comes every week to take the drugs we scavenge and produce. They bring us food, water, and more slaves."

"When are they due back?"

"Couple of days, I think. Why? You gonna kill them too?" Widow asked.

"If we have to, but for now, I just don't want to run into them on our way out of here," she said.

"You won't. Their base is pretty far away. We were in the trunk of a car for hours when they brought us here," she explained, and when the thought of her lost husband hit her like an ice pick to the heart, she forced his image out of her mind and changed the subject. "So, what are you guys going to do with all these drugs?"

"I don't know. Maybe we can use them to barter or something."

"We're going to smoke the weed," Jax said with a wink.

"Yeah, we'll probably smoke the weed," Liana agreed, laughing, but she didn't mean herself. She was too much of a control freak to let go like that. Still, it wouldn't be bad for a lot of the people at the compound to be able to take the edge off once in a while.

Before they left for home, Liana and Jax collected the bodies of Neil, the Greyhawk player who had fallen, and Widow's friends. As they solemnly placed each of them in the incinerator one at a time, Liana began to tell Widow what she was walking into back at the compound. The new people who left with the caravan earlier would be blindfolded for the trip so they would have the option to leave if they didn't like it, but Widow already knew too much because she had helped with the drugs.

"I'm afraid it's a one way ticket," Liana said, "but I promise you won't ever want to leave."

"If I could just find a place where no one beats or rapes me, it'll be paradise," she said.

"No one will ever hurt you there," Jax assured her.

"Unless you have trouble keeping secrets," Liana added to impress upon Widow how serious it would be taken if she told anyone anything about the treasure they were bringing back. "If you can't keep your mouth shut about these drugs, our..." she paused, not sure what word to use to describe Olivia. Leader seemed too innocuous after these people had served the Widowmaker, and so did every other modern word she could think of - mayor...governor...president. She realized there was only one word that fit, even though it pained her to use it.

"...our queen," she said finally, "Oblivia, the Bloody Queen, will have you killed for treason." Her words were serious, but then she softened because if she painted Olivia as a crazy tyrant, the whole story would fall apart once she met her. "Don't get me wrong. She's kind and fair, and she comes off like a fucking angel. She'll keep you safe, sheltered, and fed. But if you cross her or put her subjects in danger, you'll find out that she's actually depraved and merciless." As she spoke, Jax knew words like depraved and queen did not describe Olivia at all, but he also knew that based on the group they encountered today, Olivia had to be a ruthless dictator, even if it was just hype.

"It's true," he added. "And the queen won't just shoot you, either. She'll crucify you...slowly."

Widow's eyes grew wide. Death didn't scare her, but death by crucifixion was a different thing entirely. Later, as they made their way back to the compound, she saw the cross Jobe once hung upon still erected by the main road, the ground beneath still stained in blood, and she looked over at Jax from the passenger seat, feeling like she had jumped out of the frying pan and into the fire.

"Welcome to the Deadfall, m'lady," he said as he stopped the car, waiting for Liana to open the lower gate.

"The Deadfall?" she asked.

"It's where the living rise, and the dead fall," he said, and Widow swallowed hard, visions of the beautiful and terrifying angel Liana said ruled this place swirling around in her head as she stared at the cross in fear and awe. And it was in that moment that the legend of Bloody Queen Oblivia was truly born.

Dani was sitting on the porch of the lodge waiting when Jax finally drove up the gravel path from the inner gate, and she nearly tripped over her own feet chasing after his vehicle as Liana led him around the lodge toward the backdoor that went directly to Olivia's private residence. They had waited until after dark to return, and they planned to leave the cars locked with blankets over their contents until most of the compound's residents were sleeping. But even though Liana had ten pounds of weed in her passenger seat, the only thing that caught Dani's attention was the woman in Jax's.

"Who's that?" she demanded immediately before even hugging him.

"Are you Queen Oblivia?" Widow asked, and with his back to her, Jax quickly held one finger to his lips to silence Dani.

"This," he said, grabbing her and pulling her tight against him, "is *my* queen." And suddenly she cared much less about Widow than before.

Aiden had been waiting for Liana as well, and he walked straight for her. He stared at her beautiful face, expecting to see it marred by scratches from the glass window that broke beside her, but there were none. She was perfect, and he pulled her to him, giving her a long, intense kiss.

"Never make me leave you behind again," he breathed, and they heard Widow's wistful sigh from where she stood beside Jax's car. It made Liana feel guilty.

"She just found out that her husband is dead," she explained to Aiden.

"We'll finish this in private," he said with a glare that promised a night of sheet-gripping passion , then he left her to take Widow to join the other new members in the guarded hunting cabin not far from the back gate.

Once inside, Widow learned that she was the only one who had been told anything about their new captors beyond the fact that they would be safe and fed here, and while she shared what she knew of Bloody Queen Oblivia, Liana went straight to the queen herself to let her know what she had become.

Olivia was in her office with Alek, and she was not happy about the news.

"You have got to be fucking kidding me!" she hissed, not sure if she was more offended by the name Oblivia, the ghoulish prefix, or the fact that despite her wishes, she had been named queen.

"Queen Olivia doesn't sound very threatening, now does it?" Liana countered.

"Oh, but Queen Oblivious. That'll get your knees knocking," Olivia scoffed with a roll of her eyes.

"Not oblivious - oblivion. Like if you piss her off, that's the end of you," Liana explained.

"She has a point," Alek said.

"Really? So, when she goes out there and names you King Hell Storm, you're going to be okay with it?"

"Oh, I like that," Liana said.

"Don't even think about it," Alek said sternly.

"Then help me convince Oblivia to be queen."

"Trust me. I'm on your side here," he said, and Olivia looked at him impatiently. "Seriously, Liv. Liana's group just took down a drug ring headed by a guy called the Widowmaker. We need to sound a little more bad-assed than our boring reality."

"Exactly! Widowmaker was defeated by the armies of the queen of the Deadfall. Who? Bloody Queen Oblivia, that's who. The bitch is crazy! She'll crucify you," Liana prattled, pleased at least by the fact that even though she wasn't the queen, she was the one who created the queen, but Olivia just slumped down in her chair shaking her head. "Now, all we need is a sigil and a little mythology."

"Oh, God! Just kill me now," Olivia groaned.

At dinner that night, the new members were served inside their temporary, communal home. They were all placed together in one of two hunting cabins in the middle ring just up the mountain from the back gate. Rena had bugged both of these units so they could use them when integrating new people to make sure they could trust them before bringing them into the fold, and since those rescued from the solar farm had been blindfolded on the way in with the exception of Widow, there was always the option of dropping them off somewhere far away if they didn't work out.

While they had their evening meal under guard, the rest of the community was in the lodge where General Navarro introduced the people of the Deadfall to their queen, and to Olivia's chagrin, everyone seemed to like the idea much more than she did as they all recognized that they needed to command fear in this dangerous, new world. The mythology began to take on a life of its own, and the lodge became a mead hall as they began to share tall tales of their bloody queen.

Ten of the cruelest men ruled the Deadfall until she killed them all singlehandedly to take the throne.

She wore a cloak stained red with the blood of enemies and traitors of the Deadfall.

She walked among the dead like a ghost, and their sickness could not touch her.

She rode into battle on the back of a great, black panther named Evil who tore out the throats of those who cowered before her.

Men trembled upon witnessing the queen's fierceness, and upon seeing her beauty, they turned on their own.

The legend spread like wildfire, and though Olivia hated the idea of being called queen, she saw the value in the exercise, which brought the community together and energized them toward a common goal beyond their immediate survival. They were creating a fantasy world, but when the real world was populated by more dead than living, she was willing to play the necessary role to keep morale inside the compound as positive as they were that night because after the attack on their community, she feared things were about to get much worse. Not only did they have to worry about the larger group Monroe, Dave, and Austin had come from, now they had to worry about the group that had been trading slaves for drugs with the now dead militia at the solar farm. Olivia had their drugs, and she was terrified of what would happen if they managed to track them to her compound.

It was time to bring one of the legends of the Bloody Queen to life. It was time to crucify some zombies.

Day 46

While Alek and Jax led a small team to round up unblemished corpses, Aiden oversaw the building of the crosses, and by the end of the day, they would have murderers, rapists, and traitors hanging at the middle and inner gates. Though Aiden had disagreed with the idea of putting traitors to death, recent events had helped him begin to see the wisdom in the threat, and before the new members from the solar farm would be allowed to roam free on the grounds, they needed to get these crosses up.

Meanwhile, Rena was working to fill in all of the gaps in their video surveillance system, which would have no lapses in the camera coverage and no toggling. Though more cameras may not have prevented those men from getting inside as they had Alek's vehicle, more monitors would have meant that Savannah, who was on duty in the panic room, would have sounded the alarm much sooner, and the people of the Deadfall could have been armed and ready.

Last night before they celebrated their win at the solar farm, they mourned the lost guard and the Greyhawk who died at the farm. They burned the guard's body on the pyre in the inner ring, and they threw the bodies of Monroe and Dave into a fire pit they'd dug outside the wall. Now they just needed to decide what to do with Austin. That was Dani's responsibility, but she was getting nowhere.

She had interviewed him, and though she was willing to keep trying, she went looking for Olivia's advice because she honestly did not think he was ever going to open up to her. She found her in her office and shared what little she had learned so far.

"The only thing I'm sure of is that he's either been severely traumatized or he's working an angle to save his skin, but if that's the case, he's a great actor," she explained.

"Does he strike you as smart enough to try to manipulate you?" Olivia asked. "Savannah went to school with him. She says he was nice but not the sharpest knife in the drawer."

"My kneejerk reaction would be to say no, but I just don't feel like I know him well enough to make that determination."

"So, what do we do?" Olivia asked.

"I think maybe if we let him spend some time with kids his own age..."

"Absolutely not! Even if he didn't want to, he was willing to go along with those men, then as soon as it was clear that his group was going down, he jumped ship. At best, we can only trust him to look out for number one."

"But maybe he had been waiting for that opportunity like he told Alek. Maybe if he didn't conform, those guys would have killed him. We just don't know," Dani argued.

"I think he needs to stay in the cell until we do know, and if he wants anything at all beyond the most basic of subsistence living, he'd better start talking. We need to know if the camp he begged Alek not to send him back to is a threat to us."

Dani nodded and headed toward the door, but when Olivia went back to her work, she noticed that Dani never actually left.

"Was there something more?" Olivia asked.

"Well, I was just wondering... Has anything *changed* between you and Alek since yesterday?"

"We haven't had sex yet if that's what you're asking," Olivia said impatiently, then she sighed and put down her pen. "How can I do that, Dani? How can I just replace Reid as if he meant nothing to me?"

"It's not like that, and Reid would understand," she said. "He loves you and he'd want you to be happy, but if you're not going to let that happen, then maybe June had the right idea."

"What idea was that?"

"Remember what Liana suggested about June and Alek?"

"She was joking," Olivia insisted, rolling her eyes.

"Maybe, but June came to me with the same idea," she said, and when she saw the look on Olivia's face, she realized she needed to make it clear that she wasn't advocating it. "Don't shoot the messenger. I just told her I'd bring it up with you. That's all."

"Well, I think it's a terrible idea," Olivia said.

"Why?" Dani asked. "I mean, aside from the obvious." Olivia looked at her, incredulous. If Dani's own jealousy wasn't enough to tell her it was a bad idea, there were plenty of reasons, including June's inexperience.

"For one thing, if he gives her her first orgasm at thirty-five, she's going to fall in love with him."

"That's not always true, you know."

"Then she'll become obsessed with him. Whatever," Olivia said.

"I guess that's a possibility, but I still think you should consider it," Dani said, though what she really meant was that she figured this might shock Olivia into getting over her fear. "It would be good for June's therapy to finally commit that sin, and it would be good for Alek to not be sexually frustrated for once in the damn apocalypse. How long do you think he's going to wait for you, Olivia? At least this way you'd be in control of who he sleeps with, and let's face it, June won't steal him from you. She's not his type. Plus, it gets you off the hook for a few more weeks."

"So, that's why she picked Alek? To benefit me?" Olivia asked, annoyed.

"All of you. You get time. She gets her orgasm. Alek gets laid. Everybody wins," Dani explained.

"I'm not sure I'd call my perk on that list a win," she snarled.

"Well, I said I'd mention it to you, so I've done my due diligence," Dani declared as she hurried toward the door so Olivia could spend some time stressing over their conversation. Dani was reasonably certain that Alek would be getting into someone's panties within the next few days, and they would not be in June's.

As for Olivia, she was reasonably certain that Dani was trying to manipulate her, but in spite of that knowledge, it had begun to work. All afternoon, the idea that Alek would not wait much longer churned inside her head, tormenting her just like their resident psychologist had intended.

"There you are," Liana said as she ran into Dani walking down the hallway from Olivia's office. "I've been looking for you."

"I was just talking to Olivia. What's up?"

"Let's go somewhere private," she said, taking Dani by the arm and ushering her into a storage room off the main lodge. Once there, Liana closed the door, and Dani rubbed her arm when she was released from Liana's rough grip.

"When were you planning on telling me about the Witch of the Wellspring?" Liana demanded, and Dani froze. Only one other person knew her private name for the woman in the woods, and he was alone with Liana most of the day yesterday.

"How do you know about her?" Dani finally asked.

"Jax mentioned her."

"What did he say?"

"That you ran into a lady you thought was a witch. Why didn't you tell me about her?"

"There was nothing to tell. She's just an old lady who lives up the mountain in a shack. Olivia knows about her, and she didn't consider her a threat, so she said to just let her stay there. I wasn't keeping it from you. I assumed you knew."

"Well, I didn't, and as head of security, I should have been told about this."

"Then climb up Olivia's ass, not mine! I only saw her because I followed Olivia up the mountain with a damn chicken!" Dani snapped, angry.

"I'm sorry," Liana said, calming down. "You're right. I just thought maybe I should check her out, make sure there's nothing to worry about."

"So? Do it."

"How do I get there?" Liana asked, and even though she wasn't being harsh anymore, she still didn't seem like herself. She was impatient, almost twitchy.

"Her shack's not too far up from the wellspring. I can draw you a map," she said, and Liana pulled a small notebook and pen out of her jacket pocket, handing it to Dani. As she drew the crude map, she became even more suspicious as her friend watched intently.

"Lilo, is everything okay with you?" Dani asked.

"Yeah. I just had a fight with Aiden. That's all," she lied.

"Well, if there's anything I can do to help..."

"I appreciate it, but we'll be fine," she insisted, taking the notebook back from her.

"I'm sure you will," Dani said as Liana looked over the map before slipping the notebook back in her pocket.

"Thanks," she said as she reached for the doorknob. "Oh, and Dani? Don't mention this to Olivia. She has too much on her mind already."

"No problem," she said, but she couldn't shake the feeling that there was more to Liana's desire to visit the witch than just security.

There was.

Liana believed that Madam Levinia had brought her together with Aiden, so she was convinced that the Witch of the Wellspring could take away the obstacle standing between them. With her map in hand, she hurried off into the woods.

It was late in the afternoon when she came upon the witch's shack against the mountainside, and she waited on the stoop for a moment, nervous as she listened to a rooster crowing from inside. She almost turned away and went back home, the horror stories from her abuela swirling around in her brain, warning her that witchcraft was evil, but when the door suddenly swung open and a beautiful, young woman beckoned her to come in, she forgot all about her misgivings. The woman looked like an angel. Her brown hair shone with a halo of gold as the firelight reflected off it, her skin was smooth and pink like the inside of a seashell, and her eyes were so large as they glistened behind long, black lashes, she almost looked like an anime character.

"Come, sit by the fire," she said, her voice soothing and sweet as she shooed the hen from her seat with a graceful wave of her arm.

"Are you the woman who met my friend, Dani?" Liana asked, thinking this must be the witch's daughter or even granddaughter, and her host giggled impishly.

"I am the only one here," she said, and a smile spread across Liana's face because if this was the "old" woman Dani was talking about, she clearly had powerful magic.

"What's your name?" Liana asked.

"Does it matter? Are you here to make friends or use me for my powers?"

"I'm sorry. I..." Liana began, thinking she'd offended the woman, but she laughed again.

"It's okay, LiLo," she said in her tiny, syrupy voice, and though Liana had no idea how she knew her nickname, it became insignificant as she was offered the magic she had come seeking. The witch stood with her hands on her hips, staring down at her. "Well, come on. Out with it. Tell me what you want, and it shall be yours."

"What will it cost me?"

"Your raven haired friend brought apples and pears. Your golden haired friend brought a hen," the woman said, her mannerisms mischievous and playful.

"Olivia came to see you? What did she want?"

"She was just curious."

"She doesn't believe in magic," Liana explained.

"But you do, and I know what you've come for," she said, getting up from her chair and sorting through bottles of potions and powders on a shelf behind her. She selected a small, glass pot with a greyish paste inside that was sealed with wax, and tied around the rim was a scrap of paper with crudely handwritten words. She gave it to Liana.

"What's this?"

"Rub it on your scars before you go to sleep tonight. Use it all, then crush the glass beneath your shoe as you read the incantation. Tomorrow when you wake, you'll believe that there is real magic in the world."

"What's in it?"

"I'll tell you that if you come back for more. The spell works for one moon, then you must cast it again or the blight will return." Then noticing the confusion on Liana's face, she explained herself. "One full cycle of the moon. Twenty-eight days."

"Oh," Liana said with an embarrassed smile. "So, what do I owe you for this?"

"The first taste is free. If you return for another, we'll talk about payment. Fair enough?" she asked.

"Okay," Liana said, her instincts telling her that it was a mistake to accept such a deal, but her all-encompassing desire to feel perfect for Aiden silenced the voices. She left with her paste, hurrying back down the mountainside. She was excited to see if it would work, but she was so afraid that it wouldn't, when she got home, she hid the jar beneath the mattress in the loft where it would stay for days as she tried to talk herself into using it. It was her last hope.

Day 47

After dinner, Alek and Olivia were walking the perimeter of the stone wall to check the position of the new cameras when they were startled by a sound they had not heard in over a month. Her satellite phone was ringing. Anxious, she fished it out of the inside pocket of her jacket, in such a hurry to answer, she didn't notice the look of fear on Alek's face as she fumbled with it.

"Hello? Reid?" she asked, a huge smile already plastered across her face just from seeing his name on the display, but the unexpected joy was fleeting.

"Who?" asked the woman on the other end of the line.

"Who are you?"

"My name's Calista."

"Are you with Reid, Calista?" Olivia asked, still hopeful.

"I don't know who that is," she said.

"Then why did you call me?" Olivia demanded, her fear for her husband's safety manifesting as anger toward Calista.

"I'm sorry. I don't know anyone with a satellite phone, so I just hit redial. I thought maybe it would connect me to someone who could help," she said, and Olivia's posture fell, the phone dangling from her hand as it dropped to her side. Alek could hear the woman still talking on the other end, and he picked it up, putting it on speaker.

"Hi, Calista," he began. "My name's Alek. You're calling us on the phone that belongs to my friend's husband. How did you get it?"

"It fell off a zombie I killed outside of a hardware store on the west side," she said, and Olivia started to feel sick. Reid was in a hardware store when he called her last.

"Was it a man?" Alek asked.

"Yeah."

"What did he look like?"

"I don't know. He was a tall guy, but it was dark out, and it happened so fast. My friend got bit, and now I'm trapped here all alone. I'm scared."

"You're trapped in the hardware store?"

"It's not the store. It's the whole fucking city. I was going to go find someplace in the country to hide, but I can't get out."

"I don't understand," Alek said.

"Yeah, welcome to my world, buddy," she complained, but then she started to explain how the fact that downtown Charleston was overrun at the onset of the plague had led to her situation. "So the idiots in charge got the bright idea to blow the bridges, and when that didn't contain the dead, they put up blockades at every road out of the city from up past the capital all the way down to Iowa Street. The only way out now is on foot if you can fight your way past the hordes. We couldn't even take a fucking boat because the Kanawha River is full of corpses!"

As Alek talked to the young woman, Olivia tuned out, her whole body going numb. Even though the tall zombie could have been Reid, he could have dropped his phone and some other tall guy grabbed it before Calista ended up with it, but if they had blown the bridges and blocked the roads, that vehicle

230

Reid was planning to use to get back home wouldn't have gotten him anywhere. Olivia was beginning to realize that her hope had all been in vain. There was no spell keeping her husband alive. He was dead, and she never even got to say goodbye.

When Alek noticed the desperate look on her face, he wrapped up the conversation, offering to talk later if Calista needed to hear another voice, then he hung up. They were walking along the wall on the back of the property when he stopped Olivia and wrapped his arms around her.

"I'm so sorry, baby," he whispered, his cheek rested atop her head, and he could feel her begin to cry against his chest. "I'm so sorry."

Olivia held on tight, utterly lost, but she pulled away quickly because even amid all of the anguish she felt at the loss of Reid, she was horrified by the tiny voice telling her that it was okay to be with Alek now. Suddenly full of self-loathing, she looked up into his eyes with a sad stare, knowing she had to get away from him. There was only one thing she wanted to do at that moment anyway, something she knew was wrong and dangerous, but as the news about Reid spread its roots throughout her mind, she cared less and less about the danger until there was only one thought she was capable of thinking.

"Can you do me a favor?" she asked.

"Anything," Alek said.

"I have to be alone...just for a few hours. Could you keep an eye on Savvy? I need to know that she'll be safe."

"Of course," he said, understanding that she needed time to grieve. He was willing to do whatever he could to help her through this, and though he also recognized that Reid's death meant Olivia was free to be his now, it didn't feel like a win. Her heart was breaking, and he would rather have lost her to a returning husband than see such pain in her eyes.

She hugged him again, and he kissed her on the forehead before she hurried off alone, leaving him with her satellite phone. Since Rena had made everyone their own modified cell, the only reason she kept the sat phone on her was Reid, and now it was obvious that he would never be on the other end of that line again.

Alek went back toward the lodge to look for Savannah, and Olivia took a different route, going through the greenhouse to get to her private rooms faster. First, she opened the locked storage closet in her office where they kept the medications and took out a large syringe and two vials, then she went into her panic room and opened the secret door. Behind a retractable panel was an elevator that went down to the bunker beneath. It was one of three secret access points, and the others - the downstairs security post and Savannah's closet - were just as cleverly hidden. Olivia had told no one that the bunker even existed other than Alek, Dani, and Liana, and Savannah was still the only one other than herself who knew how to access it. As she walked through the long cinderblock hallways, past the pantry of freeze dried food, the water drums, and the weapons locker, she realized that she was going to have to let the others know how to get down here in case they needed it someday when she wasn't around. It wasn't just a place to survive if the surface became unsafe. There was also a hidden emergency exit that led to a secluded area of the woods.

It could prove useful in protecting their community, but today it was still Olivia's secret and had to remain so to hide what she had come to do. Grabbing a bag of saline out of the medical supply closet, she hurried past the room full of cots for the bedroom where she and Reid would have slept if a bomb had been dropped on the surface, and it seemed fitting because she felt like a bomb had been dropped on her life. Knowing Reid was out there somewhere trying to get back to her had made it possible for her to cling to some semblance of normalcy in an otherwise abnormal world, but now that had been taken away. Calista's call was not irrefutable evidence of his death, but after learning about the state of the roads in Charleston, she couldn't imagine how he escaped the city. There were too many variables, and if she didn't stop trying to extrapolate them all, she was going to go mad.

But she knew how to silence everything. It's what she came here to do.

Olivia's Journal
Day 47

Tonight, I'll have to find a more secure place to keep this journal because I can never risk Alek reading it again. I don't want him to know what I've done. I don't want anyone to know because they won't understand, and they won't trust that I can control myself. But I know I can. That's all that matters.

In the bunker below the compound are several rooms, one of which is a small bedroom with a comfortable king sized bed that Reid and I christened more than once while we were filling up the stores, and though I hadn't been down there in a while, the whole place was just as clean and dust-free as the last time I saw it. It stays sealed up so tight, I've never even seen a cobweb, and when I climbed onto the bed, the sheets still had the faint scent of fabric softener.

It was comforting because the smell reminded me of Reid. It almost made me start crying again, but I fought the tears. I wasn't there to mourn him. I was there to remember him, to experience being connected to the man I loved in the only way I could now.

I took the vials out of my pocket and filled the syringe, adding as much saline as I could. I'd never done this before, but I'd watched nurses inject me numerous times in the hospital. Though they usually put the needle into the IV port, I felt confident that I could do it the hard way. I was just going to have to figure out how to find a vein, and they were fairly easy to see through the pale flesh of the underside of my arm. I picked one.

Okay, I told myself. *It's just a little pin prick.* But I knew better. The Phenergan was going to burn like a motherfucker going in. The nurses always slowly added it to the IV fluids high in the line, but one time a nurse, who was either inexperienced or a total sadist, used the port closest to the IV and just squirted it in. I knew I was about to feel that intense burning again because there wasn't nearly enough saline in this shot, but the worst part about it was how excited that thought made me. It was almost sexual.

I took a deep breath and pierced my skin, the tip the needle found its target, and a tiny drop of blood surfaced as I began to depress the syringe. I felt it immediately like hot lava pouring into my vein, slowly dissipating as it crept up my arm, and *God! It was incredible!* As the pain of the Phenergan and the euphoria of the Demerol collided, it seized upon me like a full body orgasm, filling me with perfect peace and joy as I plunged the very last drop into my bloodstream.

"Reid," I breathed as I fell back on the pillow, my arm aching, and it felt so fucking good, all I could do was lie there and experience the long, delicious moment of infinite ecstasy before it robbed me of my consciousness altogether. One second, I was in heaven, then the next, I was just gone.

I woke abruptly two hours later, and before my loss had a chance to invade my thoughts, I focused on hiding what I had done. I gathered the syringe and the vials, though I didn't know what to do with them. We have very little trash at this point, careful to clean and reuse as much as we can, and the few things we do throw away wouldn't have provided enough cover in the garbage can.

I wrapped the evidence in a pillow case and shoved it in the back of the shelving where Reid and I had hundreds of thousands of bullets stored, and planning to deal with it later, I sat down in the weapons locker as I lost the struggle to keep thoughts of my husband at bay. I just couldn't get my brain around him being gone. Every bit of logic inside me said he was because that phone was his lifeline to me and Savannah. I couldn't imagine him ever leaving it behind.

It didn't make sense, or maybe I just didn't want it to. That seemed likely considering that my mind kept taking me back to what Dani said in Pittsburgh. None of the men we love can die. I didn't believe in the magic. Despite everything that had happened, *I did not believe.* Yet in the moment when I was trying to force myself to acknowledge Reid's passing, I was like the fabled atheist in a foxhole praying my heart out to whatever god would listen. Deep down I knew that Dani could have specifically said, "Reid Anders cannot die and shall be made immortal and invincible for all time," yet he could still be just as dead as if no spell had been cast at all. But I could not accept that he was gone, and every time I considered making peace with it, one thing popped into my head. Demerol.

I could still feel how the Phenergan had burned my veins, and it excited me. I knew I wasn't going to take another dose. If I did, I wouldn't stop until I had depleted our entire supply, and I had Savannah to consider. If not for her, I shudder to think what road I might have gone down.

I need to talk to her. I need to tell her what I've learned about her father because I don't have the right to keep it from her, but the thought of her grief on top of my own is too much.

And I need to talk to Alek. He thinks I'm finally going to accept that my husband's dead, and he isn't going to understand that I can't. Maybe June was right. Maybe I should get Alek to sleep with her. If only temporarily, it would still help get us through this period where I can't let go of my past, and maybe it would make me feel better. Alek has been far too good to me, and I don't deserve him or Reid at this point. I've done nothing but betray them both in my heart. I want to do right by them both as well. For Reid, that means waiting a little longer, and for Alek...

Alek deserves more than I can give right now.

Day 48

June was sitting in the lodge by the fire sipping her morning coffee before her shift in the security room when Olivia found her. No one else was around but Ravi, who was sitting at a small table against the wall in front of a chessboard. He was waiting for Phil to meet him for a match, and when Olivia came stalking across the floor toward June, he pretended to be preoccupied with setting up the board.

"Fine," Olivia said abruptly when she reached June's chair.

"What's fine?" she asked.

"If you think you can do it without falling in love with him, fine. I'll set it up."

June looked up at her, surprised and confused because even though Olivia had given her absolutely no preface for the conversation, she quickly surmised that it was about Alek. Inside, she felt her heart skip a beat, and she fought to control the involuntary cues that betrayed her excitement. Olivia didn't notice because she was focused solely on her own self-loathing. She had tossed and turned all night as even her sleeping mind haunted her with the idea that she didn't deserve Alek, and she had awakened this morning with a singular thought - that letting him sleep with June would be her penance. She didn't know what he would consider it. She hadn't mentioned it to him yet.

"And Alek wants to do it?" June asked, hoping for a resounding yes.

"I can talk him into it," Olivia said, as she continued to stand over June rather than joining her.

"I don't want it to be like that, Olivia," she protested. "If he doesn't want to, don't push the issue. I just thought that since you weren't ready, it might be a solution for all of us. I thought of Alek because I don't want to fall in love or anything. I just want to know what all the fuss is about, you know? I want to know why your diary is three volumes long and mine reads like a grocery list."

June's eyes began to glisten as she explained, and Olivia softened toward her, finally sitting down.

"I really do understand," she said. "I'm sorry. This is just..."

"Weird?"

"Really fucking weird," she said, and they laughed.

"If you're not comfortable with it, it's okay. I just wanted it to be with someone who had experience. Jax probably has the most, but I wouldn't even joke about that. Dani would crap all over herself."

"No doubt," Olivia agreed. Dani would totally freak at the idea of June borrowing her man, yet she had no problem putting Alek on the menu.

"And I thought of Alek because I just want a onetime thing with no strings," June said. "I think God will forgive me if I just try it once."

"I don't think God really cares all that much as long as no one gets hurt."

"Do you promise that no one will get hurt?"

"It's just sex. It doesn't mean anything," Olivia lied. Of course it meant something. It meant that Olivia was utterly fucked in the head for even considering this.

"Good," June said, "because I don't want this to cause any problems for anyone." Now she was the one lying. She didn't just want to get laid. She wanted Alek. He was the most perfect man she'd ever known, and *if Olivia didn't appreciate him, why shouldn't she get a crack at him?*

"I don't want any problems either," Olivia said. "And I just hope you understand if he doesn't want to do it, it's not you. Okay?"

"Why didn't you just ask him first?"

"Because I wanted to make sure I could get through this conversation before I let him know that I'm treating him like a toy I can loan out," she said, throwing in a joke to keep the mood light. In all honesty, she wasn't sure why she went to June first, but on some level that she was yet to consciously acknowledge, she wanted Alek to say no and she wanted June to know it for having the audacity to even ask. Of course, if Alek didn't want to do it, June didn't want to know.

"If he says no, maybe just tell me you changed your mind," she said.

"I'll do that," Olivia assured her, smiling as she stood up to leave, and the second she was out of sight, Ravi abandoned his chessboard and sauntered over to sit beside June with what her grandfather liked to call a shit-eating grin on his face.

"Can I help you?" she demanded suspiciously.

"I just wanted to let you know that I think you're beautiful," he said.

"Oh, Lord! You overheard!" she groaned, putting her face in her hands.

"Maybe a little, but there's no reason to be embarrassed," he said. "In fact, I've come to offer my services in case your plans with Alek should fall through."

"But you're just a kid," June said.

"I am twenty-four-years-old," Ravi complained, irritated. He realized he looked young, but he was getting tired of being seated at the kid's table, especially considering that the only women in his age group were Rena, Brittani, and Penny, none of whom piqued his interest like the fair, older woman with the beautiful red hair. He was getting sexually frustrated, and he was about to find out how frustrating June could be.

"Let me see your ID," she demanded with a smirk.

"I seem to have left it in my pre-apocalypse pants," he said, undaunted. "However I would welcome the opportunity to prove to you that I am definitely a grown man."

As he sat before her, she couldn't help but entertain the idea, even if only for a second, because as much as she hated to admit it, Ravi was a handsome man. His hair was a thick blue-black, and the color of his skin reminded her of cinnamon spice. But she had trouble allowing herself to think about him that way because he was more than ten years her junior.

"I'm still too old for you, Ravi," she protested.

"I'm not asking you to marry me, lady," he said, and when her eyes grew large as if she was offended, he reminded her of something he overhead her say to Olivia. "No strings? I believe those were your words."

"Those were my private words," she said with a scowl. "But as long as you were eavesdropping, you probably heard that I also said experienced, and I seem to recall that you had an arranged marriage at the beginning of the apocalypse."

"And why does that have to mean I have no experience? I was promised to a stranger on the other side of the world. It didn't mean I couldn't date," he said, and though curious, June was more interested in ending the conversation, so she fell back on her old habit.

"Doesn't your holy book specifically forbid that sort of thing anyway?" she asked, and he grimaced, rubbing his temples.

"You want to talk about my holy book?" he demanded, his demeanor calm despite his irritation as he leaned in close and issued a seductive warning. "I'll show you my holy book, lady."

Ravi's lips curled into a devious smile as he stood and walked away, and although she was confused about his meaning, his delivery had left June's heart racing.

Not knowing how to process the feelings Ravi stirred in her, June channeled her excitement toward Alek, who remained blissfully unaware that Olivia had offered him up. Tonight, he was on watch at the main gate with Dani. She had begun to drive him crazy with her constant questioning about everything Jax said or did while out of her presence, but he endured it patiently because now there was something he needed from her, thinking his wait for Olivia was almost over.

Dani was one of three people who had access to their medical stores, and there was a particular product he was hoping had been on that Right Way truck, something he was reasonably certain would not have been collected in any scavenging trips since. He just wasn't sure how to broach the subject. Though he came from a culture that was substantially more open about sex than the one he had immigrated into, this was still an uncomfortable request to make. But it was also an important one.

"So, you guys inventoried everything that came off the pharmacy truck?" he asked, trying to sound like he was just making conversation. Dani nodded. "Was there anything from the condoms and lube section?"

"Yes," she said, suddenly curious because Olivia's ovaries had been removed. "What do you need a condom for?"

"I don't," he said.

"So you want lube then?" she asked with a grin, enjoying his obvious discomfort.

"No," he said, looking down at his feet and pausing before sucking it up and admitting what he was looking for. "I think I need one of those sprays or creams or whatever they are...the kind that help a man..." he swallowed and the next words came out mumbled "...last longer."

"Really? Even after all that jacking off you admitted to in front of the entire oversight committee?"

Embarrassed, Alek sighed. "I only said that to make a point to June," he insisted, though it wasn't a total lie. There had been a few times in the shower when he just couldn't take the torture of not being able to fuck Olivia.

"That's a shame," Dani said with a giggle. "Chronic masturbation could certainly have helped you last longer."

"You're laughing at me," he complained, trying hard not to laugh at himself, but it was so awkward now, he regretted not just stealing Olivia's key and pillaging the supplies.

"I'm sorry," she said. "I just never dreamed a man like you would worry about that."

"Normally, I wouldn't, but things are different with Olivia."

Dani looked at him curiously for a moment before it dawned on her what had happened.

"Oh, Alek," she said apologetically. "You read her diary."

"How did you know?"

"Because I'm the reason she wrote it," Dani said, going on to explain the research she was doing before the apocalypse and how her friends agreed to take part, then she looked up at him with a serious stare. "Don't let her journal freak you out, okay? Reid had fifteen years to learn how to do that to her."

"How's that supposed to make me feel better?"

"Because you're going to be something she's never experienced before," Dani said, then she proceeded to tell him a little bit about Olivia's past, things she knew wouldn't come up in conversation between Alek and Olivia because Olivia was hesitant to tell him anything about her husband.

Olivia and Reid had met their junior year in college, introduced at a Christmas party on campus, after which they ended up back at his place, both really drunk. The next day, Olivia went home for winter break, and when she saw Dani, she admitted that Reid was the first guy to ever get her off.

"She said she'd always lied to Liana and me because she was embarrassed that she couldn't figure it out, but that excuse never made a whole lot of sense to me, so I started to think that something bad might have happened to her at some point. That's pretty common with women, you know. Everybody acts like the female orgasm is so elusive, but the truth is, a lot of the women it eludes are either with men too lazy to learn to do it right or they've been fucked in the head by some asshole who molested their bodies or their minds before they even saw themselves as sexual beings.

"June's a prime example. She's never gotten off because some patriarchal psychopath who rewrote the Bible shamed her into thinking that her clit was the devil's doorbell. But with Olivia, I always figured if there was something psychological going on, and being drunk that first night with Reid, who apparently really knew his way around a clit, kept her higher brain functions from interfering with her body's natural process."

"So, are you suggesting we get drunk?" Alek asked, struggling not to let his mind go down the rabbit hole that led to the possibilities of why Olivia might have been inhibited in the first place.

"No," Dani said, grinning. "I'm saying she's learned a lot since then. She knows what she likes now, and according to her diary, she's become very good at getting off. And you, my friend, are going to be the first new man she's been with since she figured all that out. I don't think you have a thing to worry about."

"Except living in the shadow of a dead husband who can make her come like a fucking orgasmatron," he argued, and Dani laughed.

"Relax, Alek," she said. "She wants you so bad, you could just lie there, and she'll still think it was the best sex anybody ever had. Trust me. I'm pretty good at this human psychology shit."

He looked at her with a raised eyebrow.

"Fine. I'm no good at it when we're not talking about my own life," she admitted. "So, can we please get back to Jax?"

Alek groaned playfully as he slumped down in his seat, shaking his head.

It was late when Alek's shift finally ended, and he was glad to be home. Dani's obsession with Jax had become a minor nuisance, but tonight, after an interesting conversation that yielded more about Olivia's husband than he would have liked, the insane jealousy in Dani's and Jax's relationship had reached a whole new level. As she pressed Alek for information inside the guard house, he looked out into the darkness with night vision goggles and saw someone watching them from the woods - someone who looked just like Jax in infrared. Curious, he dialed Jax's extension on the comm system and watched as the figure in the forest reached for his cell. Alek hung up before he answered, and when Jax returned the call, he claimed it was an accident.

He didn't tell Dani about it, and she didn't notice it on her own because she wasn't really paying attention. After the shift, he had planned to mention Jax hiding in the woods to Olivia, but when he got back to the room and saw her lying in bed with her blonde hair shining like gold in the dim lamp light, he forgot about everything but her like he always did.

Though he wasn't aware, she had been avoiding him all day, not sure how she was going to tell him that she had volunteered him to service June. She knew she had to find a way because she had become convinced that it was the only thing that would make it possible for them to go on, and when he slipped into bed, freshly showered and smelling like heaven, it was a struggle not to let him chase the thoughts from her head as well.

Then he kissed her, sliding his hand beneath her head as his tongue parted her lips, and she melted into him, desperate to just let her weakness overtake her, to put June and Reid and the whole fucked up world out of her mind and surrender to him. But if she was nothing else, she was consistent.

"We need to talk," she said as the kiss ended, and Alek's posture fell.

"About what?" he asked with a groan.

"I'm sorry. I don't mean to..."

"Just spit it out, Olivia," he muttered as he sat up against the headboard. He was losing his patience...the very reason this was so important to Olivia.

"I have a favor to ask of you," she said to minimize the impact, and he immediately felt guilty for getting frustrated with her.

"You know I'd do anything for you," he offered.

"Don't say that until I tell you what it is," she warned him.

"Why? What is it?"

"I want you to..." she paused, gritting her teeth then forcing the words out of her mouth so quickly, he wasn't even sure he heard her right. "I want you to have sex with June."

"Did you just say you want me to..."

"...have sex with June," she repeated.

"Funny."

"It's not a joke, Alek. I really do want you to..."

"No fucking way!" he hissed, incredulous as he stood up, glaring down at her. "Jesus, Olivia! What the fuck?"

"You said you'd do anything for me."

"How is fucking June doing something for you?" he demanded, and she reached for his hand, urging him to sit back down. He didn't want to, but her power over him was hard to resist. He found himself lured back to her bedside.

"I know it sounds crazy, but I think it could be a really good thing. June's never had an orgasm," she said, then her voice became a purr as she rolled her eyes down his body to his cock and back up again. "And I know you could make that happen for her."

"Do not stroke my ego, Olivia. This is fucked up," he growled at her, his jaw set.

"I'm being honest, Alek. You know you can do it, and you need to get laid."

"So do you," he said.

"Yes, but I'm the one fucking that up for myself. I don't have the right to fuck it up for you, too, and June promised she didn't want any strings..."

"I don't care. I don't want to fuck June. I want to fuck you," he shouted, exasperated.

"I want to fuck you, too," she yelled back, but then her voice softened, her lips falling into a frown. "I do, Alek. You don't know how much I want you, but I just can't. Not yet."

"Why not?"

"Because..." she began then stopped herself. She was about to lie to him to avoid a fight, but she owed it to him to be honest. "Alek, I'm married. I can't just move on as if Reid never existed. I don't even know if he's dead or alive."

"Oh, you have *got* to be fucking kidding me!" he roared, on his feet again. "Was I the only one who heard that goddamned phone call? I'm not trying to hurt you, Olivia, but you need to face reality. If Reid loved you, he wouldn't want you torturing yourself like this. I damn sure wouldn't if I were in his shoes! But you know what? Fine. If that's how you want it, let's do this your way.

"I'll fuck June. I'll fuck her anywhere you want, any time you want. I'll even fuck her right fucking here while you fucking watch if that'll make you fucking happy. Anything for you, *Oblivia!*" He spat the name out of his mouth like a foul taste, and she buried her head in her hands as tears pricked the corners of her eyes. He'd never called her that before, but she knew why he picked now. She was oblivious to his needs - his actual needs, not the ones she was assuming came with the territory of owning a dick.

"Alek, stop, please!" she begged, and even as furious as he was, he hated himself for making her cry. He calmed down, taking a more gentle approach as he realized that although he had yelled it in anger, he meant every word he said. He was going to do it, and maybe after he fucked June, Olivia would feel like she had suffered enough to deserve a little happiness. He sat back down on the bed.

"I mean it, baby," he said. "I may have said it like an asshole, but I mean it. If it's important to you, I'll do it."

"Really?" she asked, suddenly unsure how she felt about it now that he had agreed, and he nodded.

"Just tell me when and where."

"I don't know. I guess you guys can work that part out," she said.

"Uh-uh. If you're going to whore me out, you're going to do all the pimp work. I'll just show up and perform."

"Alek," she sighed.

"What do you want from me? I'm not going to be happy that you're only willing to fuck me by proxy, but I'm going to do it...for you. Okay?"

"Okay," she said.

"Okay," he echoed, then he laid down on the bed, his movements almost robotic. "Come here." When she laid down, he pulled her close, wrapping his arms around her like any other night, but this time, he was stiff, his anger emanating from his every, rigid muscle. They didn't say another word, and Olivia lay there for more than an hour before she finally felt his grip relax as he fell asleep.

It's the right thing, she thought, trying to convince herself.

Day 48
Late Night

Liana waited for Aiden to fall asleep, then she crept into the bathroom carrying the jar of ointment the woman in the woods had given her. It had taken her days to talk herself into trying the spell because she was so afraid of it not working, and if that happened, there was no more hope. Aiden had promised to discuss the possibility of submitting to her, but it was clear that he didn't want to, so she was left with only one viable option.

She pierced the wax that sealed the glass container, and the air was suddenly filled with a pungent stench that made the bile rise in the back of her throat. She put her hand over her mouth and nose as she began to have second thoughts, but the promised result was too tempting, even if it meant smearing something on her inner thighs that smelled like rotting skunk flesh. Taking a deep breath from behind her hand, she turned on the exhaust fan, lifted the hem of her nightgown, and began to cover the entire scarred and blemished area with the vomitous concoction, using every last bit as the witch had instructed. Then she washed her hands, placed the thin, glass pot under the heel of her right flip flop, and read the incantation.

"Souls of the Earth, and Spirits of the Sky
Destroy that which offends mine eye
Mold my flesh as I bend my knee
To serve the powers that blessed be."

As she spoke the words, crushing the glass beneath her shoe, she had expected something to happen, anything that would have given her the indication that she had done it right, but she just felt silly standing there, stinking of rancid meat and reciting poetry that was as ludicrous as it was creepy. At the very least, the lights could have flickered. Something.

Disappointed, she pulled on a pair of stretch pants and sprayed herself with perfume to try to conceal the odor, and she slipped outside to throw the glass in the garbage can.

When she came back into the bedroom, Aiden stirred in his sleep, crinkling his nose oddly before rolling over, and she slipped under the covers, whispering a silent prayer that he not be able to smell the foul reek on her thighs. Then, even though it seemed like blasphemy, she added another request.

Please, God, let this spell work for me.

Liana's Journal
Day 49

 It didn't work. I woke up this morning with my crotch still reeking, but when I pulled down my pants to look at my inner thighs, there was no difference. I'm still covered in scar tissue, and just like always during this point in my cycle, I'm getting those hard, painful cysts. I feel five of them coming on this time, even more than usual, probably because this fucking witch's brew of lizard balls and pig shit has made things worse. I'll bet that bitch is laughing her ass off right now at the poor, dumb city girl who fell for her line of bullshit, and I'd march up the mountain and rip her fucking head off this very minute if she couldn't smell me coming from a mile away. At least I'm too goddamn mad to cry about it.

Actually, that's not true.

Liana couldn't finish her journal entry. She wanted desperately to be angry, but she was really just depressed because now she had lost the last bit of hope she had left. When the world was full of dermatologists, she had spent a small fortune trying to solve her problem to no avail, and the only thing left to try was the expensive surgery to remove the affected skin, which would have left her with ridges of scars instead of the random, roundish ones she already had.

With Aiden away for a shift at the gate, she broke down on her bed sobbing. All she had wanted was to be just like any other woman, to be able to take off her clothes with the man she loved and not have him think she was disgusting because of a skin condition that she couldn't control. She didn't even know what Aiden would think if he knew. He was so attentive and understanding, it was entirely possible that he wouldn't be bothered by it at all, but it didn't matter. She was bothered. She was embarrassed. She thought the scars and acne were disgusting, and she thought they made her disgusting. It had been the background noise of her life since puberty, and now it looked like it would be until the day she died.

She cried for nearly an hour before she forced herself to start her day. She was supposed to be at a meeting with Olivia in the lodge, but she called to postpone it because she just couldn't face her perfect friend with the perfect life knowing her own would never measure up. Everyone believed that Olivia and Alek had finally sealed the deal last night, and the thought of seeing that happy smile on Olivia's face was just too much to bear.

She pulled some clothes out of her dresser and plodded into the bathroom, passing the mirror without a glance, then she stripped and stepped into the shower stall. She soaped up her wash cloth and began to scrub her inner thighs to remove the vile, useless paste, the new tears in her eyes washing away in the stream of warm water as fast as they formed, but her sadness quickly turned to curiosity when she didn't feel the texture of her scars beneath the cloth. Instead, it ran smoothly over her flesh.

She finally looked down and was amazed by what she saw. The blemishes were washing away with the soap as if they had been drawn on. Two decades of ugly scars along with the new cysts that she had felt forming earlier just vanished beneath the washcloth, leaving her skin flawless. Tears filled her eyes once more.

"Oh, my God!" she cried joyfully as she watched the colors that had plagued her - shades of pink, red, and purple - circling the drain and disappearing from her life.

When she got out of the shower, she stood in front of the mirror just staring at her inner thighs, and she had never felt so beautiful. She couldn't wait to be with Aiden tonight. She'd never have to press him to let her blindfold and handcuff him again, and she was about to get the one thing she hadn't had in years, the craving that Bob could never quite satiate. Suddenly, it was all she could think about, but Aiden wouldn't be home for hours.

Olivia's Journal
Day 49

Tonight is the night Alek is going to be sleeping with June. I wanted to get it over with as quickly as possible so I couldn't change my mind, but now the thought of them together is absolutely killing me. If I was free to be with him, I don't think it would bother me that much, and I do want June to experience what she's been denied her whole adult life. If Reid were here, given our circumstances, I might even offer him up for the job. I know that sounds like bullshit, but it isn't. I'm not a jealous person. I've set up a couple of three-ways with Vegas call girls for Reid to fulfill as much of his fantasies as I could within the rubbery confines of being with a professional. I learned that I don't mind sharing his body, and now that we don't live in the same world where everyone gets to be selfish and jealous anymore, I could easily make that sacrifice for June for one night. But Alek isn't Reid. I know I could never lose Reid to another woman. I haven't had a chance to cast the same spell on Alek since the incantation goes something like "Oh, God, Olivia, yes!"

When Alek left our room this morning, he took some clothes, his body wash, and a few other things so he wouldn't have to come back here after he finished work. He doesn't want to see me today. He said if he did, he wouldn't be able to go through with it, but I think he's just pissed at me. I don't even know why he's doing it to be honest. I don't think he wants to, and he certainly isn't doing it to please me despite his best efforts to make it look that way. He's probably doing it to punish me, and that's fine too. I deserve it.

I just don't know what's wrong with me. I don't know why I can't move on, why can't I let go. When I think about Reid, I see him fighting for his life to get back to Savannah and me, and my first instinct is to hope he's not sleeping alone and scared out there on the road somewhere. I would forgive anything if he came home to me.

So why can't I imagine him forgiving me?

Maybe it's Alek. Maybe if he were a different man, this would be easier. If he were less attractive or if he hadn't been famous before the apocalypse... My husband is an incredibly sexy man, a rugged, masculine man who makes all the ladies at the local feed store blush and giggle, and Alek is so tall, fair, and beautiful, like he was sculpted by angels. Neither would have any reason to be intimidated by the other, but I know Reid's jealousy would come on hot and heavy if he knew.

If I could just explain it to him, I'd tell him it's a good thing. Maybe it took someone as perfect as Alek to make me even consider moving on. Or maybe I'm just trying to rationalize it because I want him so much. I fucking hate myself, but every time I think of Alek, my whole body just melts. When I lie against his bare chest at night, I can feel every, tight muscle beneath my cheek and fingers, and when he grows hard against my leg, it's like a switch is thrown inside me because all I can think about is climbing atop his glorious body and straddling his steely cock, feeling it slowly ease inside me to the hilt. I almost can feel his hands on my hips, lifting me as we begin to f...

Olivia jumped, startled by a loud knocking on her bedroom door. Flushed, she shoved her diary in her nightstand and answered it, surprised to find Savannah standing there.

"Thinking about Alek?" she asked, glancing at her mother's chest with a smirk, and Olivia looked down to see that her nipples were showing even through her bra.

"Savannah!" she hissed. "Inappropriate!"

"Everyone knows he sleeps here, Mom," she said, rolling her eyes as she walked past her into the room, and Olivia suddenly felt her heart in her throat. Savannah was the last person she wanted to know about her sleeping arrangements.

"Can we please not talk about this right now. I'm already having a really bad day."

"Yeah, me too," Savannah said.

"What's the matter?"

"It's Austin."

"Savannah, I've already told you. I'm not going to kill a fifteen-year-old..."

"That's not what I want anymore," she said. "In fact, I think you should let him out."

"What?"

"I don't mean permanently. Just let him get a shower, change his clothes, feel a little normal again, then maybe I can get him to talk..."

"Savvy, I don't want you anywhere near him," she said, then she put her arm around her daughter and led her to sit beside her on the end of the bed. "Listen, baby, I know you knew him before all this happened, but you don't know him anymore. When there are no laws, our true selves come out, and maybe he showed his when he came into this community with those other two kidnappers. What do you think they would have done to Kylie, Penny, and Dani if they had gotten away? You think they would have fallen in love and lived happily ever after?"

"No, but..." she began then paused, realizing it would be awkward and likely futile to tell her mother her real motivations. She knew what he told Alek about being impotent, and though what she really wanted was to prove that it was utter bullshit, she decided to appeal to Olivia's maternal instincts instead.

"I heard that he was really affected by his time in that group," she said finally. "I think they did some terrible things to him that messed him up, and if that's the case, maybe he deserves a second chance. He's just a kid...like me."

"Then he needs to talk to us."

"That's what I'm trying to accomplish," she said. "He's not going to talk to Dani, but maybe he'll talk to other teenagers. Maybe he'll talk to me."

"Savvy, I can't risk putting you in that position," Olivia said, frustrated, but as she looked into her daughter's pleading eyes, she realized she needed to do something. "I'll talk to Liana and see if she's okay with Rey talking to Austin, but that's the best I can do. Okay?"

"Okay," Savannah said as she realized they were going to have to switch to their Plan B because even if Liana would be willing to let Rey speak with Austin, Rey wasn't capable of carrying out the ruse that would prove that Austin was a liar.

Thanking her mother, Savannah hugged her, but when they pulled away from each other, she was still sitting on the bed looking at her.

"Is there something else?" Olivia asked.

"Can we talk about Alek now?"

"Savvy," Olivia sighed, expecting her daughter to heap more guilt upon her, but what Savannah said next completely floored her.

"It's time to stop leading him on. He's a good guy, Mom, and I know Daddy would want you to be happy."

"What are you saying?"

"When was the last time you heard from Daddy?" Savannah asked, and though Olivia's mind immediately flashed to the phone call from two days before, she didn't mention it.

"It's been over a month."

"I don't think he's coming home," she confessed as her face fell. "I miss him, Mom. I miss him so much, and I know you miss him too." She took her mother's hand in hers, holding on tightly as tears began to roll down both of their faces, but Savannah quickly wiped hers away because she didn't come here to upset her mother. She came here to free her.

"You have to stop torturing Alek, Mom," she said suddenly. "I've overheard things, and I'm not stupid. I know what's going on with you two."

"Savvy, I'm sorry. I didn't mean..."

"It's okay. I understand, and Dad would too," she said. "This isn't normal life. We aren't going to live to be a hundred anymore, so we have to live faster. You *and* me."

"What does that mean, Savannah?" Olivia asked.

"It means I kissed Rey, and I'm going to do it again," she said with a shy smile. "It also means that it's okay for you to kiss Alek...or whatever it is that you grownups do together." She gave Olivia a wink that made her stifle a laugh even as tears threatened her.

"You're too smart for your own good," she sighed as she realized that her daughter had grown up so suddenly, she felt like she barely knew her. Even the teenage drama that had made Olivia ground her from her best friends the weekend the apocalypse began seemed to be a thing of the past.

"I just want to see you happy again," Savannah said wistfully. "I miss seeing you happy."

"Thank you, baby," she said, wrapping her arms around her daughter, and as Olivia cried, Savannah began to cry too. "I love you so much."

"I love you, too, Mom, and I love Daddy...wherever he is."

"I'll always love your daddy," she whispered, kissing her daughter on the side of the head as they held onto to each other, neither wanting to be the first to let go.

Olivia's Journal
Day 49, Second Entry

Savannah did the most miraculous thing. I forget sometimes that she's practically a woman, and though she didn't say anything about Alek that I hadn't already thought myself or been told by my friends, hearing it from a fourteen-year-old really put it in perspective. And the only thing that could make me more certain than my daughter's blessing would be to hear Reid say that it's okay for me to be happy without him. It doesn't mean

I don't miss and grieve him in the very depths of my soul because I do, and I always will. I love Reid.

But I've fallen in love with Alek now too. Unfortunately, it took me doing something really stupid to see that. I shouldn't have sent him with June. He should be here with me, and now that I know Savvy won't hate me for loving someone other than her father, I see everything so clearly. I should run out there right now, find him, and stop him, but I won't. I made this bed. If Alek lies in it with June, it's what I deserve, and I'll never hold it against him.

Olivia's Journal
Day 49, Third Entry

It's been about two hours since Alek's shift ended. I don't know where he is now, but my guess is that he's at June's cabin. I arranged for some of the men to take her boys night fishing to give them privacy, and I don't know what's going to happen. I don't know if Alek plans to sleep there tonight or come back here, but I won't say a word either way.

I've spent my evening preparing for the worst while I tortured myself with thoughts of what Alek might be doing with June. I took a long bath, using both of our water rations for the day, then when I opened my lingerie drawer to get a pair of panties, I noticed a new, pink babydoll nightie I'd never had the chance to wear before the apocalypse came. At first, it made me sad to see it, then I got a devious idea. I know I had sworn that I would be strong and mature about this, but I couldn't stop myself from doing what I did next.

I put the nightgown on. I looked in the mirror, and while part of me wanted to cry, most of me wanted to make Alek suffer by showing him what he was missing when he came back from June's.

That's when it hit me.

I didn't realize it until now, but I've been playing a game - a silly, juvenile, fucking game! Alek was supposed to say no. He was supposed to swear he could never be with anyone else and come running back to me, but he didn't. Now, I'm sitting here reaping what I've sewn.

I accept that this is entirely my fault, and I swear I won't hold it against him, *but why is he still there with her now?* I didn't ask him to spend the night with her. When he finished, he was supposed to come back here.

Of course, if he doesn't, I could always go down into the bunker...

Last night, I was writing in this journal when I heard Alek's knock on the door from the office. I tossed it in the drawer as I grabbed my robe to cover the lingerie because I wasn't going to play that game with him anymore, then I called out for him to come in.

"Hey," he said sheepishly as he slipped inside, and I echoed him, awaiting and dreading confirmation of what he'd done. But he didn't offer anything. He just came in, took off his shoes, and hung his jacket on the hook on the back of the door as he would any other night. Then he took off his shirt like he always does before bed, and as he stood there with his perfectly defined pecks and abs staring at me, I started negotiating with myself inside my head. Him fucking June was supposed to stop me from doing the same, but suddenly I had trouble caring if he had because I wanted him so much, my whole body ached.

Slowly, he walked toward me, and my eyes climbed from his tight jeans to his halo of blonde hair, drinking in the beauty of everything in between. When he reached me, he knelt down before me, wrapping his arms around me and laying his head in my lap. I heard him take a deep breath through his nose.

"God, you smell good," he whispered, nuzzling his face against the silk of my robe.

"So do you," I said as I detected the scent of his body wash, wondering if he showered afterward. Then he began apologizing, and my heart sank. I believed I had my answer until the only perfect words that could be spoken in that moment came from Alek's lips.

"I couldn't go through with it," he confessed, looking up at me with tortured eyes as the truth poured out of him. "I didn't want to hurt her, but I couldn't do it, Liv. I just couldn't..."

I took his face in my hands, silencing him with an enthusiastic kiss, and it was pure electricity to feel our lips meet and know that he was so thoroughly mine. With his arms around me, he pulled me against him so hard, I slid off the bench into his lap as he trailed hungry kisses toward my ear.

"It wasn't fair to her, but all I could think about was you," he whispered as he moved to my neck, and gooseflesh instantly rolled down my body. My nipples tightened, and the tiny strip of lace between my legs became thoroughly soaked as I felt his cock, growing stone-like beneath me.

"You're all I ever think about," he breathed, "and I'll wait for you, baby. I'll wait for you forever."

He caught my eyes, brushing my hair behind my ear, and a mischievous smile spread across my face as I reached down and untied my robe, letting it fall off my shoulders to reveal the sheer, pink babydoll beneath.

"Oh, fuck," he murmured as he looked me over, reaching out to touch me cautiously as if he feared it might be a mirage. He ran his fingertips down the side of my breast, his thumb tracing over my nipple as it peeked out of the half cup of the bra, but even as he trembled in anticipation, he stood firm on his earlier promise to me.

"You have to tell me what you want, Liv," he insisted. "You have to say the words."

"I'm yours, Alek," I whispered, "and I want *everything* you have to give."

"You have no idea what you're asking for, woman," he threatened as he abruptly rose to his feet, scooped me up, and carried me to the bed in such a swift motion, it made me giggle until the seriousness of his stare chased away my laughter. He laid me down, his body atop mine, and he kissed me again, his every action torturously soft and slow as I yearned for more. Sensing my desire, he slid one hand behind my head before his lips met mine again as he clutched my neck, pulling me into an insatiable kiss that was exactly what I'd been longing for. He forcefully attacked my mouth as if he couldn't get close enough to me no matter how hard he tried, even when he moved to my throat, and I heard my breath catch loudly as his teeth sank into me just shy of breaking the skin.

Oh, God, I wanted him now.

"Fuck me, Alek," I urged him, growing impatient as I felt his cock struggling against the zipper of his jeans, and my greedy fingers rushed to free it. I wanted to see it, to touch it and taste it, but he stopped me.

"Uh-uh," he said, lifting my hands over my head and holding them there. "You made me wait so long for this, Olivia. Now it's your turn to wait while I savor every, last moment."

"Oh, God," I moaned as he returned to his path, still holding my wrists in one hand as he ran his tongue from my neck to my nipple.

"Don't move your arms," he commanded, then he released my wrists. Balanced on his knees, he dragged his hands downward, making me giggle as they swept over my underarms toward my breasts. He pulled down the bodice and cupped them, pushing them together as he leaned in, taking my nipple between his teeth, nibbling and swirling his tongue over it. It excited me to feel him touch me anywhere with his hands or mouth, but my nipples are not terribly sensitive. And I didn't need the foreplay. I needed to come.

"Alek, please," I begged, my fingers clutching the pillow above my head as I fought the desire to defy his order that I not move my arms.

"Please what, Olivia?" he asked with a devilish grin. "Tell me what you want."

"I want you inside me."

"But I'm not finished with you yet," he protested, and I realized he thought it was going to be over if he fucked me.

"Do you have a problem putting your mouth where your dick has been?" I asked him with a smirk.

"No," he said.

"Me neither," I whispered, breaking his command and reaching for his zipper again.

"God, you're perfect," he growled as he gave in.

Working together, we hurriedly got him out of his jeans, and when he reached down to guide himself inside me, I saw his eyes flash as he found me dripping wet for him. *How could I not be?* I was about to fuck Alek Hellström.

Oh, my God! I thought as it hit me. In the past two months as we worked so hard for our survival, the idea of how much I had wanted him just because of who he was had fallen off my radar, but it suddenly came rushing back along with images of that first night we met in Pittsburgh, the starstruck memory colliding with the love I felt for the man I had come to know. I was on edge already, every nerve ending begging for contact, and when he finally slid his thick, majestic cock inside me, I exploded from one, single, deliciously deep stroke. Instantly, my heels dug into his calves, my back arched, and my lips trembled as his name softly fell from them. I grabbed his head, thrusting my tongue into his mouth as I writhed against him, sucking out every last bit of pleasure the orgasm had to give until I finally relaxed my grip.

"Now, you can do all those other things you had in mind," I whispered in his ear.

"Oh, my God, did you...?" he asked, his eyes full of wonder, and as I smiled shyly, his lips found mine again, breathing my name into my mouth. Slowly, he began to fuck me, and as his rock-hard cock glided against the hypersensitive nerve endings inside me, I could already feel it building again fast. He reached down, lifting one of my legs over his arm, and just the slight shift in the angle sent me spirally into madness.

"Oh, God, Alek," I cried, bucking against him and using my legs wrapped around his ass to force him in deeper as I felt myself soak his cock with warm, wet praise of its magnificence. He reared back, and I pulled him into me again as the exquisite pleasure radiated outward, sparking electricity at every point of contact between our flesh, even as the orgasm subsided.

"Goddamn, woman," he whispered, looking into my eyes as I bashfully bit my lip.

Did he think I was exaggerating when he read my diary? I wondered as he pulled my nightie over my head and started kissing downward from my navel.

Then his hands gripped my inner thighs, pushing them apart as he lowered his head until his tongue slowly made that first, faint brush over my clit, and *holy fuck!* I don't know if it was the fact that it had been almost two months since it had been touched or that I glanced down and saw Alek Hellström's eyes looking back from between my legs, but that soft touch sent a million volts of raw power coursing through me!

I gasped, the sheets suddenly fisted in my palms as his tongue swirled over me, and he played my body like a master, catching every subtle cue to know exactly when to go faster, adjust the pressure, switch up the motion until at the perfect moment, he began flickering over the tiny bundle of nerves with lightning speed.

"Oh, fuck...don't stop," I moaned, my pelvis already tilted forward in anticipation, and he slid his hands under my ass, the half moons of his fingernails digging in as he pulled me into his face. I could feel my release on the horizon, his tongue like a machine, so precise as it darted over me, and I was out of control, growling and whimpering, writhing against him, yanking on the sheet so hard, the fitted corners popped off on both sides, quickly finding their way into my clenched fists as his talents brought me to the very gates of Heaven.

"Oh, Alek, my god!" I screamed as the orgasm tore through me. The words coming from my mouth were pure impulse, and my movements merely reflex. As I arched my back, convulsing and grinding against his face, he maintained his tempo, miraculously holding his mouth against me despite that it had become like riding a bucking bronco. And just when it seemed that it might end, he did it again, his fucking incredible tongue driving me to a second, powerful climax that ended in loud, shameless praise falling from my trembling lips in a chaotic barrage of fucks and Aleks and Gods.

Finally, he released me, and I collapsed on the bed, giggling and mumbling about how amazing he was. I was so high, ecstasy coursing through my veins like a narcotic, and though I could have lain there, lost in it forever, there was no way I was going to miss sharing this rapture with Alek. I needed him to feel just as stoned and stupid, but I was in no position to take charge at the moment, capable of little more than a delighted growl when he thrust himself into me again. He was so gloriously hard, the skin stretched so tightly, he barely felt human anymore, and it thrilled me to know that going down on me did this to his cock.

And what his cock did to me was insane. Already worked into a heightened orgasmic state, even as he tried to make love to me slowly, I couldn't stop coming. I shuddered and convulsed beneath his deliciously muscular body, and he just kept fucking me, giving me no time to stop and savor. I could feel the next orgasm building while still riding out the last, and every time I came, I felt his cock twitching inside me, so close himself, I knew if

I didn't stop him, I'd never get my mouth on it like I'd planned. But I had no power to control myself at that point. He was in control, he completely owned me, and if he didn't come soon, he was going to destroy me.

Then at last, I saw that beautiful look in his eye that told me there would be no turning back.

"Come, Alek," I breathed in his ear. "Come for me."

And instantly, the only spell I've ever believed in worked its magic. His entire body tensed, he groaned my name, and with a final thrust, he buried his cock in me as I felt his hot, powerful eruption. I dragged my nails down his back, holding him deep inside as the intensity of the orgasm faded into a state of perfect bliss. Finally, his muscles relaxed, and he melted into me, his face nuzzled against mine, his lips by my ear.

"God, Olivia," he breathed. "You're so fucking...that was so fucking...oh, God, baby..."

"I know," I whispered, kissing his cheek, and when he turned his head to face me, I knew he wanted to tell me he loved me. I could almost hear his thoughts, but he didn't want the first time he said it to be after sex because that's how Alek is. As for me, I wouldn't have minded it because I'd never felt so compelled to tell him before now as I lay naked and fuck-stoned beneath him. I just didn't want to say it until he did. But I love him.

God, I love him!

Day 49
Dani

Jax had a shift at the wall with Aiden until well after dark, and Dani's last appointment of the day would be over by 5:00 PM. It was with one of the newer members of the community - Widow Six. At first, Dani had been looking forward to the session because those who came from the solar farm needed her far more than those who had been in their cushy compound since the beginning, but Widow wouldn't even tell Dani her real name, unwilling to talk about much of anything with her other than the day of the rescue.

Widow held Jax and Aiden in the highest regard, even though there had been an army of others there who helped get her out of her bondage, and Dani had difficulty remaining objective when Jax was involved. As a therapist, she should have known that it was natural for Widow to latch onto her saviors, and she should have realized that having recently lost her husband, any infatuations Widow had toward Jax would not have panned out in the end.

She was depressed and desperate to find some reason to go on in a world she no longer wanted to be a part of, and regardless, she would never have tried to act on any attraction to either man after learning of the bloodthirsty queen who ran this place.

The people of the Deadfall had embraced her legend so thoroughly that to Widow and the others from the farm, there was no inkling that this place was anything less than what they'd been told, and she was terrified of Olivia. Still, like everyone else, she wanted the queen's approval. It was something she had seen in some of the other "widows" back at the farm. They hated Widowmaker. He was a vile man who abused them daily, yet some of the women undermined the others at every turn to gain his favor. Widow Six never sucked up to him, but Olivia was different. She was loved and respected, and she made them all feel safe. In fact, if Dani had been listening to her talk with true objectivity, she might have assumed that Widow was more likely to try to seduce the queen than Jax, but Dani's jealously had taken on a life of its own.

After Widow's appointment, Dani spent the afternoon tormenting herself. Widow wanted Jax. Everybody wanted Jax. And by the time the late autumn sun began to sink, she had come to the conclusion that the only way to stop him from cheating was to control the other women if she could not control him.

When Jax got home a few hours later, he found Dani and a well-built blonde woman named Stacy waiting for him. Like Dani, Stacy was in her mid thirties and very pretty, though she wasn't quite as pretty as Dani. That was important to her, and she also hadn't come right out and said the word threesome, just in case she couldn't go through with it once she saw Stacy and Jax in the same room. Then when he walked in and threw his arms around Dani, giving her an intense kiss as he only gave Stacy a disinterested wave, she decided she could do it. It would be easy.

Jax had a habit of taking a shower as soon as he got home, and Dani followed him back to announce her plans, proud of the confidence her ability to offer him this fantasy illustrated. But he didn't see it the same way.

"Yeah, right," he said, rolling his eyes. At first, he thought it was a trap, but as Dani continued to explain that she really wanted to do this, he started to think jealous thoughts of his own.

"I'm tired," he lied. "Can we talk about this some other time?"

"What do you mean? She's in there right now," Dani protested, her fingers nimbly unbuttoning his shirt. He grabbed her hand and stopped her.

"You should have asked me first."

"Why? Is it Stacy? I can get someone else if you don't like..."

"No, it's not her. I don't want a three way."

Now Dani was the one saying "Yeah, right."

"I'm not shitting you, Dani. I'm not into it, okay? Can you just get rid of her? I've had a long day."

"You son-of-a-bitch," she muttered under her breath as she scowled at him, thinking there had to be a reason he was rejecting her offer, and she was pretty sure it had nothing to do with the lies he was telling her.

She went back into the living room and told Stacy that Jax thought he might be coming down with something, so maybe they should hang out another night, and though disappointed, she said she understood and left. But Dani didn't understand.

This was Jax Bonham. He practically fucked for a living, and he was turning down a threesome with a hot blonde? So, who did he fuck already today? Or had he cheated with Stacy before and was afraid Dani would sense their familiarity once the action started? She was convinced he was hiding something, and she knew one surefire way to find out.

She just had to wait until he fell asleep.

Day 49
Savannah

In the main lodge, Savannah and Rey stood in the hallway outside her mother's office waiting for Alek to come home from his rounds. They didn't know he had gone to June's cabin tonight, and after nearly an hour, they were starting to get frustrated. They were about to give up and go looking for him when they finally heard footsteps.

Slipping into a dark alcove, they watched as Alek approached the door that would take him through the office to her mother's bedroom. He stopped just outside, ran his fingers through his hair, and took a deep breath before turning the knob.

"What was that about?" Rey asked once he had gone inside.

"He's probably nervous," Savannah said. "I think she's finally going to have sex with him tonight."

She believed her blessing was the thing that would finally push her mother into Alek's arms, and though she loved her mother and wanted to see her find happiness in this fucked up, new world, there was a more selfish reason she picked today to offer that blessing. She needed her mother occupied tonight because she and Rey had a mission...their Plan B.

Now that Alek was in Olivia's room, the kids hurried to set the wheel in motion, calling their friends to make sure everyone was in position. Kylie was watching Liana's house to make sure she and Aiden stayed at home, and Sally

256

was watching Dani and Jax. Bella joined Savannah and Rey, and they headed up the hill to June's cabin. Her boys were off fishing, so they knew she was alone when Savannah knocked softly on the front door. June called out to tell them to hold on, then it took her several minutes to answer. When she did, she looked like she'd been crying.

"Is everyone okay?" Savannah asked, stepping inside as Rey and Bella hid around the corner.

"Allergies," June lied, and satisfied with her answer, Savvy began to work on the one adult she believed she could manipulate into helping her get what she wanted - time with Austin outside of his cell. Her mother had flatly refused, she figured Liana would be a dead end, and while Dani believed the boy needed to spend some time with kids his own age, she was just not trusting enough for this plan. Short of knocking out the guards, June was their only option.

"So what exactly do you want me to do?" she asked after Savvy explained Austin's situation and how she believed she could make a difference.

"We just want you to help us get him a shower and a change of clothes. That's all."

"What did your mother say about that?"

"She doesn't want to be associated with it because she wants people to think that she's tough on our enemies, especially with this new evil queen bit, you know? So, she doesn't want whoever's on guard duty to think that she's the one allowing it."

"I see, and why didn't she tell me this herself?"

"Same reason," Savannah lied. "Look, I promise it will be safe. He'll shower in Rey's room. There are only two ways out - the front door and the balcony that goes to the greenhouse. We'll have Bella and Sally cover the balcony, and Kylie and Ravi will be outside the front door so he can't escape that way."

"Ravi?" June asked, her mind taken back to his offer to fill in if her plans with Alek fell through. She wasn't going to do it, but she really needed to feel wanted right now.

"He's Rey's roommate, so he agreed to help us guard the door," Savannah explained, not realizing that there was anything going on between the mother of four and the quiet Indian man everyone thought was so much younger than his twenty-four years.

"So, how do you figure into this?" June asked suspiciously, and Savannah sighed, taking the calculated risk of partial honesty.

"After he's had a chance to shower and put on some clean clothes, I want to just take a minute and sit down with him. Alek said bad things happened to him in the group he was with, but he won't talk to the grownups about it. So, maybe he'll talk to me, and I guess I just thought you might understand better than the other adults because I keep thinking...what if he was just doing what he had to do to survive? What if he's just a kid like Noah, and he wound up in a bad situation? If we can't get him to talk, he's gonna die, Aunt June," she said, tugging at her heartstrings, and it was working.

"If I do decide to help you, I think I need to be there to make sure nothing goes wrong."

"He won't talk if you're there. That's why I think it needs to just be us kids, but I swear we'll be safe. We won't do anything stupid or dangerous." That was another lie. "He'll shower, we'll talk for a few minutes, then we'll escort him back to the cell. You have my word."

June sighed through gritted teeth. She knew she was probably making a mistake because if anything went wrong, Olivia would never forgive her, but the fact that a kid not much older than her own first born was sitting scared in a cell was a powerful motivator for her, particularly considering she had seen Austin turn on the men who nearly killed her.

"Okay," she said finally, "but I swear by all that's holy, if he gets away or someone gets hurt..."

"Thank you, Aunt June. Thank you so much!"

June smiled and shook her head, wary because Savvy was laying it on a little thick with the whole Aunt June thing, but already committed to helping, she grabbed her coat and followed Savannah out the door.

They went into the greenhouse to the shed in the back where two guards were stationed outside. There would always be at least two when they had a prisoner now because the last time one guard had been on duty, their prisoner ended up crucified.

As Savannah and Bella watched from behind a tree, Rey and June approached the guards, telling them they were there for the next shift.

"We're on for two more hours," one guard protested.

"I guess General Navarro over scheduled," June said, "but we're already here, so you all may as well go home and get some sleep."

That's all it took. If one of the founding members had not been present, it probably would not have worked, but when June said to take off, she did not have to tell them twice. Guarding Austin was the most boring job in the entire community anyway. Nothing ever happened.

Once the guards had started up the hill toward the new temporary housing on the back of the property, Savvy went into Austin's cell. He was lying on his side facing the wall.

"Hey, you awake?" she asked softly, and he turned over.

"Savannah?" he asked, squinting his eyes as she flipped on the light.

"Yeah," she said. "This is my house, my family's compound."

"I know. I'm sorry," he said softly.

"Come on. I've arranged for you to get a shower and a change of clothes."

"That's okay," he muttered, rolling back over.

"It isn't optional, Austin. Either get up and take a shower, or I'll have the guards turn the hose on your filthy ass," she said in a joking manner, hoping to break the ice and make him laugh, but there was no change in his demeanor.

"Fine," he said, and robotically, he got up to follow her out. With the others in tow, their guns aimed at Austin's back, they walked through the greenhouse. When they came to the saltwater pool, Rey pointed up to the second story balcony of his room and asked Bella to stand guard there. She stayed behind, waiting for Kylie and Sally, who were hurrying back down the hill to join her. Kylie would be guarding the door inside, but she didn't want to even see Austin since she was one of the girls that his companions had intended to kidnap. She was only going along with this because she wanted an explanation, and like everyone else, she wanted to know if what he had told Alek was true. After that, she might execute him herself.

The rest of the conspirators went into the lodge through the kitchen entrance, going up the back staircase to avoid anyone who might be sitting by the fire in the main room, and when they reached their destination, they knocked. Ravi came out, and Savannah, Rey, and Austin went in.

While he showered, Savannah kept time. Showers were restricted to five minutes to conserve their limited water supply, but she gave him ten because it had been such a long time since his last one. While she stood outside the door, counting down the minutes, Rey closed the blackout curtains and slipped onto the balcony that overlooked the pool area of the greenhouse. He left the sliding glass door cracked so he could hear everything that happened inside and waited to see if Savannah was going to need him.

Finally, when she called "time", Austin turned off the faucet with a disappointed groan, but even though he wished he could have stayed in there until the hot water ran cold, it had been wonderful. His only baths since the public utilities went down were in ponds and streams, and being fall in the mountains, they were also cold and brief. It was the first time he felt clean on the outside in months. On the inside, he didn't think he'd ever feel clean again.

"What happened to the guy who was with you?" he asked Savannah as he came out of the bathroom with one towel around his waist and another over his shoulders.

"He'll be back soon," she said, then she lowered her voice and gave him a smile. "I was hoping to have a little time alone with you first, so we could...*talk*."

"What did you want to talk about?" he asked, nervously looking around the room for the fresh clothes he had been promised. They weren't there. Rey had taken them onto the balcony with him. It was part of the plan.

"Just wondering what you've been up to since school let out for the zombie apocalypse," she said with a wink as she sat down on the bed and patted the spot beside her. Feeling apprehensive yet obliged, Austin sat down, trying to leave as much space as possible, but Savannah was already within just a couple of feet of the edge. He crossed his legs, holding the towel at the waist, and if not for their circumstances, Savannah would have burst out in laughter at the situation.

So many women had found themselves in Austin's position, feeling manipulated by a man who had some level of power over them, knowing they didn't want what was coming but that saying no would have dire consequences. Of course, Austin wasn't really in that position at all. Sure, he was about to get a possibly unwanted grope, but that's as far as it was going. She just wanted to know how his dick would react, and though she'd never intended to touch a guy like that at her age, this wasn't sexual. It was survival, and for the greater good, she had been more than willing to practice with Rey until she felt like she could play the vixen when she was anything but. Volunteering for this job herself had been for the greater good as well. Kylie would have pulled out a knife and cut the damn thing off, and Sally and Bella were just too scared. Savannah was driven by the determination to prove that he was a liar because he did not seem like he had the slightest problem kidnapping girls from their compound until Alek took down his partners.

"So," she said, leaning in close, but instead of talking about the apocalypse, she went straight for it and kissed him. Instantly, Austin was lost, kissing her back, responding to her like he would have before the world ended when the thought of kissing Savannah Anders crossed his mind every time he passed her in the halls or heard anyone mention her name, and for one glorious, fleeting moment, he felt normal. Then her hand sauntered down his chest until she located and grabbed her target through the towel just like Rey had taught her.

Immediately, Austin started shaking. His mouth went dry, tears pricked the corners of his eyes, and he jumped up, backing away from her, holding the towel in place to hide his shame as it fell off his hips.

"I'm sorry. I can't," he said. "It's not you, Savannah. It's me. I just...I can't."

When she looked up at the paths of salt water now streaming down his face as he stood hunched over, unable to make eye contact with her, she realized that he wasn't lying to Alek like she thought. Something fucked up had happened to this kid, something *really* fucked up.

"Hey," she whispered as she stood and slowly approached him. "It's okay. You're safe here."

Then she hugged him, and the six-foot-tall, former football star collapsed, sobbing in her arms.

After Austin had opened up to Savannah and began to share his story, it pained her to have to put him back in his cell because the lie she told to manipulate June into releasing him had actually been the truth. He was a kid who found himself in a situation where he had to play along or die, and though he yearned for death, there was a reason he had forced himself to go on for so long, a reason that hurt too much to think about.

On the balcony outside, Rey had waited quietly so Austin wouldn't be embarrassed to know that he listened to the whole thing, and Savannah asked him to wait a little longer when she went out there to get his clothes. Rey came in when Austin went back into the bathroom to get dressed, then the two of them escorted him back to his cell with Sally and Bella following, covering him with their guns just in case. But Savannah knew he would not try to run.

"I'm going to get you out of here," she promised, fighting back tears as she walked inside the cell with him.

"It's okay, Savannah. This is better than I deserve," he said, and she turned away and hurried out the door, heartbroken for Austin. She was supposed to stay with Rey for the next hour and wait for the new guard shift to arrive, but Kylie volunteered in her place because they didn't need any guards to see Savannah crying and get suspicious, especially considering the kids weren't supposed to be on guard duty in the first place. Tomorrow, they would come clean with her mother about what they had done, but tonight, the last thing they needed was somebody dragging General Navarro out of bed. It was the last thing the general needed too. She was having a very, very good night.

Liana's Journal
Day 49

When Aiden got home tonight, I had everything ready for him - dinner in the oven, candles burning, sexy lingerie beneath my dress. I had raided Olivia's closet since the new things she stocked were mostly black leather, and I was wearing a hot pink bustier that perfectly complemented my bronze skin. I couldn't wait to show it to him, and thankfully, when he saw all the work I had done, he didn't start complaining about politics like he always seems to do when I have BDSM on my mind. Of course tonight, I didn't care if *he* tied *me* up. I wanted him to see me. I wanted him to worship every inch of my body with his eyes, hands, and tongue, and he did not seem like he had any intention of disappointing me.

"Dinner smells delicious, but do I have to have it now or can it be reheated after I have you?" he asked with a fiery stare when he came out of the bathroom, a damp towel hanging low on his hips, exposing the faint pathway of dark hair from his navel down.

"I don't care if I eat at all," I said, turning off the oven, and Aiden was suddenly on me, pinning me against the counter in the kitchen.

"You look fucking amazing," he whispered as he kissed my ear.

"You should see what's under my dress," I said, but instead of taking it off me, he fell to his knees, slowly inching the hem up my legs, and chasing it with his tongue. As he got closer to the tiny pink g-string, I could feel that it was completely soaked with my excitement, and I thrust my hands in his hair, pulling his face against my crotch through the fabric. He nuzzled into me, and his hot breath sent a wave of arousal through my entire body that left my nipples so hard, they ached.

Then he looked up at me as he cautiously began pushing the skirt higher, asking my consent with his eyes, expecting me to stop him as always, but tonight there would be no stopping him. I grabbed the dress and pulled it over my head, tossing it across the room.

"Oh, my God," he growled as he knelt there, my panties directly in front of his face for the first time.

"No more rules," I whispered.

"You mean it?" he asked, and I barely had time to nod before he was on his feet, hoisting me onto the kitchen table. He pushed the clean plates and forks out of his way, and I could hear them hitting the ground behind me. Then he laid me back, grabbed the thin straps on the side of my panties, and tore them away.

He couldn't take his eyes off me, shifting them gradually from my face to where my nipples peeked through the sheer fabric of my bustier then downward, and the smile on his lips was positively decadent as he slid his hands between my thighs and parted my legs.

"I've been dying to taste you," he whispered as he leaned in so close, I could feel the warmth of his mouth on my erect clit before his tongue made the first, amazing swirl over it.

"Oh, Aiden!" I moaned, my entire body shuddering. It had been so long since a man had done this to me, and this was Aiden LaCroix! His were the eyes I saw in my mind every time I used Bob as a substitute - the deep brown eyes I had imagined looking into mine from over my mound.

He tried to tease me slowly, but there simply was no teasing me. I was too aroused, the slightest motion of his tongue like a deep tissue massage, and he knew it too! He was so pleased with himself as he made me moan, jolt, and writhe with so little effort. He realized that the challenge was not to make me come but to make me last, and he was definitely up for it.

He moved away from my clit, flickering his tongue softly all around it, and even without direct contact, I could feel the orgasm approaching. Every touch brought me closer, no matter how slight or far away from the target, and when he grabbed my calves in both hands and pushed my legs as wide apart as they would go, I finally lay trembling in the deliciously vulnerable position that had been long-denied me.

Then he stopped.

"Look at me, Liana," he commanded. I opened my eyes, gazing downward to see his tongue returning to my clit, and the cocky look in his eyes as he stared back at me said very clearly that he was about to end me. I grabbed the edges of the kitchen table in anticipation, and he pressed his face into me, darting his tongue wildly until I felt my whole body devastated by a sudden, violent ecstasy.

"Oh, yes! Aiden! Yes! Yes! Yeeeessss!" I cried as I convulsed against his beautiful face, and he kept going, bent on claiming every last bit of pleasure I had to give. I hadn't experienced this in so long, it felt like the first time, and when I finally began to come down, I wasn't even able to form complete words as I pulled away from him, giggling.

"Oh, my gah...Aid..oh, gah..." I mumbled, and he laughed as he leaned over me, kissing me gently on the forehead while I struggled to recover.

"You don't know how bad I've wanted to do that to you, mon cœur," he whispered.

"Me too," I said, but realizing I still wasn't making myself clear, I sat up and reached for his towel, intending to return the favor.

"Uh-uh," he said, grabbing my hands, and when he pulled me off the table and spun me around to bend over it, I lost my will to argue. Slowly, he began to slide his massive cock into me, inch by inch.

"Oh, God, Aiden," I moaned as he heaved my body back against his then pushed me away, all but the tip slipping out of me. I wanted more, but he was stubborn, unwilling to give me control. He grabbed my arms, folding them behind my back and using them to pull me into him, forcing me to accept his pace, and as it lifted my shoulders with each thrust, I found my body curved into an angle I'd never experienced before. His cock was suddenly hitting a sweet spot inside me in a new and different way, and it felt positively divine.

"Oh, yes," I whimpered, so stunned by this foreign sensation, I couldn't do much else. It was taking me over until I became nothing but the intense, burning pleasure inside. My breathing grew rapid and shallow. My thighs trembled. My fingernails dug into my own skin as he kept my arms held tightly behind me, and only then did Aiden speed up, fucking me ever more voraciously until we were smacking into each other so hard, it was as if our bodies were applauding his amazing skills as his hips pounded against my ass.

My toes curled, my eyes rolled back into my head, and I could tell I was on the verge of something incredible, something...*miraculous*.

Oh, my God! I thought. *Is this...is this...*

"Oh! My! God!"

The words came barreling out of my chest in an anguished growl as I experienced an explosion like never before. Suddenly, everything inside felt like pure rapture. I pulled my hands free and grabbed the side of the table with a white-knuckled grip so I didn't accidentally throw myself into the floor as I convulsed against Aiden's phenomenal cock, and it responded to my pleasure, joining me so abruptly, it surprised its master. Aiden groaned my name, thrusting deep and hard as his orgasm filled me, soothing overwrought nerve endings that still throbbed with a new, unexpected bliss.

He leaned over me, his cock now motionless inside me, and I could feel his breath on the back of my neck just before he kissed me there. I wanted to say something. I wanted to tell him how unbelievable it was...how no one else had ever done that to me...how this was the best sex I'd ever had in my life, but all I could manage was a weakly whispered...

"Ay. Dios. Mio."

"So, uh...what brought that on?" Aiden asked as he and Liana sat in the kitchen catching their breath. She was on the edge of the table completely naked as he sat in a chair, his towel draped over his lap.

"What do you mean?" she asked.

"I think you know what I mean," he said with a smirk.

"Oh. Well, the truth is..." she trailed off and sighed as she slid off the table into a chair beside him. She didn't want to make up a lie, but she couldn't exactly tell him the whole truth either. She looked up into his eyes, deciding on a very abridged version.

"I was shy about it before because I had some...*blemishes* on my inner thighs."

"What are you talking about? You're skin is flawless," he argued.

"I finally found something that worked," she said.

"You honestly mean to tell me that you deprived me of that for almost two months because you were worried about me seeing a few, little bumps?"

"It's embarrassing," she said.

It's insulting! he thought, but he didn't say anything or let his feelings show because he didn't want to start a fight on the heels of the most amazing sex they'd ever had. There was only one thing that could make it more amazing - if he was able to be as free with her as she had been with him just now - but that was not an option, at least not without a blindfold and some wrist cuffs.

Then a smile spread over Aiden's face as he realized she had just paved the way for him.

"Lots of things are embarrassing, Liana, and some things are downright insulting. I'm the one person in this world you're supposed to be completely comfortable with," he said, the combination of his harsh tone and grin confusing her.

"I'm sorry. I didn't mean..." she began, but he cut her off.

"Don't speak," he insisted, putting his finger to her lips. "Listen. You had no faith in me, mon cœur. You had a secret that was really no big deal at all, but you didn't trust me enough to give me the chance to tell you that I didn't care."

"But you don't know how bad it was," she protested, and he shushed her again.

"I don't care how bad it was. I love you," he said, and though her eyes grew wide and glazed over as she heard those words from him for the first time, he didn't even give her a chance to reciprocate. "I love everything about you, Liana, but you've been a very bad girl. You didn't trust me with the truth, and now I have to punish you for it.

"So it looks like we're going to start using the equipment in that secret room after all, but it's not going to be me strapped to it. Do you understand me?"

"Yes," she said sheepishly.

"Yes, what?"

"Yes, Master Aiden?"

"Good girl," he said, then he let his detached demeanor fade until he was once more the man she knew so he could properly remind her that his desire to be her Master was not the only revelation he made tonight. The legs of her chair scraped across the tile as he pulled her close to kiss her on the top of the head.

"Je t'aime, mon cœur," he whispered, and with her lips against his bare chest, she echoed him, fighting the urge to cry tears of joy as she held onto him for dear life.

It's after 5:00 am. I can't sleep. Earlier, I helped Savannah and the other kids try to get that boy, Austin, to talk about what happened to him in his old group. It was a good distraction, but now that he's back in his cell and everyone has gone to bed, I can't make my mind shut down. I need to know if my plan worked out for Olivia. You see, the thing is, I didn't really want to have sex with Alek. I just wanted to help Olivia finally get over her issues so she could be with him, and I knew the threat of him being with another woman would be the quickest way to make that happen. I never dreamed she'd actually let it get to the point that he came to my cabin, but at least he did the right thing.

And he's so sweet. He came here after he finished working for the day, took a shower, and had dinner with me. The conversation was so easy with him. He said I was a great cook, and he told me how pretty my hair is when I wear it down. Then we sat down on the couch and scooted close together. That's when he kissed me, and I let him because I thought maybe that's what he needed to do to realize that he couldn't be with any woman but Olivia. It was just a kiss - just a sweet, soft, *perfect* kiss.

Okay. This is stupid. I'm tired of pretending, and even if I lie to everyone else in the world, it's ridiculous to keep lying to my freaking diary! So, I'm going to try being honest for a change, and I don't even care if someone reads it someday. I've spent my whole life so worried about what other people think of me, I've barely lived at all.

So, here's the honest-to-God truth:

That kiss was everything I've ever dreamed about. He took my face lightly in his hands, looked down into my eyes as his lids slowly closed, and for the first time since college, I felt turned on by something so simple as a kiss. I'd forgotten what it was like. Kissing Jimbo had become more like wrestling with our faces because he was so rough and selfish, but Alek was different. It was gentle yet intense, and I felt a sensation in my breasts and between my legs that was so powerful, when he pulled away from me, I thought I'd die.

He slid onto the floor on his knees, and *oh, dear Lord!* I thought he was about to do things to me with his mouth, and I was completely ready, shivering and on fire at the same time, unashamed to be excited for once in my life. Then the rug was suddenly and cruelly pulled out from under me when instead he started apologizing and begging my forgiveness. He said that he wanted to be with me but couldn't because he loved another woman, and even though I was falling apart inside, I did the only thing I could do at that moment.

I told him that it was all a scheme to get him and Olivia to realize that they belonged together. There was nothing about that statement that wasn't a lie. I really did want to sleep with him. I don't think I've ever wanted anything so much, and when he left, I was so depressed, I felt like I could have just walked out in the woods and let the zombies take me. This was supposed to be the best night of my life, and it was darn near the worst.

After that, all I wanted to do was crawl in bed and cry myself to sleep, but Savannah knocked on my door, so I had to suck it up and deal with her. Then when that was finally over, the boys came back home from night fishing, so I had to pretend to be happy while I put their catch in the fridge and promised to cook it for dinner tomorrow night. After they went to bed, I tried to get some sleep, but I just kept thinking about what happened tonight and crying, so I decided to write in my journal, thinking maybe if I stuck to the lies I told Alek, I could convince myself. I should have known it was a stupid idea. I couldn't even talk myself into going and getting the darn thing until almost 5:00 am because I'd been hiding it in Olivia's office, which is right beside her bedroom. I didn't want to risk hearing Alek in there with her doing all the things he was supposed to do with me tonight.

I waited until I was certain they'd be asleep, but I still swear I heard her crying his name. Freaked out, I grabbed my journal and ran, trying to tell myself it was just my imagination torturing me. Now I can't get it out of my head as I sit here in the corner of the lodge writing this. I have at least another hour to wait because I can't go back home and risk my boys waking up and seeing how puffy my eyes are from crying all night. They'll know because their father made me cry like this plenty of times. But I'm not comparing Alek to Jimbo. I'm not even mad at Alek.

How can I fault him for being a good man? I just wish he could be *my* good man, but that's never going to happen now, especially if Olivia had sex with him last night. I could never compete with her. I don't know how to do anything other than just lie there and wait for it to be over, but I don't think it would have been like that with Alek. He could've taught me things. He wanted to. He said it himself. He said he would have been honored to be the first to share something so beautiful with me. That's what he called it. Beautiful.

God! I wish he had just been an a-hole! It would have made everything so much easier. I want to hate him. I want to hate Olivia. Actually, I do kinda hate Olivia. She gets everything. She had a rich husband who worshipped the ground she walked on, and now she has the most perfect man in the world as her lover.

And I have nothing. Nothing at all.

June closed her journal and took another drink of the hot chocolate she had made earlier. It was cold now, but she didn't even care enough to warm it up. She was just killing time. Once her boys woke up, if they found her gone, they would automatically come to the lodge for breakfast, then she could sneak home the back way so she didn't have to see them until she could get the swelling to go down around her eyes.

As she sipped her drink in front of the fire, a door opened on the second floor that overlooked the great room, and Ravi stepped out quietly, trying not to wake his roommate. He had planned to grab something to eat before his morning shift at the rear gate, but when he saw that June was sitting below, he slipped back into his room to grab the prize he'd obtained on the scavenging mission the day before. He had been looking for a particular book for days, volunteering for every assignment until he found it after looking under the mattresses and in the nightstands of more than a hundred homes.

With his gift for June in hand, he crept down the stairs, not wanting to draw her attention just yet, and she remained unaware of him until he was standing behind her chair. Then he cleared his throat, and she jumped.

"This," he whispered seductively with his Indian accent as he slid the tome over her shoulder, "is my holy book."

Without another word, Ravi strode off into the kitchen without looking back, leaving June staring at the well-worn hardcover before her, her eyes wide, her mouth gaping. She didn't know what the words Kama Sutra meant, but the weird, stylized drawing of a man and woman entwined on the front gave her the general idea.

She looked around casually to make sure no one had seen him give it to her, then she hid the cover behind her journal and hurried out the door, biting her lip as her smile threatened to show itself for the first time since Alek left her the night before.

Day 50
Dani

268

In the cabin next door to June's, Dani had gone straight to bed, not even wanting to talk to Jax, but before she did, she drank a large glass of water that would be guaranteed to wake her up before the sun because she didn't want to set an alarm and risk waking him as well.

Around 4:00 AM, the water did its trick. As Jax lay sleeping, his beautiful, naked body sprawled over the bed, the tattoos on his arms lit by the moonlight, Dani gave him a long, wistful stare before she pulled on her winter coat and boots, armed herself, and headed out toward the back gate to see the one person who could help her. Even though the last time she had come out in the woods alone had been terrifying, she was determined to get inside Jax's head and put an end to this torment one way or another, and when she finally passed the wellspring and saw the flickering flame up ahead, a feeling of peace came over her. She hurried toward the light shining through the cottage window as the cold wind blew through her hair, and she soon arrived to find the witch standing on the porch waiting for her.

"Let's get you warm, child," she said, putting her shawl around Dani's shoulders like a loving grandmother, and once she was sitting inside in front of the fireplace with a cup of tea in hand, Dani found herself suddenly telling the woman everything that was on her mind. When she finished, the witch looked her in the eye with a hellish grin.

"Why scale this mountain and risk your life amongst the dead just to borrow my power when you could have it for yourself?" she asked.

"I don't understand," Dani said.

"I can show you what's in your lover's heart, or I can make you the earth beneath his feet, the fire in his soul, the water that quenches him, and the very air that he breathes," she whispered.

Maybe it was the way she romanticized it that sucked her in, but suddenly it all seemed so easy, instantly transitioning Dani from a desire to see inside Jax's mind to a zombie-like willingness to take whatever magic she was offering.

"How does that sound?" the witch asked.

"It's all I ever wanted," Dani admitted, not realizing how literal the old woman meant her words.

"Close your eyes," she said, and as Dani complied, the witch sat in the chair facing hers, grasping her hands and muttering under her breath. Dani couldn't understand what she was saying, unsure if her words were just spoken too softly or if they were in some foreign tongue as a strange light began to emanate from the old woman's eyes. It started out as two faint, ice blue dots, but when it burgeoned into a single ball of energy, she could see a thin magenta membrane around it that grew until it engulfed them both. Mesmerized by the colors of the light and the hum of the spell, Dani felt herself lulled into a trancelike state, her limbs heavy with the same hazy feeling she remembered from Madam Levinia's, and she found it comforting since she credited the gypsy with bringing her together with Jax.

Jax. He was always the first thought she had upon waking in the morning, and now he was the last thought she remembered having at all...

Day 50
Olivia

Olivia woke entwined with Alek. It wasn't the first morning she had opened her eyes to find herself in his arms, but it was the first time they had been naked. In the hazy moments between sleep and full consciousness, she reveled in the sensation of his warm, hard body against hers, and even when he began to stir, she didn't feel the slightest twinge of the guilt that had kept her from consummating their union for so long. It just felt right.

"Good morning," he whispered, and as she looked up into his eyes, they both started giggling, immersed in an absolute bliss that quickly turned into desire as she felt him grow hard against her leg at the slightest movement.

"Again?" she asked excitedly, just as ravenous as she had been the first time even though they had woken and made love twice in the night already, making up for so much lost time.

"Again," he growled as he rolled her onto her back. She wrapped her legs around his hips as he slid inside her, and soon, just as he promised her a month ago, she was screaming his praises so loud, he had to smother her cries with a kiss to keep her from drawing the attention of everyone in the compound.

"You don't need to worry about the noise, by the way," she assured him afterward as they lay side by side. "The walls are thick, and even if they weren't, I don't care who hears."

"Then I don't care either," he said because his only concern was her feeling uncomfortable, but she wasn't. She had finally committed to her new life with him, and as soon as he left for his shift at the main gate this morning, she was going to run straight to Dani and Liana to gush about how perfect last night had been. But first, she wanted to write it all down in the brand new journal she was starting this morning.

After Alek got out of bed to take a shower, she retrieved it from the bookshelf in her office and started reliving every last, delicious detail, but there was so much to write, she hadn't even come close to finishing when he was ready to leave for work. He came over to the bed and sat down, reading over her shoulder.

"That good, huh?" he asked, and she snapped the book closed.

"You were there, you tell me," she said with a wicked grin.

"It was the best night of my life," he whispered, then he kissed her as he stood to leave for work. "And I want to do it all over again tonight."

"Oh, we're going to do more than that," she purred, licking her lips as she stared at his bulge, which was already growing at the thought of it.

"I can't wait," he growled, smiling down at her, then he glanced over toward her lingerie drawer. "Wear the black one tonight." He winked at her then forced himself to turn away lest she tempt him back into bed. It had occurred to him to ask her why she was wearing lingerie when he came home last night, but he decided that it didn't matter. He was too happy now to care.

Leaving Olivia completely enamored, Alek headed off to the wall where he had first watch with Jax in the guard station, and he had so much he wanted to talk about. It wasn't that he was the kind of guy to brag about his sex life. It's just that he had never experienced anything like Olivia, and she was the only thing on his mind.

"Are you sure she wasn't faking that?" Jax asked when he told him how many times he made her come. He was skeptical because he had seen plenty of women fake it, but so had Alek. For the last decade of his life, most of the women he met were actresses.

"I'm sure that's what it sounds like, but trust me, it was real. I could *feel* it. She would just gush inside...and tremble...she broke out in gooseflesh all over... It was fucking amazing to know I was doing that to someone," Alek said, and Jax was fascinated. Every night of his life since he was eighteen women tried to convince Jax Bonham that he was a sex god when in fact, he had been a fairly selfish lover. He just didn't know it until he met Dani and realized what it meant to make love to a woman. He wasn't thinking about himself anymore. All he cared about was pleasing her, and he was good at it...or at least he thought he was until Alek showed up talking about getting Olivia off a hundred times the very first night they slept together.

"How?" he asked. "How did you do it?"

"I don't know. I think she's just wired for it. I didn't do anything special," he said, but even as he said it, he realized it wasn't entirely true. He'd never been so invested in experiencing anyone like he was with Olivia. Orgasm hadn't been his goal. He went into it last night wanting to touch her, taste her, please her in every way, and his own pleasure was heightened as much by the fact that he was deeply in love with this woman as it was by how incredible it had been to make love to her. She was perfect - from the way she clung to him, forcing him deeper inside, to the words she whispered in his ear, commanding him to come - and being able to get her off like that was as satisfying as his own orgasm, maybe more. He just didn't know how he did it.

"Well, if you figure it out," Jax said, "tell me. I want that for Dani."

"Does she not come when you're fucking her?" Alek asked.

"She does, but it's all about the clit with her. It's not the same thing."

No, it is not, Alek thought with a wistful smile as memories of last night threatened to make him hard right there in the guard house with Jax. He turned away, staring out the window at the cold, cloudy winter day, trying to think of something helpful to say to his friend when he noticed a figure in the distance coming up the winding road from the second gate.

"Hey, check this out," he said to Jax, and they both picked up their binoculars to get a better look at the lone man in a heavy winter coat walking toward them. The morning sun reflected off his mirrored glasses as it peeked out from behind a cloud, making it impossible to see his face, but he had a rifle slung across his back, and when he was on the final stretch to the gates of the Deadfall, Jax and Alek picked up their own rifles and headed out of the security station.

Jax had assumed that Dani left for a shift earlier than his when he woke to find her gone, but instead, she was near the mountaintop, lost, disoriented and, abruptly ripped away from vivid dreams - terrifying dreams that still haunted her conscious mind even though she couldn't remember what they were about. The sun had risen, and she was aware of the brightness even before she looked around and noticed the heavy shadows cast on the ground as it shone through the trees where she had slept.

Trees? she thought with a sudden jolt of adrenaline. *Oh, my God!*

Dani was still in the woods, and now she wasn't sure she had been sleeping at all. She was upright, and she could hear dead leaves crunching on the forest floor while she roamed around the mountain. As the sound grew, it was all she could focus on until she realized she wasn't the one making it. There were corpses coming at her from all directions - worn, rotting corpses that ambled along slowly, groaning and reaching for her as they came closer. Their foul reek filled her nostrils as she knelt and scrambled for her gun, but she couldn't get a grip on it. She could see it lying on the ground in front of her, yet it seemed to slip through her fingers every time she reached for it.

Panicked, she sucked in a deep breath to scream for help, but the sound that came out wasn't her voice. It was a low rumbling noise that reminded her of the groans of the dead or the howling of the wind. No one would hear her cries as the horde of corpses closed in around her, reaching out with boney fingers to grab her, but their hands passed through her as if she had no form.

Mystified, they sniffed at the air, trying to hone in on her as they began wandering in circles like dogs chasing their tails. They knew she was there somewhere. They could smell her, but they couldn't find her. Worse, Dani couldn't even find herself. She thought she caught a glimpse of her hair blowing in the wind out of the corner of her eye, but when she turned, she saw nothing. On the ground, her clothes and weapons lay scattered, and though she could see her pants, her shirt, and even her shoes clearly, she couldn't see her own feet. She could feel them, but they weren't there. Confused and unnerved, she slowly raised her hands in front of her face to look at them only to discover that she had no hands nor eyes with which to see them. Yet she could see. She could see, smell, feel, hear, and taste everything around her.

What am I? she wondered, and as she heard the old witch's joyful cackling in the distance, she realized she had been transformed into something beyond human. But she wasn't sure if she had been blessed or cursed.

Olivia finished her journal entry. She didn't have to be anywhere for a couple of hours when she was scheduled to train one of the new people from the solar farm at the security station. After she had chronicled all four events with Alek since the first time they made love last night, she took a shower, got dressed, and picked up her phone to track down her best friends, but before she could dial, it rang. It was Liana.

"Hello?"

"Hey," Liana said, and before she even had to chance to tell Olivia what she wanted, Olivia started talking. She was too excited to share her news about Alek.

"So, should I come to your place or are you coming to mine? I need to tell somebody all the wonderfully nasty, little details about last night," she gushed, and though Liana would have loved that because she had some wonderfully nasty, little details of her own to share, now was definitely not the time.

"Olivia..." she began then stopped. Right before Olivia called, Liana had spoken with Aiden, who was at the main guard station with Alek. Aiden had news that he elected Liana to deliver to her friend, but after the way Olivia had opened the conversation, Liana had no idea how she was going to tell her. Unable to bring herself to say it, though she felt like a coward and a terrible friend for what she was about to do, she took the easy way out. "They really need you at the front gate right now. I'll catch up with you later, okay?"

"Is everything alright?" Olivia asked, suddenly worried.

"I think you'd better just go see for yourself," Liana said, then she hung up quickly before her friend could ask any more questions.

"Okay..." Olivia said warily as she slipped the phone into her pocket. She grabbed her coat and headed out through the lodge. It was bitter cold when she stepped onto the front porch, and she wrapped her scarf around her head as the first flurries of winter began to swirl in the air above the Deadfall. They melted on her cheeks as she made the short walk to the front of the community, and when the gate came into view, she could see a man standing just inside, bundled in a heavy winter coat with a fur-lined hood that blocked much of his face. The rest was obscured by sunglasses and a thick, unkempt beard, but this was a man she knew instantly in spite of all of that.

"Oh, my God!" she cried as she froze in her tracks. Her heart was beating out of her chest, and her mind was assaulted with a barrage of feelings from extreme joy to devastating angst as her beautiful memories of last night suddenly felt like a crushing weight upon her soul.

"Olivia!" the man called out, his voice cracking with raw emotion as he hurried toward her, his arms wide to embrace her, and in the guard house window over his shoulder, she caught a glimpse of Alek, his eyes filled with desolation as he felt a knife twist in his heart because everything was about to change.

With tears streaming down her face, Olivia looked away, unable to maintain eye contact as she spoke the name of the man who had fought the dead for two months just to see her face again.

"Reid," she breathed softly, and he nearly collapsed as, at long last, he folded his arms around his beloved wife.

Day 50

Alek stood frozen, his head hung, his eyes on the floor. He couldn't look at her because if he did, he wouldn't be able to say the words he knew he had to say. He had made her a promise he never thought he would have to keep, and now it was time to pay the piper.

"I'm happy for you," he lied. "I'll move my things into one of the trailers up the hill after my shift."

"Alek, you don't have to do that," Olivia said.

"I said I would step aside if your husband came home. I don't want to cause you any problems, Liv. We'll just pretend it never happened."

"Pretend what never happened?" she demanded. "That you never helped me get through the toughest time in my life? That you never came in here and protected me and my daughter when we needed it the most? That you never had the patience of a saint with me even though you deserved far better than what I gave you? Alek, there's no way I can pretend those things never happened."

She walked over to him and lifting his chin, wanting him to look her in the eye as she got to the point.

"I don't want to lose you, Alek. I don't know what's going to happen, but I can't let you go because..." She paused, searching her brain for words she hadn't said out loud since she was teasing the cute Swedish exchange student in high school, and when they came to her, she had to gather the courage to say them. She looked up into his eyes, her own full of tears, and said...

ABOUT THE AUTHOR

After leaving southern California, Lilly Black lives in the southeastern United States with her husband of twenty years.

LILLY BLACK

www.lillyblackauthor.com

www.ingramcontent.com/pod-product-compliance
Lightning Source LLC
Chambersburg PA
CBHW021951170626
46808CB00001B/110